Three Farmers on Their Way to a Dance

Three Farmers on Their Way to a Dance

RICHARD POWERS

WEIDENFELD AND NICOLSON
LONDON

Contents

We guess as we read, we create; everything starts from an initial mistake. . . . A large part of what we believe to be true . . . with a persistence equalled only by our sincerity, springs from an original misconception. . . .—MARCEL PROUST, *Remembrance of Things Past*

"Everybody," said Knudsen, explaining the demand for the automobile, "wants to go from A to B sitting down."—ANNE JARDIM, *The First Henry Ford: A Study in Personality and Business Leadership*

Chapter One

I Outfit Myself for a Trip to Saint Ives

Cats, kits, sacks, wives: how many were going to St. Ives?

FOR A THIRD OF A CENTURY, I got by nicely without Detroit. First off, I don't do well in cars and have never owned one. The smell of anything faintly resembling car seats gives me motion sickness. That alone had always ranked Motor City a solid third from bottom of American Cities I'd Like to See. I always rely on scenery to deaden the inconvenience of travel, and "Detroit scenery" seemed as self-contradictory as "movie actress," "benign cancer," "gentlemen of the press," or "American Diplomacy." For my entire conscious life I'd successfully ignored the city. But one day two years ago, Detroit ambushed me before I could get out of its way.

The Early Riser out of Chicago dropped me off alongside Grand Trunk Station, a magnificent building baptized in marble but now lying buried in plywood. I lugged my bag-and-a-half into the terminal, a public semidarkness stinking of urine and history. Subpoenaed relatives met their arriving parties under the glow of a loudspeaker that issued familiar, reassuring tunes.

One hundred years ago, the Grand Trunk must have quickened pulses. Pillars of American Municipal balanced a fifty-foot vault on elaborate Corinthian capitals: America copying England copying France copying Rome copying the Greeks. A copper dome with ceramic floral trim bore the obligatory inscriptions from Cicero and Bill Taft. Now the station's opulence left it a mausoleum, empty except for the Early Riser executives who threaded the rotunda in single file.

I fell automatically into line, sensing the station's layout. The soaring ceiling seemed out of proportion to the size of the hall. When my eyes adjusted to Detroit's industrial-grade light, I received a shock, the same shock I had felt as a child when, at a public swimming pool, I saw an old vet unstrap and remove his leg before taking a dip. The antique terminal had been similarly amputated: the corridor I walked down was not the station's length but only its width. The Grand Trunk had been sent packing: plywood sheets boarded off palatial wings and multiple gates, leaving only this reduced chicken run between a lone arrival platform and the main exit.

Transferring trains in Detroit was the cheapest if not the most expedient way of getting from Chicago to Boston. Drastically cut fares promoted a new route, the Technoliner, for the first month of its run. The line subsequently folded, the technolinees long ago forsaking Detroit for Houston and northern California, and even longer ago forsaking trains for planes. Another case of our railway being behind schedule. Nevertheless, I sank as low as Toledo to take advantage of the reduced fare.

When I'm in money, I can leave half-eaten meals in restaurants along with the best. I've worked hard at overcoming a natural stinginess. But when I'm out of money—a cyclical occurrence paralleling America's boom/bust economy of the last century—I easily fall back on old habits. This trip found me once again short, having just spent a year in the Illinois backwoods on a small business project that did not pan out. "Pan out" comes, I assume, from the prospectors' days. Flash in the pan. I spent my early thirties in isolation, chasing flashes in the pan.

With my technical background, I knew that I could find work in Boston providing I could put down a security deposit on an efficiency and still have enough cash left over to dry-clean my interview suit. My money margin, marginalia in this case, did not worry me so much as the immediate problem of how to spend the six hours between the Early Riser and the Technoliner in a city I had, until then, celebrated by avoiding. It was me against motion sickness in the city autos built.

But as sometimes happens when killing time, I would come across something in my brief Detroit layover that would kill not just six hours but the next year and more before I came to terms with it. Sifting the downtown for novelties that might deaden ten minutes, I did not imagine that the next ten months would find me obsessed with everything I could learn about Motor City and the fifth-grade farmer who put it on the map.

When I made my stopover, Detroit had already been undergoing a manufactured and heavily publicized rebirth for some time. The emblem of this new era, the Renaissance Center, may be the single most ambitious building project of recent times. Its five black towers outscale the rest of the city the way Chartres Cathedral dwarfs its surrounding town. Four cylinders flank a central, massive pillar, each hanging black glass over girders in disguised International Style.

But if the city were not already dead, would it need a rebirth? The name "Renaissance Center" resembles an ad campaign declaring Sudso "All the cleaner you'll ever need," or a restaurant assuring, "What we serve is really a meal." And just as when telling an old widower that he looks well we mean he ought not to push his luck, the leading citizens of Detroit, in naming the Renaissance Center, implied that they would be pleased if the city could, at this point, break even.

The size and opulence of the center meant to attract tourists and conventioneers into double-A, self-contained luxury. The palace executed its purpose too well. It drew people (read money) up and away from the surrounding businesses, and because the towers were so self-sufficient a village, the people never came back out. The area surrounding the Renaissance Center showed the signs of a hasty evacuation and rout. Gravitating toward the towers, I passed row on row of brick, triple-decked residences standing vacant, their windows and doors broken open to reveal nothing inside.

I figured that the Renaissance Center (dubbed the Ren Cen by those who make a living truncating all words into monosyllables) would be good for a half hour. The inside was a contemporary version of the Grand Trunk—the multileveled, involuted architecture that had delighted me as a boy of six, when I still believed in Tom Swift and urban renewal. I ordered a meal, reading the menu right to left, in a disk-shaped restaurant floating on a moat in the central tower, spinning, gradually but perceptibly, driven no doubt by a thousand Asian coolies chained to a mill-track on a hidden lower level.

My training in physics made the huge spinning plate seem an unintentional homage to the last, great empirical experiment of the nineteenth century. In 1887, the physicists Michelson and Morley set out to measure the absolute velocity of the earth through the ether field. The two scientists floated a gigantic slab on a sea of mercury, on the same scale and setup as the slab I now rode. They shone a beam of light through a prism in the center and back to mirrors on the perimeter, reasoning that light flowing in the direction of the ether stream would travel faster than light flowing upriver. But Michelson and Morley found no difference in light speeds, regardless of orientation. An international calamity followed in 1905, when Einstein, a Bonn patent clerk with no reputation to lose, suggested preserving the velocity of light at the expense of the concept of absolute measure. The century was off to a quick jump out of the gate.

I came across an account of this experiment again much later, after pursuing the Henry Ford hoax through the infant century. But at the time, I drew the comparison casually. I waited until the disk completed one full rotation before disembarking. Since I don't smoke or drink and swear unconvincingly, symmetry is my only vice. Escaping from the Ren Cen, I walked counterclockwise for a few blocks to reverse my dizziness. I sat down on the nearest set of steps. A bum approached from across the piazza and requested a quarter for some suntan oil. I explained that I needed it to dry-clean my interview suit and he left me in peace.

Nearby, a vintage '50s statue depicted a green, cupreous titan hefting a petite, state-of-the-art, Waspish couple in one hand and either a globe or an automobile—I can't remember which—in the other: Spirit of Detroit. Two lawyers fist-fought over a parking space. A woman sold clods of earth out of a shoe box. A man with ventriloquist's dummy explained to an indifferent crowd that the present secretary of state was the Antichrist. A prominent clock harped on the fact that I was doing a rotten job marking time. If I was going to make it to the Technoliner intact, I'd need better diversion.

I bused to the Detroit Institute of Arts. Now the finest of this century's paintings will never make up for our concurrent botch of everything else. Art can only hope to be an anaesthetic, a placebo. The best artists know that patients always fake their symptoms and must be tricked into diagnosis before treatment can take place. The last thing I expected to find at the Institute was a mystery, a work of art demanding to be tracked down, a trail unfolding indefinitely, approximately, the way memory tries "recoil," or "recommend," or "record," coming as close as "recoup," but never alighting on its real object, "recover."

The foyer of the Detroit museum opens onto yet another Grand Hall, a high-vaulted, Euro-sick, stone rectangle entirely unfit for displaying works of art. Rococo satyrs and curlicues alternate with heat-duct grills in a confused architectural legacy. In 1931, in the depths of the Depression, the Institute's Arts Commission, backed by Edsel Ford, asked the Mexican muralist Diego Rivera to use the room for a fresco commemorating the greatness of Detroit.

It was an odd marriage: Edsel Ford, whose father was the first among capitalists, in cahoots with Rivera, the notorious revolutionary who secured Trotsky's political asylum in Mexico. Rivera, the Third World champion, praising the city whose chief icon is an enormous electric sign tallying new autos as they come off the assembly ramp. Diego, who once incorporated a wall fuse box into a mural, working in a room the gaudy copy of Bourbon splendor. But Detroit and Diego shared something critical: both were in love with machines.

The Institute put up ten thousand dollars of Edsel's cash, embarrassed to offer "the only man now living who adequately represents the world we live in—wars, tumult, struggling peoples" such a meager sum. They suggested he limit his work to fifty square yards on each of the two larger walls, one hundred dollars per square yard, by some esoteric formula, considered fair for a man of Diego's stature. Thus the Fords, standing in for Michelangelo's papal patrons, might have suggested the fellow not do the whole ceiling, but just a little bit above the altar. Rivera grew increasingly ambitious in guilty compensation for the gringos' liberality. Edsel, finding out that Diego meant to cover all four walls, upped the ante to twenty-five thousand.

The Institute told Diego that they "would be pleased if [he] could possibly find something out of the history of Detroit, or some motive suggesting the development of industry in this town." They did not suspect that the huge man would cart his bulk through all the factories of Detroit, holing up for over three months at Ford's, Chrysler's, and Edison's plants, sketching thousands of preliminaries. Rather than appease the room's rococo anachronisms, he blitzed them with a vision swept up off the factory floor. And in the final work, the curlicues and satyrs go unnoticed, lost in Diego's mechanical vision.

Rivera worked behind a screen for two years, an hourly laborer painting sometimes sixteen hours a day, in a room whose glass roof created greenhouse temperatures of over 100 degrees. Journalists, glimpsing the work in progress, declared that the murals, far from praising the city, would "knock Detroit's head off." The unveiling provided plenty for all those who secretly love a thunderstorm. The crowd stood baffled by the revealed work, seeing no historical allusions or civic allegories, no lineup of leading Detroit power brokers. The public flocked all the way out to the museum to see what they were forced to see every other day of the week: ordinary, characterless people chained to endless, sensual machines.

Diego had committed the principal subversive act: he painted the spirit of Detroit in all its unretouched particulars. Strings of interchangeable human forms stroked the assembly line—a sinuous, almost functional machine—stamping, welding, and finally producing the finished product—an auto engine. Men in asbestos suits and goggled gas masks metamorphosed into green insects. Languorous allegorical nudes mimicked the conveyor. The frescoed room showed the spirit of Detroit from a much closer distance than the comfortable, corporate copper titan I had passed on the street outside. Viewers at the unveiling found themselves inside Detroit, just as the mural-men crawled in, around, and over their creation, striking a mutually parasitic relationship with metal. Diego had painted a chapel to the ultimate social accomplishment, the assembly line, a self-reproducing work of art, precise, brilliant, and hard as steel.

Bishops and businessmen instantly mobilized to destroy the frescoes. It is not hard to read subversion and heresy into the average work of a person's hands. The task becomes easier when the work is ambitious, joyful, and revolutionary. Rivera's was a duck shoot. Even those who had not yet visited the museum found a garden variety of blasphemies in the work. People saw a ridiculous Saint Anthony tempted away from his foreman's plans by an allegory nude's legs. Depression-sensitive capitalists saw in the figures communist-inspired proto-humans. A panel showing the inoculation of a child burlesqued the Nativity.

Diego's compliment—that Detroit reveled in the vitality of the machine age—became, in the mouths of its interpreters, an insult. Edsel, the people declared, had been taken in by a piece of dangerously populist propaganda. An organized outcry of radio broadcasts and written petitions culminated in the *Detroit News* saying that "the best thing to do would be to whitewash the entire work completely."

The work stood. Those cooler minds in the opposition knew that whitewashing turns an ambiguous work decidedly subversive, whereas a busy and ambitious mural was its own death kiss. Left alone, it would date itself more and more each year, playing to an increasingly disinterested house until one day, with the roots of civilization still intact, it would pass a magic milestone and become that perfectly harmless, even socializing item, the historical artifact.

I knew nothing of all this as I stood in the mural room between trains, nor did I suspect that I would be caught up in finding out. Viewed from inside the factory, the self-reproducing machine demanded allegiance or resentment, but denied the possibility of indifference. Technology could feed dreams of progress or kill dreams of nostalgia. The old debate came alive in Rivera's work with a new strangeness. The machine was our child, defective, but with remarkable survival value. Rivera had painted the baptismal portrait of a mutant offspring, demanding love, resentment, pity, even hope, but refusing to be disowned.

With new eyes, I noticed a minor panel on one of the small walls, off to the side of the conveyor murals. In front of a sculpted dynamo more erotically contoured than any nude, a white-haired man sat at a monolithic desk, face pinched into an amalgam of benevolence and greed—Ford or Edison or De Forest or any of a dozen crabbed industrialists and innovators.

In this face, the face of our times, lay all the evidence I would need to break the hoax. to crack the mystery. Had I recognized the composite face for what it was, I might have saved a year spent tracking down the other leads: Detroit, Rivera, Ford, the auto, mechanical reproduction, portraiture, ether, relativity. When we don't know what we are after, we risk passing it over in the dark. The Chinese played with fireworks for hundreds of years without inventing the gun. Edison thought his moving pictures were just toys. The physician who first set out to discover appropriate anaesthetic dosages discovered, instead, addiction. And I, thinking the clues to my discomfort lay elsewhere, turned my back on this crabbed face and left the hall.

By the time I reached the far end of the adjoining hallway, I was in an extreme state of agitation. I had forgotten all about my connector. To calm myself, I began repeating an old nursery rhyme: While I was going to Saint Ives, I met a man with seven wives. Rivera's murals had upset me deeply and I thought only of getting away from them. Putting one last corner between myself and the factory, I wheeled smack into a mounted photograph: three young men from the turn of the century stand in a muddy road, looking out over their right shoulders. I knew it at once, though I had never seen it before. How many were going to Saint Ives?

The photo caption touched off a memory: *Three farmers on their way to a dance, 1914.* The date sufficed to show they were not going to their expected dance. I was not going to my expected dance. We would all be taken blindfolded into a field somewhere in this tortured century and made to dance until we'd had enough. Dance until we dropped.

Chapter Two

Westerwald Farmers on Their Way to a Dance, 1914

And somewhere from the dim ages of history the truth
dawned upon Europe that the morrow would obliterate the
plans of today. —JAROSLAV HAŠEK, *The Good Soldier Švejk*

THREE MEN walk down a muddy road at late afternoon, two obviously young, one an indeterminate age. They walk leisurely. One
sings:

—Carrots and onions and celery and potatoes. Such thin fare!
If my mother had served up a little meat more often, I might never
have left home.

He sings in German, but with a Rhenish or even a foreign accent. He is the taller of the two young-looking figures. Both wear
matching black suits of a heavy material that scuds up in creases
about the elbows, even when the boys straighten their arms. The
singer's hat is taller, more ostentatious, worn more jauntily than
the other's. But this does not destroy the paired impression the
two give. The bone running from the eye ridge down into the nose
has the identical arch in both faces. They may be brothers. All
three carry canes; the singer waves his in a simple, monotonous
sweep, conducting his own performance. Carrots and onions. Carrots and onions. It is the first of May in the Rhineland Province
of Prussia, 1914.

Their way is a pressed-dirt cow-and-cart trail through stark farmland that tapers, at a few hundred meters' distance, into a gentle roll. Earlier, a spring shower turned the crushed gravel and dirt mixture of the road into a muddy silt, no good for walking. Pools of water stand where horses' hooves have torn up the center of the road. The three keep to one edge or the other, where the relative safety of high ground above the packed-down wheel ruts protects their shoes. The singer wears long, flattened, gradually pointing shoes that exaggerate his dandyism. This fine, city-crafted style— the height of fashion this month—will be scorned very shortly and called "dreadnoughts," after the new battleships. Those of his double are sterner, more sober. The third figure, who wanders absently off the road or into the mud more frequently than the prettier two, wears shoes that, with the largest degree of flattery short of lying, could be called well kept up.

The third loiters behind the others in a fit of abstraction. He runs an experiment on how loosely he can hold a cigarette between his lips. It drops to the ground several times before he can perfect just the proper angle of droop. His shoulders hunch forward in his brown suit, of a lighter material than the others' but still fit for special occasions. The third one walks a while carrying his arms stiffly at his side. He stops, examines and rearranges his posture, then takes off again, arms flying. He undergoes this stop-and-change every so often, tilting his head each time to observe the effect. His cane serves sometimes as a weapon, sometimes as a prop, sometimes as excess and troublesome baggage. When he looks, for a change, at his friends up in the road ahead, a glance brought on by the sudden halt of song and bickering, he notices that the singer is walking backward in an exaggerated cakewalk, aping him. The lagging figure retaliates with a rude gesture of his own, and the two now obviously young men grin at each other in disarmament.

Faintly over the newly planted fields comes the odor of the last five years' compost and fresh manure. With this smell, equally faint, comes the sound of an orchestra. Only a stray note or phrase ripped out of context can be heard, the way a letter from a loved one, lying folded for many years, shows only spectral, illegible marks and a dissociated "I hope you are . . . "

The short one of the matched pair speaks:

—Peter, Hubert: listen. Hear that? Brass bands. I knew it would be brass bands again this year. These people, they're very good people at heart but they have villagers' imaginations. Never traveled out of the Westerwald, you understand? I'm sorry I've made the two of you come so far for a brass band.

He uses a surprising number of words for one whose walk and dress are so succinct. Until the speech, he had kept silent except to return the harpings of his twin. This burst of words carries the demure figure through his bouts of intervening silence.

His match, the singer, Peter, looks for the music but cannot find it. The rear figure, Hubert, still posturing with cigarette, scowls in impatience. But Peter looks curious, amused.

—Oh Adolphe . . .

He calls to his circumspect lookalike, giving the name a playful, effeminate sing-song, a long "e" on the final syllable.

—. . . that's not a brass band, you scoundrel. That's a full orchestra with violins. Oh, *I've* got it, Adolphe. You're *not* taking us to the charming town of Luden's May Fair, quaint as such a spectacle must be. You dog-darling. You're walking your newfound brothers all the way to . . . Vienna!

Peter explodes on the name of the city and pounces, kissing Adolphe sloppily and repeatedly, grabbing and swaying him about in a waltzer's grip. The smaller boy pushes off the prankster with Teutonic severity, disbursing, briefly, a thesaurus's listing for "insane." He straightens his ruffled clothes, adjusts his tie and starched collar. His eyes dart to the joker, now doubled in laughter, and, straightening his hat after the attack, he attempts to imitate the rakish angle of the other's.

Hubert, still lagging, gets off a good cackle at the brawl, uncontrolled and childish. He speaks with all the control of a bad tragedian trying to deepen his voice.

—We're not going to no dance *or* no Vienna. We're going to May First Soviet.

He says this as an American child of the same era might say, "We've got to go kill Jesse James." The others work at paying him no attention.

—It's not So-*veet*, Hubert. It's *So*-veet. And say *the* So-veet, not just So-veet, or people will think you're talking about a place.

Hubert only grins feebly, and hangs his cigarette steeper from his lips. Still ruffled by the surprise Viennese attack, Adolphe smoothes his suit again, and checks for his billfold in his inside vest pocket. During this entire journey, he has not let ten minutes go by without checking for this same billfold. And there is no one in all of Germany clever enough to sneak up unnoticed through these thousand acres of flat absence to filch his billfold. Still he checks the place of value every few minutes, instinctively, to prove its firm reality.

Peter resumes leading the caravan, moving ahead briskly. He sees a lost Westphalian sparrow hopping in the fields just off the road, trying to get at the April seed in the furrows. The dandy bobs his head in a grotesque parody of pecking, resembling for a moment those frightened children who believe that neck exercises can prevent the horrors of double chins and goiters. Bored, he starts to sing again:

—I might never have left home. Leave home. Leave ho-ho-hoo ho-ho-home.

Then, by association, he starts a new tune:

—How long you have been away from me. Come home, come home, come home.

This second song is livelier than the first, so Peter begins automatically to walk a shade faster. The new tempo soon carries him a few hundred paces ahead of his companions. When he realizes this, he turns on the other fellows and folds his arms. They draw closer, and he shouts:

—Orchestra, Adolphe.

—Brass band, Peter.

They are still more than a mile from their destination, the music's source. The music carries that far because of the dead stillness in the spring, 1914, air. Sound travels at about 1089 feet per second at freezing, and increases about 1.11 feet per second for each degree Fahrenheit rise in temperature. This crisp May Day is a perfect 68 degrees, so the speed of sound today is around 1129 feet per second. In five seconds, the music—whether it is Bavarian Beer Hall or Viennese Woods—travels 5645 feet, the little over a mile that the three boys are from the site of the May Fair. Five seconds at eighty-five quarter notes a minute means the waltz they hear is already two measures in the past.

The few notes that do make it this far are long over by the time they make themselves known. Modulation replaces modulation; in two measures' time the song the boys hear is no longer the song being made. The boys have only outdated music with which to create a belated present. The stars on a clear winter's night have perhaps novaed a thousand years back, but persist as an undeniable current event. The realities of the past become true only when they intersect the present. Then, only, do they become present, known, regardless of what has happened to them since. Only when grief sets in—grief, like sound, that varies with the temperature of the air—does the past in fact die.

Peter loses his lead to the more businesslike Adolphe. He lags, lost in a reverie, pronouncing out loud the name "Franz Joseph." He says the name again and again, in as many different ways as he can dream up. One permutation draws the "z" sound out to freakish proportions, then slides it into the "yo" beginning the second word. Another variant imitates the clipped sounds of a Prussian accent—"Frans Chosip"—a dialect that rings false in Peter's mouth. He speaks, chants, and sings the words until they assume a foreign, deranged quality. When Franz Joseph refuses to respond to any of the entreaties, Peter grows bored. After a few minutes, he resumes his animated, teasing voice, giving it the singsong quality of rhyme that accompanies a game of hide-and-seek.

—Adolphe. A-dol-phee. Maybe, Adolphe, Alicia will . . . A-lee-sha is going to be at the May Fair, Adolphe. And maybe she will want . . . you know, Adolphe.

Adolphe stiffens, reddens, and checks his inside vest pocket.

—Shut up, you would-be brother of mine, or you'll get this cane but good. I swear it.

It is a perfect, unwitting imitation of von Moltke, the old Franco-Prussian War general. Peter pays him no attention.

—Oh Hubert. Huu-bee. Huu-uu.

He pronounces the word to pun with the Dutch word for "how." It now becomes obvious that Peter himself is Dutch.

—Maybe some girly who doesn't know any better will give you your first little nip-and-tuck at the May Fair, Hubert.

Hubert's face contains no quality of age. It is a clay mask that conforms to the thought of the moment or any preconception of the observer. He removes his worn-down felt hat and passes his hand over the creases in his forehead, creases that seem deep enough to be the product of sixty years or more of garden pain.

—Women like So-veets the best. So-veets have the biggest stalks.

—Don't say stalk, Hubert. People will think you're just a child. Say pole. Then people will know you really have a big one.

The boys push each other and laugh. They tell one another exactly what they will do to which girls if they so much as dare show up at the dance.

While wrestling in sport in this way, the boys call one another "brother" in a way that real brothers, growing up together, never would. A cart appears, heading toward the enclave of woods that harbors the music coming from the fair. The boys break off scuffling and try to make themselves look presentable. Middle-class farmers in the cart greet Adolphe familiarly as they pass, but the cart does not stop. Peter grimaces at an imaginary spot of mud thrown onto his suit by the horse's hooves.

—*Verdomme!* What do these crazy peasants think they're doing, hey, Adolphe? Reckless drivers.

Adolphe and Hubert laugh as Peter brandishes a fist and pantomimes a fantasy-revenge on the distant cart.

—People in this valley are still in the last century, Adolphe. Everybody moves so slow they're all going to be asleep before they get to the May Fair. All sleeping; Frederick Barbarossa, asleep in the Kyffhäuser, his long red beard growing for centuries. But he'll wake up and lead Chermanee to greatness, hum, 'Dolphe?

Adolphe makes no answer. Recovering from the interruption of the cart, he heads down the road again. He straightens his hat back to its former, sober angle.

—Adolphe? Are you sleeping, Adolphe? What this sleepy valley needs are a few big Dutch automobiles. Speed, hum, 'Dolphe? Buy me an auto, A-dol-phee? We had an auto in Holland.

—You lie, brother.

—No, honest, brother. We did. Tell him, Huub. Hu-ub, tell the kind man how everybody in Holland has an auto.

—Well, being Flemish, and a So-veet, I can't say.

—Oh pooh. You're about as Flemish as that cow over there. Yaaa, yourself, you big bovine.

Adolphe returns to the others, and to good spirits. He asks:

—Say, what are you, anyway, Hubert? I mean, what nationality?

—I told you, I'm . . .

—Don't listen to him, Adolphe. He'll tell you stories all day. He's worse than a Prussian when it comes to lying. Truth is, a girl friend of Mama's—cute little ham pattie too, but pushing the middle years now—got knocked up and probably got a telegraph from the womb about the trouble this one would make. She was too busy to care for him, so my father—that is, our father, Adolphe—was big enough to make a place for him in our home.

—Shut up, you. Your pants are open and your intelligence is showing.

—Aw, sniffle in your hanky, orphan.

—Quiet, Peter, and take the log out of your own eye. After all, you're *both* living on *my* mother's generosity now.

Adolphe's eyes shine with a triumph that had not come into them until now. The three continue fairward in a renewed silence. Westerwald Rhineland consists of deceptive distances that swallow up and separate the intimate, populated enclosures. Not two hours by cart from Cologne, the region the boys travel nevertheless conceals certain roads that threaten to collapse, just beyond the next seductive rill, into total isolation. The landscape varies from violent, wooded ravines to the boredom of unmitigated open spaces. Just outside the warmth and well-lit hilarity of evening villages lie bogs of solitude. Activity on the road and in the air falls to nothing as the boys draw near the hidden May dance.

Something breaks the spell of silence. A man pedals a bicycle along the dirt track from the direction of Adolphe's mother's farm, a farm lying on a clean bevel in front of Cologne, as if threaded on the great spires of the cathedral there. He balances a rucksack full of gear on the front bicycle fender. The three watch curiously as the man hollas and stops, with some difficulty, nearby. He is bearded, perhaps thirty, and wears knickers, gaiters, and a wide-brimmed hat. With the nonchalance of one asking for directions, he calls out:

—You're wearing your Sunday clothes?

To rural reserve, the boys add the guarded manner saved for the very odd.

—Yes . . . that is . . . there is a dance.

—Of course there is a dance, my young man. Germany has held May festivals for thousands of years. Goes back to the Romans—wine bashes, the spring goddess, Flora, that sort of noise. Now I'll wager you young fellows didn't know you were headed to a heathen ritual, heh?

The boys hang spellbound. They cannot figure out how to respond to this strange-talking older man decked in bohemian hat and gaiters. Hubert is the unlikely ambassador for their faction. He takes a chance:

—Are you So-veet?

The cyclist, beginning to unpack his rucksack, curls his upper lip in a sneer of amusement and distaste.

—Social Democrat.

Hubert looks inquiringly at his stepbrother Peter, who mumbles, uncharacteristically softly, that the two are similar, so he thinks—roughly equivalent. Hubert is ecstatic.

—See! I told you that the rich folk can become So-veet too.

The man unpacks photographic prints and plates, which he begins laying out by the side of the road. Adolphe warns him that the way is muddy, but the man pays no attention. Addressing Hubert, the man adds:

—So we're political, are we? You wish to point out to me that the left has made May first some sort of workers' demonstration day, is that it? Well, they're still relative newcomers compared to the Romans and their Flora. Still, that's fine. Make some noise in the world is what I say. Just don't fall afoul of the laws. But why talk about governments and all on a fine evening like this one? Here. Come here and have a look at these.

Despite their reservations, the boys examine the photographic work he has spread out by the side of the wheel track. Adolphe gives a shout of recognition on seeing the image of two landed farmers who work several hundred acres near his mother's.

—Ha! Look at Herr Jacob all puffed up in his evening dress. Isn't he just the important man in his photograph?

Then, embarrassed at his sudden profusion, perhaps thinking

that he has just unknowingly wounded the pride of this strange man, he lapses into his customary reserve. But the man slaps his hands together, delighted with Adolphe's response.

—Exactly! See how he has stopped being the Herr Jacob that you talk planting with and has become, in front of the lens, somebody else, something more serious. He has stopped being just an individual with a certain year of birth, a certain year of death—God preserve him, you understand—and, for the sake of the unseen audience, has joined himself to the stream of the universal, the type of the well-to-do working man. The *idea* of Herr Jacob, if you will.

Now it is the cyclist's turn to be embarrassed at his explosion. He shrugs, then turns back to his unpacking. He draws a stand, some unexposed plates, and a wooden box camera out of his sack. Peter, poking about, begins to come back tentatively into his own.

—Oh *now* I see, Mr. Philosopher. You'd like to sell us some pictures here on the grounds that they show . . . whatever it is you said. The Ideal.

—Peter! What a suggestion.

—Not exactly, young fellow, but I knew you would be a shrewd one. Your jawline proves it most definitively.

Peter puts his hands to his face, suspiciously. Meanwhile, Hubert's face, which previously, hanging cigarettes and practicing revolution, might have passed for sixty, has in his childlike delight over the photos slipped several decades back to its actual mid-teens.

—Look! My buddies, look at this. Maastricht. I've been there. I *live* there. I mean Peter and I used to live there, huh, Peter? The new tool factory. When were you over there, old man?

—Sad to say, Mr. Soviet, but that is a tool factory in the Ruhr. So many of these are springing up these days that it grows increasingly difficult to tell one from the other. Yet it delights me to no end that you should mistake this one for another in—shall I say—your hometown?

—The revolutionary is a citizen of all countries at once.

—What he means, sir, is that he now lives with me in my mother's house—over that rise there; we're mostly turnips this year—and that he's in the process of becoming a naturalized German.

Peter, caught running his finger over the edge of the wooden

— 25 —

camera box, responds with all the flippancy of guilt.

—I come with the package. Two-for-one relatives. What does this instrument perform?

—That, friend, is my outdoor portraiture camera.

—Outdoor . . . ? Now there's a rich one. I'm good with machines, you know. Not a child. I understand the science of these things. Portraits, if they are to be good ones, need to be done in the studio. Something about strong sunlight blackening or blurring the film. Or like that. Am I right, *opa?* You are trying to sell us something. Are you French?

—On the contrary, my young jawbone. All the images you see here were made with my outdoor camera.

—You ride a bicycle instead of an auto, and you tell lies for a living. I cannot think of a worse combination.

Adolphe is shocked at his double's accusation, and apologizes by proxy. The photographer invites Peter to look closely at the images and notice the surroundings: here, the Luden row houses, the ridge of woods across from the Ainsbach fields, or the expanse of Neanderthal valley behind a study of two shepherd children with facial defects. Peter denies the proof.

—I tell you, you magician, I've seen all these tricks before. Sure, these were done with cameras. But indoors, in front of backdrops painted to resemble these parts. Very cleverly painted, too, I might add. The illusion of the natural is very convincing.

Portrait photographers at this time always double as oil landscapists. While their backdrops are seldom convincing enough to pass for nature, they can make nature pass for a backdrop.

—The effect would be very artistic, very artificial—almost perfect—if you could keep your subjects from dropping pose at the last minute. Or did you sell the good ones and think you could pass off the remainders on know-no-betters?

The bicyclist continues to look from one younger face to the other, with all the attention and dispassion of a botanist engaged in species identification and nomenclature.

—I can see that the only way I'm going to convince you of the reality of outdoor portraiture is to do one of the three of you. Here, now. The three of you on this road, as I saw you when I rode up.

—See? I knew you were trying to sell us something.

—No, this one will be for science's sake only, and for the archives: a personal record of the conversation we shared today.

His disclaimer collides with the flattered look that had come across Adolphe's face. Adolphe liked being selected as good photographic material, and is sorry Peter has spoiled it. He tries to appease the photographer.

—But if . . . supposing we . . . ?

—But if any of you wish to meet me at this same spot next Sunday and look at the results, then we can talk terms if you wish.

Peter takes charge of the boys, attempting to marshal them into a pose that will reflect the sheer heroism of being young. He argues with the photographer, who says he does not want a pose but a natural grouping: the same arrangement they were in—walking along toward Luden—when he interrupted them. Peter demands to know where the craft is in that. The photographer threatens to pack up his bicycle and leave unless the boys behave. Anxiously, Adolphe warns that the sun is going lower and that they had best shoot the picture now or lose the chance forever. And also that they had better hurry on soon to the fair or risk losing the better part of that as well. Peter teases Adolphe that Alicia has no chance at the May Queen because he, Adolphe, by far the prettiest in the Rhineland if not the empire, will sweep the balloting and become the first-ever May King.

The first plate is spoiled because Hubert drops the cigarette out of his mouth and bends down to pick it up just as the photographer opens the lens. The second has got to do because he has no more plates and cannot make his customary backup image.

As the man collects his photos and packs up his gear, Hubert asks him if he belongs to a trade union. The photographer says he scrupulously avoids organizations and advises the boys to do the same. The talk drifts easily from the weather to planting conditions and on to politics, with the photographer deploring the recent Zabern Incident, in which an army officer exploited and humiliated Alsatians. In an unconvincing imitation of someone much older than he, Adolphe warns the photographer not to talk disrespectfully about the Kaiser. The photographer asks Adolphe:

—What do you think the Kaiser had in mind by raising the army to eight hundred thousand men?

Adolphe, again sounding as if he has just recently heard his father say the same thing, replies that he is sick and tired of alarmist talk about war. Such talk shows a selfishness of nature, a weakness of will, and a clamoring for sensationalism. Daily routine is enough, and people shouldn't go about talking war to liven things up. And besides, military service is an honor.

Three men, only one of them native to the area, are photographed as if they are walking to a not-quite fair. One lags a little behind, cane at a rakish angle, undisciplined hair curling out from under a beaten-up hat. His lip shows the first sign of down. His jaw seems to contain an extra joint just above the chin. Despite ill-behaved ears and a nose that will be too fleshy in old age, he is redeemed from ugliness by eyebrows that recurve into grace. He hangs a cigarette from full, Flemish lips. His dark eyes carry the accumulation of several decades' pain.

In front of him, a brighter-looking man turns three quarters in a more arrogant attitude toward the camera. His too-long nose seems even more equine in that the nostrils can be seen from head on. Eyes and mouth share a concord of irony that cheek fat and a minute chin cleft attempt to undermine. His left hand closes finger to thumb, in a gesture of covert aristocracy.

In the lead, the youngest face, oldest in years, seems in danger of being routed totally by a starched white collar. His pose is a successful imitation of the middle figure, although rigid in a way suggesting autonomy, or attempted autonomy, as if accusing the model of doing the copying. The arch over the eye is pure nineteenth century. The effect is of a young man trying to preserve something not wholly understood.

All three have stopped left foot in front of right, looking out over their right shoulders at an observer present but remarkably unobtrusive. Behind them, empty fields.

Alicia is at the fair. She lost the May crown to the middle Jacob daughter. Nevertheless, the boys fight for a rotation of dances with her. Hubert asks her what she thinks of the Soviet. Peter tries to put his tongue in her ear. Adolphe asks her what she thinks the Kaiser had in mind by raising the army to 800,000 last year.

Chapter Three

Accommodating the Armistice

. . . Opticians' shops were crowded with amateurs panting for daguerreotype apparatus, and everywhere cameras were trained on buildings. Everyone wanted to record the view from his window. . . . —MARC ANTOINE GAUDIN, *Traité pratique de la photographie*, quoted in Beaumont Newhall, *The History of Photography*

MARCHING: what five minutes before might have passed for a mid-sized Ford sedan badly in need of a tune-up now unmistakably became marching. Mays listened to the regular stamp of feet hitting the concrete coming from somewhere in the neighborhood of Clarendon. Ascribing direction to the sound at this point, from eight stories up, was largely speculation, interpolation after the facts. And this noise, definitely marching now, left only the faintest of tracks. That Peter bothered with it at all testified to the less than hypnotic hold of the work in front of him on his desk.

Facing Mays across an impenetrable barrier of potted plants, Moseley, Peter's colleague, continued to seek the lowest level permitted by his office chair, happily cutting, rearranging, and pasting a manuscript in front of him as if the trampling noise could be nothing more serious than a rattling radiator. Thirty years in the Powell Building—a noisy twelve stories of poured concrete—had conditioned Moseley to ignore all aural phenomena aside from the 5:00 all-clear bell.

But neither editor could cultivate ignorance for long. An affected sergeant's accent called out drill in the street below:

—Hawp, hawp, wan-te-doop, ga-dinkity-dinkity, hawp.

A concerted shuffling following this epileptic outburst signified a change in squad formation. Snare drums fired off in snappy precision. Mays, perhaps because this was the first parade he'd ever heard without seeing, wondered that no one had ever pointed out to him that marching feet do not move metronomically but in a lopsided, trapezoidal one-*two*, one-*two*. Armies lurch; the listener does the smoothing out.

Mays's interest in what was going on outside the office window gradually escalated, starting with disinterested head bobs, so as not to alarm his cellmates. He coughed, fussed with papers, turned slowly toward the lone window. Peter's precautions were lost on Moseley, on the far side of the plant wall. The senior fellow breathed heavier, in raspy sforzando, but continued shuffling sheaves. The army marching in the street below would have to ambush him in his pretended ignorance.

When the marching grew louder, Peter caught the eyes of Caroline Brink and Doug Delaney, the other half of the technical masthead of *Micro Monthly News*. The eighth floor of the Powell Building allowed this eye contact by means of the advanced concept of Modular Officing. "Modular" was an interior decorator's euphemism for obscuring the fact that the walls separating the editors went only halfway to the ceiling. Moseley, for his part, had tried to rectify this modularity—a violation of his constitutional guarantee of oblivion—by lugging in potted plants one at a time on the commuter shuttle, to build an organic barrier.

—Sounds like the Germans got the East Coast in the divvy-up, Captain.

Dougo Delaney had gotten his first laugh in Mrs. Rapp's 2-B, when, being asked by the teacher how he was going to learn math if he kept asking for the washroom pass, he had responded, "Process of elimination." He addressed and saluted his superior, Caroline. Brink, ignoring the irony, asked:

—Where's that coming from?

Mays felt an urge to tell her not to end a sentence in a preposition, but could not decide if "from" was one. He had always been a little too slow for the obligatory, sadistic office patter. To identify the marching, he would have to stand and crane. He declined to lower himself to active observation. Instead, he addressed the potted-plant barrier:

—Aren't you going to have a look, Mr. Moseley?

—No. They're a couple blocks away. Can't see them from here. It's nothing, anyway.

His denial galvanized the other three. With a look of complicity, they moved from their modules to the window: if Moseley says they're too many blocks away to see, then they're here, in plain sight below the window. Mays's suspicion—that there was something remarkable, worth looking at, outside—received a last ratification in the unswerving wrongness of the wheezy fellow across the way.

—Brink, come hold my legs.

Delaney, supine on the window ledge, resembled a tackled halfback trying to sneak the ball ahead over the first-down mark. Snares, bagpipes, and drillmaster had been driven aside by the typical parade brass. The new sounds dissipated into random, drunken snippets of "Turkey in the Straw," the Marines' Hymn, and an obscure version of "Columbia, the Gem of the Ocean." Particles of Americana collided against each other on the eight-floor trip up the side of the Powell Building, a Brownian motion of regimented anarchy.

Mays, too, had gravitated to the window, but could see only Delaney's graceless posterior there, Caro keeping it in place. He thought to offer his help, but knew she had the better build and stamina for the job of anchorperson. Moseley, claustrophobic, pushed his wire rims higher on his papier-mâché nose and said something about the musicians being two blocks away. Delaney blandly came within a few centimeters of killing himself on his way back inside.

—Gentlepeople of the press, God damn that son-of-a-bitching Mr. Powell. Off the record, of course.

Not content merely to verb a noun, Delaney was moved by the extent of boss Powell's crime into participling one. Worse than not getting Veterans' Day off, the staff of *Micro Monthly News* had not even been told they wouldn't be getting the holiday. Not reminded that this was anything but a routine workday, they'd been deprived of the vicarious bitterness that is often more gratifying than the holiday itself. Delaney began making up for lost time.

—Veterans' Day, you lousy proles. Three quarters of Boston must be out there. Party hats, floats, confetti, buxom young women twirling those white rifles . . .

He grabbed Brink and began half-waltzing, half-polkaing her around the office. He accompanied himself by singing, "O Caroline, My Caroline" to the tune of "O Maryland, My Maryland," a song he evidently assumed fit the occasion by being vaguely patriotic. In fact, the song is highly separatist, encouraging acts of violence against the same soldiers of the Union marching in the street below. Brink made her Managing Editor's face and attempted to free herself. Moseley, without changing the cadence of his cutting and pasting, pronounced his judgment on the proceedings, coming dangerously close to unlawfully impersonating an Old Testament prophet:

—Adenoids.

His diagnosis, a malapropism for "adrenals," implied that Delaney was under the dim influence of sex glands that, if humored, would go away as soon as he gave up the bad taste of being twenty-six.

Mays, roused by the prospect of novelty, decided to have his own look at the parade. He did not yet know that there is no better way of spoiling the exotica of the *Thousand and One Nights* than to visit contemporary Iran. Nor did he yet know how involving, beyond all reasonable expectation, a simple act of eavesdropping can become.

The ledge made him nervous, and he linked his feet on a runner pipe in the absence of the anchoring Caro. Although this limited him to half of Delaney's extension, he craned out far enough to see that the commotion eight stories down was not a parade but the breakup of one. Delaney had deliberately and maliciously lied: three quarters of Boston were not in attendance, nor were three quarters of Back Bay, Copley Square, or three quarters of those who worked on the immediate block. By the time the remarkably perfunctory parade passed outside the Powell Building, not even three quarters of the marchers were still present.

Delaney, despite Brink's protests, was still singing in four and dancing in three, with terrifying effect. Seeing Mays prostrate in the window, he broke off.

—Peter, no! Don't jump. Powell says he'll agree to the raise.

Mays came back into the room, registering disgust on the roof of his mouth behind his right front teeth. He had gone to the window in hopes of a spectacle, and had come away instead with a vision of dissolution: wandering battalions, batteries of tubas and euphoniums breaking for the curb in relief, infantry out of sync, jaded clarinetists stopping in mid-note, trumpets draining spit from mouthpieces, clowns tearing off their bibulous noses, small-fry politicians beating hasty retreats, whole regiments pouring into waiting buses.

Delaney resumed the vacated window post with a suicidal leap. Mays, seeing him dangle over the edge, sat down on the office floor, overcome by sympathetic vertigo. Caroline joined him. Her hair fallen and temples swollen from the waltzurka, she did not look like a technical editor specializing in integrated-circuit components and the ostensible big chief of the *Micro* group.

—Great, isn't it? Veterans' Day, and we're working.

She hit into an unassisted triple play. It was by no means great, they were certainly not working, and it was not even Veterans' Day. That is, it was not November 11, the anniversary of the armistice of the Fourteen Points, commemorating the end of the First World War. The day on which first one and then the other of two young men of draftable age looked out of a window on what one thought of as a parade and the other as a disappointment was October 29, 1984. An act of Congress had created the discrepancy. Some well-meaning legislator, presumably concluding that the day on which the belligerents in the world's then largest cataclysm had chosen to sit down and end hostilities fell too close to Thanksgiving, succeeded in moving Armistice Day, which had become Veterans' Day in light of subsequent events, to the fourth Monday in October, a movable feast and legal holiday. Powell broke the law; instead, any employee of Powell Trade Magazine Group could take Good Friday, "as needed."

Unaware of how history had been rewritten, Mays sat on the floor contemplating Brink's overbite and considering his professional relation to her. For weeks after signing on with *Micro*, rather

— 33 —

than attack his first assignment (a somewhat dense piece of prose called "New Printed-Circuit Board Adds Reliability to PCM-type Trans Codes"), he had tried to decipher the loose hierarchy of jobs and job titles of the Powell eighth floor.

At the top was Powell himself, an Annapolis grad who made brief appearances to relieve himself of nautical metaphors at the expense of the under-20K set. Each trade magazine in the Powell holdings—such titles as *Synthetics World* and *Modern Brick Journal*—had its own sector. Brink headed up the Electronics Sector, being the only one on the masthead with a real knowledge of the material, most other competent people taking the same higher-paying jobs in industry that Mays had fled.

In a class to himself lay Moseley, who had put in a thankless ten years in engineering before being farmed out to the trades as an anachronism. Moseley's father had told him that the survivors of the century would be the electronic technicians, but had failed to predict their rapid obsolescence. Moseley was what the press called "an analog guy"—he'd learned all his electronics before 1965 and could be of no possible help on a magazine dealing with contemporary digital technology. Delaney, who had to bring his flashlight batteries to the store to ensure his buying the right-size replacements, enjoyed torturing Moseley with lectures on the simplicity of digital—"a mere matter of On or Off"—using obscene finger gestures as visual aids. Doug Delaney had gotten on the magazine as a fluke—"I borrowed a résumé"—and remained there through the magic of inertia. Mays had survived in the vortex of positions at Powell Magazines by using Delaney's simple advice: "When in doubt, interface."

While Delaney hung out the window, Brink gathered her breath for a return to micro-normalcy, and Moseley shuffled paragraphs. Mays, trying to recall from grade school the background of Veterans' Day, conjured up a hybrid image in his mind of Lord Kitchener and Marshal Foch, the two meaning nothing to him apart from the moustaches.

—Peter, get over here. You've got to see this. God. A magazine cover. A bacchante.

Until then, the highest tribute Delaney had ever paid a woman in public had been "amazon." Mays, the compensatorily diffident

— 34 —

superior, joined him at the sill. Without even a finger-point from Delaney, Mays locked onto the figure at once: a woman at once implausible, standing violently apart from the river of jugglers, scouts, vendors, and soldiers that threatened to take her in the undertow. She forced her way upstream, west, while the world all about her insisted on another direction altogether. Even aside from this salmon-perversity, she would have stood out at once from the busy scene as the figure that did not apply: she wore a full-sleeved, gathered, embroidered, bias-cut, hobble-skirt dress from out of the last century. She carried a clarinet. Her hair—a brilliant strawberry red—fell all around her in ringleted profusion. From eight stories up, she seemed to be listening to something, in pain, petrified, in parade-gladness, or simply lost, out of joint in time.

Late in October, the Berkshires having collapsed the week before, the vets began piling back on the subway to make it home before more leaves fell. As Acting Editor, it sat with Brink to order the Electronics Sector back to work. But Caro'd gotten caught up in a story in one of the competing trade journals about a mainframe chip that replaced rooms of computers and sat comfortably on two fingertips. Moseley continued to collate and excise, Delaney to resuscitate vaudeville. Peter Mays alone remained fixed by the temporary and remarkable frame that had opened up in front of him, a shock of red hair—the view from his window.

Chapter Four

Face of Our Time

The wrinkles and creases on our faces are the registration of the great passions, vices, insights that called on us; but we, the masters, were not at home.—WALTER BENJAMIN, *Illuminations*

AT THE TIME of my shock in the Detroit museum, I knew just enough about photography to hold up my end of a conversation, providing I had only to nod in agreement. I managed discussions of photography the same way I got by in all matters outside my own too-specialized technical vocation. I use a time-honored formula: for each discipline I've memorized a half-dozen personalities and an equal number of broad technical terms. From there, I simply string together judgments, always pleading subjective bias: "To me, Weston's compositional sense is so much more interesting than Strand's depth of field." I'd played the same game as a child, using those decks of feature cards in which the ears, eyes, nose, and mouth of any face fit equally well on any other.

The bluffing game works because we think of history as the work of individuals. Politics produces Jeffersonian Democracy, the Monroe Doctrine, or Seward's Folly. A history of music invariably becomes Bach and the High Baroque or Debussy contra Wagner. Even a field as objective as Mathematics marshals under proper names: Venn diagrams, Fourier transforms. The discoverer becomes the discovery.

The great physicist Max Planck claimed that the advancement of knowledge actually follows quite a different path than the one this cult of personality indicates. The climate of the times, according to Planck, rather than some timeless quality of individual genius, fosters the invention. Thus Newton and Leibnitz developed the calculus simultaneously and independently. This idea, which has been called Planckian, gains authority in having been proposed by one of the century's great physicists. But it would insist of itself that the time was merely ripe for its own proposing.

Bluffing works because listeners impose sense on fragments. When I mention Nijinsky, you know exactly who I mean, smoothing out the snags between the dexterous faun and the aging, confined lunatic. In cementing a familiar name to an adjective phrase, I am simply the amiable volunteer from the audience, pouring one colorless liquid into another. My conversant is the magician, causing the resultant fluid to shine with the colors of the rainbow.

But at the Detroit Institute, seeing the black-and-white print of three young men from early in the century, I felt my dilettantism become urgency. I knew that the old bluffing game would not get me through this one, that my passing knowledge of photography was no longer enough. "Compositional technique" and "depth of field" were no longer the issue. Who made this? Under what circumstances? What did it signify?

Stung by three casual glances, I felt that the photographer had stumbled across a great discovery, caught, by talent and chance, an image of great importance, and that no one would have rescued that moment from obscurity if he had not arrested it on film. My first response, triggered by my passing resemblance to one of the figures, was to find out the photographer's name. And later, if possible, to find out and hide away the names and identities of those three young men.

I snuck a sideways look at the identifying tag, crib sheet for an important test. I half-expected to recognize what was written there, but the tag meant nothing to me. It identified the photographer as August Zander, an Austrian. The room contained no other work by the man. The photograph's identification tag turned out to be in error on three counts: in the spelling of the surname, in the nationality, and in the tacit proclamation of its correctness. A variation on an old puzzle goes: This sentence have three things rong with it. The first is the agreement, the second, the spelling of the word "wrong." The third thing wrong is that there are only two things wrong. That third thing set me back several months in pursuing the hoax.

Where I had been in a hurry to kill time so that I could catch the connecting Technoliner back to Boston, I was now in a hurry to linger in the room a long time, longer than I had, fixing the image in my mind. The odd notion occurred to me that if I had a camera I could take a snapshot of the photo and thereby possess it the same way the photographer had captured the three figures. But I had no camera, so I had to document my alarm with the less reliable instrument of memory. And my memory has never been close to photographic.

Detroit had laid the groundwork for my agitation, with its cult of mass production. Rivera's mural played on that agitation, surprising me with a thousand square yards of paint, a chapel to the greatest and most awful of human constructs—the machine. I had left the assembly-line altar with my whole sense of balance destroyed. Out of nothing, three farmers offered a foothold. The three men on a muddy road seemed to me an entrée of immense importance, but to what, I was still unsure.

The mechanics of my profession called on me to do a little research—modest stuff, periodicals indices—from time to time. I had lived in Boston before and knew those places where I could answer questions quickly. I found a cheap room in The Fens—the university ghetto, a short walk to the public library and a bridge away from Cambridge. The room was clean and the bugs did not keep me awake at night. Finding work was tougher, as I refused to sign any forms releasing personal information for inclusion in my file. I finally landed a position downtown. I sprang for a subway pass as soon as it got cold, and set about my new life.

Aside from having once spent a month and a half asking everyone I met if they knew a song with the words "a lingering lass in her party dress," a line I knew from somewhere but could not place, I had never been obsessed. And even after the first few weeks of researching the photograph, I did not yet admit to obsession: a glance at the *Xerxes to Zygote* volume of a multivolume encyclopedia in passing. Slight facial resemblance was not enough motive for irrational interest. I laughed off my curiosity. Dismissing is one of the great pastimes of those setting off into the dark. In a short while I accumulated enough absence of data to convince myself that there had never been a photographer named Zander. Austria in 1914 could produce no artist capable of creating the work I remembered seeing in Detroit just weeks before. The man simply did not exist.

One night in 1910, August Sander, a German then working in Austria, while doing menial chores, hit upon the idea of an epic photographic collection to be called *Man of the Twentieth Century*, a massive, comprehensive catalog of people written in the universal language—photography. The work would be a meticulous examination of human appearance, personality, and social standing, a cross-sampling of representative types, each fitted into a sweeping scheme of categories and subcategories.

Incredible as it seems to us now, Sander believed, without irony (that peculiarly twentieth-century defense), that hard work could complete such a document. It took a man of the nineteenth century to conceive of *Man of the Twentieth Century*. Sander was born in Herdorf, a mining and farming village east of Cologne, in 1876, six years after the Franco-Prussian War, during which the provisional governor escaped a besieged Paris in a hot-air balloon. He had only six years of schooling.

His memoirs describe the Siegerland of his boyhood as an idyllic and varied paradise. "There were impressions daily," he wrote, "and every day brought new experiences." A dreamy child, he loved more than anything to listen to the herdsmen tell their ghost stories in the twilight. He learned to draw and paint, sealing himself up in landscapes. The idyll came to an end when August went into the mines at the age of thirteen. Labor below ground left Sander a pragmatist for life and marked his documentary project with grim toughness. Sander's early descent into the mines contributed to his being one of the first to train the camera on the uglier face of humanity. Before Sander, photographers used their machines solely to isolate beauty: upper-class portraits, vases of flowers. But Sander's monumental document would include a section of portraits entitled "Ill, Insane, and Disabled"—no art that does not acknowledge the asphyxiating life underground. Yet despite this pioneering social realism, Sander remained a miner, suspicious of the *avant-garde* and of ideas, more comfortable with the Westerwald farmers—the ill, insane, and disabled—who were his real people.

After years in the mines, the young Sander was one day called on to assist a traveling photographer, one of the breed that springs up in the wake of a developing technology, surveying the mining district. Sander led the man to a hill overlooking the entire mining valley. He writes how, still a boy, he was suddenly struck by how a human invention could stop the fluctuations of nature and make permanent even those qualities as accidental as the shadows of moving clouds. Sander had a vocation.

Both financial and critical success came almost at once. His early work as a painter helped him master the gum arabic process. This technique let the photographer brush and scrape the developing print, touching up in the lab the mistakes of the studio and the subject's face. Although Sander later gave up the gum process, declaring his hatred for "sugar-coated gimmicks, poses, and false effects," his early mastery of the touch-up technique earned him his own studio and the financial prosperity to renounce the process.

In these early years, he supplemented his income by bicycling from his studio in Cologne into his familiar, rural Rhineland. He took impromptu portraits of the local population, becoming one of the first to spread photography outside the privileged and middle classes. Technical advances permitted short-exposure images out of doors. Several of his poorer rural subjects got their first taste of photography on Sander's weekend trips into the Westerwald. In this way, Sander led the movement to bring serious and commercial photography out of the artist's studio.

Sander always considered photography a trade, a livelihood earned by hard work. Art and income were bound together. In addition to documenting the working class, Sander specialized in commercially lucrative commemoratives. He photographed emigrants departing for America. He produced soldiers' keepsakes. Those works that he could not sell went into shows, where they almost always took prizes. Then in 1910, at the age of thirty-four, he hit upon, overnight, the final shape of his life's work: that comprehensive catalog of faces that would record, with German thoroughness, life in the new era.

From then on, Sander worked at his human encyclopedia, stopping only for the century's two interruptions. The year of the three farmers photograph caught him at an early career peak. Two major honors had just come his way. The Berlin Museum of Arts and Crafts purchased six photographs for an exhibition honoring international photography pioneers. Additionally, the Deutscher Werkbund, a Cologne design association, recognizing in Sander and his medium that middle ground between the trades and arts, between forward-looking technology and reflective portraiture, commissioned photos for an exhibition linking progressive architecture with advancements in industry.

Unfortunately, the Kaiser did not attend this exhibition. Wilhelm had not yet been informed of any progress in any field since Frederick the Great. European balance of power—or a failure in the balancing act—preempted Sander's career ascendancy. A reservist, he was called up to serve in the medical corps. He stayed with his unit in Belgium and France until defeat in 1918.

Sander retaliated with his own historical indifference in the years following the war. As the Weimar Republic brought Germany into its most economically depressed sixteen years in modern times, Sander commenced the most productive period in his life. Blessed with that unusual combination of architect's vision and laborer's obeisance, Sander continued his hopelessly anachronistic cataloging through the general disillusionment that followed the First War. He ignored the century's first principle of positivism, which forbids us to talk about what we cannot know. Instead, he did the only thing that could save a work too naïvely ambitious to salvage: he made it larger. As his portfolio of faces grew, as his subject matter—Man of the Twentieth Century—doubled twice in his lifetime, Sander responded in a way possible only for one limited to six years' formal education. He expanded his classifications of facial and human types to include the terrible new categories of the times.

Sander, the uncontroversial, comfortable, middle-class craftsman, crossed the public will in 1934 when the Reich Chamber of Visual Arts destroyed the printing blocks and burnt all available copies of a volume of Sander's photographs called *Face of Our Time*, the first installment of *Man of the Twentieth Century*. *Face of Our*

Time, a microcosm of the larger work, followed the same arch-form, beginning with Westerwald peasants, creeping up the economic and social scales, peaking with creators and inventors, then descending through urban compromise, squalor, and illness, concluding with an ominous image of an unemployed man on a Cologne corner.

The Nazi suppression of *Face of Our Time* ended Sander's overt work on *Man of the Twentieth Century*. The ban seems at first an arbitrary exercise of police power. How could such harmless images, in the hands of a respected craftsman, be subversive? Sander was no more political than normal. His party, just left of center, was one of the most popular of the day. True, the man who wrote the foreword to the book was Jewish, but a converted Catholic. Sander's son, Erich, was actively anti-Nazi, but the thin book could hardly be found guilty of complicity with Erich.

But *Face of Our Time* was found guilty. Sander's gallery of anarchists, minorities, and transients crossed the view of the German people the Nazis were trying to foster. And Sander compounded his sin by presenting these dregs alongside the industrious and the propertied without editing or commentary. Sander removed himself from the seat of photographic judgment, deferring artistically in favor of real life. The Ministry of Culture, intent on its own version of the face of our time, might have forgiven an aesthetic error more than the proclamation of objectivity. Confronted, Sander gave up portraiture for harmless landscape and nature studies. The ban was the century's way of confirming that the enormous cataloging project had been doomed from inception.

Sander's camera crossed the authorities in another tragic way. His son Erich published anti-Nazi pamphlets on a private press until the police tracked down the machinery and destroyed it. The father offered to help his son by reproducing written tracts photographically. Thus Erich, who on any of several bicycle trips into France might have emigrated and ensured his safety, instead remained in Cologne and continued distributing subversive material. Father and son worked together on the project, an appendix to *Man of the Twentieth Century*, drying prints on clotheslines on their roof. An anticonspiratorial wind blew a loose page down to the courtyard below into the hands of a citizen eager to earn social credit by denouncing a stranger. Secret police came for Erich at four the next morning, and he received a ten-year jail sentence. A few months before the end of his term, Erich, unable to convince his guard that he was suffering from a sharp abdominal pain, died in prison of a burst appendix.

Sander survived a decade deprived of his calling, subject to periodic searches and seizures of negatives. But throughout it all, he never stopped archiving, scrutinizing faces, rating individuals for the lens, exposing and developing in the mind, a mind that left no evidence of aperture or silver nitrate. His house near Cologne was gutted by Allied bombers bringing their purifying and simplifying fire. His forty thousand negatives, hidden in the cellar, survived.

It seemed a sign that the interminable compilation would continue after the relatively short war ended. Then, in one of the ironies of modern times, petty looters, in the anarchy of the war's closing, set fire to the bombed structure and destroyed the entire collection.

In later years, Sander no longer entertained any delusions of completing his portfolios. Yet he continued to work over his remaining negatives. A few later books appeared, refusing to admit that their supporting volumes—the ones that would flesh them out—had been blown away. No longer strong enough to bicycle into the Westerwald, Sander remained at home polishing and refining a few isolated cornices from which we might induce the magnificence of the intended mansion. The awards and accolades continued to pour in until they finally accomplished their intention, rendering him today an honored and almost totally forgotten figure who does not even rate an entry in our larger multivolume encyclopedias. Sander has slipped into semifictional marginalia.

Clearly Sander's camera could no more exhaustively document Man of the Twentieth Century than a mechanical planetarium can exhaust the night stars. Yet his work completes itself in failure. The shattered, overambitious, unfinished work seems the best possible vehicle for its undemonstrable subject. From integrations over tens of thousands of mechanically reproduced prints, extant, maliciously destroyed, or never taken, emerges a sitter by turns willing, self-destructive, reticent, demure, but never, not even in the sum of all its unsummable parts, not through naming and categorizing and endless, industrious compilation, never, ultimately, catchable. The incomplete reference book is the most accurate.

Sander's work is everywhere shot through with such paradoxes. His embracing the mechanical portrait marks him as modern, as does his rejection of pretty nostalgia. Equating beautified photography with deceit, Sander worked with silver-salt papers that always represented moles as woefully molish. He saw the facts as the century demanded, in stark images of a one-legged Great War veteran, an aged syphilitic, or blind street urchins signing furiously with hands. In a 1927 exhibition credo, he writes:

> We must be able to endure seeing the truth, but above all we should pass it on to our fellow men and to posterity, whether it be favorable or unfavorable to us. Now, if I, as a healthy human being, am so immodest as to see things as they are and not as they are supposed to be or can be, then I beg your pardon, but I can't act differently. . . . Therefore let me speak the truth in all honesty about our age and the people of our age.

But this very belief that he could get at the objective truth dates him, marks him as an anachronism. The nineteenth century had held to the doctrine of perfectibility. Aside from a few holdouts, most of the thinkers of the last century believed in the upward spiral of rationality, which would at last triumph over the imperfections of nature. Sander forsook such meliorism in favor of dispassionate observation. But the main current of the new century broke with reason altogether, embarking on a course of eclectic irrationality. Even the cold machinery of the camera was turned, by the true moderns, to the cause of surreality, absurdity, and abstraction by such devices as composite doctoring, odd and illusory angles, or trick exposures.

Sander rejected the innovations of the *avant-garde*, continuing his single-purposed, conservative work. The guiding metaphysic of his most shockingly modern portraits dates to the medieval pseudosciences of physiognomy and phrenology, two category disciplines that claimed exact correspondences between facial and skull types and personalities. Sander updated the theory for this century: a good statistical sampling of photos can prove a nervous thinness in the salaried class, saturnine brows on the propertied.

His family tells of how Sander would chase down an interesting face until the harassed individual threatened to call the police if not left alone. He abandoned a reverence for higher things and turned his lens instead toward the details of the street. His work celebrates the isolated case: a civil servant's vacuous smile, the tight-lipped, too-fashionable sneer of a socialite, an unemployed vaudevillian warding off hunger with a shrug. The title of a later volume of Sander's photos, *Men Without Masks*, betrays his love of the undisguised particular. The widower's daze and his sons' sadness are their own best document.

In a 1931 radio broadcast (the year of Diego's frescoes) Sander explains:

> More than anything else, physiognomy means an understanding of human nature. . . . We can tell from appearance the work someone does or does not do; we can read in his face whether he is happy or troubled. . . . The individual does not make the history of his time, he both impresses himself on it and expresses its meaning. It is possible to record the historical physiognomic image of a whole generation and, with enough knowledge of physiognomy, to make that image speak in photographs. . . . The time and the group sentiment will be especially evident in certain individuals whom we can designate by the term "type."

The man obsessed with the involutions of particular faces sought in them the type of our Face-in-General. Sander unmasks the individual only to restore to the denuded figure the mask of the clan. The images in *Face of Our Time* attempt to remove the obtrusive presence of the photographer in order to call full attention to the photographic object, the face of our time.

But clinical diagnosticians soon learn that their personalities help fire or defuse their patients' complaints. The photographer who practiced dispassion and removal becomes instantly recognizable by his absence. Sander, at the same time as those working in physics, psychology, political science, and other disciplines, blundered against and inadvertently helped uncover the principal truth of this century: viewer and viewed are fused into an indivisible whole. To see an object from a distance is already to act on it, to change it, to be changed.

After watching a thousand encyclopedias and references skip from Zambia to Zanzibar, I began to suspect that my Detroit Zander did not exist. The dozen casebooks I took apart suggested that Austrians had made remarkably few contributions to early photography. Because I could not find a second opinion, the photo of the three farmers grew progressively less distinct until it seemed a collection of shapeless gray tones: two, perhaps three men in the year of outbreak of war, one looking vaguely like me. The too-familiar is the last recognized. Paged in a crowded terminal, we remark on the unusual coincidence of someone else being here with our name.

Day after day, I tried to recall the sense of unsponsored obligation the photo had made in me as I waited for the Technoliner. The moment seemed intent on joining all the others I had lost— those August evenings arguing over love on the darkened lawn, or Saturdays on the fence rails behind a vacant lot, singing to a ladybug that her house was on fire and her children in danger. I was losing the moment of the photograph, losing the photo itself, as if my memory were no better than a bad director who relied too heavily on the slow dissolve.

I began grabbing for long odds. Between technical assignments at work, I read anything remotely related to that lost day: Fodor on Detroit, *Britannica* on Rivera and the War. Winter came. I positioned my desk to look out of my upper-story office window onto the Mass. Turnpike. My six-month review judged me satisfactory, with unmet potential. The city government survived a graft scandal. Sixty thousand people in Greater Boston were out of work. I stopped reading the papers. Increasingly interested in finding out about another man of the early century who, like Sander, parlayed a few years of formal education into world renown, I passed, without knowing it, the point where I no longer could recall those three faces.

Sander, ever the archivist and documenter, kept, for whoever might stumble on them, meticulous records of his own development. In one recollection he writes:

I put in the plates and began my first photographic tour, to a hilly part of the village from which I photographed the landscape where the mines were. In the evening I developed the plate, but when I finished, a second village was reflected in the clouds. At first I thought I had made a double exposure and was very depressed about the picture. When the plate was dry, I went with it to our village physician and told him what had happened. The doctor said it was not a double exposure but a Fata Morgana—a mirage, a reflection in the air. This was my very first photograph.

Chapter Five

Trois Vierges

The pallor of girls' brows shall be their pall. . . .—WILFRED
OWEN, "Anthem for Doomed Youth"

THREE WEEKS after the brief May affair, Peter Kinder, formerly
Dutch of Maastricht, and Hubert, called Minuit, of unknown nationality became officially registered Germans. To simplify a difficult, sometimes impossible process, they acquired German parents.
As both boys had parents still living, they had to fabricate deaths
for purposes of the adoption.

In fact, Peter's mother, the woman who, together with a growing addiction to novelty, had lured Jan Kinder away from Adolphe's
mother, still lived in Holland's South Limburg Province, just over
the German border. Of French extraction, she succeeded in
changing the man only to the degree of getting him to answer to
"Jean." She could do nothing to reduce his appetite for change and
conquest, a taste that even brought him, for a time, back to his
German wife. On each of Jan's subsequent border incursions back
into the Westerwald, Adolphe's mother continued to yield dutifully to him, in secret, out of the technical obligation of matri-
mony.

When the old campaigner died in January of 1914, his Dutch-
French consort, Peter's mother, could no longer see any reason to
keep the boy. She applied to Jan's German wife, who had long
before remarried without benefit of divorce. The letter was a combination of plea and innuendo. Adolphe's mother, unaware that
Jan's death freed her from any threat of bigamy trial, bought the
blackmail. Over the feeble objections of her second husband, she

opened her home to a new son with all the dumb acceptance she had always shown his father. Falsifying the adoption forms, Peter trusted that his blood mother would accept her official, paper death with the same docility.

Hubert's paper lies, on the other hand, lay closer to the truth. Although his mother could be traced and even possessed by any German immigration officer with enough capital and interest, his father was unknown, even to her. She had given the boy the surname Minuit after the Dutch national hero and buyer of Manhattan. For his part, the boy had taken it into his head that his father was some Flemish man of action. Foisted on Peter's mother before Jan's death, he had been accepted by her without objection. Coming across the border as a surprise auxiliary clause in the treaty between Jan Kinder's two women, he was taken in by Adolphe's mother with a similar silence.

Europe was rife with such transients, and families stayed continually ready to swap loyalties and annex newcomers. This constant exchange of doorstep obligations drew families of all nations grudgingly closer until, at the turn of the century, miscegenation and ties bound together everyone from these farmers all the way up to the cousins Edward VII, Kaiser Wilhelm, and Czar Nicholas. Optimists used this interdependence of relatives to prove that European war was impossible.

But apart from the custom of shifting households, women were naturally inclined to open their doors to the odd child Hubert. Naïveté and geriatric suffering formed so absurd a combination in the boy's face as to evoke instant empathy. Hubert met the first condition for inspiring love: he gave off an aura of cruelty coupled with basic helplessness. He was at the mercy of others. Many times one or the other of his *mère-moeders* would catch themselves looking at one of his ineffectual, sadistic acts—chasing a squirrel with a penknife or threatening a town banker with class warfare—and would predict in loud, maternal voice how the world was not meant for old children, how he was due to suffer at society's hands. For this he would curse them, but mispronouncing the profanity or drooling on himself in his anger, he thereby confirmed them. It was their own laughable callousness these women saw in Hubert and took pity on.

So in late May two adolescents perjured themselves on notaried paper about the state of their real parents and received ones of a new nationality in exchange. They took the name of their legal father, Schreck, a name Adolphe had already adopted after his mother's remarriage. In his heart, if not yet consciously, Adolphe, being the oldest of Jan Kinder's sons, toyed with the idea of changing his name back so that his blood father's line might not lose its last record.

The new father of three held part-ownership in a moderately prosperous Westerwald farm. He hedged against the uncertainties of crop raising by investing heavily in British colonial ventures. The new international investing, like the exchange of unwanted children, supposedly drew the Continent together, making it unlikely for any country to sever its own economic interests. But international investment, like international charity, was in its infancy, and it would be some time, if ever, before either presented a good substitute for war.

The naturalization of the Dutchman and the self-proclaimed Belgian had lain dormant in paneled offices for several months before the adoption. Following the adoption papers, citizenship became all but automatic. On May the twenty-third, the two became German. The change made almost no effect on their long-term appearance, although Peter spoke all day in a thick, indeterminate accent and walked with a limp, imitating what he took to be a commonly recognized German type. Under Peter's direction, a covert naturalization celebration went on for some time. Farmer Schreck frequently wondered aloud with middle-class inarticulateness why he could not get at least as much roguing out of three strong German adolescents as he had formerly gotten out of one.

Outwardly at least, Adolphe showed no sign of infection from Peter's and Hubert's foreign contagion. He looked on his own seniority—a year and a half over Peter, three years over Hubert—as a grave responsibility. In public, he reprimanded them with the severe kindness of a schoolmaster intent on forging a new Leibnitz, Kepler, or Euler. But in the evenings, when the family gathered to read from Goethe or the Bible, he found it increasingly difficult not to snicker at his half brother's coarseness, which Peter always passed off as misreadings: "Abraham beshat Isaac. Eh? Sorry. Abraham begat Isaac, that is. Excuse me, my parents. Stupid of me. Stupid Dutchman."

Together at these sessions, the two older boys delighted secretly in Hubert's total illiteracy, the child's complete inability and refusal to learn to read: "What use is this gibberish to me? I'm a worker, a So-veet. There are people who read and people who shoot and I'll tell you right now that when the big change for the poor comes I'd rather have one bullet than all these words." The same speech could have been punishable by imprisonment a few years back, before the abrogation of Bismarck's socialist laws.

Adolphe would step in at these outbursts, sparing his parents their show of righteous indignation. In truth, the legal father grew to enjoy Hubert's childish outbursts in that he could then watch his first adopted son go to work with the well-loved arguments of the right. Adolphe adored arguing politics with Hubert. And when either backed themselves boyishly into a dialectical corner, they did what all good political theorists do: they made up figures. Adolphe continued to argue his father's conservatism well past the day when it could do him any good.

Alone, Adolphe would practice talking, something he rarely did in public since puberty. He tried for that jaunty growl of Peter's. Soon, he began copying his new brother more brazenly. He caustically called his old friends "villagers." In talk when the topics went beyond him, he'd wave his hand as Peter always did, saying, "X squared, y squared, z squared."

His father's moral imperative, however impaired, would at least see him through the month. Alicia Heinecke, the not-quite May Queen, seeing a deadline of June 18—Adolphe's nineteenth birthday and the start of his compulsory military privilege—set to work courting him with regional efficiency. She contrived to monopolize most of his free time during the busy spring farming months, working hard to appear demure and inaccessible for one so much around. One becalmed, prematurely hot day she had him for forty minutes. They walked together in Truller Woods in silence. Her silence, more than any other single characteristic, always evoked Adolphe's gratitude and thereby his love for her. Soon, however, Alicia compromised the silence with a parliamentarian's grace.

—Adolphe. . . . I have to tell you that . . . I'm missing . . . something.

Adolphe was at a loss as to how to parse the message, until his vanity suggested a solution.

—Oh sparrow! You're missing your man Adolphe because he's in the fields so much? Is that it, little one?

Neither winced at the nineteenth-century endearment. In lovemaking alone, Adolphe resisted the taint of Peter, who called any woman who would listen to him "my meatpie." Adolphe referred to himself in the third person, a character actor reluctant to see himself in the romantic lead. His affectionate response increased Alicia's nervousness.

—No! I mean, well yes, I do miss you, my dearest. But no. I mean I'm missing something else. I've *been* missing something else.

Adolphe tried to recall what trivial promise he'd failed to keep, what keepsake he'd braggingly promised her. He had not borrowed anything from her, to the best of his remembrance. He felt the sick suspicion that the euphemism stood for some article of clothing they had lost, left behind when collecting themselves after an innocuous fumble in the oak leaves. He pictured her mother, huge over her, demanding, "Where is your . . . ?," and her father, larger, demanding the same of him. He could think of nothing diplomatic to say to her, nor could he fully interpret the nature of this crisis. His silence roused her from nervousness to violent resentment.

—I'm. Missing. Blood.

For one horrible moment he imagined that she meant for drinking. She was a vampire, pale at night, in a thin gown, red-spattered, crouched over fallen barnyard animals. She was saying that their courtship, so perfect and placid until now, overlooked only one thing—her insatiable need for his jugular.

He shook off the thought and gave himself a quick, primitive, approximate lesson in physiology. The rough implication of her words was more serious than the Moroccan Crisis, the Franco-Russian alliance, or any foolish thing in the Balkans. He did not know if the trifles he and Alicia had engaged in until then could actually have left her impregnated, but if there were any chance at all, however unlikely, he had only one honorable course. He lifted his head to an angle of commendable arrogance, and, as if he were already a career soldier, a lifer in the Prussian Army, said only:

—*Du.*

With the informal second-person pronoun, Alicia realized that she had succeeded in using a time-tested, shopworn trick to hasten, against the deadline of conscription, a promise of marriage.

He celebrated his birthday with pomp, got married with the blessings of both sets of parents, and received his call-up with residual good sportsmanship. Never pretending to be a wife of the bivouacking variety, Alicia remained in the Westerwald, passing time and living for the occasional weekend leave. The lie concerning the missing something was revealed in a moment of weekend tenderness. Before Adolphe's return to his regiment, she spoke dreamily about how they ought to start making this soldier's child. Conception took place that evening in an act of militant retribution.

'Dolphe's new uniform did little to change the standing between the three amateur brothers. Peter, ever flexible, simply changed "Have you heard the one about the Rhinelander?" to "Have you heard the one about the infantryman?" Hubert asked how hard it would be to overthrow the commanding officer and seize control of his regiment. Adolphe brought new facts (if the camp rumors he ate for breakfast could be called facts) to the perennial political debates. Adolphe continued, during leaves, to argue politics with Hubert all the way up until the day the Kaiser declared he would not recognize any more political parties, only Germans. If the two had still been in communication then, they doubtless would have continued to argue about what good Germans were to believe.

But by the time the Kaiser used this edict to dissolve the Reichstag and put Adolphe to work for his stipend, Peter and Hubert had left the country. Juggling their citizenships as if so many hoops and plates, they crossed back and forth over the Dutch border with impunity. Allotted two free days every few weeks, they packed up dangerous secondhand bicycles with sack lunches and a change of clothes. They pedaled the thirty-five miles to Maastricht to visit their no longer legally living mothers. They rode, walked, forced, and nursed their machines over the taciturn terrain, sometimes worse off than if they had gone by foot.

Hubert pedaled distractedly, caught his trouser legs in the exposed chain, serpentined as if a slalom skier, and continually went off the road with gritted teeth and squawks of surprise. Soon he discovered that he did better if he did not smoke and kept his eyes on the portion of road his wheel pointed toward. Peter crouched low, shoulders to handlebars, as he had seen the riders in the motocross do. He wrecked his throat making engine noises, and rubbed his right hand raw by pretending that his hand grip was a throttle. He became adept at running down chickens.

On the second of such bike trips, Peter created a sensation in his old neighborhood by showing the photo that the boys had purchased in installments from the eccentric from Cologne. He explained how this one was better than a formal studio portrait because it showed them as they were, really, on that day, with no lies or covering up. An old Dutchman, dubious, remarked that they had been taken: if they wanted "as they were" they could look around them anytime and get it for free. If they were going to pay good money for a photograph, it ought to be for "as they ought to be."

But Peter's mother adored the image. More fond of it than of her foisted son, she wanted to keep it in her oak press along with the rest of her life's prizes. The boys explained that they had to rotate possession with Adolphe and Alicia. They promised to bring the photo along on every bike trip when it belonged to one of them.

The city of Maastricht was and is the largest in South Holland, but still drops off abruptly into fields indistinguishable from those in the Westerwald. The city itself is a railroad nexus and an industrial manufacturer of glass, ceramics, textiles, and paper goods. But the surrounding fields, which in winter circle around the city like packs of wolves, have not changed since the Hapsburgs. A city wholly intent on producing useful material goods, Maastricht is large without luster or cosmopolitan quality. Detroit might be a good American analogy.

Natives would object to this description, pointing to the eleventh-century church, the Roman antiquities, even the rich historical overtones of the city's original name—Mosae Trajectum, the ford over the river Maas. But they would be clouding the issue. The town lives first and last for industrial production. It makes things, things that can be used.

Peter, brought up on the narrow cusp between the urban center and blank fields, enjoyed ridiculing Adolphe, lording it over him merely because in the Westerwald, Jan Kinder had had to walk to work in the fields, slaving there for fifteen hours a day, whereas in his second life in Maastricht, the boys' mutual father took the train each day to a ceramics factory, working there only twelve. To Peter, this represented a metal-pipe dream, a vision of progress and mechanical betterment. Given a transmission long enough and a gear box to put it in, one can move the world.

Maastricht doubled as the capital of Limburg Province. Limburg stands in relation to the rest of the Netherlands as, once again, the Midwest stands to the U.S. Limburg permits the continued existence of Amsterdam, just as Michigan permits the continued existence of Boston, the East Coast. Yet both provinces have second-class standing. Both cultivate customs so different from those of their sophisticated partners as to have little in common with them aside from language and a loose federal hegemony. Both are the object of ridicule of the more cultivated if dependent parts.

From early times, Limburg changed hands as often as a block of short-term investment stock. A string of changed allegiances attest to a contrary spirit. Like Bohemians and Parisians, Limburgers oppose everything. They cheered the revolt from Spain, but out of apathy fell back into Spanish hands soon after the creation of the Netherlands state. The United Kingdom of the Netherlands later reclaimed the province and with it the resentment of the populace. Limburg has always harbored French sympathies except for those periods in the seventeenth and eighteenth centuries when parts of it fell under French control.

The separation of the area into Belgian and Dutch halves in 1831 left each part hankering to trade places with the other. The creation of Belgium by the Great Powers in that year was an experiment in the idea of buffer states: an attempt to keep two fighting dogs apart by dangling a piece of raw meat between them. More remarkable than the idea's illogic was its success. Guaranteed by the underwriters, Belgium's neutrality had gone unimpaired from 1831 to the year of Peter and Hubert's bicycle trip. But to Limburgers, Belgium meant just another national state to resent.

To a Limburger, separatism was a pastime, avocation, religion. Freud once compared the replacement of the id by the ego to the Dutch draining of the Zuider Zee. The analogy relates Limburg to that part of the mind that has always been fully conscious, high and dry: congenital resentment, homelessness.

Native contrariety alone could not explain why Peter, with an adopted mother near at hand, had to cycle all day to see a mother he had signed away. For Peter had become a naturalized German to the extent of believing that kindness ought not to take you more than a mile or so off your path. A long bike ride, like excessive personal grooming or sticking with a too-difficult book, had to rest on a higher motive. Peter had begun frequenting a tobacconist's widow who kept an aromatic shop in Peter's blood mother's old neighborhood.

This woman had a son two years older than Peter, and between mother and son they pushed near six hundred pounds. For this woman's company, Peter had forsaken a Gertie of some plain beauty and dangerously buck teeth. In public, he preached an idolatry of the perfect and beautiful woman. But his tastes thus far in his brief life always took him toward the grotesque. The widow kept an army cot in the back of the shop, surplus from the Sedan confrontation. There they had sex in all but the technical sense of the word. On account of an unshakable fidelity toward her dead husband, she would not permit him genuine intercourse. Instead, she made soft cavities out of her excess flesh that did just as nicely. This was the closest he had come to what he bragged to his new brothers about having accomplished years ago.

For the woman's part, she kept the boy around to liven up a remarkably dull trade. Her husband was dead, her son married, and tobacco was only good for a smoke. The boy's anarchy was her only amusement. He would walk about the shop yawning, then suddenly pounce on the longest, thickest maduro cigar he could lay hands on and hang it in suggestive pantomime from his front trouser crotch. She would laugh, screaming, "Liar," "Dreamer," or "Novelist," the three being roughly equivalent to her.

The two of them invented a game in which she would retreat into the back room and he would stay behind the counter until a customer came in. Then, in answer to anything the client might say or ask, the mock proprietor would repeat the last few words of the phrase, inflecting them as needed.

—Young man, I'm looking for a birthday gift for my husband.

—Your husband?

—Yes. He smokes a pipe. Have you any recommendations?

—Any recommendations?

—You know. . . . This brier pipe, for instance. It looks like it gives a good smoke.

—It gives a good smoke.

—I must say, young man, you are not being very helpful.

—Not being very helpful!

—Now don't you get huffy on me. I want to speak to the owner. You know, the heavy woman.

—I know the heavy woman.

While not very good for business, this routine always sent the tobacconist's widow into hysterics. She peeked through the draw curtain to witness the transactions, sometimes giving them away with her cackling. In a corollary game, they would watch people pass by on the street and rate them as to how many rounds of the echo game each would last before losing temper: "Now there's a pompous ass; I bet he'd not go more than three. Note that gullible sap. You could get him to twelve, easily." Later, this became abbreviated to a nod of the head and a grunted "six" or "eight."

In visits to the tobacconist's widow, Peter slowly worked out his moral code. His disposition and makeup did not encourage sticking to principles for very long, but for the interim, at least, he'd devised rules of behavior running something like: going outside bareheaded beats wearing a hat that might be thought silly. If someone is to be taken in, make sure you are on the delivering end. And most important, in conversation, jokes go over better than current events. This last precept was to take him well into the Great War before it failed him.

Hubert was the big loser on these bike trips. With his mother seldom free and Peter consorting with a petite bourgeoise, he could only suffer desertion with the same placidity with which he had suffered Peter's cruelties along the way. The fluid, folded age lines in his face came from his never knowing when he was being hurt by someone. What marked him alternately as a case of crib death and one of senescence was his continuing halo of resigned bafflement, a look that seemed to remark: I had better find something to do for two days.

To kill time, he would head down to Hoog Straat and the public fountain. This piece of northern propaganda, commemorating the most recent retrieval of Limburg by the Dutch, meant to bribe the province into a semblance of nationalism. Alabaster was cheaper, if not as immediate as agricultural reforms. The poorer element of Maastricht, however, were able to do their wash in it. Incapable of thinking figuratively, Hubert misinterpreted the fountain's brass inscription: In Dutch Hands Alone. He thought that meant only Dutchmen could put their hands in the water, and that his new German papers made him anathema. So each trip, without fail, he bathed his whole torso with all the urgency and delight of a criminal.

He broke laws with the same sense of constructive accomplishment that other boys got from building little model towns. A blow here and there for the cause, mosquito bites on the fat buttocks of burghers. If he'd owned a pick and shovel, he would certainly have been out destroying a road somewhere. Instead, he loitered below the windows of the state-run charity grade school, waiting for lulls in history lessons to yell out his own interpretations of the past and prescriptions for the future. He twice received lazy warnings from languid, mounted constables.

The anonymity of an industrial city also allowed him the freedom to do shameful things. To Hubert this meant not masturbation or blasphemy, but playing streetball with the local urchins. The first two sins he looked on as agreeable obligations, something a mature, responsible person ought to do regularly—like work, or talking politics. But he felt real shame at not being able to give up streetball. This shame marked his first passage out of narcissism into guilt, out of childhood into adolescence. A few more years might add a brand of Catholic contrition for the sins he committed so cleanly now. With the process initiated, only a small leap of years would lead him into the final shape of shame: adult indifference.

The children who gathered in the alleys in the early afternoon played a game that vaguely resembled soccer in that it used a round ball. None was yet in his teens, so Hubert cut an odd figure among them, feet taller than the rest, blocking and checking as if in a professional match. The children called him *opa:* Grandfather. While *opa* committed brutal penalties, Peter called his girl friend's son "sir" and Adolphe received weekly letters from Alicia, two years his junior, beginning "My Dearest Child." Age is more moldable than clay. The streetballers revered *opa* as their greatest curiosity until an eight-year-old named Sjefke stole center stage by appearing in an eye patch after having had his eye put out by his father.

Aside from these activities, Hubert split his time in Maastricht pretty much evenly between a fourteen-year-old girl named Wies and a retired laborer named Willy. Wies, a policeman's daughter, loved men to an extreme, and was never out of their company for any length of time. But she threw them all over the instant Hubert hit town. The most severe of lovers, she meant to save people. Hubert, more than any single person she had ever met, was in serious need of salvation.

Their courtship never varied from a strict routine. Hubert arrived unannounced at her parents, always surprising her in some degree of intimacy with a new cousin of hers. Flustered, she would introduce and summarily dismiss the crestfallen relative. Hubert then would take Wies out walking, usually to a place where they gave out yesterday's bread for free. The daughter of a moderately well-off police officer, Wies always offered him money. His rejections of charity—"What use has a So-veet for money?"—were to her a powerful aphrodisiac. Watching the boy gnaw on stale bread aroused her even more. She would begin by leading him to some dark public park, all the while saying how the Lord planned each person's life, if they would only stop being foolish and selfish in rejecting Divine Will.

When she reached the part about those short-sighted people who thought they were put on this earth simply to experience pleasure, that was Hubert's cue to lift up her many-layered greatskirts and begin playing with her underclothes. He overruled her modest objections, polemicizing, "So-veets have no use for God." This pragmatic argument served him well. Wies, a girl of very low sexual threshold, would in minutes be heaving under his hand. After climaxing, she would begin to cry, striking him with all the violence possible for a fourteen-year-old daughter of a policeman. Her blows rapidly became equally violent strokings of Hubert's trousers, as if the worst and best course ever allowed is retaliation. He never took much longer than she.

When a calm and awkward grace descended again on the two, he would fill the odd silences by telling her everything he knew about communism and the socialist movement. In three minutes, he exhausted his store. Love, after the exchange of indoctrinations, had to adapt to silence. He would laugh the laugh of a barnyard animal, shrug, and leave her to find her way home alone. And so, in the unconscious race on the part of the three brothers to preserve a disintegrating childhood, Hubert won without contest. He had not yet seen his love any way except fully clothed.

On leaving Wies, he generally went to Willy's. This old fellow slept only for half-hour stretches during the morning and afternoon, and he was always ready for company at any hour. At Hubert's age, Will had already compiled five years' experience as a brick carrier. Outfitted with a curved plank that sat on his shoulders, a notch cut in it accommodating his head and neck, he carted carefully stacked pyramids of bricks from the ovens to waiting trucks. At Hubert's age, Willy's single motivating desire had been to get a job inside the factory, preferably working the ovens. Inside jobs paid fifteen cents more a day than carrying, and it was easier on the spine. When he finally earned his promotion, he rested content for several years, secure in knowing more about bricks and brickmaking than all but a very few people on this earth.

After a time, however, that sense of superiority grew thin, and Willy had to look around him for other novelties. A true Limburger, he hit upon discontent as a consolation. He had read about the Second International in a newspaper that had been short on copy and run an account of the great movement of the left as a filler. After asking himself, "The Second International what?," he thought no more about it until some of the younger hands at the brick plant started talking strikes and trade unionism. At that moment he put the two together and experienced one of those rare, lasting descents of understanding that sometimes kill the normal state of daily incoherence with one of demanding simplicity. He could combine a moral cause with a gratifying belligerence to achieve that almost unattainable happy marriage: justifiable martyrdom. He had come into his heritage.

Largely uninformed about the labor movement except in spirit, Willy did not stop talking worker revolt from that day forward.

He followed Europe's flirtation with common property and progressive government with all the devotion of a sports fan backing an underdog team. His new enthusiasm, however, did little to alter his brick production one way or the other.

Hubert was not the only young person who learned his politics from Will, but he was the only one to devote himself to it with the seriousness of the master. Willy knew that Hubert was the only crab in his brook, so he groomed the boy carefully. Although no one knew who in all of Belgium, Holland, France, or Luxembourg Hubert's mother had procured to father the boy, it was certain that Will was not the one. But equally certain, Hubert came dutifully on each Maastricht visit to sit as a disciple at this man's feet.

Since his forced retirement, Willy had grown increasingly vocal. His declamations reached the point where the town police had to lock him up regularly for what was called Disruptive Conduct, a catch-all, part-political, part-civic charge that took very little in-court proving. The arrest usually took place around the twenty-fourth of each month, so that Willy would appear on the prison rosters on the first of the following month, thereby counting toward the precinct's tax-credit calculation. It was in following one of these arresting officers once, intending to bomb or at least throw stones at his house, that Hubert instead had met the policeman's daughter, Wies.

Hubert arrived at Will's house on the last day of July to find his entire world changed.

—Hubie, I want to tell you before you go shooting your mouth off outside my house that we're working things a little different these days.

—What different? We're going to warm your gun up some, Oom Will?

Hubert had continual designs on his "uncle" Willy's gun, a twin-barrel shotgun that Will hunted ducks with on the lakes that fed the Maas. Hubert was convinced the public needed physical prodding to realize what was good for it. He didn't want to use the gun so much as just to brandish it menacingly.

—We're not going to use the gun, but we *are* going to start using a lot less of your mouth, little man.

—But Oom Will, you said So-veet will not be silenced until the breaking of the last chain.

—That's poetic, son. From now on, we're going to undertake the silent revolution.

—You're joking. You're testing me. That's not policy. That's not the way the pressed worker goes about getting control, eh, old man?

—Let your gums sleep a bit, Huub. I'm tired of going to jail. No more. The place smells bad. They put poisons in your soup and fifteen men in a room all have to shit into a single bucket. That's embarrassing for a man with my condition.

Will alluded to his second favorite topic of conversation. Temperament and the chemical atmosphere at the brick plant had combined to inflict him with ulcerative colitis. His bowel movements could not, by any stretch of semantics, be called statistically normal.

Hubert sat out on Will's front porch, listening in stunned disbelief to the change in policy. The single Dutch stoop, one of a house-row of hundreds, was little more than a bump in the narrow stone walk. Lazy foot traffic had to detour around the two conspirators. Will pointed out a foot patrolman across the street.

—They've been after me for two weeks now. But they won't get me this month, providing you keep your trap shut. Tomorrow starts August, and I'm out of the lion's den. Now talk, normallike, about anything except the you-know-what.

Without the old familiar topic, Hubert was lost for conversation. Besides, he needed full concentration to figure out how his world could change so totally and irrevocably without warning. So Willy did all the talking. He skillfully stretched out talk about the weather, taking even longer than a technical reporter would need to write it up. He went on to tell three dirty stories that were, aside from changes in locale and cast, variations on a single punchline. He fought heroically to keep the law on the far side of the street. Yet after weather and pornography, conversation had no place to turn except to current events.

—Hey, Hubie. See the headlines this morning? I'll tell you, little man, the Germans are going to go through Belgium like THAT.

He shouted the last syllable, using a fierce swipe of his pen-

— 62 —

knife at the loaf of bread they'd been eating to demonstrate his point. The Kaiser two years earlier had made a similar swipe in the air, using the same figure—"My armies will cut through Belgium like that"—in front of a startled visiting British staff officer. Now Will was not telepathic and shared nothing with the Kaiser, aside from indiscretion masquerading as shrewdness. It was simply one of those gestures—the sudden appearance of dandelions in spring, the flu in late fall—that become ubiquitous. Millions repeated it throughout the coming week. Nevertheless, the police officer, an old friend, was across the street in seconds.

—Hello, Willy. Pretty dangerous words, those. You wouldn't be planning anything, would you?

Within a half hour Hubert appeared at the tobacco shop trying to catch his breath. Peter hated having his ward show up here at the scene of his crime, and expressed his anger in an unwitting but accurate imitation of an American capitalist.

—This better be important, you little toad, or we're going to tie you up and burn you all over with cigars.

—They came and arrested Oom Will. They got him in prison.

—Again? That's all? You came here against my orders to tell me that? You're feeding me yesterday's news as stew.

The vogue expression meant the hot item was old hat. Happens all the time. And so things do, with only the level of boredom changing.

—And, and . . .

—And what, you epileptic?

—And the German armies are going to cut through Belgium like THAT.

The gesture lacked something without a stale loaf of bread for prop. Yesterday's news as stew. This time, however, Peter acted. In the space of three slow breaths, he evaluated the reliability of his brother as a news source, weighed his personal versus collective responsibility, and at once came to a course more resolute and defensible than the German Schlieffen Plan or the French Plan 17. He walked to where the widow was tidying up and threw himself consequentially into the act of sorting cigars.

—Think you could find some long-term work for two Dutchmen?

Hubert surfaced briefly from bitterness long enough to knock on Wies's door. She was surprised to see him back so soon after their last parting, and her visiting cousin's condition was more compromising than usual. But Hubert's agitation showed he was in great trouble. As such, her sainthood rose in her like a glamour stock until she felt willing to do anything for him, beginning with following him unquestioningly into the street.

Once outside, a silent Hubert herded her along with shoves and prods. She objected, demanding information. She complained that he hurt her. But she fell short of calling to the passers-by for help. His purposeful behavior infected her; she felt a certain destiny waiting for her at the end of the block.

Without thinking, Hubert sensed that the only place with enough solitude for the job in question was Will's now vacant home. A nesting instinct: if Hubert did not puff out his neck like a pigeon, it was because he needed the muscles to hold his cigarette in place at this brisk pace. Will, shuffled off by a policeman who was in a hurry to make the August first deadline, had not had time to lock up the place. Hubert forced the door and pushed Wies inside.

—Now. Start talking God.

—But Huubje, we already . . .

—Shut up and start it. Now. "God grows angry when . . ."

He twisted her arm, not well or effectively enough to hurt her. She began hastily, knowing exactly what a request for the speech meant. Her voice carried no tone or purpose, as far away and tinny as a wireless.

—. . . Too, God grows angry at those who throw his temple away on pleasure. God gives each human. . . .

The rite began as usual but soon took a wrong turn when he ripped through her frilly, grotesque underclothes, which offered only modest resistance. Cut through like that. This time, there were no recriminations after.

He at once demanded to know if she was pregnant. Stunned, she giggled. She thought he suspected her of trying, in a few months, a bribe of the Alicia variety. She called him a pet name, a diminutive, and told him not to worry, that the evil of the day was sufficient thereunto. He struck her with a force that stunned even himself.

For the first time, this orphan frightened her. She reasoned correctly that one so naïve as to think a woman could feel the moment of conception was beyond protecting, beyond saving, beyond even nursing into a reconciliation with the world. Innocents always present the most danger. She had to give him the correct answer to his demand, but she had no idea of what answer he wanted. She could not know that, taking his brother Adolphe's example, Hubert had developed the notion that soldiers off to war were secretly obligated to impregnate someone. She offered a very tentative yes.

Immediately he bent into a grin: her old playmate Hubert. He called her every lovename, mostly edible foods, that he could think of. He gave her the May Day photo, carefully folded into quarters, that he had stolen from Peter for this purpose. She played along until she saw a chance to escape from the house. With great difficulty, he wrote something on a scrap of paper and forced it into her hands. She did not look at it until reaching the security of the policeman's home. There she carefully opened the scrap to reveal where a shaky hand had spelled out a much-practiced word, a German surname.

Hubert stole Will's shotgun. After all, Willy had taught him well that a man with moral cause stands outside the law. He took, also, a half box of buckshot scatter shells. What's good for the duck was good for what he had in mind. He biked the Maas ford into Belgium, where the river, with no apparent change, became the Meuse. He headed upstream, where in about fifteen miles he expected to find Liège and the Belgian fortresses. He rode about five miles, even managing to stay on the road for good stretches at a time. He spent the night sleeping soundly in a hayrick.

In the morning, the owner of the property found him taking eggs out of a hen house. Hubert explained that he had left a pack of cigarettes in the nest to pay for them. He said, in addition, that he was going to help repel the Germans from his native Belgium. The farmer scoffed at the idea, pointing out that the Germans had co-signed the guarantee of Belgian neutrality. The farmer's wife ended the ensuing debate by hard-boiling the eggs for the monkey-faced boy, and making her husband give back the cigarettes, with half a pack of Belgian brand thrown in as a gift.

Hubert bicycled through midday, wondering what he and Will would talk about now that there was no more Soviet. Maybe Will would get used to jail again and they could go back to the old ways, which were best, after all. His riding grew erratic under these complex thoughts. An explosion very near him knocked him clean from the bike.

Under the impression that the German invasion had begun, he lowered his shotgun in the direction of the commotion, unloading one barrel, then the other. The recoil hurt his shoulder. Belgian engineers, demolishing bridges in the event of a German advance, went down hurt or seeking cover. An incredulous gunner opened up an automatic small arm in the direction of the bicyclist. The repeating weapon continued to go off, nervously, even after vacancy had taken hold in the air.

That day, the Germans violated Luxembourg at a town called Trois Vierges: the Three Graces, or virgins.

Chapter Six

Two Leads on a Fata Morgana

You see what I'm doing: there was an empty space left in the trunk which I'm filling with hay; that's how it is in our life's baggage; no matter what we stuff it with, it's better than having an empty space.—TURGENEV, *Fathers and Sons*

—I found my thri-i-ill
In John Stuart Mill. . . .

DELANEY'S VOICE strongly resembled a Phantom jet in the hands of a developing nation. His strafing run had as objective a reticent molded-plastic-cum-printed-circuit-card that generated what the magazine referred to as "fully user-programmable" coffee. The machine, however, had long ago rewritten its own software, and now refused to wander from REHEAT MODE. Although the machine's microprocessor could make decisions in milliseconds, it invariably decided to do the same thing time and again: bring the water to 65 degrees and dribble it miserably into the waiting flask. The U.S. Army had, at Ardennes, 1917, devised a method—big pot of lukewarm water with grounds stirred in—that beat the IC technology in both taste and throughput.

Delaney, having changed his tune this quarter hour ever so slightly to "I found my thrill in diddling Jill," perhaps knowing somewhere in his voluminous preconscious that by cashing his checks on Powell Trade Magazine Group, he morally obligated himself to accomplish at least a little something each morning, annexed a cup and made his best imitation of a straight line toward Mays's module.

—Do you realize that if I stretched out your small intestine it would reach all the way to the latrine and back? Save you the trip.

Mays concealed what he had been working on and filled his face with a polite, functionary look. He had been raised under the moral imperative that considered impoliteness a far more serious crime than, say, killing a loved one, so he was always attentive. He adopted the servile attitude of the smaller of two dogs that, after token resistance, ends a scrap by rolling over and baring its throat.

—Doug, I've got this job, see? Maybe Mr. Moseley would like to chat.

In fact, Moseley had taken a rare break from red-penning manuscripts to work on his pet project: the noise vacuum. In the plan, a microphone sent incoming sound to an analyzing loop, which built a sound wave exactly inverse to the source. Where the natural-source sound wave had a crest, the machine's resultant wave formed a trough, and vice versa. The two waves thus summed to a resultant wave of zero: silence. Moseley worked on his circuit whenever Delaney went on a spree. At the sound of his name, Moseley adjusted the wall of plants around his desk, closing a dangerous gap in the shrubbery barrier.

Delaney had no intention of taking Mays's hint.

—Dougo, can't you at least go through the motions of doing some work?

—I belong to the union, I'll have you know.

—Do you want us to be overtaken by the competition?

Mays alluded to regular pep talks that Caroline—Madame Chairperson, to Delaney—gave the staff in meetings or parceled out in discreet memos. Brink, not by nature a competitive person, normally had no more sympathy for the underdog than had the average American citizen since the Spanish-American War. But when it came to *Micro*'s standing with regard to its competitors in the trade press, Caro grew fangs.

A triumvirate of interchangeable magazines competed for what might loosely be called "market share" of the early 1980s' microcomputer design readership. The trade press being to real magazines what government prop films are to Hollywood, rival journals cannot "compete" in any except the literal sense of the word. Still, the chief editors of *Micro News*, *Monthly Micro*, and *Micro Monthly News* viewed each other with the mutual animosity of diplomats, devoting less time on articles than on badmouthing the enemy.

Distinguishable only to themselves, the three magazines maneuvered around one another for undisputed control of the design engineer. But as with Orwell's Eurasia, East Asia, and Oceania, complete superiority was impossible. The market had a random reader distribution built into it. Each magazine hired the same coveys of pollsters to produce "independent reader surveys." Each survey, regardless of the most sophisticated statistical tampering, remained adamant: at most two hundreths of a percent swing in preference over the last six-month period. If one of the three obtained a flukish one percent or more "market" lead, the other two would tacitly cooperate to bludgeon the giant down to a humble equality.

This inviolable deadlock resulted from the magazines' being in all respects interchangeable. They ran to the same number of pages. They carried the same four-color, full-page ads. (The slogan of the day in the leading industrial parks was "Saturate the available outlet-organs.") They received identical press releases and converted them into roughly equivalent dialects of technobabble: "Ease Dual Process Control" and so on. Most important, each magazine kept close watch on its competitors, expressly prohibiting innovation. One former chief had been dismissed for proposing a title change not containing the word "Micro." Any innovation that did sneak through was instantly and mercilessly copied by the two rival presses until it became a harmless status quo.

Executives of each book played an elaborate, felonious espionage game: spies and industrial thieves stole confidential editorial schedules and sold them to rivals, who then promptly tailored their own calendars to match. Each staff, knowing it was the object of espionage, made it easy for spies to collect the desired information without ransacking too many valuable files. Nobody wanted escalation: the other fellow might retaliate if you hid your secrets too well. That could only end with everyone thrown back on their own resources.

Color spreads in each magazine harped on niggling differences between the books in an attempt to convince potential advertisers of the dangers of appearing in either of the inferior rags. *Monthly Micro* began a slander campaign against *Micro News*, running a photo of an old man dressed from the turn of the century propping himself up with a cane and perusing a copy of *Micro News*. The book trailed a foot of spider webs complete with black widow spider. A caption asked: "What's so new about *Micro News*?" The ad lamented that the rival's "lead time"—a favorite term of indefinite meaning—was so long that many components were obsolete by the time they were reviewed in print. The text did not mention that, in this field, the design life of new introductions averaged four months.

Micro News retaliated within two weeks—no lead-time problem here—distributing a glossy flier carrying an enlarged *Webster*'s entry for "monthly." The headline screamed: "What's so monthly about ten times a year?" The ad pointed out that two *Monthly Micro* issues, the so-called "Product Bonanzas," tried to pass as double issues simply by calling themselves the May/June and the November/December issues. The broadside asked if any serious professional in so voluble a field could get by without "data update" for as long as sixty days. Mays, on first reading the copy, remarked that he had gone without data update for the first seventeen years of his life, had been updated only intermittently since then, and didn't see why he needed it monthly now.

Micro Monthly News—Brink, Moseley, Mays, and Delaney—like so many third parties of the past, might have profited handily by sitting on the sidelines. This was Mays's personal choice. He sat, each day, on the sidelines in a sort of religious frenzy. But Caroline, perhaps under pressure from hidden executive superiors, perhaps convinced that every major power had to bloody its hands a bit to lend itself credibility, encouraged *Micro*'s ad staff to draw up its own manifesto. Theirs was a gem of cross-reference. It reproduced reduced versions of the two previous attacks, one on each side of the page. In the middle, sans serif, it asked: "Caught in the cross fire?"

The ad pointed out that magazines intent on pointing out the shortcomings of other magazines often did so at the expense of good coverage. The whole shooting war ended up with the declaration: "While others exhort, we report." Delaney, realizing that the catchphrase would never reach the rhetorical heights of, say, "Speak softly and carry a big stick," burlesqued it about the office as "While others bicker, we snicker." So Mays, knowing how much Delaney enjoyed throwing himself into the competitive fray with a faked Mohammedan zeal, alluded to the cause in an attempt to get Dougo to quit torturing him and resume torturing the coffeepot, Moseley, or some other inanimate object. But this morning Dougo could not be swayed.

—Say, what are you working on that's so important that you don't have two minutes to chat with the fellow who taught you everything there is to know about Schmidt Triggers? Deadline got you down? Lonely? Suicidal? Constipated? Perhaps you need . . .

Mays had to intervene at once to keep Delaney from going into his half-hour Madison Avenue free association, which began with an indictment of toilet bowl ring, moved blithely through a docu-drama on killer satellites to arrive at a panel discussion (Doug doing all four voices) on the relevance of the Magna Carta in today's go-get-'em world. Desperate, Mays uncharacteristically fell back on the ploy of trust.

—How would you go about locating a woman with red hair?

For a dissociative schizophrenic, Delaney struck Peter as being remarkably quick on the uptake.

—Once I saw Gene Kelly trying to locate Vera-Ellen, only he didn't know she was Vera-Ellen, thinking instead that she was a certain Miss Turnstiles. Ha! I scoff at his naïveté. Anyway, he found her finally, in the fourth reel. Now as finding a blonde in New York must be roughly four times as difficult as finding a red-head in Boston, the tart in question ought to show up in about twenty minutes.

—How about some constructive advice?

—In good time. First, you have to do this nifty soft-shoe routine down in the subway.

—Get serious for a minute, will you?

Delaney instantly went into his Lytton Strachey impersonating Oswald Spengler imitation. It was much more convincing than Mays doing Caroline.

—I tried contacting the Commonwealth of Massachusetts Registry of Motor Vehicles. They'll release statistics pertaining to hair color, but no names, addresses, or phone numbers. I tried to buy customer lists from the hairdressers down on Newbury, but they thought I was a Fed or deviant or something. Isn't there a lobby or special-interest group for redheads?

—Have you tried NOW? Really, my friend, this is not *Ivanhoe*. Contemporary woman is not yours for the hunting down. There's a new consciousness about, a new . . .

Peter made a rude suggestion involving Delaney and a Susan B. Anthony silver dollar.

—Besides, you're going about this all wrong.

Mays steeled himself for the "There's more than one fish in the sea" speech. A favorite of Delaney's, it ran: "There's more than one fish in the sea. There's more than one cow in the slaughterhouse. There's more than one 'l' in 'constellation.' " Instead, Doug said:

—She also plays the clarinet.

With some embarrassment and much discomfort, it occurred to Peter that he had not adequately disguised the obsession that had had hold of him for the last several weeks.

Delaney had never gotten past Hank Williams, while Mays himself was stone tone-deaf. Fa and la, like most monosyllables, made him nervous. When the two asked Moseley how to go about finding a redhead musician who looked about mid-twenty from eight stories up, he threatened lawsuit if not left alone. Mays was already in trouble with Brink over a delinquent column; a lawsuit would mean back to working for a living.

Yet between them, Delaney and Peter managed to work up a few leads that would occupy Mays at least enough so that he did not have to rerehearse the conversation he would have with the mirage-woman when he finally caught up with her. He had a script written for each of many possible meeting places: Supermarket, Public Library, Hospital, Casbah, Combat Zone, Côte d'Azur. She would say, "It took you long enough." He, with a flash of Sherlock or Oliver Wendell Holmesian deadpan, would say, "I hadn't much to go on." With a provocative orange-juicy look about the eyes, she'd say, "You didn't want it to be easy, did you?" And then he'd say and then she'd say.

The imagined dialogues always seemed to flow more freely than his overdue "Accumulator" column. Half the world suffered from *esprit de l'escalier*, staircase witticism, in which, on the way to bed, the victim recalls the chances for funny sayings missed during the evening. But Mays belonged to the camp suffering from *esprit d'entrée*, in which the victim must endlessly prepare all wit in advance. Those not suffering repeatedly under the delusion that they've forgotten to lock the door on leaving always subscribe to a mania that won't let them hang up the phone until they've gotten directions three times.

Delaney suggested that Peter get hold of a parade manifest. City Hall, he explained, held for six months a roster of all participants registered for public events. This protected the city from potential lawsuits. America in the '80s produced ten lawyers for every engineer, and *Micro* was printed proof to how much trouble the engineer could make. Lawyers could create ten times the havoc, so the city barricaded itself behind a wall of protective paper. Japan, on the other hand, produced ten engineers to each lawyer, and it was little wonder that they were cleaning up in what *Micro* styled the "Technowar," a conflict in which Delaney saw himself as a sort of Ed Teller.

City Hall, it seemed, made documents such as the parade manifest available to the public. Mays wondered how a lug like Delaney knew such a timely piece of obscuranta, but thought it wise not to inquire too closely into the matter.

Between the two of them, they also scraped together a meager roster of the area's musical institutions: the Symphony, the Conservatory. Neither mentioned the suspicion that the redhead was more than likely a high school twink who marched in the school band to be close to her beau, or a career woman who dusted off the Selmer on weekends and holidays because it beat standing on the curb picking cotton candy off the kids' clothes. Mays harbored and Delaney encouraged the notion that this was the daughter of two survivors of Belsen who'd dropped out of a surgical residency at Mass. General to pursue the diminished seventh.

As each new tangible avenue of attack joined the list, Peter grew more morose. Did the hunters for Pluto, the coelacanth, or the *Andrea Doria* feel sullen at closing in on the quarry? If not for this morning's chance conversation, not being able to put Delaney off, he would have gone perhaps another six weeks searching for a head of red hair, using all the method of the famous drunk searching for a way away from the lamppost. In the end, as always, he would arrive at a cheery oblivion, lulled into a forgetfulness appropriate to the matter's inconsequentiality. What had made the figure, swimming upstream against the crowd's current, so compelling was her aura of otherworldliness: her clothes, her carriage, her bearing all contributed to making her seem a vision glimpsed through a closing shutter. And visions were not meant to be approached up close.

Brink pounced on the conspiracy from out of nowhere. Breaking in mid-sentence, Delaney tried to cover up their activity:

—And so, you simple-minded clot, your shallow ideas about the feasibility of a gigabyte address decoder fail to show even cursory familiarity with the state-of-the-art. Consider the alpha particle . . .

—Who wants to know what about musical groups?

Mays, too exhausted to keep up his guard any longer, confessed. Brink mentioned that her boyfriend belonged to the Cologne Chamber Music Society. Delaney asked how the fabled twosome were getting along of late. The Managing Editor reminded him that times were very tough and that overpaid copy boys were luxuries. He counterthreatened, saying he knew of two books that would jump at a person of his qualifications. She said "jump at" would just about describe the encounter. And he said and she said.

The idea of Caroline having relations with men struck Mays as incongruous. She was attractive, in a professional way. Her near-corpulence went against his late-twentieth-century taste for the anorectic. But she was entirely too congenial to be mixed up in the sordid affair of sex. Mays had met Lenny Bullock, Brink's boyfriend, for want of a better term, at office parties when both men had been duly oiled. Even the haze of alcohol could not lessen Mays's suspicion of what the cad must certainly be doing to the unsuspecting and frowsty Caroline.

—He's unbelievable. You can sing a tune once and Len has it by heart. He's studied with professionals, you know. He walks around the house singing, you name it, Brahms's Fifth, the way you or I might sing "Wedding Bells Are Ringing."

—Are you in the habit of singing about wedding bells?

With that, Delaney made a timely and Continental exit to the coffeepot. Brink went on at uncharacteristic length about how Bullock could provide Mays with an entrée to the Boston musical scene. He had never heard her speak of anyone outside of De Forest or Edison with such reverence. The more she spoke, the more Mays stood by his first impressions: Bullock could only charitably be called unbalanced. A transient when transience was fashionable, he played the American extended adolescence for all it was worth. Finding himself at last in adulthood and totally unqualified to do any meaningful work, he'd sashayed into stockbroking—"got registered," as the jargon had it (handguns, historic houses, and stockbrokers). Society had tamed the erratic fellow by co-opting him into the mainstream. For its largest threats, society reserves success.

Despite this success, despite the fact that he frequently took home to the place he shared with Caro over seven thousand dollars in one week's commissions, Bullock was heavily in hock. Unlike most other heavy borrowers, he adored talking about his debt. The first thing he ever said to Peter, by way of opening line, was that a man's worth could be gauged by how much he owed. The same evening, he told Mays that he had an investment that could net him 8K for 2, "K" being jargon the two professionals shared. Lenny had probably gotten the lead the same place he'd found out about the new Brahms symphony.

Mays thanked his boss as deferentially as his personality allowed, and said he'd get in touch with Leonard, who would certainly be a help. Secretly, Mays filed all thought of the fellow under "Insect" for safekeeping.

—Say, what are you so hot on music for all of a sudden? You're usually so serious and aloof from that sort of stuff.

Mays observed silence, considering a three-part series on public television titled "Young Mays: His Seriousness, His Aloofness." He wondered if "seriousness" were a word. Serity. Seriosity.

—It's next March's special report on music synthesis chips, isn't it? Damn it, Peter. That's fine, first class. We're not even out with the Christmas issue, and you're planning ahead for spring. You're going to be a first-rate editor after all. A damn fine editor.

"Damn" was going to need a lot more time in Caro's mouth before her body stopped rejecting it as foreign tissue. Nor did Peter like the sound of that "after all." But at least she was back to the magazine and off the topic of humans and the relations thereamong.

Moseley suggestively rustled several manila envelopes, and Caroline, shocked into sense by the rare sound of office supplies at work, grew circumspect and slunk off to her cell. In the jungle of indifference Mays had cultivated toward the older man, he planted a twenty-four-hour flowering gratitude. Moseley, in peace at last, resumed his red-penning.

The remaining day, already reneged, had to be gotten through on the installment plan. Delaney buzzed by Mays twice more, once forcing him into the degradation of discussing professional sports. Caro, compensatory, remained shut up in her module. Mays wrote two words and lapsed, wrote two more and lapsed. He tried to force his memory—which he imagined to be an inch deep and just left of his crown—to reproduce the aerial view of that Veterans' Day. But the more he strained, the more distant and ubiquitous that antique, upstream figure became.

When the five bells sounded, Mays dredged up, instead of the memory he was after, a spontaneous tune from out of his old church hymnal: "Now Thank We All Our God." He did not know that it had been the German national hymn, sung spontaneously by Berlin crowds on August 1, 1914, the day of mobilization. Nor could he imagine how it sounded on the clarinet. It was merely his way of giving thanks for the end of another thankless day.

Chapter Seven

Portraits in Gum Arabic

The world that used to be and the ideas that shaped it disappeared . . . down the corridors of August and the months that followed.—BARBARA TUCHMAN, *The Guns of August*

AND SO after only a very short time in Boston, I had lost both the mystical impression and the physical sense of that Detroit photo. I had come across those faces by accident, but it was also the gradual accumulation of daily accidents that blurred and overexposed those faces in my mind. For the three figures on the muddy road had no names to anchor them in a more solid bed of association. Stories stick in the mind longer than near-religious sensations.

And to admit it, the forgetting made my life less anxious, more comfortable. We're lucky that our memories are so much less physically persistent than they might be. Being able to forget a broken arm usually makes up for the annoyance of bad memory. But this time, the trade-off was a bad one. If the weakness of memory protects from repeated regashing, it also postpones the cut of necessary surgery.

I could no longer voluntarily call to mind the subject of the black-and-white image that had moved me so profoundly. Yet I had moments, admittedly more and more isolated, seemingly spontaneous or brought on by slight associations, when the urgency and clarity of those three farmers, looking out over their right shoulders, came back to me with all their old force. I felt very much the old widower who, fifteen years after the death of his wife, wonders what could be keeping her so long this fine morning.

But I could no more sustain those clear slices of quarter hour when the farmers once again came down the road than the widower could preserve his confusion. When I was able to make out the shapes of those black suits and canes, my feeling revived so strongly as to seem the one instant of lucidity out of weeks of wasted time. At my office, on hearing a proper Bostonian say "Revere," I mistakenly heard the surname Rivera, and was at once back inside the assembly-line murals in Detroit. My sense of returning sanity was so strong that I instantly got on the phone before the conviction could escape and made reservations for the next flight to Michigan. I had very nearly completed the deal when the clerk put me on hold. The piped music, technomorphia, was quite definitely *not* "There's a Long, Long Night of Waiting." I felt rather foolish and broke the connection.

Convinced that my memory was deteriorating, I began to keep a notebook. I would stay up late, and under the influence of black coffee I would fill pages with forced recollections and exercises in concentration. I would wake in the mornings, eager to see the revelations waiting in longhand on the pages. I would reach for the still-open book and read over what I had written down the evening before. The small part that was legible I found romantically incoherent.

Most of my time I spent in calm disinterest. While I could not remember the urgency of the picture, I had forgotten also to worry much about forgetting. My work was technical enough to lose myself in, but not so difficult as to require any real concentration. In the evenings, I continued research on those leads I could remember from my Detroit hiatus, but I had lost sight of the end. No conspiracy developed. On weekends, I stuck to my Baedecker, doing walking tours of Boston. The Freedom Trail was my happy monotony.

The interruptions of memory, however few, were fierce enough to force notice. Three men walk down a muddy road at late afternoon, two obviously young, one an indeterminate age. When that mechanical reproduction came back to me, I felt the shame of neglect that I always feel in those dreams in which my father, who gave in to cancer when I was twenty-one, comes and sits on the end of my bed, saying, "You've forgotten me? What do you think I am, dead?" The farmers, looking out over their right shoulders, accused me of the same crime. Their look at the lens, when clear, seemed a call to experience something I knew nothing of.

Stronger than their accusation was my fear that any sudden moves on my part might dissolve the image once more. But the fear generally did the chasing off by itself. I seemed headed for a time when the anxiety of memory would soon be present without any sense of its constituting image.

I did not know it then, but I had no cause for worry. What seems a detour has a way of becoming, in time, a direct route. I would have to follow a strange, indirect circuit to arrive back at that day in 1914, but I would get there in time. To identify those would-be dancers, I had first to submerge myself in their dance.

By winter, I received my first raise, on the order of 2.5 percent. Against a national inflation of 14 percent, this represented a sizable pay cut. The vice-president of personnel (people in the vernacular) rushed to assure me privately that this did not reflect the quality of my work. He said I was one of the few who carried my weight in the office. But then, I've always been rather light for my weight.

But our business, this fellow explained to me, was one that prospered or panicked in proportion to the stock exchange, and a sustained loss of confidence in equities caused an equal loss of confidence at the executive level at our end. "Trust begets trust; lack of trust begets lack of trust." Or perhaps it was the other way around. I've never been very good with economics. It made sense when he said it.

If I had been twenty-five still, I might have argued against his circularity. But I didn't care about the money, and only wanted to be free from his office. I thanked him for the 2.5 percent, and hoped that would cut the interview short.

It did not. This fellow, who had mercifully left me alone until that day, now began an in-depth analysis of how America had to go about getting back on the track of economic recovery. These theories seemed the product of an unhappy home life. His wife, no doubt, would not let him keep a pet. From a discourse on the steady crumble in capital value of most of the country's technical blue chips, he rowed across an ocean of similes back to a discussion of my salary review: I was a serious worker, perhaps too serious. My problem was that I threatened morale, and thereby production, with my standoffishness. Why didn't I mingle a little bit more? He allowed me to leave only under oath that I would attend the office Christmas party.

When the day came, I lugged myself out to the president's house in a wealthy South Shore suburb to keep that promise. The train out took two hours, pleasantries an hour and a half, the turkey raffle a quarter hour, and toasts and caroling another forty minutes. I was about to consider the four and a half hours of Saturday a total loss when I made my most important discovery since the photograph. I met the office's immigrant cleaning woman, Mrs. Schreck, with whom I had had no prior contact outside of cryptic, cellophane commodities, apparently chocolate bonbons, she sometimes left as presents on my desk.

She was a strong woman, though obviously at least a decade in violation of the forced retirement act. Letting her work on was perhaps the only decent felony our mutual employer had ever committed. We spoke while looking over our host's treasure of artifacts, a large collection he maintained as a hedge against inflation. Mrs. Schreck held one of these, a German ambulance driver's cap from the First World War, and delivered herself of a marvelous private story. As she told me, in almost impenetrable accent, a harmless detail from her early life, I found her words opening a way back to the photo, a way that I thought had been closed to me for good.

I was back on the scent. And though it was the stink of the past, it had the aroma of something new and strange.

In 1913, Charles Péguy, then forty and an unlikely combination of poet, journalist, Socialist, and Roman Catholic, made the famous and often-repeated statement that the world had changed less since the death of Jesus than it had in the last thirty years. He described, for his millions of contemporaries, the concurrent horror and excitement of geometrically accelerating culture.

Hidden in Péguy's formulation is the idea that each tool, each measurement, each casual observation of the nature of things—even Péguy's—accelerates and automates the acquisition of the next tool. The first rock-chipping rock logically extends itself, along a series of ever-shorter steps, into the assembly line and the self-replicating machine. This increasingly steepening curve applies to every endeavor where the product of growth contributes directly to growth's progress.

As with free-falling bodies, it seems apparent that such quickening change, whether evolutionary, cultural, or technical, cannot accelerate indefinitely but must reach some terminal velocity. Call that terminal velocity a trigger point, where the rate of change of the system reaches such a level that the system's underpinning, its ability to change, is changed. Trigger points come about when the progress of a system becomes so accelerated, its tools become so adept at self-replicating and self-modifying, that it thrusts an awareness of itself onto itself and reaches the terminal velocity of self-reflection.

Trigger points represent those times when the way a process develops loops back on the process and applies itself to its own source. A billion years of evolution eventually, along an increasingly steep curve, produces a species capable of comprehending evolution. After Darwin (or, as increasingly metaself-conscious scientific historians argue, Alfred Wallace, or even the previous generation of anonymous naturalists), evolution cannot ever follow the old path again. Having reached a trigger point, natural selection re-forms itself as conscious selection. Even if we, the product of but now the proxy agent for evolution, choose not to directly help or hinder the cause of a particular species, the result still becomes primarily a product of mental rather than environmental choice. If one buys nothing else from Marx, whose ideas may be the trigger point of economics applied to itself, he is at least untouchable on quantitative changes becoming qualitative ones.

In the process of psychological adaptation, the trigger came with depth psychology and Freud. Now that our culture is glibly aware of defense mechanisms, the self can never again defend itself in the old ways. Art that was once a product of psychological mechanisms is now *about* those mechanisms and—the ultimate trigger point—about being about them. The Industrial Revolution cusped in the computer, a machine capable of designing its own replacement.

Gödel pulled a trigger point on mathematics, using a formal

system to demonstrate the incompleteness of itself as well as any system strong enough to prove its own incompleteness. Planck, Bohr, Heisenberg, and other co-conspirators similarly turned physics back onto itself, bringing a new reflexive element into the limits of the discipline. (A by-product of physics' trigger, Los Alamos represents a trigger point in the history of warfare.) Change in these fields does not stop at the trigger point. Only the curve of progress reaches a critical moment, the second derivative goes to zero, and a new curve begins, pushed forward into a new country.

So what of Péguy's—and hundreds of others' concurrent with him—triggering observation that culture and its tools had changed more in thirty years than in the previous 1900? Culture had finally created people who were not only the passive product of but also the active operators and commentators on their own culture's acceleration. Culture had replaced its own by-products more and more quickly until it arrived at a trigger frame, one whose members knew of and were synonymous with the fact of their own replaceability. No longer just a changing culture, but a culture of change.

The artifacts of societal behavior came down the turnpike of years, a decade doing the work of the previous century, two years overturning a decade, adding new combinations of content and epiphenomena, threatening, in the years before 1913, a Malthusian catastrophe of population. Then, as when the velocitized particle in a cyclotron slams into a waiting plate and transmutes it, the accelerated cultural change, released by the Péguy pronouncement, slammed into and transmuted the old societal iron into a new metal. And all about, people breathed the air of a new planet, the new qualities of concurrency and self-reflexiveness.

Cultural change had achieved the old joke of the runner so fast that she passes herself on the road. By 1913, changing tastes, doctrines, isms, theories—which once obeyed the old model of sequential cultural progress—now replaced one another so rapidly that they overran each other, collapsing into the spontaneous. The *avant* grew so far ahead of the *garde* that they lapped and began running side by side. The Futurist Manifesto of "faster," having reached a terminal velocity, could only become a doctrine of "all-at-the-same-time." And this simultaneity still holds true today, with

Third World militarism, bank-by-mail, television game shows, the rebirth of orthodox religion, conceptual art, punk rock, and neoromanticism thriving side by side.

Hyperprogress transmutes, paradoxically, into stillness. It is *still* true that things have changed more in the last thirty years than in all the time since Christ. Since it is *still* true, then *nothing* has changed since Péguy. Social culture has taken tail in mouth and rolled a benzene ring. Art takes itself as both subject and content: post-modernism about painting, serialism about musical composition, constructivist novels about fiction. At that, the century has become *about* itself, history about history: a still, eclectic, universally reflexive, uniformly diverse, closed circle, the homogeneous debris in space following a nova. Nothing can take place in this century without some coincident event linking it into a conspiratorial whole.

Péguy himself suffered from the self-modifying nature of his own observation. His life changed more in the year following his statement than it had in the forty before it. All his eclectic, simultaneously held beliefs—Catholicism, mysticism, socialism, aestheticism—paled before the Ism that he received at the Battle of the Marne, only a month after the start of the war. Separate casualty figures for the Marne are difficult to determine, but at least a few hundred thousand received baptism into the same terminal belief as Péguy's. And they have held that faith now longer than any living conviction. It may well turn out to be the century's triggering and most durable religion.

The squeezing of any trigger point results in some explosion. The Great War was the century's way of catching up to itself. For Simultaneity to set itself up as the new governing condition, it had to clear a spot for itself out of the rubble and clutter of royal dynasties, imperialism and colonialism, moribund belles-lettres, top-heavy property systems, and the grip of nostalgia so often confused with historical precedent. The curve of cultural tradition had outrun itself, reached its trigger point of self-reflection, and just as a sonic boom results when an object catches up to and pushes ahead its own sound, so the twentieth century propagated a considerable shock on catching up with the twentieth century.

An unthinkable number of individuals—over ten million, if the number means anything—did not make it through the catching up. Nor did any aspect of the old order make it through untouched. The violence of that cesarean section is written into every trivial detail, every congenital and hidden memory of our waking lives.

The incidental cause of the war—"some foolish thing in the Balkans"—seems even at this late a date wholly arbitrary, largely irrelevant, and only moderately interesting. Hašek's Good Soldier Švejk, a Czech veteran of the Balkans and obedient volunteer for the new conflagration, by turns certifiably imbecilic and insanely lucid, has the last word on the blind lead of the royal assassination:

> "I'd buy a Browning for a job like that. It looks like a toy, but in a couple of minutes you can shoot twenty archdukes with it, never mind whether they're thin or fat. Although between you and me, Mrs. Muller, a fat archduke's a better mark than a thin one."

The "cause" of the war—the events of June and July 1914— seem now to be nothing more than the clumsy working out of intrigues and diplomatic pressures laid out for some time before. The telegrams between royal first cousins at the head of states, the secret deals, forced ultimatums, blank checks, and eleventh-hour regrets can no longer be fully or satisfactorily unraveled by anyone so distant or implicated as ourselves. Again, Švejk's mis-explanation is as good as any:

> "There'll have to be a war with the Turks. 'You killed my uncle and so I'll bash your jaw.' War is certain. Serbia and Russia will help us. . . ."

His alliances may have turned out all backward, but he has the spirit of the thing. The war resulted from the common attitude summed up by England's Foreign Secretary, Sir Edward Grey: "If we are engaged in war, we shall suffer but little more than we shall suffer if we stand aside."

But was the war necessary? A.J.P. Taylor observed after the fact that "No war is inevitable until it breaks out." This lucid epigram makes a formidable effort to preserve the best of humanity—reason—from its worst, fatalism. But one might as well say that no one ever got hurt jumping from a tall building until hitting the pavement. In an environment where Austria-Hungary thought that the Germans assumed that Russia believed that war between Serbia and Austria-Hungary was inevitable, not to mention France, Britain, and Turkey all rushing to position themselves advantageously so as not to be preempted by others' positioning, Taylor's statement seems snared in a circular tangle: "No war is inevitable until one or more parties believes it to be inevitable, or until one or more parties believes that another believes it to be inevitable."

Social developments often collect such a massy inertia that years pass before a tendency shows its results. The private automobile provides a good illustration. Ford perfected the under-five-hundred-dollar automobile in the first decade of the century, but it took another seventy years for this country to find itself hostage to oil-rich nations, increasingly susceptible to respiratory and oncological diseases, unable to get from A to B except through private ownership, and every fifteen years acquiring enough highway fatalities to level the city of Houston. Similarly, the war may have resulted from some agent long since vanished, caused by the past, but seemingly inevitable to the present. Perhaps the dead dictate necessity to the living.

Barbara Tuchman raises this possibility by suggesting that von Schlieffen and the German General Staff, although guilty of laying down the immediate plans of destruction, acted under the centuries-broad umbrella of German thought. The invention of total war lay tacit in Fichte and Nietzsche, who urged the strong and culturally superior to achieve their rightful dominance; and especially in Hegel, who described continual upheaval as the instrument of progress and change. The French were likewise under the spell of an equally well-worn tradition of progress. Henri Bergson's doctrine of *élan vital* maintained that vital force, or the French, would triumph over base material, that is, the Boches. Thus the war had long ago started in the entrenched belief in progress and the triumph of the Great Personality.

Nineteen-thirteen was a time richer in Great Personalities than any since the Renaissance. Vienna and Paris—arguably the two best representatives of the warring factions, the one outgoing and monarchical, the other incoming and anarchical—boasted between them Freud, Picasso, Wittgenstein, Proust, Apollinaire, Schönberg, Webern, Berg, Gide, Jarry, Debussy, Klimt, Stravinsky, Bernhardt, Mahler, the General Hospital physicians and scientists, Stein, Meliès, Krauss, Werfel, and Rousseau, to name only a few, breaking off before the list stales the palette. The era is often described in paraphrased lives of these individuals, a forgivable practice, as the time seems to have seen itself in the same way. It is as if the last gasp of the old way of progress—successive leaps made by individual genius—would only give way to the new era of simultaneity by blowing itself out in one final burst of fecundity.

Then, perhaps, the war may have been made necessary by some genetic predisposition in humans. The love of the moribund, the belief that the sickly and perverse hold more possiblity for experience than the status quo, has been our times' epidemic of preference. But an opposite mentality, a perennially unfounded optimism, is equally to blame for catastrophe. Consider that almost every observer at the time, from the ignorant to the overly informed (with the exception of a few powerless pawns at the heads of armies such as Kitchener and von Moltke), went on record in predicting a short war.

This optimism came in part from reasoning about the new weapons technologies: dividing the total available European fighting men by a reasonable kill rate for field-emplaced artillery and machine guns gave an estimate of a little over four weeks before all draftable men of both sides would be dead. Others argued that European nations had become so economically interdependent that none could survive a war of attrition. Nor could a modern war government remain in office after more than a few months of fighting. In Proust's *Remembrance of Things Past*, the officer Saint-Loup, mastering the paradoxical art of political reasoning, explains to the sickly civilian Marcel that the war would not last beyond a handful of weeks because neither side was making plans for it to do so.

Yet to say that the war was necessary because of social tendencies laid down long before does not absolve the casual individual of his act of complicity. The heads of state who acted under trumped-up charges have to be held accountable. More subtly, every individual who gave in to the context of deteriorating trust contributed to it through his or her own omissions: the woman anxious over admittance to Oxford, the brickmaker in Holland, the German landed farmer, all guilty in waiting for history to blow over, guilty in assuming that death could never happen in their lifetime.

There is no pinning down necessity after the fact. Every speculation on the origin of the Great War putrifies after a point, stalls in postmortem abstraction. "It's bad," says imbecile Švejk, "when a chap suddenly gets caught up in philosophizing. That always stinks of *delirium tremens*." Explanation of cause must at some point turn back to recounting of effect, back to the ugly fact.

And yet, of the war's consequences, the most material are the least important. The more than ten million dead, an unthinkable number now or then, made only the smallest dent in the steady doubling and redoubling of the world's population. In fact, influenza alone took more lives than weapons did during the war's last two years. Over twenty million surviving casualties mattered more. As a result of increased medical technology, countries had to reabsorb, for the first time on so large a scale, the maimed and amputated. Sander's objective, unprecedented portrait of the one-legged, uniformed veteran pandering in the street for loose change, an image later taken up by painters George Grosz and Otto Dix, salutes this new social caste.

Changes in warfare—the tank, warplane, submarine, poison gas—incomparable horrors, remain at best tactical devices, quickly outdated in terror and effectiveness by the arms of the next generation. War in this century has been largely a field test for new technologies. Nor do most historical texts, in such phrases as "the entire map of Europe and her colonies was redrawn," get the point. The colonies simply changed hands. The colors of the map changed, but in small tailorings and alterings, not touching the flawed system of national states itself.

Of the much touted far-reaching political changes, the League of Nations and the Weimar Republic were little more than failed experiments. The Russian Revolution, entrenched more firmly, cannot be denied. What exactly it signifies, however, is open to debate. In short, the political revampings were far-reaching only in that they established a system so volatile it broke down almost at once into a second, far more horrible conflict.

Perhaps the war's central consequence is not the first that comes to mind. Europe lost its innocence and importance by pushing warfare to the cusp point: fighting making itself known to itself through the irreversible practice of total war. Every citizen, not just paid soldiers, now became a direct protagonist in war in ways never before imagined and never afterward escaped. From aerial bombardment to the sinking of passenger vessels to the economic front, war's totality now included each individual. Nowhere was this new totality clearer than in the occupation of enemy territory.

The German program for victory, derived from Clausewitz, called for total subjection of occupied territory through the cultivation of fear in civilian populations. Their strict, timetabled march through Belgium did not allow for the terrifying setbacks of guerrilla warfare. With turn-of-the-century naïveté, the Germans tried to solve the problem of snipers firing on soldiers through a series of public proclamations. To the German General Staff, whatever was proclaimed became legal, even if it flew in the face of every war convention yet laid down. Citizens found guilty of subversive activities would be shot at once or sent to Germany for hard labor. And, establishing the most important intellectual precedent in this century, they declared that each entire village would be held hostage and punished for the work of so much as one rebellious bullet.

The German army of occupation legislated what peace had been powerless to promote and the atomic bomb was to enforce as a terminal inheritance: every human being was now to be held accountable for its neighbor.

But in the early days of the war, none of these consequences was immediately obvious. The war had reached a deadlock; month after month, commanders sent men over the tops of trenches, refusing to believe that the last debacle would be repeated. At the Somme, desperate for a breakthrough, the British regressed to the eighteenth-century tactic of the "slow walk": thousands of men almost linking arms, walking stately into waiting machine-gun nests.

Europe was stalemated in a static front. War had reached that transmuting moment. It had become self-reflexive, self-knowing. It would now go on forever. It was about itself.

Yet on the morning of November 25, 1915, New Yorkers awoke to a *Tribune* whose headlines declared:

GREAT WAR ENDS
CHRISTMAS DAY
FORD TO STOP IT

Chapter Eight

Static Front

Each man would die of the disease of his own class if war did not reconcile all the microbes.—JEAN RENOIR, *Grand Illusion*

WILLY'S SHOTGUN used exploding shells. These made it easier for the old Socialist to continue hunting ducks, which had become a good deal smaller and faster than when he was thirty. "Evolution," he explained to Hubert. "We hunters keep bagging the fat, slow ones and the survivors are breeding a super race. The last century had it easier. They didn't have evolution yet."

Will would sit in his duck blind before sunup, his pants all beshitted by ulcerative colitis, waiting for a flock to fly overhead. Any birds would do, since he could no longer see well enough to care. If the probabilities seemed reasonable, he'd raise his shotgun over his head, close his eyes, and try to cover his ears with his extended upper arms. He would have liked hunting a whole lot more without the noise. Releasing both barrels dropped birds with surprising frequency.

The same exploding buckshot shells should have made Hubert deadly at the twenty yards' distance he was from the detonating crew. But he shot hastily, falling off his bicycle. Possibly, in believing this handful of Belgian engineers to be the advance guard of a German army several million strong, he had not felt the need to aim. Buckshot, scattered in any direction approximating east, would necessarily contribute to thinning out the enemy. Inexperience, too, weakened his aim. This was, after all, Hubert's first real war.

For these reasons, Hubert's buckshot spray, which ordinarily would have cleaned a butterfly from the side of a barn at five hundred paces, did not make an auspicious contribution to the opening of the war. The left barrel sliced way wide, most of the lead pellets falling into the Meuse tributary that the Belgians meant to unbridge. The pellets lay in the sluggish current, growing sizable algae beards over the next several decades.

Part of the right barrel went into the dirt, throwing a clump of chick-pea gravel into the groin of one engineer. This man doubled up in pain and went down, thinking he was dead. In fact, he sustained no permanent injury at all. The location of the wound, its slightness, and the pathetic, ribald thoughts he'd had on impact might have made a good barroom story in middle age had not the fellow gone and gotten killed only ten days later, brained by a somewhat larger piece of masonry dislodged by the German 420-millimeter siege guns brought up against Liège.

A third spray of shot scattered into the arm of another engineer, slamming him to the ground. This man felt only the vague impression of having grazed his sleeve against something soft. He felt nothing more of his wound until after the commotion had died. Then he saw the blood welling up under his sleeve. Cutting his shirt off at the shoulder, revealing the sticky mass of the wound, he fainted with pain proportionate to the visual horror. He was sent off to Antwerp in the north, to a hospital specializing in the new techniques of prosthetic parts.

His new arm, mobile and cosmetically passable, kept him out of the theater of war over the next five years. Much later, on days when morosity did not have him by the throat, he played a game with his grandchildren in which he was a mechanical man, occasionally made by Hitler but just as frequently a spontaneous product of Borneo or Africa, and they were Pilots, the only race congenitally capable of stopping the metal creature.

After the danger had passed, after the disturbance came to a quick end, after even the machine gun realized it was the only sound and shut up in embarrassment, the crew rose to their feet to examine the corpse of the enemy that had fired on them. They saw a sight beyond easy explanation. Here was no professional soldier ("murderer," as Ford had read in McGuffey's *Fourth Eclectic Reader* in a section called "Things by Their Right Name"), but a boy with a French face, Dutch shotgun, and Belgian cigarettes, the ones the farmer's wife had given him that morning.

Following several rounds of obligatory European debate—only two liters of Burgundy short of being a picnic—most of the men agreed that the child must have been driven mad by the sensationalism in the newspapers circulating everywhere, a madness only remarkable in being a few days ahead of the median. Having decided this, they forged ahead twenty minutes later to decide that they had not much time to decide what to do with the body. They thought some more about this while completing the bridge detonations that had originally startled Hubert.

The bridge work did not require all the men's explosives. One or the other said it would be a shame to let any part of Mr. Nobel's invention go to waste. Dynamite, like the tractor or assembly line, was for the greater use of mankind—a labor-saving device. Why not save on the labor, let alone the cost, involved in digging this crazy boy's grave?

The plan won instant approval. The crew planted the remaining charge in a nearby fallow field. The explosion left a middle-sized crater, large enough for Hubert, the shotgun, and his bicycle. (A year later, when Henry Ford spoke with President Wilson about his foolproof plan to end the Great War, he loosened up the President with a joke of his own invention: a man asks to be buried with his Ford because it has pulled him out of every hole so far.)

With his burial, Hubert finally triggered his long-coveted mass movement. He was at last a revolutionary, the first to occupy a field that would fill to capacity with Belgian and Flemish citizens found guilty on the principle of collective responsibility. After the war, each place, including Hubert's, would be decorated with white stones bearing the ubiquitous inscription:

1914
Fusillée par les Allemands
(Shot by the Germans)

The next generation of Belgians made use of the same inscription, with only the date changed.

In the relative comfort of her policeman father's house, Wies sought safety from Hubert's attacks of the night before. She said nothing of the incident to her parents, naturally, who knew little of the boy's existence. Their plans for their daughter—education, in Paris if possible—kept them from noticing anything so slight as the impediments of reality. There were matters of more concern and excitement loose in the world; her father had taken a knife graze across the neck three days before, and still repeated and clarified the details for his family each night over dinner:

—A marriage fight, cat-and-dog. Every footer on the force will tell you that that's the worst a fellow can come across. Give me anything—an armed robber, crazy man, drunken students, auto accident—just don't send me into matrimonial bliss gone wrong. The Bremmers, on Schunk Straat, married sixteen years. Everyone says here's an ideal couple. Then the call comes Tuesday the Bremmers are at it, and I say to myself that I'm all in. Sure enough, I come in the front way to break it up, and the two of them turn on *me*. The little woman charges with a fruit peeler: "My husband's been beating me for years and I love it. You get out." And she gives me one across the neck. I'm lucky just to make it out the pantry. Don't talk to me about international huzza; I've got my hands full with the domestic.

And for many nights running, the family would proceed to lamb with mint jelly or stewed chicken so pungent that no amount of current event could dispel the taste.

After a few days of hiding out at home, Wies grew used to her safety and so no longer felt or needed it. She wondered about what had come over Hubert. He had always been two parts crazy, laughing like a wolf and slobbering like an infant. But this last trip had been worse. He began by swearing that his brother Peter could not make him return to the Westerwald. He told horrible stories about what he would do to the rich if he ever came across any. Wies tried to quiet him by telling him how dangerous it still was to speak such words in Maastricht, even for a boy. But he only pinched her forearms until she said he was not a boy and could talk as he liked, anywhere.

Then came the attack. Wies went home afterward and washed out her sex with warm salt water, an old wives' contraceptive she'd heard about somewhere. Two weeks passed, while she by turns dreaded and hoped for some word from him. Visits from the cousins petered out. She sat safe, anxious, in the sitting room of her father, the law.

She passed time with the novelty of newspapers. At first the stories made no sense to her, but soon she grew used to their cadences. She thought it strange that the Germans fussed so much over Belgian Limburg while against Dutch Limburg they raised not a finger. She felt the guilt of unearned favoritism. Beyond that, 1914 did not much touch her. She lived in a neutral country. Hubert's madness was all that she knew of the world's.

Bored with her police-state home, certain that Hubert would not in these times return to Germany, and curious about what the boy could find that was more fascinating than she, Wies set out to locate her displaced love, without any leads. His blood mother, ordinarily evasive, was now unreachable. In stabilizing the province for the outbreak of war, Limburg officials put many citizens under house arrest and swept suspicious elements into quarantine. The net caught Hubert's blood mother, who'd committed no crime greater than wondering publicly which of the two armies, French or German, would be better business.

Wies had similar problems finding Hubert's friend Willy. On the day that the Maastricht police, with apologies, released the old man from his monthly revenue stint, Limburg officials picked him up for much tougher grilling. They released him only after he'd agreed to sign thirty-four different documents, oaths, and affidavits. Once free, he could not recall anything he had put his name to. The general gist, though, was that he denounced everything political he'd ever thought or said, and acknowledged that the instant he stopped behaving he'd be back in the jug.

On the day that Wies came calling for him, Will simply closed the doors and windows on her, hoping that no one had seen the girl who knew the boy who heard the man who said the crazy things that the signature denounced. That swallowed the fly. That Jack built. That was going to St. Ives. Under this policy of strict non-involvement, Willy survived a good, long, apolitical while, and became among the first in the area to enjoy the boon of postwar, government-subsidized housing.

Aside from Hubert's streetball friends—and Wies would have

gone to them if she thought they could have helped—only one other person in all Maastricht either knew or cared about Hubert's existence. This was the one person Hubert forbade her ever to try to meet: his brother Peter. Hubert kept the two from meeting simply because for two years he had bragged to Peter that he never knew any of the names of the women he had "done over." Until Wies, Hubert's claim was at least as valid as the Kaiser's assertion that Germany had to invade Belgium to prevent a French violation. The logic of the null set cannot be challenged, and a false antecedent implies anything.

When Wies arrived in his life, Hubert, for the first time accountable to a nonempty set of done-over women, could no longer make the claim honestly. So he simply kept her away from Peter and hoped to make the brag last a little longer, absence of evidence to the contrary. He was ashamed to tell his adopted brother that he returned to the same woman again and again, grew familiar with her, even called her by name. Somewhere he had learned that sex and familiarity could not negotiate except unilaterally. He was not ashamed to admit to one or the other, only the two in combination.

For her part, Wies thought Hubert kept her from Peter out of shame for the other. The fellow—cast on poor Hubert by the machinations of the state—must have some fearful abnormality: perhaps he was a leper, or a Swede. Only on the day when she set out willfully for the tobacco shop did she worry that the brother, too, might be touched; perhaps a pathological Catholic. Hubert had always enjoyed her religious scoldings when they played the kissy game. Peter might be a reverse sort of apostate. Most likely, she'd get a beating from both brothers: once for being a devout, once for wantonness. She slunk, head down, toward the tobacco shop as if the whole process of heaping up new pain were somehow inevitable.

Not pain but much the reverse waited for Wies at the widow's shop. She recognized Peter at once from the folded-up photo Hubert had given her the night he went away. Even with a burlap clerk's smock replacing the beautiful dark suit he'd worn that May Day, even where retail confines destroyed the airy memory of that muddy road, Peter wore an unmistakable smirk of confidence as much a product of the arch of bone around his eye as of his personality. He dispensed cigars to the customer ahead of Wies as if he were a hero of that school of novel, still popular in this year of dynastic crumbling, a royal heir forced in infancy into peasant upbringing by some vast conspiracy.

Wies's turn came to be served, and she stepped forward to the counter. Peter looked up from dirtying his hands in the greasy cash till and at once put off his business face, letting his eyes dilate. She was afraid for a moment that he recognized her: what did he see so arresting? But he said nothing more committing than:

—*Hemel!* You are too pretty a woman to be doing your own shopping. And in this sort of shop, too. Where's your lady's maid, eh?

He spoke with mock opprobrium, meaning to imply that no pretty and modern girl could take seriously the taboo on female smoking. Certain of his facial muscles went so far as to suggest that her being here in the smoke pit even excited him.

Wies felt a sudden springing up of well-being, a relief almost as physical as the one she felt each evening on shedding her dress stays. She was back on familiar territory; it had been too long since she had sat in the parlor with a Wednesday admirer. Peter's speech, as familiar to her as the Christmas story from St. Luke, put her at her ease. There would be time for her errand later. Peter's grace, like a lazy evening, had to be taken at its own pace. The moment for her mission had been lost. She would come again to the right moment, after a while. Hubert had been missing for days; rescuing him could wait as long.

—Yes . . . I'm looking for some small smoking item that might be appropriate for a . . . cousin of mine. Maybe some kind of . . . tobacco that he could . . . smoke.

—Tobacco for smoking. A novel idea, that. I'm no professor, but I bet the combination might just work.

Peter had a way of making his speech affable and appealing, drawing his listener into a pact of conspiracy by blowing air out on the first consonants of words, puffing his cheeks, even spitting a little, the way he used to do during his five-year stint in school when he could no longer contain his hilarity at a master's stupidity.

—How old did you say this cousin of yours is?

—I didn't say, sir. But he's about your age. Is that important? Different tobaccos for different ages?

—About my age, hmm? Say, you're not intending to use this little gift item yourself, are you? You might get big brown splotches breaking out all over your beautiful skin. Look here; see what working in this thankless shop brings me?

He craned way out over the counter toward her, lifting his head and baring his jugular, so that she could see up under his fine jawline. At the same time, he reached out and put his hand lightly on her nape, guiding her authoritatively toward the blemish.

Wies was home free, on extremely firm footing here. Through long practice, she considered herself the best examiner of toothaches, skin imperfections, and somethings-in-the-eye in the working-class quarter of Maastricht. She made the appropriate ghastly sucking in of breath. She pulled out all the stops, going so far as to reach out with one timid, overly shaking third finger to touch the area—a normal birthmark—as if it were an infected animal capable of transmitting the increasingly popular phenomenon of germs even through her cotton confirmation gloves.

The August day was hot, and smoke shops stood particularly low in popularity. Perhaps the start of the war, too, kept the normal clientele at home. Not anticipating a long war, the Dutch did not start queuing for and stockpiling staples for another five months. They stayed home from the shops to take part in a sophisticated form of ambulance chasing: the habit of tobacco stood no chance against a stronger addiction to the tabloid press with its line engravings of the shifting fronts.

For this reason, the First War kept the smoke shop mostly empty and kept the tobacconist's widow out of the shop preying on war rumors. Peter came from behind the counter and began conducting Wies about. He placed his hand in the small of her back, guiding her in the manner popular on the dance floors that year. Having familiarized itself with that fascinating but too local area, his hand began playing Balboa in search of the Pacific.

He talked to her at great length about cigardom, making up names and curiosities when the facts weren't enough to distract her from what his hand was doing. Yet she showed Olympian skill at asking an ingenuous question while turning in such a way as to return his hand from its perch in Peru to its remote port in Spain. She knew by heart the old formula for compound interest: delay is the way to compound the crime without losing the criminal's interest.

Their sales talk followed the basic pattern of he proposing and she disposing. He steered her starboard toward a box of the cheapest, garden-variety panatelas, fabricating:

—Perhaps your cousin would be charmed by a gift of these remarkable eleganta. They were first brought back by one of our early explorers of Java. This fellow discovered a tribe there that smoked these by putting the lit end into their mouths. Like this. Don't laugh, you. This tribe turned out to be cannibals, and that explorer lost three quarters of his men.

—Oh, awful! I don't want to hear.

—But did that explorer care about the dangers? Of course he didn't. He thought of only one thing: how to get this cigar back to Holland so he and Her Majesty could make a mint.

—And . . . he made it back? Alive?

—No. He mailed it back parcel post. Say, you're not too much upstairs, are you? Anyway, that's what makes we Dutch great. You and that explorer: neither smart enough to get distracted. That's why the Huns better leave their mitts off us, or they'll be tied up with an enemy too dumb to know when to quit.

—You're Dutch?

—Limburger, if you please. What did you think, Latvian?

—I thought he said . . . Oh, no reason.

—So what do you say, miss? Elegantas for the cousin?

In each instance, she would remove her glove, pick up the sample, smell it, roll it between her fingers, replace it in its box, and give the shelf the pat of extreme unction. Visibly aroused, Peter warned her that this was a good way to get "nicotine sores," but made no effort to restrain her. And after each ritual she would say, with disarming, nostalgic regret:

—Why no, I don't think that's quite the thing for my cousin.

And they would sail to another bin. Aware that the obstacle had to be surmountable if it were to raise desire, Wies encouraged Peter to open a second front. She let the garments of her greatskirt brush unrestrained against Peter's arm. The effect at that time of a light brush of fabric is beyond the imagining of a modern. The century's progress killed that sensibility. Submarines, battleships, welfare, radio, the psychological novel, exploding shells, the computer, depth analysis make it no longer possible to confuse a graze with contact, suggestion with the deed.

Peter returned pressure for pressure. He began to brush her leg accidentally as they walked, apologizing at first, then acting without cover. His sales pitches suffered a steady attrition until they deteriorated to "Your cousin care for this?," and finally, "You like this?" With the most delicate schedule, he worked them into the shop's back corner, not visible from the street but still not without danger.

Peter had a strong sense of the impossibility of the situation but had learned, along with one hundred million other Europeans that hot August, how small a step it really was over the bounds of the possible. Wies faced yet another shelf of merchandise and waited for the inevitable, momentarily visited by a stillness that seemed to come from somewhere out of her past, settling on her like an old friend. When, against all odds, Peter managed to lift all her undergarments in one smooth motion, she did not so much as flinch, but stood with the docile fatalism of August corn. She only smoothed down the front of her skirts so that, from head on at least, she seemed the least molested. Somewhere behind her, Peter was asking her something. She found that the question went away if she ignored it.

He asked if she liked his free hand on the back of her thigh. Soon, he forgot such trivialities and attended to the job at hand. He moved to open his trousers and found he had already done so. He guided himself forward to take her from behind. He drew back, momentarily stunned as a crossed synapse caused him to believe he had touched a wet sea mammal that had made the two hundred miles overland from the Zuider Zee for the express purpose of lodging itself up her dress.

Instantly the impression passed, and he found his way inside her. She turned her head and made her face partly visible for the first time since he touched her. Her lids, cheeks, and forehead lay slack over her skull in abandon. She held a cigar in wet lips, puffing imaginary smoke out of the corner of her mouth, pantomiming a corporate higher-up who sees all things going exactly per plan.

She must have learned such luridness in Maastricht, as she had never traveled. The play-acted smoking aroused Peter even more than the anonymity of rear entry. He held on and pushed into her with adolescent severity.

Whether she faked or felt an ecstasy did not concern Peter as much as it did men later in the century. His anxiety came from another source altogether, for almost at the peak of their acceleration, she half-screamed:

—Peter!

He came instantly, prematurely, inside her. The next moment the whole incident vanished without trace. He grabbed her by the shoulders and swung her around, his nails making half-moons in her exposed skin. Without speaking, he demanded how she had come to know his name.

—You are . . . that is, you are called Peter? Peter Schreck? I am right?

She took a chance, appending the Christian name Hubert had mentioned so often to the German surname he had labored to write on the scrap of paper the night of the attack, the night he went away. Peter's response to her accusation became forever unreadable as he turned, head down and away from her.

—Your brother Hubert came to me several nights ago and . . . acted so strangely. Then he left and has not come back since. Have you seen him?

Peter replaced his clothes as she spoke, then walked with all the old impudence back to the front counter and cash till. Wies followed him, near hysterics, doing no better than repeating:

—Have you?

Her dress was still mostly décolleté. Peter stared at her, at her hands, which still held the cigar she had used to mime wantonness for him.

—One Spanish panatela comes to one quarter guilder.

—Peter?

—All right, take it for free, then. I'll pay for it out of my wages.

—Your brother, Hubert. He may be in trouble.

Weeping now, variations on "What have I said?" took her all the way to the shop door while he said nothing. She opened the door, ringing a small brass bell meant to warn the widow and Peter of a customer's entrance. Hearing Peter speak, she turned with infinite relief toward him, her rubbery face already composed in joy and forgiveness. But the boy only said, for no one's benefit in particular:

—I have put my bread in a cold oven.

Having touched the seam between need and cruelty, Wies found she wanted no more of male love for the rest of her waking life. She returned home, growing closer than ever to her parents and to the evening newspaper. And frequently over the next weeks, she would remove from the back of her press and reexamine the two documents—one mechanical, the other handwritten—that could change in so short a time from nostalgic keepsakes to legal leverage, should she find in the days to come that the seed of either boy left her in need of documentary proof.

That evening, as the tobacconist's widow mocked, Peter wrote to the Schreck family in the Westerwald, knowing that they, perhaps even more than the imprisoned blood mother, would care about Hubert's whereabouts. He wrote: "I told him not to, but the fool has gone and mixed himself up in this international business, and I can no longer be the protector of his safety. Your son, Peter."

The couple forwarded the information to Adolphe, assigned to a corps of von Bülow's army in the middle of the German West Front's right wing. Mail remained sporadic but mostly reliable through the end of the war's first year. They warned Adolphe not to answer any questions about his two brothers, should anyone come poking about the camp, as many had already come by the farm.

Adolphe got off two letters of his own the night that the mail caught up with his advancing column. He wrote both letters standing at ease in marching formation, while his regiment waited outside Namur for officers to unsnarl the traffic caused by two failed gasoline engines. The first letter was to corps headquarters, forwardable to the appropriate authorities, reading: "The evader Peter Kinder Schreck can be found at . . ." He was not yet twenty, and had to be forgiven having had no chance to consider the other names for loyalty.

His second was his weekly letter to his wife, differing from all its predecessors only in slight details. It began, "My baby Alicia: I am in a new country!"

Chapter Nine

Selling the Market Short

MAYS STEPPED into the back corner of the elevator, put on his best act of contrition, and waited for the button to the fourth floor to activate itself. He hated asking favors of inanimate objects, especially man-made ones. It was humiliating when they wouldn't co-operate and humiliating when they deigned to condescend. The metal doors slid shut, but the car remained still. At last Mays, beaten, moved toward the button panel and pleaded to be taken up. He who exalts himself will be humbled, and he who humbles himself will be humbled.

Following a timid jab of the finger, the elevator, after waiting an authority-challenging second, lunged into a slow assault of the upper stories. When the doors again slid open, they revealed a slick, Swedish-modern anteroom with walls coated in the tragically fashionable gunnysack material that monks had at one time worn for self-punishment. On one wall, foot-high burnished letters identified a major East Coast stock brokerage which, in a fit of creative invention, named itself after its three founders.

Ten yards past the door, Peter had to choose between a Teletype news wire spitting out data and a woman making mechanical clucking noises into a bank of switchboard buttons. A self-contained, mass-production line, this woman manufactured precise, identical greetings—"Good morning Phillips," and "Please hold"— converting them into neat packages of electromagnetic disturbance through the intercession of Dr. Bell's machine.

Mays thought it odd that everyone who called should be named Phillips. After a few hundred calls, it dawned on him that she was not saying good morning *to* Phillips but good morning *from* Phillips, that is, the firm's senior partner. Mays wanted to warn the woman that impersonation was a felony.

He opted instead for the safer prospect of the news ticker. Not that the woman's glossy dress and ballpark figure intimidated him. Formerly a woman of her looks ("Primo vintage," said Delaney, who still couldn't "get a handle on what all this consciousness-raising racket was all about") reduced Mays to a conversational level midway between Cal Coolidge and bread mold. Now, however, as she was a brunette, she could no more move him to "please hold" than the old Liberty posters could move him to buy bonds. Red; red was the issue. Auburn, perhaps, but not a tint-type lighter.

A perusal of the news wire led Mays to believe that it must have been a primitive means of communication at one time. Stories smudged their blue ink across a perpetual roll of newsprint. Mays read in mute admiration; his contemporaries were busy moving and shaking various parts of the globe as he looked on from his cheap seat in the pit. On the far side of the linkup, never directly visible except through the electronic moving finger, were the doers, people who through obstinacy of genetics had the rare ability to make something, however inconsequential, happen. Latching on to these deeds were the reporters—stooges like the gang back at *Micro*, newshounds hanging around the courtroom turning some sordid accident into COP SLAYS CON, blamed bringers of bad news, glorified middle-persons mucking the data with personal bias—whose only power lay in passing the info on to the Teletype.

Once the impartial machine had hold of all the news that fit, it sent it violently into the hands of the thousands of information brokers on the receiving end of world events. This class, although not of the real current of history, were privileged in that they would interpret the data coming out of the wire and sell it to the event-illiterates. And yet, Mays noticed that in the click and hum of this model office, the information brokers went to the well only for explanations after the fact. Sea Board Shipping down a handful of points by three o'clock? Check the wire, and sure enough: the *Lusitania*, reported sunk at noon.

Low on the totem pole came the class of perennial eavesdroppers who, like Mays, found themselves day after day gazing into the data stream (the only natural resource left to contemporary life), seeing but unable to comprehend the prolific chattering of the ticker. To these scavengers all tabloids were tarot; they gathered in knots of bodies outside appliance stores whenever Management left color TVs running in the showcase. The tons of newsprint spewed daily out of wire machines, if unintelligible, could at least divert.

Mays, having renounced the Church at puberty, Marx upon taking his first job, and the *Scientific American* when partial differentials began to elude him, had of late become a card-carrying scavenger of the first rank. He let the network news run in the living room of his Back Bay flat each evening as he worked halfheartedly in the kitchen to approximate a balanced meal. He had, in fact, arrived at Phillips, Please, and Hold for privileged data, for a market system. He had come to find out through the wire what he could not find out alone. He had come to ask Lenny Bullock for help in finding a redhead.

When Brink had suggested ingenuously that her beau could work Mays into Boston's musical power structure, Peter swore he'd call every name on the Veterans' Day parade manifest before soliciting help from the fellow. In a business where behavioral aberrations were job prerequisites, Bullock stood out among brokers at Phillips as the unacknowledged legislator of mania-depression.

Peter had last encountered the man at a party at Caroline's hopelessly upwardly mobile digs on Route 128. Brink and Bullock Inc. had hosted an embarrassing office get-together on a Tuesday night, the invitations announcing the motive as "chat, burgers, and volleyball." The memory of Moseley feebly attempting to take part in a team sport made Mays wince.

Filled with culinary zeal, Lenny had made about four times too much food. While his guests threw themselves ineffectually against the meal, trying to go over the top and occupy a hill of pork and beans, he held forth on how the U.S. should have taught the Russkies a lesson when they had the chance, and how the Marshall Plan was money flushed down a toilet. Caroline let no guest leave without taking home a half gallon of potato salad. In a hasty exit, Mays forgot his apartment keys and had to go back to the bash for them. He returned to find the party long dispersed, with Brink in the kitchen washing the dishes by hand so they would be clean enough to put in the dishwasher and Bullock out back mowing the lawn by flashlight.

Naturally, when Caro offered Lenny's help in solving a problem no one entirely understood, Peter did not rush to close the deal. That was before he had learned, seat-of-the-pants style, exactly how many redheads, clarinetists, and combinations thereof were milling about on the eastern seaboard.

The first illusion that his search for the exotic figure dispelled was Mays's belief, picked up through grade-school propaganda, that culture in this country was readily accessible to the little person. Concert ticket prices alone had nearly reduced him to selling his blood to the Red Cross in an attempt to make his editor's salary stretch from the first to the fifteenth. He'd started out attending Symphony concerts, intending to knock out several clarinets in one sitting. He'd stay only long enough to make sure that all the ill winds were old, male, and bald.

This meant surviving the first piece, invariably Beethoven's *Fidelio* Overture. After several hundred hearings, Mays still did not like the work. Perhaps he was impervious to things not immediately useful. For utility, *Fidelio* ranked right up there with parsley and napkin rings. He'd never quite gotten the hang of the arts in general, ever since he'd missed three weeks in the sixth grade. He came back from a bout with mono to find all his friends post-Renaissance, with him still raging in the Middle Ages.

After exhausting the local orchestras, Mays progressed to the rarified atmosphere of chamber music. He'd go through the weekly performance listings in the papers, making a prepass for clarinets and a second search by gender. Although less expensive to attend, these concerts made him extremely claustrophobic. First the violin would go *noodle*, then the cello would go *noodle*, and by the time the clarinet got hold of the noodle and ran it over the goal line, Mays was humming the theme song from *Twenty Thousand Leagues Under the Sea* and wondering nervously if the little hall held enough air for all the heavy breathers.

Besides these longhair recitals, he also frequented a brood of football halftimes, a brace of USO galas, a pride of nightclubs, a clatch of coffee houses, and an exaltation of church choirs. At the end, he was broke and exhausted, and had found no phantom. Twice he was almost arrested for charging through crowds after women with the right coloration. Ultimately, he would have doubted the figure's existence in the light of so much statistical evidence if Delaney had not also seen, pointed out in fact, that upstream parade anachronism those months before.

Yet he still would have avoided Bullock, so great was his distaste for the man or so great his love for the impossible search, had not the matter been taken out of his hands. His eternal anticipating, attending, or recuperating from the latest concert caused his editing at *Micro*, which had never been much more than a euphemism, to settle a comfortable notch below travesty. Delaney, pleading altruism, squealed the matter to Caro. ("What's more important, a minor friendship or the best goddamn electronics rag west of Bangor?") It marked the third time Mays had been kept on the trail by well-meaning friends.

After Dougo told her what was up, Citizen Brink called Mays into the inner sanctum sanctorum for a little tête-à-tête. Throughout the whole hoopla, Peter began to develop a profound respect for Moseley simply because the old guy left him alone. During their closed conference, Caroline refused to take any phone calls, although the incessant ringing caused more distraction than taking the calls would have. She demanded to know what the big idea was.

—Could you be more specific?

—Don't be evasive, Peter. You saw some woman out of a window, and have taken it into your head to hunt her down? A tad dime-storish, wouldn't you say?

—Yes.

—Yes what?

—Yes . . . ma'am?

—Dash it, Peter.

Mays appreciated being present at the first use of the word "dash" since Kipling. Somehow, though, it fit Caroline better than her earlier forays into stronger profanity.

—Can you tell me what use such an escapade could possibly produce, I suppose?

Brink had the irritating habit of saying "I suppose" for "I wonder."

—No use, I'm afraid.

In fact, his wayward salmon-woman made a fine triumvirate of the useless along with parsley and *Fidelio*.

—There's no explaining it, chief.

—Everything has an explanation.

—Well then, the reason I'm chasing this stranger is because I refuse to believe everything has a reason.

Brink played with her paperweight, the world's lightest, CMOS, nonvolatile, programmable computer. She'd picked it up at a press conference as a coverage bribe. Her whole office was swamped with such techno-memorabilia: silicon wafers embedded in plastic, posters of processor command sets, photos of Edison and Ford on camping trips.

—If you're that desperate for human companionship, why don't you take out a personal ad in the weeklies? A lot of losers do that. You know: Straight White Male looking for females, all races, colors, creeds, for meaningless relationships. Contact . . .

—I've tried that already: Redhead Clarinetist, Vets' Day Parader, must meet. Name spot and time.

—Cripes. Couldn't you have fixed on someone nearer at hand? You couldn't even have seen this woman very well from up here. Did you notice the teeth? Teeth are very important. A lot of redheads fall down in the teeth department.

Peter was now nauseated. Caroline talked of sex with the same clinical curiosity and wholesome attitude with which she approached a product showcase. That was decidedly unhealthy. Mays was all for taking sex out of the classroom and putting it back in the cloakroom. Besides, his attraction to the figure was if anything collectorial, not sexual.

—Well, she's thin, from what I could see. And she seemed, I don't know, antique, somehow.

—Thin? Antique? Listen, there's a nursing home up by Mass. General not four blocks from here . . .

—Not antique, then. Out of place. Like a memory that you can't quite get a bead on.

And for some reason—there are always reasons that reason cannot comprehend—Mays imagined the same woman, in the same gathered skirts, stepping onto an entry dock somewhere in the last century.

—Now Peter, you're putting me in a bind. I'm sure you see why I'd like to keep you on as an editor . . .

Mays distinctly did not see. The only explanation was that Caro had to settle for semicompetence, as all the truly competent were in industry, making the big bucks, instead of in trade journalism, writing about them.

—. . . but I really don't need another Dougo.

The reason she needed the first was not entirely clear.

—Here. Take this eight dollars right now, get a cab to Lenny's office in Cambridge, and have him straighten out this thing once and for all. I tell you he knows everyone in the Boston music industry. And I just hope you know what you plan to do when you find this woman.

Only now, staring down at the frenetic news ticker, did Mays realize that Caroline's last question had been the clincher. Nothing cures longing like a dose of success.

The trip to Bullock's office, admittedly a long shot, was no longer than many trips he had recently made. He brought along his parade manifest, a prime-number sieve on which he had penciled out each name as he eliminated it. Bullock might, at very least, help him eliminate a few more, bringing the total down to several hundred. The opiate spell of the Teletype clack was broken by a greeting from across the room:

—Nicky!

The reason Bullock insisted on calling Peter "Nicky" was lost in antiquity. Mays had only one suspect hypothesis: his last name reminded Bullock of a famous baseball player's and, by free association, of this player's only contemporary peer, whose first name

sounded vaguely like Nicky. This tortuous synaptic route must have
burned permanently into Bullock's mind on their first meeting, for
it now offered the neurological path of least resistance. Mays, long
ago having elevated diffidence to the level of a cult, only smiled in
recognition at the greeting, but retaliated by calling back:

—Leonard!

As with all overly fastidious people, Bullock was too compensatorily casual in public. His full name made him wince, and he
put forward "Len" as if giving orders. Most of his friends compromised at "Lenny." His was the miser's generosity, the man who
invites guests for dinner to show how magnanimous he can be over
cigarette burns in the priceless Persian rug. He would, of course,
have insisted on being addressed by his full title, complete with
middle initial, if he thought he could get compliance. Barring that,
he faked affability. As on the Exchange, he who conceals the most
wins.

—Leonard, good to see you after all these . . . weeks. How
are things going with you?

Mays had started adult life asking "How are you?" but this late
in the century, had switched to the greeting that was each year
earning more and more of the market share.

—Not too bad, Nicky. Of course, the market's gone to hell in
a half-track, and it's been pretty rude about it, too. Bonds have
saved my ass. I'll tell you, my friend, I can give you the number
of a great little convertible I've got a line on. Heavily discounted,
a real bargain. It would break every exchange regulation for me to
tell you, but four years from now you'll be thanking me for buying you in at the bottom of this godforsaken slump.

—Four years from now, Leonard, we'll both be dead.

—What are you talking about? Jesus, you haven't gone and
joined the doom patrol, have you?

Mays, as startled as Bullock by his own oracular pronouncement, did as he always did when the conversation turned serious.
He clammed up.

—Look, Nicky. I'm talking nineteen, twenty, maybe twenty-
two percent per annum. *After* taxes.

—Thanks, Leonard. I prefer to *spend* my money.

In the ensuing silence, both men realized they had gotten to the conflagration without first shaking hands. Bullock bluffed his way out of the deadlock by affecting extreme good humor.

—OK, friend. Who needs wealth beyond their wildest expectations anyway?

He pulled Peter away from the wire and ushered him unceremoniously into a combination salt mine/entertainment area. Bullock's desk was impeccable: unbroken ranks of trust prospecti, Standard and Poor's stock guides, and back issues of *Certified Trader*, a trade-press journal expressly for brokers. Mays recognized this rag as another of Powell's magazine sectors, floor three.

If Brink did fire him, Mays could get Delaney to fake him a résumé and he could get on this other masthead. He'd already worked out the details of a great market system: buy low, sell high. Bullock could serve him up a steady source of speculation, innuendo, and blatant fabrication, the stuff the trade press thrives on and enshrines on the editorial page. The arrangement would benefit Bullock too, who could show himself and his clients confirmation of his own rumors in print. Brokers, like General Staffs, want nothing more than to be able to believe their own communiqués when they filter back to them through the chain of command. And rumors, once in trade print, tend to fuel themselves into fact. For if enough of the public believes the report that a given investment issue is about to fall, they will make it happen. Forget the bit about how no bear market is inevitable until it breaks out. Bears break out when the first fellow asks, "What if?"

Kitty-corner to the spotless desk was a suitably disheveled lounging cubicle consisting of an oval coffee table and two aggressively Scandinavian chairs. The office furniture, while not as progressively modular as *Micro*'s, nevertheless was designed to anticipate all considerations except the human body. Violent scoops of polyethylene might have passed for hardwood if it weren't for a certain pattern of cross-graining that conspicuously repeated again and again in each chair. As Peter came down in one, his eyes caught a notepad on the table stamped with the Phillips logo and stenciled *From the Desk of Len Bullock*. In red-pen calligraphy, there appeared a flowery scrawl: "Shld be w. 250K min per an." Bullock leaned over and snatched the pad nonchalantly.

He sat down affably and reached around to the file drawer on the bottom right of his desk. His hands still concealed in the drawer, he poured from a bottle, conjuring up two plastic cups. He served, and whispered:

—Kahlua. It can pass for coffee in these parts. It's every able body for itself in this profession, so we're safe.

Mays watched him slug the stuff down.

—Come on, drink up, drink up, ye Princeton men. Thiamine or something. Puts hair on your ass. It's on-the-job description in this office. You think the rest of these goons could go day after day, watching their profit line crumble like the Maginot, without hitting up a bracer?

—How do you get it to steam like coffee?

—Trade secret. Nontoxic.

Mays drank, with the pleasure of calculating that Brink was now paying him in excess of $5.37 an hour to get stewed with her boyfriend. Unable to think of a way to get the conversation ramped back up, he reached back into racial memory and came up with:

—So, really Leonard. How are things with you? I mean really.

But Leonard did not answer at first. He had become engrossed with punching up stock quotations on a terminal that lodged itself on the table between the two. Mays had ceased to exist. In another minute Len lapsed into a simulated conversation that attested to a good deal of practice on his part.

—*Pas mal.* I mean, I don't have cancer. And after cancer, what's the number two killer? Everybody knows it's boredom. And that only gets me a couple times a week. So I can't complain. After all, there's no known treatment for the big B, is there, Nicky? Nothing you can do except kill it by overfeeding.

—I'm glad to hear that you're doing well. Are you doing anything with yourself, Leonard?

—Len. Doing? I make a living. Playing some hardball with the big boys. Let me tell you something, Nick. If you're interested in becoming a big boy yourself, there are a lot of positions opening up. The way our nation's finest industrials are going, more than a few of the big boys came to work on Monday and found their personal belongings in cardboard boxes in the hall.

Mays had nothing to say to this striking pronouncement, and said so emphatically.

—Yes, my friend, the little disturbances at the bottom produce large waves at the top. The upper branches start to wobble and the whole roost comes down. There's a lot to say for being a little fish down at the bottom, wouldn't you say?

Mays agreed without hesitation, though in his heart he believed that fish of whatever size did better in water than at any height in a tree. Bullock took a swig at his plastic cup, continuing to punch inquiries into the machine and to watch the readout intensely. As he spoke, his voice grew increasingly reminiscent of early Cagney. He sounded as if he wanted to take a grapefruit to the entire stock market.

Mays watched Lenny screw up his face into cheerful sadism with each piece of bad news that flashed across the screen. He tried to imagine the guy at Thursday night meetings of that group Caro had mentioned—the Cologne Chamber Music Society. Brink said he knew everyone in the music circuit; he probably sold them tax shelters between movements. The only explanation Mays could find for a person like Lenny being musical was that it kept him occupied one night a week, leaving only six more to kill. Lawn mowing by flashlight was good for another two, and he could always bring his work home with him.

But why music? It seemed so insubstantial a quantity for a man of Bullock's obsession, so delicate, so few chances for spoils. Just then, Bullock must have punched up an issue that pleased him, because he began singing light opera. Mays knew the aria only from the old Warner Brothers cartoons—the tune they played whenever the rabbit tortured the bald guy with the speech impediment.

And at that, Mays hit on the connection between music and market mania. One dealt in bulls and bears, the other in crescendos and diminuendos. But both were about hidden movements, contexts, wordless proofs. Both made the small self feel part of something larger, companies on the one hand, an oceanic feeling on the other. Both dealt in cult objects, collectibles. Abstractions made the best purchasable commodities. And both could be played by the small investor.

—Dum, ditty-da dee, diggity. While the big boys fall, the little fish sometimes come up smelling like a rose. Look here, Nicky.

Bullock spun the lazy Susan that held the terminal until a stock summary sat staring Mays in the face. The neat columns and rows meant nothing to him. He was no good with foreign languages; he had failed his first year of French, not being able to repeat *Je m'appelle Jacques* for the simple reason that his name was Peter. In his first four weeks at *Micro,* he sat for days at a shot, looking at long articles he was supposed to edit, hoping Moseley could not hear him giggling in devastation. The same dissociation struck him if he said the word "couch" twenty times in rapid succession.

In a minute, he began to pick out stray shreds: YH and YL had to be year high and low; O for open, CL for closed; B, bid, A, asked. The issue was a certain Trans-Air Transport, up considerably since that morning. It had to be the item that Bullock had tried to sell him twice now. Mays looked up for confirmation, but Bullock had already gone off in search of other conquests and was now emptying the ashtrays.

—For every loser, there has to be a winner. It's that simple. A buyer for each seller. Zero sum. Impossible to get anything more elegant, more moral.

Mays declined another Kahlua and wondered how Bullock could find anything on the impeccable desk to straighten further. Len put all the periodicals in razor-sharp formation, then carefully mussed one up.

—Viciously moral. Because two points down hurts you more than two points up helps. A big boy has to sink for a little fish to rise. Or to put it still differently . . .

—Leonard, I used to be in sort of a hurry . . .

—I was *just* going to ask you what I could help you with, Nick. I assume you came here for a reason, that Claire Booth Luce doesn't pay your way over here to turn down *sure-thing tips.*

Nine dollars and eleven cents, thought Mays. Having lost his last chance to pace the thing properly, he rushed out his story. The feeling he got from blurting out the history of his construed fixation was similar to how it had always felt when peeing in his pants as a child: pleasant for the first few seconds, then decidedly uncomfortable.

As much as possible, he tried to tell the saga of red hair from the eighth-story window from the detached, dramatic view of a professional storyteller. Perhaps because the whole scenario seemed so ludicrous, it now seemed important to make the tale as interesting as possible. To seduce and hold Bullock's interest was the main thing, and to do that, Mays embellished the plot, depersonalized the "I" until he appeared to be talking about someone else. He paid huge attention to details, which at times threatened to take over the story line. Carried away, he made his recent life come across like *Moby Dick,* at least with regard to the love interest.

There is some stranger, someone with the aura of another time, he wanted to meet: was that all, was that the extent of it? Mays had no idea what story Bullock was hearing. Barring some hidden clap-, laugh-, or sob-o-meter, he had no idea of how things went over. For the time being, at least, Lenny had stopped his compulsive straightening and seemed mildly taken in. After finishing his elaborate plea for assistance, Mays sat in the storyteller's shame.

—A red-haired musician? Not in any of the area's regular ensembles? She marched in the Vets' Parade, but is not in any of the bands listed on the roster. You're sure you haven't crossed any names off without more than probable cause? And you say she plays . . . ?

—The clarinet.

—The oboe.

—The clarinet.

They had reached the same impasse as those telegrams between first cousins beginning "Dear Willie" and "Dear Nicky," concerning the reining-in of Franz Josef and the Serbs.

—The oboe, although from eight stories up, I can see how you might have confused the two. Still, we've got to be accurate in these matters, as I can tell you, having chased a few mirages down in my time.

Mays was too excited, exhausted, or deflated to ask the obligatory "Do you know her?" He sat passively as Bullock once more rooted through the mass of printed matter on his desk. This time Lenny removed a few journals, exposing some books hidden in a second rank behind them. He removed a fat volume, one of those *Bluff Your Way Through the Great Personalities of the Last Hundred Years* books. Each page carried a small biography and a glossy photograph. Stockbroking, primarily sales work, meant coddling the client's special interests, whether Dizzy Dean or William Dean

Howells, Bill or Bertrand Russell, knowing all the right people, even if all the right people were already dead. That, then, was why Mays was such a problem case for Bullock: until now, Peter had been remarkably indifferent to the cult of modern personalities.

—Here we are. Take a good look at this photo. Unless I'm wrong, this ought to look mildly familiar.

It did. It was Mays's mirage, or very close to the image still in his mind after months of embellishing. The black-and-white photograph of poor quality, probably from the turn of the century, showed a beautiful woman lying in a coffin, her arms crossed over her breasts. Even in black and white, her hair seemed a strawberry mop.

For all her familiarity, Mays still could not name the woman. He glanced to the opposite page, cheating on one more test that chance and the past had thrown his way: Sarah Bernhardt, French actress and perhaps the most famous woman in the world at her flourishing, asleep, not dead, in a golden coffin given her by an admirer.

Mays looked up at Bullock in total incomprehension. Bullock, for the first time that meeting, stared directly at the quarry.

—Come on, Nicky. It's a perfect afternoon for history.

Chapter Ten

Flivvership

I have the answer, but I don't yet know how to get it.—attributed to the mathematician Karl Friedrich Gauss

HENRY FORD received the same formal education as Sander—through the fifth grade. Afterward, he was immediately conscripted into farming, the Michigan equivalent of the Siegerland mines. At the end of the last century, the two presented roughly equivalent fates: both crushed the body and snuffed the soul, under either earth or Earth.

Both Ford and Sander escaped through the machine, though neither did so completely. Both felt a nostalgia for the lost life that would have killed them; at sixty, Sander wrote memoirs of the idyllic mining valley, while the aged Ford complained that no one in the country was minding the farm. Both Sander and Ford, despite their mechanical allegiances, made the Earthbound Man the foremost category in their respective archives of *Man in the Twentieth Century*.

Their resemblance stops there. Sander freed himself by developing a peculiarly twentieth-century trade, a technical craft in an age when mechanical know-how was a saving grace. But he never escaped what Walter Benjamin calls "the portraitist's nostalgia." Only through the retrospective eyes of a photographer could he embrace the mechanical progress of the times.

Ford, however, went on record in the year of Sander's *Three farmers* . . . saying he "wouldn't give five cents for all the art in the world." (His son Edsel made up for this, paying Rivera $25,000 for his factory portrait.) With one exception, Ford's life brooked no commemoratives; his solution was a machine not of retrospect but of revolutions per minute. His auto and tractor would pull him out of every hole he might come across, transferring the murderous work of his childhood—the demands of farming—onto the machine, thereby reducing the amount of hard labor involved in going from A to B.

Sander joined vocation to avocation, mastering a satisfying life. Yet his life's work, *Man of the Twentieth Century*, like the century itself, remained unmastered. Ford mastered the century early on, becoming the most powerful fifth grader of his day. But in paving his own internal landscape, he went no farther than the science of mass production could take him.

Of the great Americans of the early century, when the Great Individual theory of history still applied, Ford was the most paradoxical. Morgan, an old creditor, closed an era when he died in 1913. Wilson was an ambivalent Ivy Leaguer. Edison, an ambitious utilitarian, had a bad habit of spitting tobacco juice on the floor. Norris and Dreiser were just journalists with consciences. The Wrights, Dodges, and Firestones were no more complex than today's garage entrepreneurs. Ford alone remains an enigma, the improbable meeting of pragmatist and idealist, innovator and reactionary, peacemonger and war profiteer. His friend John Burroughs once characterized him:

> Notwithstanding his practical turn of mind, and his mastery of the mechanic arts, he is through and through an idealist. . . . He is as tender as a woman, and much more tolerant. He looks like a poet and conducts his life like a philosopher. . . . His car and his tractor engine typify him—not imposing, not complex, less expressive of power and mass than simplicity, adaptability, and universal service.

The *Detroit Saturday Night* doubtless would have clumped Burroughs's appraisal with other cases of Forditis: "What we would like the world to think about Pa." The *Chicago Tribune* called him a dangerously ignorant anarchist, and was sued for saying so. Hitler praised him in *Mein Kampf* as the only American who understood the enormity of the Jewish problem, and escaped litigation.

Henry evokes not so much admiration or contempt as amazement. He embodies the unsolvable paradox at the heart of modern man. In 1915, with the war well into its second year, while armies of occupation initiated the practice of collective responsibility, Henry Ford arrived at the incredible decision to act as an individual. He planned to dispense with state diplomacy and use the collective will of individuals to end a war that involved, directly or indirectly, every nation on earth.

For as large as his empire was, it had grown on the principle of mass production—bringing the machine to the worker on the *worker*'s own good time. The first automated assembly line was a masterpiece of design, revolutionary only in scaling machinery to fit the size and speed of the human worker. In Ford's boyish industrial dream, the machine catered to the individual both inside the factory and out. He ran the auto plant that produced over 60 percent of the country's cars as if he were a meddling grandfather. He tried to enforce the sobriety of employees, making his old enemy, the press, comment that the only way to test the breaths of fifty thousand workers was with an assembly line.

Most of his contemporaries accepted the war, citing Napoleon's prophecy of 1814 that in a hundred years, the Continent would be all autocratic or all republican. This explanation fed the front and kept the home fires burning. Ford's peace plans were only a shade more simplistic. He remembered the *McGuffey's Fourth Reader* lesson "Things by Their Right Name": "soldier" by its right name was "murderer." Europe was making millions of men murderers: a simple problem requiring a simple solution.

Ford's solution was nothing if not simple. Fill a large ship full of celebrities, dignitaries, and common folk, and sail it—the first-ever "missile for peace"—at the continent of Europe. Once there, the party could serve as a mediating forum for "continuous negotiation," where the belligerents could work out their grievances civilly. This ship would be organized and funded by private individuals. No nation, state, or collective organization could give it official recognition.

The Peace Ship probably seemed less crackpot in 1915 than it does today. A widely supported international pacifist movement had been active before the war. Two enormously influential prewar books, Nobel laureate Bertha von Suttner's *Lay Down Your*

Arms! and Norman Angell's *The Great Illusion* convinced many that sword and ploughshare were of interchangeable alloy. Eternal peace seemed a mere matter of collective, vocal insistence.

For his own part, Ford had great cause for believing in the power of idealism and individual conviction. Much of the United States and Europe had caught Forditis, a hysteria that left its victims calling for the farmer's canonization. Ford was universally admired for his Horatio Algerian biography. Admiration became gratitude when he put his car within easy reach of the median income. Gratitude became outright worship when he instituted the unheard-of minimum wage of five dollars a day. The popular poet Edgar Guest rhymed:

The children laugh where they used to wail and the eyes of
    parents glow
With the happiness they used to think only the rich could know.
And this is the work of Henry Ford—all this the future scan
And find in him a friend who lived and thought of his fellow
    man.

At the peak of Forditis, Ford began to believe his own image as the hero who "thought of his fellow man." The times found him preparing to mint his own coinage, not to pass off as legal tender but nevertheless preserving the size and material of a Lincoln cent. In place of the Great Emancipator, the coin bore the silhouette of another liberator, the man who made it possible for America to get from A to B sitting down. In place of *In God We Trust*, the penny—the six cents he was awarded in the *Tribune* libel suit minus the five cents he wouldn't give for all of art—bore the inscription *Help the Other Fellow*.

Now if the diplomats and heads of state had perpetuated mass, pointless killing of Europe's young, sustaining the whole thing on a thin, self-supporting tissue of lies, wasn't it perhaps time, Ford reasoned, that a plain-sense idealist stepped in and put himself in charge of ending the foolishness? Ford was about to help the other fellow with a vengeance.

In late November of 1915, Ford granted an interview to the

Hungarian Rosika Schwimmer and the American Louis P. Lochner. The two had come to ask Ford to aid the peace movement. Before the interview could begin, Ford disconcerted the two with typical midwestern matter-of-factness: "Tell me what to do." The pacifists had no set program aside from a vague goal of instituting a process of mediation by neutrals. Ford adored just this sort of sketchy problem in engineering, and he leaped on a nervous joke put forward by the American concerning a floating ark of emissaries. A material answer for a material problem: the Peace Ship was born.

Within days the three chartered a Scandinavian custom liner, the *Oscar II*, issued invitations to various luminaries, announced a press conference, and arranged a meeting with the President of the United States. An astounded Wilson sat in the White House listening to Ford, whose leg, throughout the meeting, dangled over the arm of a chair. The President thought the whole thing an elaborate joke until Ford insisted he would set sail inside two weeks, with or without the blessings of the United States. Wilson could not be chained to so definitive a course on so little planning. He lauded the principle but could not back the effort. When the meeting ended and the President excused himself, Ford grumbled out loud that the Princeton and Johns Hopkins graduate had shown himself to be "a small man."

No minor political setback was about to stop this mission. Ford, with a keen sense of how much history depends on right-sounding jingoes, busied himself with inventing aphorisms, leaving the trip plans to subordinates. He came up with "Let's get the boys home by Christmas," but someone pointed out that even if the *Oscar II* sailed the following day and all Europe agreed to lay down their arms the instant Henry touched shore, such an event would still be logistically impossible. Undaunted, Ford quickly changed the line to "Let's get the boys out of the trenches by Christmas."

Good attendance at the news conference flustered Ford, whose public speeches included one of the shortest on record. Addressing a boys' scholarship program, he had managed to get out: "Congratulations. I only want to say there's no such thing as No Chance." At the Peace Ship promotion, he didn't do much better, opening:

A man should always try to do the greatest good for the greatest number, shouldn't he? . . . We're going to try to get the boys out of the trenches by Christmas. I've chartered a ship, and some of us are going to Europe.

This press conference touched off an explosion exceeded only by German 420s along the front. The press trotted out irony, ridicule, satire—the showhorses reserved for idealism and revolutionary works of art. The *New York Tribune* ran its sardonic headline about Ford personally ending the war by Christmas. The *New York Herald* called the Peace Ship "one of the cruelest jokes of the century," though the century was only a few years old. The *World* did one better, resorting to parodic verse:

> I saw a little fordship
> Go chugging out to sea,
> And for a flag
> It bore a tag
> Marked 70 h.p.
> And all the folk aboardship
> Cried "Hail to Hennery!" . . .
>
> And so, without a quiver
> The dreadful task they dare
> Of teaching peace
> To France and Greece
> And Teuton, Celt, and Bear.
> Ho for the good ship Flivver,
> Propelled by heated air.

If the mission were as self-evidently obtuse as these judges insisted, there would have been no point in pointing it out so vehemently. The mission would wash up impotently, a shipwreck on Europe's coast, and that would be an end to it. The journalists seemed to need to sink the mission before it started. Some New York papers were more friendly. The *Evening Post* praised "his generous act of knight errantry," saying it would "be acclaimed by thoughtful hundreds of thousands the world over as a bit of American idealism in an hour when the rest of the world has gone mad over war and war preparedness." The *Times* said the effort could do "as little harm as good." Ford's effort varied with the observer.

Scores of copy-starved reporters represented the one class that did not unanimously turn down berths on the *Oscar II*. Of the other invitees, just one of forty-eight state governors sailed, and only a handful of lesser politicians. Turnout was better among the prominent clergy, though none who sailed is today a familiar name. The writers, activists, and speakers who attended were similarly obscure. Teddy Roosevelt declined for the leading figures, calling the venture a travesty that ought to be forcibly stopped. Not one "person of the first rank" chose to cast their lot with the Peace Ship. Jane Addams, who had booked to sail and who alone had given the boat some small credibility, backed off at the last minute, begging illness. Even Ford's close friend Edison praised the idea publicly, but declined to take part. On the dock at the ship's send-off, Ford offered him a million dollars to sail. Edison applied more than his usual deafness to the offer.

Many rejected invitations with a rudeness that placed the Peace Ship on a moral par with the war itself, preferring the hideously destructive to the laughable. Yet others sent florid testimonials, as if well-thought words could replace the body in person. Vachel Lindsay, Luther Burbank, and Helen Keller were particularly eloquent in declining. Besides the core delegates—fewer than twenty workers from various loosely organized peace committees—the ship's manifest was filled out with businessmen, students, and obscure citizens, representing a cross-section of little Americans everywhere. Less than a couple hundred went to St. Ives, insisting that the ludicrous was better than the bloody.

Any attempt to evoke world admiration failed when the send-off degenerated into a free-for-all. One passenger took it on himself to serve as a master of ceremonies, generating hoopla and getting the crowd to chant hip-hip-hooray for Ford, the respected clergy, and well-wishing luminaries. When Edison showed, the MC invoked the crowd to give a big hand for "the fellow who makes the light for you to see by." Two of the departing passengers pulled a stunt of doubtful taste, getting married by the ship captain, to the great delight of the crowd. The marriage was later annulled for having taken place in port. A wisecracking practical joker sent a present of two caged squirrels and a note saying they'd be sure to feel at home on board with the nuts.

The ship pulled away to brass bands and cheering crowds as if that localized, drunken spot of New Jersey had already signed a separate peace with the entire world. Before the boat got a few hundred yards, an onlooker jumped from shore and swam after it. Fished out by police, he identified himself as "Mr. Zero," swimming, according to one source, "for public opinion," and according to another, "to ward off torpedoes." These details attest to the full attendance of a voracious press corps that, in this year of Serbia's being overrun, Italy's entering the war, Germany's using poison gas for the first time at Ypres, the *Lusitania*'s sinking, the Gallipoli campaign, Zeppelin bombings, a new British government, major works by Picasso, Lawrence, and Pound, the first great motion picture, *Birth of a Nation*, and Einstein's theory of general relativity, had no better use for its time than ridicule.

The plan to correct social ills with the collective wills of individuals ran into trouble even before it reached the battlefield. That is, the battlefield met it halfway across the Atlantic. Ford began the journey affably enough, scolding a young female passenger for smoking, and telling jokes and homilies over communal meals in the ship's dining room. Soon, however, begging a sea-induced virus, but more likely suffering from overrealized idealism, he retired to his stateroom into total seclusion. Rumors spread about his illness—he was dying; he was already dead. A gang of reporters broke into his room. They explained to an enraged and healthy Ford that Morgan had been dead six hours before anyone knew, and they weren't going to be scooped on another story that important. And so the ambassadors were left to concoct trouble by themselves without any help from the top.

At first the traveling journalists complained of a lack of newsworthy events aboard ship. They radioed back bland tidbits about the diet, fashion, and pastimes of the peace pilgrims. Then came the first major meeting. The representatives agreed to draft a manifesto summarizing their beliefs and outlining their platform for action. One might marvel that such a document wasn't drafted long before Mr. Zero chased the boat out of Jersey. But then, Trois Vierges hadn't waited for manifestos explaining the need for war.

A steering committee of delegates drew up a declaration for the group condemning not only European hostilities but also the American program of preparedness. When it came time to attach signatures, a considerable number refused, requesting the striking out of several clauses and demilitarizing of rhetoric. "Thank heaven," some gentlemen of the press were overheard to say. "At last a story has broken."

The world press had a holiday reporting the quarrel. Cartoons pictured two doves clawing each other, attempting to yank an olive branch out of the other's mouth. Editorials suggested that the peace pilgrims, if they had set out to teach heads of state a lesson, were doing a fair job. The papers, milking the drama for its copy value, forgot to report that the Peace Ship delegates settled their debate without a single gassing, maiming, or amputation. Following the blowup and hoopla, Ford withdrew even more. As soon as the ship docked in Oslo, he was whisked, reportedly under doctors' orders, back to the U.S. without the betrayed peace party knowing. But before this covert exit, he managed to give one press conference. In front of an incredulous band of journalists, he refused to talk of anything except his plans for a new tractor, then going into production.

Deserted by Ford and a steady trickle of disillusioned delegates, the core party made its way through neutral nations, raising a meager commitment for continuous mediation. A whittled-down group passed into Holland and took up the long, boring, and invisible work of negotiation that had little to do with front-page coverage. The remaining pilgrims hoped they could be more obstinate than the mass obstinacy of national states. They could not. Two years later, they drifted apart, the project abandoned. When the armistice came, it was virtually identical to the very first peace proposal generated by this committee.

The Peace Ship met the goals of its initial charter. It provided a high-profile forum for concerned individuals. It established an alternative peace channel for the belligerents, depriving them of yet another excuse for continuing an obviously hopeless struggle. Ford had only said that "a few of us" were going to see about getting the boys out of the trenches by Christmas. And a few did try. But in the eyes of the world, the Peace Ship was an anachronistic joke, a gesture of monstrous egotism that failed miserably.

One encyclopedia after another refers to the Peace Ship as a bizarre side comment in Ford's personal history.

Only in the biographies and primary sources does the story of the *Oscar II* start to become interesting. One biographer suggests the whole mission was sabotaged by a hostile press corps, scuttled in Jersey Harbor by advocates of the inevitable. The ship sank, says this biographer, not from its own overweight idealism, but because the world refused to ballast it with belief.

Ford himself held the press responsible for the failure. But when asked if he resented the coverage of the Peace Ship, he replied, "It suited me all right." Ford the industrialist gained from the losses of Ford the ambassador of private will. The *Oscar II* succeeded, Ford was quick to point out, in taking war talk off the front page and putting peace talk in its place.

As Ford left the initial press conference, reporters called after him for a final message. He responded, "Tell the people to cry peace and fight preparedness." When asked what he would do if the expedition failed, he said, "I'll start another." But he did not start another ship. His subsequent campaigns were not so admirable.

In an interview with Ford, John Reed, himself predisposed to events of conviction shaking the world, tried to get Ford to say he would do it all over again. Ford said he would leave the bigwigs on shore, sailing instead with the folks from his own village of Dearborn. And that indeed would have been something out of the ordinary: an obscure midwestern town adrift on the Gulf Stream, unsponsored, ready to intrude unasked between warring parties with ultimatums of humanity.

Yet who but an obsessive narcissist could have initiated such a voyage in the first place? The plan may have been already ruined by the motive of its sponsor, his fixed need to force his fellow man to love him as he felt he deserved. This would explain Ford's retrenchment following his humiliating return from Europe. In explaining the failure of his peace gospel, Ford hinted that he had discovered the real cause of the fighting. The Jews had started the war in order to profit from it. For the next decade, a gang of Ford news writers and history editors waged war against the "Hebrew network" with all the idealistic vigor with which the ship had waged peace.

Frustrated narcissism also explains Ford's complete reversal following America's entry into the war. He became one of the country's most committed armorers, transforming his River Rouge auto plant into a war machine. He swore he would not make a profit off the hostilities, promising to return every penny—in legal tender, "In God We Trust," not "Help the Other Fellow"—to the government after the war. He did not. Such altruism easily seems the work of a man caught in the drain of self-love.

These interpretations of the Peace Ship's failure, however interesting, represent minority opinions. By far the largest body of comment holds that the mission failed for obvious reasons—anyone paying attention would see that the Great War was precisely the death knell to actions like Ford's. The Battle of the Frontiers had shown that something irreversible had happened to the scale of human events: certainly the man who had automated the Tin Lizzie should have known that.

The change was everywhere—in warfare, industry, the arts: a sudden shift into numerical modernity, a new, mass scale. Quantitative change had become qualitative, and the war, with its seven thousand dead per day, set the standard. The newspapers had to laugh at 150 in a boat. It was the old joke of a mismatch in scale: a judge fines a criminal ten thousand dollars. The criminal reaches into his pocket and begins counting change. An astronomer says the sun will die out in a billion years. A terrified voice at the back of the hall asks the lecturer to repeat the prediction. "I said the sun will die out in a billion years." "Thank God," says the relieved voice. "I thought you said a million."

The vast majority of biographers—so numerous that the ingenious holdouts are as impotent as Ford was against the majority's war—imply that Ford's action belonged to another, lost time. Tilting at windmills may have been admirable once, but tilting at carbines, as the General Staffs repeatedly found out, cut nothing. In the words of Mies van der Rohe, whose homogeneous International Style would rebuild a decimated world, "The individual is losing significance; his destiny is no longer what interests us." Those ten million in a position to argue would not rise again from the cratered mud. Hereafter, only the Collective counted.

Ford was an evolutionary backwater—a tonsil or an appendix—and the Peace Ship was his surgical corrective. He had acted as a nineteenth-century leading citizen voting his conscience, and had returned a shell-shocked creature of the new landscape, with theories of conspiracy to explain his helplessness. "Learned a lot on the P. Ship," he wrote in one of his journals. He did not think it necessary to spell out what.

But out of all this Us comes a We. At the office Christmas party, Mrs. Schreck, the cleaning woman, explained in thick accent that she left chocolate bonbons on my desk in the evenings because she had seen my photo in the New Employees section of the company newsletter and had vowed to save me from terminal thinness. She spoke while massaging the shell tear in the ambulance driver's cap, one of our host's collectible artifacts from the First War. I identified the insignia on the cap, having come across it in my random search for the 1914 photo. She was delightedly surprised.

—So many of the young live in this year alone.

She spoke of her childhood. And it was from Mrs. Schreck that I first learned of the incredible story of the *Oscar II*. She spoke of how, as a child in her early teens, she had dined each evening to her father's lectures on current events and world politics. She learned from him to equate the word "German" with destruction. Her father wept openly for the burning of the library at Louvain, and swore lifelong hatred against everything German. One winter's evening in the war's second year, he announced with the first trace of hope since the invasion of Belgium that a great American inventor was coming to Europe to put an end to the fighting. Her entire family, in awe of anyone who could understand the new machinery, let alone make it perform on command, at once believed that this foreigner could do the miraculous.

At first I attributed the odd, moving story to the elaborate embroidery of memory. But I was the more deceived, finding in time every detail she had carried around inside of her for three quarters of a century to have its counterpart in documentary fact. I would even find an equivalent to her girlish hope. Mary Alden Hopkins, a magazine writer and Peace Ship passenger, temporarily abandoning objective journalism, wrote:

> One hundred and fifty everyday people have been brought face to face with a great idea—the thought of world disarma-

ment. There's no escaping it, short of jumping into the sea. . . .
At times, the vision comes to all of us—mystic, veiled, and
wonderful. Then common sense revolts. Yet we dare not treat
the vision with contempt. A ship of fools crossed the Atlantic
in 1492. A ship of fools reached Plymouth in 1620. Can it be
that in this ship of fools, we bear the Holy Grail to the helping of a wounded world?

At the Christmas party—still another Christmas those ten million boys would not be out of the trenches by—Mrs. Schreck's
story gave me a clue to finally identifying those fellows in the photograph, giving them the names I had been trying to recall ever
since my stop in Detroit. But I was not quick enough to pick up
the clue, and had still a long route to trace before circling back to
it. Without knowing how much she had revealed to me, Mrs.
Schreck asked:

—How does so thin a *jonge mannetje* know so much of the long
before?

In a scattered recounting, several times losing the thread, I re-
traced for Mrs. Schreck my haphazard research. I described, poorly,
the photo I had sought, curious, even as I spoke, over what it was
I had been so anxious about. Between her weak English and my
poor description of what I only partially recalled, I was not surprised on coming to the end of my story to find her sitting very
still. But it was not bored politeness that had ossified her.

—I know your photo many years now.

She spoke as if admitting something under duress. The fellow
I was looking for, she said, tapping the shrapneled cap as if it stood
for nationality, as if it alone could explain the pathetic coincidence, all the pathetic collisions of hope and ridicule and horror
and joy, the memory of a place long ago lost but even, at this distant decade, never too far from hand,

—Is German.

Chapter Eleven

Conspiracy of Equals

"From my mother's sleep I fell into the State."—RANDALL
JARRELL, "The Death of the Ball Turret Gunner"

UNTIL THE WAR BROKE OUT, life in the service had done little to
stop the change in Adolphe that had begun when the two foreign-
ers invaded his home and became Germans. Peter especially had
infected him, an irresponsible child influencing an older boy prematurely set in his ways. Very early on, Adolphe's adopted father
had taught him that disorder and pleasure were forms of insanity.
The daily routine of Westerwald farming, more poisonous in the
boredom than in the physical strain, made the boy age directly
from twelve to eighteen, skipping the years between. But when
Peter and Hubert came to conquer the old world, Adolphe began
making up for lost time.

On the farm, his changes had all been covert. He would cock
his hat to match the angle of Peter's and snicker at an obscenity
or two, but when put to the test, when called on by his parents
to uphold Cross and Crown, he performed magnificently. The old
spell of order still kept the aroma of otherliness under lock. If his
mandatory conscription had not come just in time, Adolphe would
have passed into adulthood having reached some more or less unsatisfactory compromise between the two. But war, by definition,
removes the need for compromise.

On first falling into the warmth of his battalion, Adolphe was
pleasantly surprised. He found it much easier to disobey his superior officers than it had been to defy his parents. After all, his
parents had given him everything; his section corporal, on the other

hand, gave him only three bars of soap stinking of rotten animals, a mobile cot too heavy to be worth carrying, and a metal mess kit whose sheet-pressed plates, spoons, and cups stacked neatly inside one another, folding away compactly. For two hours after being issued it, Adolphe took the kit apart and reassembled it, delighting at the cleverness of the designer who could come up with such a marvel of economy.

But Adolphe's joy ended and his spite for the chubby corporal increased upon discovering, on looking over at the next bunk where another nineteen-year-old lay deep in concentration over his own mess kit, that he was missing a part—a four-inch soup bowl. Adolphe complained at once. The corporal said that the kits were always issued complete; Adolphe must have lost his bowl. He would not be able to get a new one short of dying, reincarnating, and reenlisting. Adolphe called him a pig, and was sent up for his first disciplinary review.

Instead of having only one Peter and Hubert to provoke him, Adolphe now ate, washed, slept, drilled, and suffered with a hundred of both. Germany, unable to anticipate the implications of total war, committed the same error as the other major powers. Each nation lumped infantry together by place of origin. One wrong turn at the Somme and entire towns were lost. So Adolphe's section was made up exclusively of nineteen-year-olds from the Westerwald, many of whom had been at the May dance only two months earlier. Basic training was their summer camp. Even rigorous drill beat farming; what boy wouldn't choose bruises over boredom?

Because all the boys knew one another, if only remotely, and because they were all away from home for the first time, the Westerwald section each evening transformed the barracks into a free-for-all, or what passed nicely for one. As soldiers in the world's most disciplined army, their bashes were in fact extremely limited. But to these boys, and especially to Adolphe, just staying up evenings until ten, going into paper debt at cards, and singing softly and communally seemed the nearest, sweetest thing to anarchy on this overplanned earth.

It was the last, the singing and toasting, that proved Adolphe's true baptism into unchecked Peterism. Normally during the group singing and Teutonically restrained roughhousing, Adolphe sat on his cot, hiding his social ineptness and showing an imbecilic grin. Then one evening, about two weeks into his tour, a compulsion came on him, one irreconcilable with his basic character. A verse came into his head of its own accord, a parody of the battalion theme, an old Protestant hymn going:

> Oh My God, nothing will come to us
> Not the smallest harm
> Except through Thy will.

Adolphe's parody came to him spontaneously, a sign that it was for public enjoyment. He waited for a lull in the festivities, then grabbed the floor to everyone's surprise. In what he thought to be a good Berlin concert-hall accent, but sounding more like a Munich sausage vendor, he announced:

—Ladies, for your listening pleasure, express from Bayreuth . . .

And in his clean, still high operatic tenor replete with stage vibrato, he belted out:

> Oh My God, what will become of us?
> The smallest balls
> Belong to our sergeant.

The barracks exploded, beginning in beery German delight and ending in all-out French hysteria. Adolphe became an instant folk hero. The youths stamped and applauded, banged their mess kits and called for more. When the display continued, military police poured into the room and threatened to arrest the next man who spoke. In the ensuing silence, someone began humming the hymn. At once, the whole troop set to sea on four-part hummed chorale with ostinato giggling.

The hilarity continued after the MPs left, if only on the reduced level of shared imagination. Every boy made the pilgrimage over to Adolphe's cot to congratulate him on a fine piece of work. Each boy, therefore, committed an act of complicity with the deed. Yet one boy, never to reveal himself, practicing collective responsibility, in the light of the next day identified Adolphe for the authorities as the agent of the evening's anarchy. This time, the discipline review sentenced him to a short confinement.

In less time than he had known his brother Peter, Adolphe had already compiled a record worthy of an amateur political agitator. But Adolphe had no pretensions, political or otherwise. Nor was he growing cynical or losing the old working-class deference to authority. He was not trading respectful propriety for worldly nihilism. He had only learned from his Dutch half brother that foolishness went over better in public than gravity.

Even Alicia's having defrauded him into marriage did not shake his faith in the institution. He continued to write her in high formality and decorum. He always sent along the bulk of his army check, making no mention of the antics that were winning him fame. For he had become the Westerwald section's Holy Clown: deliberately missing spots while shaving, pretending heart attacks, pantomiming the chaplain alone in the vestry with the communion wine, or drinking near beer through his nose. These harmless games passed the time of conscription. At tour's end, he meant to give them up and return to the serious work of farming without any more hypocrisy than the devout Protestant who sets aside his whorehouse days on reaching maturity. But how could he explain this to his wife (now definitively pregnant) or family without undue alarm?

Then came August. An abnormally hot summer reached peak heat. The Kaiser, through an infinite variety of commanding officers' accents, announced Germany's hour. He dissolved the Reichstag, ended domestic pettiness, and decreed that every German soldier must now be both a model of fighting efficiency and an example of Perfection of Will: go ye therefore and teach all nations, even unto the ends of the earth.

Adolphe heard the pronouncement on the parade ground with a thousand other soldiers. He joined in the spontaneous cheering, yelling louder than he thought physically possible. The shifting, confusing scene of reports and counterreports, the strain of waiting during the last two months, the anxiety over international events too large to ignore and not small enough to understand, now resolved, self-evident, into parade-ground euphoria. And for the first time since the May dance, Adolphe felt free of the irritating question that had never left him, the one put forward casually by that photographer on that lovely late day now lost forever except in the picture (Who had the photo? He should like to see it again): the Kaiser had built up the army—so simple now; if Adolphe had only been able to answer the fellow at the time—because he knew, with royal foresight, as early as that fine spring, that Germany would be called on to go to war and had to be ready.

The photographer's question about the 800,000 troops had torn a hole in Adolphe without his even being aware of it. It had altered everything—the May dance, Alicia, the daily work on his father's farm, the evening readings of Goethe and the Bible. Nothing remained intact after the photographer had poured in his ear the possibility that collective higher-ups were moving and plotting events outside Adolphe's control and not necessarily in his best interest. The photographer's suggestion—that the will of Germany might not, after all, be just a benevolent extension of Adolphe's own hopes and wishes—was the wound that had left him open to infection from Peter. It alone, he felt sure, had led him into his recent foolishness.

And thinking of that foolishness there on the parade ground, Adolphe turned from joy to self-conscious shame. As soon as his fellow infantrymen took time out from their own exaltation, they were sure to notice him and wonder what sort of emissary for the German Will he'd make abroad. His battalion would not want to be represented by a rhymester and clown, holy or otherwise.

Adolphe at once stopped his wild jumping, tucked in his shirt, checked his nose for visible snot, and waited passively for an officer to come up and tell him that he, of course, could not go to the front, but would be shot or held in the brig for the war's duration. Instead, several nearby soldiers began battering him with their shoulders, saying, "Germany." The fellow immediately behind him jumped on his back and gave him a packhorse spur in the flanks, shouting, "Paris! Calais! London!" Another voice explained excitedly that the letters in the names Frederick Barbarossa and Kaiser Wilhelm summed to the same value using some complex numerological scheme.

Slowly, it occurred to Adolphe that he was being given another chance. Either by the wisdom of the authorities or by accident in the general uproar, he had been absolved; the great campaign restored him to a state of grace. Never again anything but blameless. He began to cry, and it only increased his joy to find that he could will the tears to stop.

Redemption was the order of the day. In England, another boy, Rupert Brooke, hurrahed in the harvest and welcomed the baptism of

> . . . swimmers into cleanness leaping,
> Glad from a world grown old and cold and weary,
> Leave the sick hearts that honour could not move,
> And half-men, and their dirty songs and dreary,
> And all the little emptiness of love!

The celebration of boys about to come into their heritage washed Adolphe cleaner than he had been since a child of six, when he had tried to stop the cook from slaughtering farm animals. He felt a forgotten wholeness, each part of his self in concord with every other. The solution to the photographer's challenge had been at hand all along, and it only took his choice to see it. The answer was as simple and pleasant as relieving a full bladder: if the state's will was not his, then his will had to do the bending. He had to dissolve the part into the whole, after months of insisting that the whole conform.

Everywhere across the parade ground, boys arrived at the same revelation. Soon the commanding officer reigned in the celebration, which had become a shade too Gallic in effusion. He conducted the now-homogeneous lot of farmers in a rendition of "Now Thank We All Our God," and the antique tune gave the impression that the confederation of petty principalities had dissolved into empire centuries instead of only years before.

Adolphe strained to hear the hymn's cadence. The parade ground was so large, populated with so many singers that it took the tune—traveling about 1176 feet per second this 78-degree day—almost two full seconds to travel from the front of the reviewing stands to where Adolphe stood. Rather than forming a good, national unison, the hymn propagated through the mass of voices from its epicenter. Yet the lag did not trouble Adolphe; the important thing was that his clear tenor, so lately wasted on satirical broadsides, now joined the melody in a common urgency: a man should try to do the greatest good for the greatest number of people.

From his parade-ground awakening on, Adolphe carried a mental checklist with him at all times that imparted an air of gravity to even his smallest actions. People began to take him for a fellow with much schooling because of how long it took him to do even trivial things. He picked his teeth as if giving a refutation of Thomist philosophy. Yet his behavior, for all his deliberation, was in fact simpler than ever: before doing anything from cleaning his rifle to defecating, he merely asked himself how he could act to give an observing Frenchman the most shame at not being German.

So he rejoiced on hearing that the Schlieffen Plan did away with the reserve, calling for every corps to take up an active combat position. With this spirit he marched ponderously into Belgium in the wake of those horse cavalry and sabers intended to shame six Belgian divisions and gun emplacements off the map by sheer casual waste of troops. And with this spirit, waiting on a Flemish field—the same field as appeared in a thousand van Eycks, Memlings, and van der Weydens but, most recently, in one Bosch— he wrote the letter informing on his brother.

'Dolphe reported his brother as a favor to Peter. Such peace had come to him since resolving his internal debate that he felt compelled to spread the feeling to the Belgians, the French, and most of all to his brothers Peter and Hubert. Peter had the old Jan Kinder insatiability, the old argument of state and self stamped on his face: the arched brow bone at odds with the equine nose. Adolphe could help Peter to a parade-ground reconciliation. Even Hubert, although not a Kinder, still confused on politics, could find great peace, and 'Dolphe would help him to it when he got the boy's forwarding address.

He wrote to his love, Alicia, all deceptions now forgiven, with a missionary's zeal. He tried to use his fifth-grade vocabulary to describe how purgative was the serious responsibility of being inside a new country. For Adolphe, the son of Jan Kinder only in the congenital sense, had never traveled outside his farm's district. Until this walking tour of the Belgian interior, his trip down the muddy road to the May Fair had held all the exotica of the conquest of Peru.

He struggled to write, against the dual barrier of illiteracy and marching formation, about how the war was a preventative, a final, natural ascent into a new world order, a simplification of borders, and an elimination of the old, violent ways of national states. As he saw it, both Germany and Belgium stood to gain from this mutual trade agreement. With grammar corrected and syntax smoothed, the same ideas made the rounds in every home-front newspaper.

At home, Alicia had at last caught up with her own fiction. Although only ten days late with her period, she knew that her body had finally fallen in step with her ruse. She read Adolphe's first letter from a foreign country out loud, as if her fetus could find nothing more fascinating than its father's theory of nations, his pallid prose description of 200,000 men in gray suits on a dirty road:

> We wait for some men to repair a few gasoline engines in trucks that have stalled, blocking the column. Peter should be here. He says he can fix any auto in four and a half minutes. He lies, because our vehicles, at least, are very complicated and don't like to run very long. They say the engines came from America, but I don't see how that could be, on account of the Atlantic Ocean. They say England won't fight and the Turks are with us. And so, Dear Alicia, I remain your love, Adolphe. Go to my parents if you need them.

All was set for the first large engagement, the Battle of the Frontiers. The six Belgian divisions, although pushed aside, had badly upset the German timetable. Now the Germans faced seventy-four allied divisions—a million and a half men. To Adolphe and his equally uninformed comrades, the engagement stood for the whole war. Despite his careful adoption of the German General Will, Adolphe would not be involved in the battle. On August 15, a few days before the action that would be inconclusive in every respect except in taking 300,000 lives, a hidden command yanked

Adolphe's untrained section from the front and earmarked it as an occupation force.

For the invaders found the Germanifying of Belgium more than they bargained for. The inhabitants of this insignificant and annoying country resisted the acquisition of *Kultur* for some reason that the Germans neither anticipated nor understood. The resistance ranged from refusing to make dinner conversation with quartered officers to destroying supply dumps and communication lines. The Belgians even stooped to the criminal—shooting at German soldiers from hidden places. These actions the Germans found unforgivable. In each occupied town, the conquerors posted handbills declaring the actions wholly outlawed and punishable without trial. The obstinate Belgians ignored even these appeals to reason.

Initially, the German occupation force comprised mostly men in their forties and fifties, too old for the front but not without worth in the war effort. Fully mature, these men could serve as arbiters of taste and order, exemplars, living proof of the superiority of the new ways over the old. And naturally, a fellow could use guns against unarmed civilians well into a ripe old age.

But when the acts of terrorism continued, the aged caretakers met their match. Although it meant depleting the active combat arm, the German command had no recourse except to beef up the occupation force with units from the line. First went the July draftees, who proved insufficient. The following week the two-month trainees, including Adolphe, were pulled from the advance and sent back.

To be on a dusty road in one's first foreign country, only a good day's walk from one's second; to spend every hour drunk on adrenaline; to hear bullets on three sides, and not know whose had the upper hand; to listen daily to how the precipitous campaign, the one that would end war for good, was about to begin; to stand among thousands of newborn; to dissolve one's small self in the stink of dense squares of infantry; to go unwashed for days; to shit in hand buckets, feeling as if the body had never had so wonderful a purging; to have come so far since three months ago in May; to feel, in short, that all history led up to and would culminate in nothing short of a useful death, and then just as suddenly to be found wanting, guilty on the technicality of inexperience, and to be assigned to a post amounting to little more than a glorified police box is bitter. The combination inoculated Adolphe against his brief flirtation with history. Deprived of certain destiny, diverted into a man-made lagoon the instant before flowing into the cold ocean, Adolphe reached his trigger point and began the final change that would make him, despite his unusual end, a more than representative Face of Our Time.

Those at the front had only death to deal with. The interior lines, on the other hand, had to cope with What If. I might have been there; I should have been there; why wasn't it me? To those who have at last touched tragedy—the bankrupt, the automobile victim, the fellow put to use by his nation—these, even if crippled or killed, have gone through the thing, replaced horror with experience. To these people, the dreaded trumps are played, the uncertainty removed, the little scene over. Public and private make their local compromise, and the sufferer can go on living, stripped of concern, in a postmortem world. But to read the daily casualty lists and honor rolls from the relative security of a small town behind lines holds more horror. One habituates to the worst of tragedies and expends it. But imagination goes on, varied, insatiable, offering no accommodation.

Adolphe's sufferings exceeded any he might have sustained at the front because they grew unconfined in his imagination. The sketchy, elliptical rewrites in the day's press, following the rigid German guidelines for battle reportage, left him enough room to maim himself many times over each hour. So Adolphe settled into occupation, with the front moving farther away daily. He might have survived a pitched battle of fact, but stood no chance against one of fabrication.

Staff assigned Adolphe's section to a town called Petit Roi, population eight thousand, in Belgian Limburg. They stripped the group of trainees of potentially valuable officers for return to the front. Four older men remained to supervise the two hundred boys' pacification of the village. The boys thus were on their own in converting the local populace.

The unit went to work at once issuing proclamations. Adolphe's first job was to mix the cornstarch paste for sticking these orders, and amendments to orders, and amendments to amendments on every vacant square inch in Petit Roi. In one week, the town went from plaster to newsprint, a surrealist's kingdom. Print everywhere—on buses and cars, inside and out; on lampposts, so that one had to walk a small orbit to read one line; on the sides of houses, shops, and churches; even on sidewalks and streets, for those who looked down when walking.

A citizen of Petit Roi—renamed, by proclamation, Königen—needed only to stand still for print to come into view. The gist of all these congressionally worded charters, manifestos, articles, and clauses was that the occupation force could do whatever it pleased without the benefit of proclamation. Natives gathered at the freshest issues—pasted on top of older handbills, building up a paleontologist's dream—and shook their heads grimly.

—Jo. Says here that all business transactions must be conducted in German or Flemish.

—Now how in hell am I going to do that? It took me thirty years to get my cows to understand French.

'Dolphe's role in the war soon grew beyond that of paste mixer. With a blank check to rewrite local politics, the occupation force kept on as much of Town Hall as had the good sense to collaborate. They deposed the other officials, replacing them with their own number. Catching the spirit of politics, they created several new offices in the process, naming Adolphe Contraband Council. This meant he had to go door to door, systematically checking for proclaimedly illegal material.

He checked for food hoards, subversive literature, French literature, wireless equipment, and especially firearms, explosives, and homemade weapons. Adolphe wrote:

> My Alicia chestnut, not only do they resist us but they even hate us. I cannot understand; we are fairer than fair to these folk. Yet reports keep coming in from villages like ours that civilians have actually fired on German soldiers, there only for keeping order! I cannot believe it.

By "cannot believe," he meant that anticipating was worse than taking a slug in the back.

On his rounds, Adolphe uncovered enough evidence to aid belief. He took the town's manifest—supplied by the Council of Records and Information, another nineteen-year-old set up in Town Hall—and went house to house, a traveling salesman, checking off each visit. At almost every place, he found some device that could be construed as a weapon: antique fowling pieces, handmade powder-firing lead pipes, farm tools mounted on poles, even piles of sharpened sticks.

Adolphe was incredulous. No one could have serious hopes of using these against technological weapons. Even an untrained child with a carbine could hold off a whole Petit Roi with pointed sticks. Only then did he begin to understand the extent of the town's hatred for their cultural saviors. The townspeople stockpiled weapons without hope of using them, out of the need for some mute demonstration.

One day he arrived to check the house of what the roster had as the Després family. Adolphe was nervous; he had learned to expect trouble in proportion to how French the surname sounded. But this family had gone out, all except a young daughter, perhaps sixteen. He asked her a few questions in his gentlest Contraband Council's manner. She would not cooperate.

Adolphe was hurt. Normally he would have searched the place without stopping to ask questions. He had already wasted several minutes trying to appease her, and only because she was young and female. And even though he gave her this special attention, she insisted on being as obstinate as every other Belgian. But he had already committed himself; now he would not search the place until he had her as an accomplice. He slammed down his hand on the nearest solid piece of furniture.

—Enough nonsense. You've read the handbills? It says there that you have to cooperate with me.

—What is it that you want?

—I don't want anything, only you have to be polite to me, as to another person, or this whole thing doesn't make any sense.

—I can be polite, if that's what you want.

—It's not what I want, it's what you have to be. And not because it says on the proclamations, but because you want to. One person to another.

—I can be polite, but I cannot want to be polite. Is there anything else you'd like of me?

—That's a very French answer. The war is taking care of answers of that sort.

The girl stood still and said nothing.

—What's your name?

—Comelia Després.

He checked the list. She was not lying. He looked at her. Docile, she was not perhaps as attractive as his Alicia, who had not written him in some time. He tried to think, to decide if taking this woman would be proper behavior for a representative of the German Will. On the one hand, it would be forceful, determined, and a victory of the dominant over the weak. On the other hand, it did have an element of crudity, of low behavior, and probably would not go very far to improve diplomatic relations in the village. The war was to clear the way for the New Man. This new fellow would take what he wanted, but at the same time would be above base desires. It was all too confusing, as confusing as his being consigned to this role behind lines.

He did not, of course, want to be unfaithful to his Alicia, at this moment growing big in the belly and waiting patiently for victory and his safe return. He could avoid betraying her by calling this Belgian girl, at the instant of taking her, by Alicia's name. Perhaps he did not desire her at all. It was not at all simple.

He did not inspect the house properly. Rather than spend the bulk of his time in the crawl space and cellar—the most likely spots for concealed weapons—he grew top-heavy, loitering on the upper floors, particularly interested in the girl's bedroom, which she shared with a younger sister. Here he searched meticulously—in drawers, under and behind furniture, even among the bed sheets. He stopped short of cutting into the mattress with his bayonet.

During the investigation, the only noteworthy item Adolphe discovered hung on the wall by the door. A photograph showed two figures dressed in antique costumes or, rather, suggestions of long ago as dreamed up by a modern costume designer. The figures, actors, portrayed a small boy and an older woman. The boy extended his open palm, proudly showing off half a dozen small seeds. The woman held hands over her face, going through the stereotypical gesture of weeping. Below the image, a caption in Dutch read: *De moeder van Jan is niet tevreden met de boonen:* "Jack's Mother Is Not Pleased with the Beans."

Evidently the photo came from a series illustrating the old fairy tale of "Jack and the Beanstalk." Out of context, with no surrounding story, the image moved Adolphe. He felt drawn to it; it promised a slow grace. His eyes were changed, although he could not say what, if anything, he saw in the photo. The stilted, ill-printed, technically deficient image of two exaggerated thespians in sorry costumes miming a scene from a maudlin tale whose moral—useful things don't always appear useful—had nothing to do with the war, his part in the war, or this Belgian girl who hated him for no good reason reminded him of something, and Adolphe decided he must possess it.

—Is this yours or your little sister's?

The girl looked away. She did not answer.

—How much will you ask for this? As a remembrance of you.

—I will not sell that to you. You will have to steal that.

A sadness came over Adolphe. He had never lost a close relation and had kept relatively free from bad news. But he recognized this feeling without being able to place it. The sun rested, deep-set against an aqua sky. Belgium was warm, sunbaked in September. The usual barrage from the front came in over the still-neutral Belgian air. He'd spent too much time on this house already; others waited. He had reached a point beyond which there was no passing.

Adolphe thrust his hands into his pockets, sounding their deep places. His hands went down, farther down, until they touched bottom, and loose change. He drew up the coins and counted out a third of what they had given the photographer only three months before: half, because the photo was half the size of the other, and two thirds of that, because this image had only two figures to the other's three. Leaving the change, he took the photo off the wall and went downstairs and out of the house. At his back, he heard the unmistakable rustling of absolute silence.

That evening in billet, he drew out the picture and freed it of its unwieldy frame. He tried to discipline himself to look hard at the picture, with all the attention a foot soldier could muster. He looked for some detail, some clue or link that might point at why he felt the stupid image meant something. He had seen the actress-mother before, and felt he ought to know her name.

Slowly, out of his aesthetic stupor, he became aware of a commotion outside, firing and voices. The soldier in the bunk next to him shot up and whispered:

—Assassins!

Two other fellows nearby said he was going out of his head. They said it was still the sounds from the front, only weather and a shift in winds made them seem louder than usual.

Adolphe looked at his photo. The little boy stretched out his arm proudly; the mother hung her head in shame. Two ways of looking at the same beans. He heard the firing again. Perhaps the shots were closer; he had not yet decided. He was deep in the first of May, hearing not shots but dance music. He mouthed out loud—the only way of being sure if he had actually said them once—the words:

—Brass band, Peter.

Chapter Twelve

The Love Interest

First, there is always a long-sustained condition of great mental expenditure or one established by long force of habit, upon which at last some influence intervenes making it superfluous, so that a volume of energy becomes available for manifold possible applications and ways of discharge.—SIGMUND FREUD, *Mourning and Melancholia*

MAYS HAD NEVER BEFORE noticed how much the Charles River Drive resembled the S curve at Le Mans. The machine responsible for revealing the likeness was Bullock's minute sports car, into which the two now crammed. Lenny had told Mays the model—something Italian ending in "i" or "o," sounding like those genus and species names that had stumped Peter altogether in the ninth grade.

Mays sat in what could only be the co-cockpit, the curb looming in the distance over his right shoulder. He chanted to himself such phrases as "The wheels hugged the pavement," and "The sleek little machine nursed the rail." He had only a vague sense of what these meant. They came to him spontaneously out of the vast warehouse of cultural quintessence he'd absorbed over a quarter century. Airfoil, rpm, turbocharge: the awful pressure of the *Zeitgeist*.

He experimented with willing the veering cars and trucks out of their way, as Bullock broke for daylight in a far lane. The red-haired woman had eluded him for months, but it now seemed, as with any self-respecting matinee, that he had only to survive the obligatory chase scene to pin her down at last. Not that he placed too much hope on survival: out here in the traffic, Bullock's *bon mot* about the number two killer after cancer being boredom took on a whole new dimension.

Until his interview with Bullock over a hot quote machine, Mays had been content to chase after the eternally elusive woman with the usual ineptitude of the modern male. Having come this far, he might grudgingly concede to risk his life for the cause, but not in an Italian car. He would signal for a stop; perhaps if Lenny started braking now, Mays could hop out somewhere in upstate New York.

The wind and excess g-forces plastered Bullock's cheeks back and pulled his lips into a grin. He had not spoken a word since identifying Mays's woman as Sarah Bernhardt back at the brokerage. He had concentrated on the immediate objective—speed. Mays glanced at him, and, helpless against the narrative voice that always took over in times of crisis, dredged up the description "eyes glued to the road."

Putting the machine on cruise control, Lenny turned toward Mays and saluted. The gesture was unmistakable: the low-slung cockpit, the wind-pressed face—Errol Flynn in *Dawn Patrol*. A slow dissolve into the next scene and the wing commander would go stoically to the duty roster, find the names Len Bullock and Peter Mays, draw a heavy line through them, and mouth the words "*Adieu, mes amis.*" Len screamed something above the traffic:

—Perfectly safe!

At first, Mays thought Bullock had said, "Murder is great," but dismissed the possibility as unlikely if not out of character. The nominal driver took hands off the wheel to pantomime physical laws, zooming them about, tilting and waving, proving that the faster a body went into a turn, the more it would resist tipping over. Making eye contact with the other fellow, Mays nodded eagerly. He was certain Bullock was certifiable. He could not remember enough college physics, however, to disprove the contention, long ago having forgotten everything except a maniacal professor who regularly screamed at the class that centrifugal force did not exist but only seemed to. And once again, as he had done so many years before, Mays wondered what could be the difference between a real force and one that only seemed real.

Not surprisingly, a glance at the speedometer showed that Bullock had murdered and disposed of the gauge. What use could such an instrument have for him? To a fellow like Bullock, there were those that measured speed and those who lived it. Mays sat back in his cockpit, put his little fingernail between his canine and first bicuspid, and threw his lot solidly behind the camp of the measurers. Barring a notion of where they were headed, he had somehow to determine how fast they were traveling there. He remembered enough physics to know that velocity was distance divided by time. Finding feet per second, he could multiply up to miles per hour, exactly reversing the process he always used to calculate his pay in seconds. In this way, Mays could determine how fast he was traveling when he died.

The clock on the dash read 5:25. That seemed impossible; it couldn't be later than a quarter to. A furtive glance at Lenny's wrist showed 5:31—worse and worse. Mays thought back to the digital on Bullock's desk at the brokerage: that one ran fast as well. A conspiracy of clocks; the sick feeling struck Peter that the man sitting next to him, one hand on the steering wheel, deliberately set all his clocks as much as forty-five minutes forward.

Such a habit could only come from Bullock's believing that to be on time was already too late. Lenny had the disease of the dieter who, losing weight, still buys clothes one size too small, or the husband who tramps about in the garden beneath his wife's window until he at last he discovers the tracks of infidelity, those he himself has just made. Though Mays could still have gotten legitimate seconds from either the dash or Lenny's wrist, he abandoned the measuring project: whatever the cardinal number, it was sure to be off the red zone of his personal speedometer.

When they finally develocitized somewhere downtown, Mays extricated himself from the cabin and looked for the carrier and helicopter the navy always sent out for just such situations.

—Leonard, if you really wanted me to buy that Transport issue you're so hot on, you might have used some subtler form of persuasion. You know, broken my fingers or something.

—What? You mean the car ride? Come on, Nicky; I've never even gotten a ticket that wasn't at least partly the other fellow's fault. Besides, you think I'm going to crack up a machine I still owe twelve K on?

—I'll buy the whole Transport company and have them bring

me over on a troopship before I ride with you again.

Bullock gave a superior snicker and suggested they "duck in somewhere and have a mug." Whatever he meant by that, Mays would do it, providing it wasn't too septic. The chase scene had dealt a severe blow to his white count.

Mays had an aberrant fondness for greasy spoons, and for a single happy moment thought they were headed for one called The Feed Bag. Because he lived alone, he ate out continually. The only way he could afford to spend six dollars on a sandwich was by knowing that a fancier place charged seven. Also, the worse the place, the more the clientele left one alone. Only the rich had time to involve others in their psychopathies.

But Bullock ushered them past the lowly Feed Bag into the seat of opulence, a place called The Trading Floor. Velvet and brass sat in judgment, instantly turning Mays against the spot. Entering along an oaken balustrade of sorts, he went right to work on demolition plans. Brink could do the electronic explosives. Delaney could create a diversion. And Moseley could shelter him from the law behind a complicity of potted plants.

The staff of The Trading Floor greeted Bullock as a regular. Men in cutaway collars and women in starched linen gave Mays proprietary bobs of the head, tacit acknowledgment of the importance of any business transacted in this place. Underneath their circumspection, Mays felt sure, lay the lurid boxing fan or concertogoer. They waited for the big boys to break, the shareholders to snap, jump to their feet, and execute business takeovers with sharp table implements. Meanwhile, the staff assumed the decorous indifference of the serving class.

A young man in glorified bellhop suit led them to a table.

—This is your spot, I believe, Mr. Bullock?

Mays noted the bill that changed hands. If Brink and Bullock Inc. ever got into serious trouble with their debt, they could always come to The Trading Floor and ask this boy for a loan against future tips. Did Len bring Caro here, or did he reserve the place for important clients? If so, what were the two of them doing here now?

Mays felt decidedly out of place. The joint reeked of departed decades—the glory days of Teddy Roosevelt, Taft, and American

Imperialism. Not a cornice dated a day past the Treaty of Versailles. Someone had gone to great effort and expense to outfit brass moldings and darkwood daises with motifs that might have been picked up at any vegetable-and-fruit stand for eighty cents a pound. Each recessed ceiling panel contained a cloud scene in oils and mother-of-pearl inlay. The only similar sky scene Mays had ever before witnessed was in a dive where a falling fan had torn clean through the ceiling.

—Listen, Leonard. I didn't bring any cash. Let's go across the way to that Feed Bag place. I can trade my watch for two Reubenses.

Bullock shushed him just as the headwaiter came up, leading a demure woman in Edwardian Downstairs getup.

—A pleasant afternoon, gentlemen. This will be your waitress, Miss Stark.

Mays commenced to mumble a "how do you do." An icy look from Bullock cut him off.

—Two private lines to the exchange at either end of the bar, a news wire in the corner, and a tape . . .

Bullock waved the headwaiter off with practiced nonchalance. The fellow backed away, continuing to offer assistance until too far off to hear. The anachronistic Miss Stark settled her linen bindings and stays, and attended to the place settings. Mays took another look around the room, which had altered considerably since the headwaiter had pointed out the amenities. While the hardwood and burnished metals still gave off the unmistakable aura of lost times, here and there from out of the turn-of-the-century trappings poked the strange fruit of the present: cathode screens, dot-matrix printers, and above the mirrored and marbled bar, a twelve-foot green phosphor ticker reading out the latest spasm of common-stock transaction. The clients of The Trading Floor needed their data in a steady, real-time stream, no doubt because all fixed money was as deeply in hock as Bullock.

After having to adapt to the rich, darkened, opulent feel of brass and oak, Mays caught himself regarding the data machines as the anachronisms. Host had become guest, and to his eyes, dilated in the gaslight, there seemed no way one could have grown smoothly out of the other. And yet the mechanical altars of information seemed somehow of the same stuff, the same aura as the marble and mother-of-pearl. Mays had read somewhere—either the *Britannica* or *Culture Comix;* he could never remember sources—that after the White Man had brought radios to Polynesia, the form of the knobbed box began showing up in totems.

Bullock said he'd pick up the tab and that Nicky was not to read the menu from right to left. Mays was busy watching the ineluctable Miss Stark—twenty-five if she was a century—set the table. She doled out the silver in quirky genuflections. Her employers had evidently instructed her at great length in the protocol of place setting, protocol now as universally extinct, except in preserving cults, as the Model T. But they lived on, an unconvincing fossil record, in the jerky formality of this woman.

Despite her ritualistic behavior and her Trading Floor livery, Miss Stark seemed, in the face, a woman of unmistakably contemporary bone structure playing dressup. If he laughed appreciatively, perhaps he could get her to roll her eyes in secret agreement. But he hadn't the nerve to try such a stunt in such a place. When Miss Stark completed the service and left, Bullock said:

—She's going to get a big, fat tip.

—How do you figure?

—I start with a maximum of twenty-five bucks and subtract a dollar for every word they say. When I go to a restaurant, I want to be waited on. If I want chat, I go home to Caroline.

The two men looked over their menus, reproductions of 1910 handbills, in silence. At what seemed the perfect moment, Miss Stark reappeared. Mays held his breath and hoped she didn't blow a day's income by getting garrulous all of a sudden.

—Gentlemen?

Bullock looked over at him, eyes alight, delighted at finally finding a member of the serving class who could, if keeping to an equally succinct good-bye, gouge him for twenty dollars. They ordered. Miss Stark, without condescending to write anything down, evaporated in silence.

The two were at last face to face with no interruptions. Mays sat next to the last fellow he would have asked for help, who was about to reveal all. Peter's search for the phantom redhead, which had gone from dull picaresque to detective thriller, was now to reach its denouement here in this electronically outfitted, ivory-enameled monument to *laissez-faire* and the *Maine*. And Mays had suddenly lost all interest.

For one, his mind had habituated to the too-frequent setbacks and diversions—the false leads, the claustrophobic chamber concerts, the titillation of red hair at the far end of a city block—until now he felt more comfortable in the sheer plod of pursuit than in the possibility of arising victorious, bloody, but unbowed. For another, the desire for the redhead, if it had ever been desire per se, had long ago become just a motive for getting up in the morning and searching—for some thing, any thing—if only to overcome the sloth he suspected was at the center of his personality. He might even have dropped the whole escapade some time back had not friends and chance conspired to keep him on the track.

Finally, he'd been so long getting used to and at last enjoying the idea that this search was hopeless, that the phantom woman was immeasurably beyond the caliber of any female he might meet in the flesh, that it stood to reason any woman Bullock told him about could not, by definition, be *her*. He still coveted the chase and wanted to resume it. But he had no need for any lead Bullock might give him over a T-bone, with one eye on the twelve-foot ticker tape above the bar.

Mays had no hobbies, religion, or social convictions. His job held no interest. His friends, be they ever so humble, and love affairs, be they ever so transient, grew predictable after a while. Things, he had always felt, stayed interesting only until they revealed their underlying behavior. But the chase had been arbitrary; it *had* no underlying pattern, and so might have remained nominally interesting forever, providing he never closed with the quarry. But he had made the mistake of fixing his obsession on a woman who, however ethereal, had in fact at one time, even from eight stories up, a real, bodily existence. Now he had to pay for that mistake, to sit still and listen while the compulsive Bullock told him who (there's the rub) that person was.

Bullock smirked slightly with dramatic showmanship, enjoying the role of man with the facts. Throughout the ensuing speech, Mays wished for a copy of the criminal code, so he could see if what he wanted to do to Bullock really carried all that stiff a penalty. While Lenny gave his view of the facts, Miss Stark brought on the meal without a word. Lenny paused politely when she came by the table, but Mays waved him on impatiently; if he could stomach the facts, so could innocent bystanders.

—Puzzles like this, Nicky, always involve some moment of insight—the instant of aha. The solution comes in a flash, all at once, so simple and obvious you wonder why you couldn't see it before. But seeing the answer requires jumping out from under bad assumptions. Take the one about the two men who play three games of chess and each wins the same number of games without drawing. You see the puzzle in a magazine and become obsessed with it. You stop taking meals and baths. You decide the thing has no answer. Then one day a year later you wake up at midnight and realize that you'd assumed, falsely, that they were playing each other.

Habituated as he had become to digression, Mays wondered if there were a simple way of hastening Bullock down the path toward revelation. Perhaps throttling him and yelling, "Get to the point" might do the trick.

—Not to belittle the basic attraction of *cherchez la femme.* I know that finding this redhead cheesecake is more difficult than an exercise in logic. Only you—and I, when you first put it to me—had some bad assumptions about what you were going after.

—Meaning?

Mays was perfecting the art of the dangling interrogative.

—Meaning you came into my office asking me to help find a red-haired clarinetist. Your givens are all wrong.

—All right, oboist. Whatever you say. I didn't get a good look at her.

—It's worse than that, my friend.

—She's not a redhead? She's not a woman?

—Funny, Nick, but that's the skeptical spirit. I mean to say that your phantom of delight isn't even a musician.

—Not . . .? Come on. I *saw* her, playing in the parade. That is . . .

Mays felt only disgust and fatigue; he had just gotten mugged, and was trying halfheartedly to talk the thief into giving his credit cards and license back. He had no energy to object any more strenuously.

—Fascinating, no? You look out through a window onto a thin

frame of fact, and create all the rest out of an initial mistake.

—But you yourself said she played the oboe.

—I said no such thing. She was *holding* an oboe. A tremendous clue. I kick myself now for being so obtuse. There I was, going through my memory of every woman instrumentalist I know. When I gave up the notion that the instrument belonged to her, the whole scene came back to me in one piece. I'd *seen* your image, and on the same day, too.

—Impossible. This was downtown, and you were . . .

—Assumptions, Nicky. The exchange is closed on Veterans' Day. I was kicking around downtown, doing errands and killing time. Caught a bit of the parade. Your redhead was fairly prominently showcased, before the floats broke up. I didn't dwell on her, though I saw she had the goods to turn a head or two. I was preoccupied with the oboe. It wasn't right. Pan doesn't play oboes. He plays reed pipes.

—Mind speaking English, bwana?

—You see, she wasn't carrying the oboe at the time. That belonged to the fellow on the float next to her. Nijinsky.

Mays had had enough. He wanted to forget the whole thing, head home, catch a little prime time, shower, rack out, then look for work tomorrow under an assumed name. Fixations were supposed to be clean and simple. This one could not possibly be worth unraveling.

—Seems some civic luminary hit on the idea of sprucing the parade up some. Rather than another year of just having the dour vet crazies get in formation and limp down Commonwealth Avenue in the memory of regimental splendor. Add some local color, a dash of exotica.

—Clowns, brass bands, the usual stuff? Yeah, I saw all that. You mean to tell me I've been chasing down a majorette?

—Not at all. Just the opposite of your usual parade filler. I'm talking something peculiarly Bostonian. Too many universities here. Smell your pits and six grad students want to write dissertations on it. No, I'm talking about a Parade of History. A Floating Documentary of this Veterans' Cementury. Something to that effect.

—Sorry, still don't follow you.

—Look, you have your parade manifest handy?

Mays handed over the manifest and went on patently addressing himself to his meal. He had regressed from the beef to a taste-
less excrescence billed as Potato Skins. Bullock examined the roster.
It cross-indexed each alphabetized name by sponsor and activity.
Mays had already crossed out all those not related to music. Bullock ran his finger down a dark, heavily crossed-out area.

—Let's see . . . here's the ticket. *Great Personalities of the First
World War Era.* Awkward title, but to the point.

Mays looked up sharply from playing with his food. He'd noticed the listing and several like it a hundred times without attach-
ing any significance to it. Extraneous filler: "A tableau of the great
men and women dominating the period of the Great War." Its
sponsors included two local art museums, the New England chap-
ter of the American Society of Concerned Scientists and Engineers, and the Triple-A. Mays followed Bullock's thumb down the
roster.

—A perverse idea, if you think about it. Here are all these fellows sent off to another continent to fight, and why? To make the
world safe for democracy. And they get maimed or gassed or killed,
and then they come back and can't get work and have to become
gangsters or bootleggers. Finally, seventy years later they have to
march along in a parade that treats the whole thing like a prettified
photo in the *Golden Book of History:* an actor playing Einstein, one
playing Freud. An actor dressed up as Nijinsky, the satyr in
Afternoon of a Faun, but with oboe in place of panpipes, for
Christ's sake.

Mays blushed unconsciously. He had always thought the piece
had been about a baby deer.

—But before I regress totally into bleeding hearts' club, allow
me to point out your actress, playing Sarah Bernhardt.

And Bullock's meal-greasy thumb came to rest under the pen-
ciled-out name "Kimberly Greene." Mays felt overcome by anti-
climax. Knowing the name depressed him tremendously.

—I don't see how all this follows. How do you know that's
her? Just because she's listed on that float doesn't mean . . . All
right, I'll grant you your basic theory, but how do you know that
that is her?

—Because, chump, the "Great Personalities" float had a ready-made local celebrity to cast as the world's most famous actress. But you wouldn't know that, would you? Too busy with your microchips to keep current with the arts scene. Caro is exactly the same way. I say, "Isaac Stern is in town. Let's go see him." And she says, "Isaac Stern, the inventor of the low-conductivity relay?" Why does everyone have to choose between one cult or the other?

Mays did not particularly feel like admitting that despite his job he was technically illiterate, and despite his recent spate of concertgoing he still had no entrée to the cult of culture. Isaac Stern was the smart fellow in third grade who took off for Yom Kippur.

—You mean this woman is famous?

—Bernhardt?

—Greene.

—Small potatoes. A local talent who's made a name for herself doing a revue of famous women from the past. The Divine Sarah is one of her specialties. She's got a one-woman show that's been running forever at the Your Move Theatre: *I Dwell in Possibility*. The critics raved over her Virginia Woolf, but found her Margaret Sanger somewhat sterile. Get it?

Mays decidedly did not get it, and probably would not have even if he had been paying attention.

—And you've seen this show? You're certain it's the same woman?

—No. I only see shows with casts of thousands. But she's on the parade roster, no? The papers praised her Bernhardt to the skies. She was a natural for the "Great Personalities" float.

The evidence strongly suggested that Sarah Bernhardt, Kimberly Greene, and Mays's *idée fixe* were one and the same. Here was an explanation of the quality of antique displacement he had seen in the figure even from several stories up, the quality of fierce nostalgia that had kept him on the search for so long. Yet the idea of an actress playing herself playing another actress playing an old stage role for a Veterans' Day Parade seemed the most recursive, unlikely thing he'd ever come across. But then, Mays had never read much history.

—But if you doubt the explanation, put it to the test. Her show's at the Your Move, on Boylston.

He gave rudimentary directions, and suggested that Mays call the papers for information. Then he excused himself, saying he'd only be gone a minute. Mays watched him walk to one end of the bar, to a vacant terminal resembling the one at the brokerage. Bullock began punching up quotations. That's why they had to eat at The Trading Floor instead of The Feed Bag. Caroline's boyfriend had an even more violent sickness than Mays had before realized: he was addicted to information.

Gradually, the serious evening diners began to replace the afternoon business-drinking crowd. Looking out the window for the first time since entering the bar, Mays jerked slightly on seeing the advance that evening had already made. For the first time in a long while, he had no particular need to get home, to keep to a strict timetable. He felt slack; the mere fact of evening no longer implied he had to be here or there. He no longer had the mystery to organize his time.

From across the room, he watched Bullock punch up a few more stock quotes. Miss Stark returned, this time so perfectly preserving the illusion of Edwardian decorum that Mays had to resist the urge to ply her for information on Sarah Bernhardt.

—Will that be all, sirs?

Peter wondered what he had ever done to this woman to deserve the plural. At least three mouthfuls of every course remained on Bullock's plate. Mays blanched, hearing in his memory his immigrant mother lecture on how millions of children—usually Indian but sometimes, for variety, Chinese—would kill for such scraps. Mays, not wanting to be killed by children of any nationality, had long ago perfected the technique of clearing his plate, and even at so fancy a place as The Trading Floor, he had sopped up all the beef juice with a spare roll when no one was looking.

The refusal to finish his meal seemed to fit with the rest of Bullock's personality, though. It was cut from the same cloth as the enormous personal debt, the consolidation loans, the forty-five-minute-fast clocks, and the midnight lawn mowing. Mays resisted the temptation to clean off Bullock's plate, too, with one enormous wipe of the tongue, although he would like to have seen how such a move would register on the woman in black linen.

—Yes, that will be all, ma'ams.

He watched her face as she bent to clear away the china. Either she had not heard the joke, or they had her well trained. She didn't even contemplate grinning. She placed the bill face down on the cleared table and said, in the same strain of ancient accent:

—We hope you have enjoyed your meals.

Mays decided not to report this spate of verbal activity to Bullock. Intent on transferring as much as possible of the twenty-five-dollar surplus value from the broker back to the Edwardian anachronism, he decided to say that she came by, cleaned up, slapped the bill down, and said, "Here," a grand total of two words, good for twenty-three smackers. He was, after all, a technical editor by vocation.

But so excited was Bullock when he returned to their table that Peter never got the chance to lie for the woman.

—Listen, Nicky. This is absolutely your last chance. Are you buying in or not?

Mays could not, even by violent force, fit the words into any smooth continuity with what they had been discussing. Buying into Bullock's theory about the redhead? Buying into his share of the meal? Buying a ticket to *I Dwell in Possibility*? As customary when confused beyond recall, Mays said nothing.

—You'd better decide now. I'm heading back to the office and can put a ticket in for you for tomorrow.

Suddenly things clicked. The whole business meal, the opulent, archaic restaurant, the unraveling of the elusive woman had all been, to Bullock, just another sales pitch. Lenny had strung him along, indulged him, and had hoped that, by disabusing the client of his little fantasy, he could pick him up on the rebound and score a big sale of that issue he had hounded Mays over for so long: Trans-Air Transport. Shut up and buy bonds.

For a moment, Mays understood that all such mysteries at last come down to a question of double-entry bookkeeping, that after dalliance with red hair, one had always to come back to questions of profit and loss. But a perversity on his part made him refuse to give in just yet. Only now the object of his perversity was no longer the antique woman he'd seen from eight stories up, hereafter called Ms. Greene, but the improbable image of a one-legged actress stumping the boards and sleeping in a golden coffin.

—Trans-Air? I don't know, Lenny. I've always found the idea of airplanes a bit, you know, tentative.

—Jesus. I'm not asking you to ride in them. Just buy into their equity.

—I know. Only, airplanes go up, and you're never sure how they're going to come down. Why just today, in your office, I was reading on the wire about this plane in Chicago . . .

—Nick, I've got to get back . . .

—Do you have anything more down-to-earth?

—*Autos?* You want to buy autos? Jesus, Nicky. Haven't you heard what the Japs have done to Detroit? They've leveled it.

A day that will live in infamy, thought Mays.

—Sorry, Leonard.

Bullock grunted. Brusquely, he gave over the cost of the meal with twenty-five extra dollars and specific instructions to tip the waitress by the prearranged formula.

—And with the leftover, get a ticket to this woman's show. Then when you return to sanity and are ready to talk reality principle, come back to the brokerage. But you'll never have another chance like now.

When Lenny had left, Mays decided willfully to betray the bequest and leave Miss Stark the full twenty-five dollars as legacy. Having reached that decision, he stretched out his empty hands palms down, placing one on the heavily starched tablecloth and resting the other carefully in a pool of gravy accidentally spilled by the prim Edwardian as she removed the boat. Again, he felt the queasy responsibility of being without sponsor or commitments: he never brought work home from the office, there was nothing of interest on television that evening, he'd written his mother only five months ago, and Ms. Kimberly Greene, merely by existing, had removed the last possibility of enchantment in life. He had absolutely no place to be more than where he was.

Like any other revelation, this profound feeling lasted only long enough to be displaced by another, more powerful one of bodily discomfort. He had to go to the loo, and announced the fact out loud to no one in particular.

On seeing The Trading Floor's bathrooms, he no longer mourned the loss of his revelation. He would have sacrificed twice the profundity to see such a place. The sinks were a smoky gray marble, the floor a rich mottled mosaic of hexagons, the mirrors polished to perfection with a floral trim that threatened to swallow up his reflection in a pastiche of petals. The fixtures were of semi-precious metals, including faucets in the guise of dolphins that spit water in upward parabolas. Mays turned them on and off several times in succession, delighting in watching the watery arcs spurt and die.

He felt happier among all this grotesque ornament than he had at any time since the pseudo-Veterans' Day. The overabundance left him positively oceanic, and he only regretted not being able to stand unobserved in the corner and watch the brokers from this place's heyday unbutton their tailored flies and take their privileged pees. Hats and canes, the original executors: how did they differ from the current breed of Bullocks?

The toilet stalls were no less opulent than the privy foyer. The doors and toilet rims were of an amazing dark wood that Mays suspected was no longer manufactured. The water tank sat ten feet atop a lead pipe, and Peter was in a great hurry to evacuate so he could pull the chain, a flushing method entirely novel for him. The side walls, cut from the same quarry as the basins, were pasted over with printed matter. For a fellow whose folks had always forbidden reading matter in the john, this was heaven on earth.

The document taking by far the largest area of stall walls bore the title "Securities Exchange Commission Regulations for Registered Representatives." Mays felt as if he were reading taboo material, not for laymen's eyes. He imagined a broker, constipated, who nevertheless made good use of his otherwise lost time by checking to see if everything he'd done that day was aboveboard.

He bogged down in the turgid legalese. As he finished what his mother, even well into his maturity, insisted on calling his "business," he began wishing that the authorities had posted "Famous Actresses" or "Great Personalities of the First War Era." Even as a child, he had adored the four-line thumbnail biography, complete with legends and wild claims beginning "Sarah Bernhardt did not change the history of acting. She *was* the history of acting."

Mays stood and began fastening himself together. As he did so, he automatically read the text that bobbed up to eye level. "The New York Stock Exchange closes in observance of the following

— 158 —

holidays:" He jumped from Jan. 1 to Jul. 4 without thinking. But after going from Labor Day to Thanksgiving, he stopped, backed up, and made the leap again. No Veterans' Day—either original armistice or congressional rescheduling. Bullock had lied about seeing the parade.

The familiar feeling of having been cheated rose up in him and Mays could not dislodge it. He lowered his head to the marble basin and began to douse water over his face with a fury directed not just at Bullock's lie but at the whole trail of lies, misrepresentations, involvements, false leads, and ambiguities that had obscured his way, destroyed any hope of his coming to a thumbnail biography not dependent on his or others' interpretations. The deeper he pursued the mop of strawberry hair, the more her identity seemed grounded in willful reworking or clumsy observation. Worse, under the stream of cold water arcing from the dolphin's mouth, Mays sensed that an even more elusive string of interpretations led well beyond that day at the window, beyond the concerns of Delaney, Brink, Bullock, and Ms. Greene, back through a tangle of years, even involving and outdistancing the Bernhardt herself.

If nothing else, Bullock's lie restored to Mays the sense of having to be somewhere, to meet a deadline. His lethargy following the afternoon's revelation fell with a steady douse of water to the hexagons of the porcelain floor. He left the sanctuary of the opulent commode and returned to the dining room, resisting the temptation to go to the news wire at the end of the bar and get current on the day's disasters, further tragedies of travel by air, sea, or land. No more hunting of clues; if some conspiracy indeed lay in wait for him, he would fall into it willingly with the satisfaction of having brought on, at least in part, his own inheritance.

Midway in his down-and-out pattern toward the door, a hand hooked inside his arm and restrained him. Instantly recalling the trauma of being caught shoplifting at the age of nine, Mays began to protest his innocence, saying he'd left the meal money on the table and someone must have walked off with it. Turning, he found himself confronted by the full-fruited face of Miss Stark. She stood exactly Mays's height, and her eyes were rolled back in a burlesque of long-suffering.

The laundered Edwardian had disappeared. In her place stood

a Mack Sennetient comedienne who, by a puff-pastry joviality to her cheeks, gave off the impression of being caught in a punchline too ludicrous to explain. She had an animated face, photogenic, with refreshingly mundane brown hair and an expression that might, if caught by the shutter, have seemed ironic, but, when allowed free movement, passed well beyond irony into relish and good humor.

—I need your help. Will you play along for a minute? I'll explain later.

Playing along in hopes of a later explanation had become a sort of religion with Mays. That he could actually help someone by doing so had never occurred to him. He nodded acquiescence.

They stood facing each other for two beats. Then she tightened her grip on his arm and nuzzled up to him, steering the cargo to a distant table. As they approached, a figure rose in a flourish of Old World grace. Even Mays, who had all his history from late-night costume reruns starring Garbo and Charles Boyer saw at once that this fellow was the genuine article. His Continental clothing, unlike Miss Stark's set copy, hailed from the heyday of The Trading Floor.

Like a good Aristotelian, Mays never guessed at people's ages beyond labeling them as Beginnings, Middles, or Ends. This fellow was the clearest-cut End Mays had ever met. The gentleman's act of standing called out for a good traction kit. Miss Stark glossed over the scene with introductions.

—Mr. Krakow, I'd like you to meet my fiancé, Mr. . . .

Before she could add to the heap of falsehoods and misrepresentations, however well intentioned, that had just nauseated him a moment before, Mays interjected:

—Peter Mays.

An ineffectual blow for accuracy. After blurting this out, Mays hoped, with some embarrassment, that he had not upset Miss Stark's plans. Gauging by her expression of gratified relief, matters were passable.

Mays took the old man's proffered hand, afraid that even a light touch might break the intricate and antique mechanism beneath the skin. Contact contracted the old fellow's muscles, the way an electric shock galvanizes a dead frog's legs. He began to speak quickly in a thick, virtually indecipherable European accent.

Mr. Krakow combined apology, congratulations, reminiscence, homily, and asthma attack into one tortuous siege of syntax, seemingly without connective tissue or logic. At first, Mays thought he detected a story line about childhood in Vienna, but when his drifting attention returned to the man's monologue, he found the topic had wandered on to the beauty of Miss Stark, Peter's luck, and the doddering obtuseness of the man himself.

—But most you, please, my two young friends, have you the knowledge how my heart goes forth with your way. Will you join me at my table for the evening meal?

—Dinner? Well, I'm afraid, Mr. Krakow, that Peter and I have . . .

Once again Peter, afraid of this woman's least embroidering of the facts, interrupted:

—We've plans to go out this evening. But Miss Stark and I would be pleased to eat with you on another occasion.

An odd formality had infected Mays's diction. He and Krakow made long, full-eye contact. Mays imagined he could see the man's eyes go soft, insubstantial, even as he looked at them, losing ground to the proliferate folds of cheek and eyelid, beaten down mostly by all they had taken in in a century's time. Mays had the unpleasant sense of being just another sight at the end of a long line of travelogues. He felt a tremendous urge to recant, to go back on what he had just said about he and Miss Stark having plans, to spend the evening with this fellow, to put in front of those liquid eyes the obscurities he had come across in tracking down the Vets' Day mirage, to see what history could make of the mystery before experience softened the man's eyes altogether.

He opened his mouth, but this time Miss Stark cut him off. She made the perfunctory good-byes for all three parties, and the two men again shook hands. Mays tried to form a permanent memory of what that hand felt like. Then Miss Stark steered him back to the door, saying:

—Thanks so much . . . Peter. I'm really embarrassed to have done this to you. But that man is off his nut. He comes in for dinner three times a week, dressed in a thousand dollars of antique clothes and carrying on about the Old World, like he did just now. He's convinced that I am the perfect image of his dead wife. Gives me the heebie-jeebies. A bit on the ghoulish side, wouldn't you say? Anyway, I thought I could use you to shock Arkady back to the present.

Her words had precisely that effect on Mays. He was once again without conspiracy, Bernhardt forgotten, in a snooty restaurant with a waitress who, despite the getup, was graced with a decidedly contemporary attraction. She still had his arm, still gave off the look with which she had initially accosted him. Her words, when she spoke, were saved from the inflection of sarcasm or cynicism by a component of seemingly congenital affection:

—So what are these much rumored "plans" we have for this evening?

—A show. The Your Move Theatre.

Chapter Thirteen

Great Personalities of the First War Era

Cultural fatigue is sometimes preceded by a kind of euphoria, a last flare-up, which forecasts the impending collapse.—GERHARD MAUSER

IN FOLLOWING a path back to the world of the First War, whether opened up by the portal of a photograph or by a casual remark from first hand, the amateur historian finds the wayposts populated, as if the past were no more than a sum of portraits done in gum arabic and brushed into representative perfection for the lens. Each book on the period circles back to the same names again and again, names that are held up as symbolic of the spirit of the times. Choose one at random—the day's most adored redhead—and find it done up a century later as if she meant from the start to cross and weave together, with the help of outside editing, all the chief personages of her era.

For someone as famous as Bernhardt, the editing by observers obscures her real self almost completely. Just as the minerals in water replace the cells of a fallen tree, legend crystallized her life until she became her observers' rumors. At the end, we all become edited copy. With the famous, the process simply starts sooner, while the subject is still alive. Bernhardt aggravated the situation, cultivating and believing her own legends. Her capricious memoirs read like gossip sheets. Her biographers—related to Sarah by blood, love, and scandal—all have personal reasons for perpetuating the Bernhardt legend. Only three facts concerning Sarah are agreed on: she was a household word from palaces to hovels, she lied obsessively, and she was excessively thin.

She was born in a half dozen houses at once to a score of parents. She was most probably of Dutch descent, although her accent bore a hundred cultivated traces. Her childhood is anecdotal at best, with no record of her six-year formal education. Sarah made sure never to recount her colorful rise to fame the same way twice.

Every account of the Great Sarah embellishes on a notorious coffin that the actress supposedly traveled with and slept in. Some sources transmute it to gold plate, others make it rosewood lined with satin. She communicated with spirits while lying in it. She slept in it to gain the power of dead thespians. She did it to shock France, to shock the world. She entertained in it. She took lovers in it. One reporter called it a "sepulchre built for two." Robert de Montesquiou, the model for Proust's Baron Charlus, reportedly administered a black funeral mass over Sarah as she lay in it.

For her part, Sarah claimed that she had begged her mother to buy her the box when she was fifteen. Perennially ill, with a habit of coughing up blood, she had been condemned to death by various doctors. Afraid of an ugly bier and eager to get used to a state she'd be in for a long time, Sarah procured the coffin for aesthetic reassurance and practice. The December 1903 issue of *Theatre Magazine* imports the legend into the New World:

> When Mme. Bernhardt is world-weary, she gets into this coffin . . . and covering herself with faded wreaths and flowers, folds her hands across her breast and her eyes closed, bids a temporary farewell to life. A lighted candle on the votary table at her left and a skull grinning on the floor add to the illusion.

So perfect a journalistic knowledge of the details surrounding Madame Sarah's coffin came not at first hand, but from a photograph of the actress in her rosewood bed. The details survive in countless mechanical reproductions. Sarah had herself so photographed at least twice in her long life. The first amateurish attempt shows a teen-aged Bernhardt in repose, ill-focused and poorly composed. The second, improved by experience, is a luxurious scene, the model for the journalist's florid imaginings.

The obvious contrivance of the document, rather than dispelling the legend, only adds to the pyre. The age of mechanical reproduction creates a new celebrity worship. We read about Garrick and Booth, study their careers and roles, digest descriptions of their gestures and eccentricities, but they remain strange to us. About Sarah we may be in total ignorance but simply *seeing* her lying in state creates the illusion of intimacy. We need only pretend that we, not the photographer, composed the scene.

The Bernhardt legend rests on many such intimate scenes. She made and squandered several fortunes. She frequently went from obscene wealth to deep debt in a matter of days. When bills grew pressing, she simply dipped her hand into a bowl full of precious rings given to her by lovers, pawning a scoop. The sum always covered the debt in style. Her least expense was immoderate. One winter, she spent two thousand francs feeding the sparrows of Paris.

Readers visited, via the tabloids, her notorious menageries. Apes inhabited the attic, lions ate live quail, snakes reigned in her front rooms, disrupting her soirées. If her scripts called for animals, she used live ones, no matter how dangerous. She was a pantheist, once refusing to walk on a carpet of lilies laid at her feet by Oscar Wilde. Wilde, no slouch at flamboyance himself, went to his own coffin in the first year of this century, insisting that the three women he would have most liked to marry were Lillie Langtry, Queen Victoria, and Bernhardt.

She traveled to engagements in a private train, the Sarah Bernhardt Special, an entire car reserved for her alone. She wore heaps of fur, even in summer. Yet this woman, who decorated her rooms in endless damask, also gave extravagant sums to anarchists' soup kitchens. She befriended Vaillant, amused and moved by this man's childish idealism. The memory of childhood poverty and an innate love for the phantasmagoric drew her to this fellow. When Vaillant's bomb exploded in the House of Deputies, the naïf bragged that:

. . . a hundred deputies lay wounded on the floor. . . . Everywhere I have been, I have seen the same wounds and

— 165 —

tears and blood. Tired of this life of suffering, I aimed my
bomb at those who were primarily responsible for social misery.

Their friendship ended with the anarchist's hanging.

Audiences poured in, first to see the performer, then to see what
everyone else flocked to see, and finally to see the Personality whose
scandals filled the popular press. In an age of propriety, her affairs
with leading men, paupers, and Ducs of all persuasions were
thought necessary for one of her stature. If she kept clear of politics after the anarchist debacle, she did not shy away from heads
of state. She was brooched by Louis Napoleon. Rumors prolifer-
ated about her relations with princes and ministers of all nationalities. In 1910, when nine kings gathered for the funeral of Edward
VII, they mourned, besides their own coming disintegration, a long-
time Bernhardt paramour. If Bernhardt had slept with all the men
the papers implicated, she would never have had time to appear
onstage. She fueled her own notoriety, saying of her son, "I could
never make up my mind whether his father was Gambetta, Victor
Hugo, or General Boulanger."

Among those linked to her is the Italian poet Gabriele D'Annunzio. His musical drama of 1913, *La Pisanelle*, concerned a
beautiful medieval prostitute who, captured by pirates, dances
herself to death, smothered in roses. Former Prime Minister Cle-
menceau, leaving the opening of *La Pisanelle*, remarked to a reporter, "D'Annunzio is the last of the troubadours." Parisians could
not be bothered with such fluff. They were busy rioting at Nijinsky's barbarically innovative ballets, hissing his minimal movements and still poses in Debussy's *Afternoon of a Faun*, for which
he dressed in a satyr's suit but carried no panpipes. Responding
to the broadsides attacking his performance in Stravinsky's *The Rite
of Spring*, the dancer, shortly to go incurably mad, ushered in an
epoch with the phrase "Grace and charm make me sick. . . . I eat
my meat without sauce Béarnaise."

Squeezed from the artistic spotlight, D'Annunzio made his mark
on another front altogether. At the outbreak of war, Bernhardt's
consort returned to Italy, where his skills in writing and oratory
were instrumental in bringing Italy into the war on the side of the
Allies. He became the most daring ace in the first Italian air force,
as if the transformation from anachronistic rhymester to pioneer-

ing biplaner were the most natural step in the world.

After the war, D'Annunzio involved himself in the dispute over the port of Rijeka, also called Fiume. The secret Treaty of Paris promised the city to Yugoslavia, but Italy would not renounce its claim. D'Annunzio took matters into his own hands, marching his personal army of Italian free corps on the city, establishing an independent nation opposed to both belligerents as well as to the rest of Europe. There D'Annunzio introduced a costume of black shirts, one he later re-created for his future employer, Mussolini. When poets become activists become Fascists, we arrive at the heart of the century. But D'Annunzio too, as a youth before the war, was a lover of Madame Sarah.

Now, everyone in the world was not a Saradorer. Max Beerbohm lampooned her from across the Channel. George Bernard Shaw accused her of having a whole arsenal of "capitally vulgar" sensational effects. Henry Ford used his newspapers to discourage his employees from attending this immoral woman's American tours. When she could, Sarah dealt with such detractors head on. She went after the libelous Marie Colombier with a horsewhip in one hand and a stage dagger in the other. Three continents exploded with news of the attack, spilling many times the words that Colombier had written in the first place. The only way to handle reporters was to give them good copy.

Men and women alike stood in the wings, called from the balcony, wept over performances, massed to train stations and ports, chased after this red-haired wraith as if she possessed some fabulously important secret, worshiped her well into old age, followed her into the new century. All, that is, with some important exceptions. For one group of men and women entered the century by a back door which in time became a grand foyer. In 1900, when Sarah was the toast of every respectable table, a different banquet was under way across the Seine.

There was another play in town besides Sarah's production of Racine's *Phèdre*. In a single night's performance four years before the century began, this play established itself with its first word: *Merdre*. Shee-it. The opening-night house rioted for a half hour before the play could reach its second word. For six weeks afterward, all Paris was dueling.

Ubu Roi was written by Alfred Jarry, a man who single-handedly raised derangement to the level of religion. Jarry opened the floodgates of that movement with the military name: the advance guard. By his death in 1907, every practitioner of radical art—Picasso, Matisse, Pound, Joyce, Stein, Satie, Stravinsky—owed something to the diminutive Jarry and his obese King Ubu. Yeats sat in the house on opening night, cheering the play on against its detractors. Yet afterward, he wrote of feeling an extreme sadness. After the refinements of his own verse, of Bernhardt and Brahms, there had to be a reaction against so much beauty. Sadly, he wrote the century's obstetric: "After us, the Savage God."

But Jarry and the *avant-garde* of the first decades were not so savage as they first appear. They are not so much antibourgeois as bourgeois *ad absurdum*. The artistic vanguard wedded the logic of the middle class to that class's unadmitted dreams. Jarry merely emphasized the underside of the intimacy brought on by mechanical reproduction: the camera, in encouraging us to identify with the photographed scene, *always* lied. It cropped, it recolored, it double-exposed. Lenses blurred the distinction between private dream and public, mass-reproduced logic.

Jarry simply stood Bernhardt on her head, sensing that people did not pack the theater to see stodgy old *Phèdre*. They came to see the woman who slept in coffins, let wild animals roam about her house, and kept kings as lovers. The public came to see the Bernhardt. Jarry simply affected the inverse of this relation, thereby discovering—with Planck, Einstein, Freud, the Cubists, and the stream-of-consciousness novelists—the intermarriage of observer and observed, dreamer and dream, worshiper and stage celebrity. He became his fictional King Ubu.

Transformed into fictional royalty, he built himself a castle—a hovel standing on four rotting planks, which he called, through the machinations of dream logic, "The Royal Tripod." He pedaled about on "that which rolls." He brandished firearms in public. He consumed heroic amounts of alcohol and ether. He initiated Banquets, lavish bohemian parodies of Sarah fêtes. At these several-day-long bashes, guests threw one another out of windows and gave long speeches glorifying squirrels or metal bolts or pieces of poster torn from kiosks. Jarry's feasts were object lessons in how to love and ridicule a thing at the same time.

As King Ubu, Jarry let his speech grow lavish and grandiloquent, even as he sank into addiction and squalor. Somewhere in the charade, he passed the point of role-playing into belief. He induced in himself a divine schizophrenia not unlike the Divine Sarah's, driving himself simultaneously into self-proclaimed Great Personality and obscure Everyman. King Ubu, self-made schizophrenic, addressed himself by the royal "We." Only on his deathbed did he revert to first person. For several days, semicomatose, he repeated, "I search, I search." In his last lucid moment, Jarry asked for a toothpick. Given one, he held it devoutly in his hands as if it were the object of his delivery and final happiness. After his burial, his friends held a banquet.

The great task of Jarry and the *avant-garde* was to force two things to occupy the same place at the same time: public and private, celebrated and obscure, serious and ludicrous. One tool that helped instigate this pursuit of the simultaneous was the automobile. Tearing along at fifty miles an hour, the new century saw its familiar landscapes collapse along the axis of travel, breaking the old barrier of time, shortening the space between Paris and Vienna until the two seemed synonymous. The car inspired action paintings, superimposed photographs, tone clusters and polychords—a whole art of the simultaneous. Movements and manifestos equated the auto and speed with power and beauty. Marinetti and the Futurists found in the car further good: danger, audacity, revolution, and war. Again, in their worship of the private auto, the *avant-garde* did not oppose Sarah's values so much as democratize them: each to her own Bernhardt Special.

So the showgoing public polarized violently into camps for Queen Sarah and camps for King Ubu. Yet by far the greatest number of those in the early century—both celebrities and those millions who left no document of their ever having lived—were untouched by the controversy between the personality-become-actress and the playwright-become-personality.

Count Zeppelin was busy keeping his airships from blowing up. Diesel had disappeared, with both German and British espionage agencies blaming the other. (The inventor had, in fact, killed himself after suffering huge losses in the market.) The Czarina Alexandra was staying up late with her hemophiliac son; recently, she had found a man who could stop the bleeding. De Broglie, Planck, Heisenberg, and Einstein were interpreting the discoveries of their Miracle Year. Mahler kept together the Ninth Symphony, in which things fall apart. Sun Yat-sen was busy freeing half a billion people. The suffragette Emily Davison threw herself under the King's horse at the English Derby, and by this vote, recorded in a remarkable photograph, abstained from the theater for good.

The Wrights tinkered, Stalin wrote news copy, and Kafka stamped official papers. Hearst incited his reporters to denounce ragtime. Schweitzer wrote about Bach and set up camp in Africa. And Alexander Fleming, the fellow who identified the most important substance of the century, was busy putting out a thousand petri dishes, waiting for the chance spore blown from a brewery to mix with the mucus from a runny nose and reveal the antagonistic action of penicillin. Finally, there is the innumerable class of those who might have advanced beyond the achievements of any of these mentioned. Where is the Sarah of mid-century? Where is Ubu's heir? As one poet-journalist put it, in Flanders' fields.

So the reports of these times circle back to Bernhardt and her enormous popularity. Biographies document endless anecdotes: crowds near hysteria, duels, Days of Glorification, parades—a worship so great that on her first visit to America, hearing an incredulous reporter exclaim, "New York didn't give Dom Pedro of Brazil such an ovation," Sarah said drily, "Yes, but he was only an emperor."

In her twilight years, Sarah only tightened the hypnotic grip she had on the public. In March of 1914, while Ford perfected his automated plant and Sander bicycled into the Westerwald, Bernhardt, yet a third celebrity with only half a dozen years of schooling, in debt to the hilt, stood on the stage of her own Théâtre Sarah Bernhardt and received France's greatest award: Chevalier of the Légion d'Honneur. That summer, the seventy-year-old took her latest hit on the road, electrifying the provinces as if she were a girl of eighteen. She'd returned to her summer home for a brief vacation when the newspapers started to carry accounts of the troubles in the Balkans. When the news of August first arrived, Bernhardt is reported to have said, "Dear God! Why does civilization keep on receding?"

The gallant French front, which was to sustain itself on *élan vital* and red pantaloons, fell apart in the first month following Germany's devastation of Belgium. France had left the route through Belgium only lightly covered, daring Germany to bring Britain into the war in defense of Belgian neutrality. Each day the German columns advanced until the fall of Paris seemed certain. The government was evacuated to Bordeaux, leaving Gallieni in charge of the city. Still Sarah refused to leave. She had nursed soldiers in the occupation of 1870, and insisted on doing the same this time around. But when intelligence revealed that her name led a list of Great Personalities the Kaiser wanted captured and brought back to Berlin, a hysterical Paris forced its Divine Sarah from the city.

On the morning of her departure, her son had extraordinary difficulty in securing a taxi to take her to the station. He searched for over an hour, finally turning up one sorry excuse for a cab. Sarah instructed the car to go by way of the Champs Élysées for what might be a last look at the beautiful thoroughfare now belonging to a lost time. Arriving there, she saw a scene that caused Gallieni, the defender of Paris, himself to cry out, "Here at last is something remarkable."

The way was jammed with five hundred cabs rushing an entire army of men to the Battle of the Marne. The taxi portage was the last act of heroism from a lost world. An officer stopped Bernhardt's cab, reprimanding the driver for not falling in for the bizarre conscription. He threw open the door to evict the passenger, and stood face to face with the third most famous woman in France after Jeanne d'Arc and the Virgin:

> I beg your pardon, Madame, I didn't know! Go chauffeur, take Mme. Sarah Bernhardt to the station, then come back and put yourself at our disposition. . . . Go with a tranquil mind, Madame.

And then he repeated the catchphrase that all France was rallying around: *Ils ne passeront pas*. And while it was technically true that the Germans did not pass, one needs the cynical rejoinder, invented later by boys at the front, to tell the truth about the next four years: "And neither will we."

Sarah left for Bordeaux. There a flare-up of an old knee injury, first contracted when jumping out of a stage parapet, grew so severe that it forced surgery. Sarah went into amputation almost eager for her war wound. Fantastically, not even losing a leg at the hip ended her career. She burned her wooden leg and appeared onstage in a chaise. She was again a marvel, and the public had more cause for adulation than ever. An agent for Barnum offered ten thousand dollars for the severed limb.

Sarah demanded to play for soldiers in the field, insisting on going, escort or no. The authorities set her up in a tent near the front and announced to a division of battle-shocked men, who had just spent a year under the Germans 420s, gassed, bombed by airplanes, and slaughtered by the carbines, that they were about to see the great Sarah Bernhardt perform. The soldiers watched in silence as a horribly aged woman hopped about onstage, mirroring their own mutilation, shouting out lines in the remnant of a voice once called the "Eighth Wonder of the World," a woman who could not move without extraordinary effort, bandying some ludicrous patriotic pap, refusing to believe that she was hideous, that she was not still irresistible to her old, faithful lover, the audience, and, in her obstinate refusal, forcing reality to meet her halfway. The soldiers reportedly broke out weeping, many of them calling out, "To arms!"

Badly strapped for funds, Sarah turned to that source of income she had considered little better than prostitution: she made films. Seeing these, hearing her Victrola recordings reveal the paradox of mechanical reproduction: the lens insists, "Here is her physical evidence. See how the film follows her, fits her into any viewer's world." But there is no fitting her world to ours. We are left to pick out of the reproduction the auburn mop, the other-worldly movement, to reconstruct, despite the machine, the cult of this personality, what it was that made all the world chase after this figure. But her contemporaries chased the red-haired Sarah forward in time, into the promise of a new century. We can at best chase the reproduction backward for some misunderstood resemblance.

Sarah spoke her roles for the camera, performing for the deaf machine exactly as she had done onstage, ignoring that the camera could not reproduce her glowing articulations and alexandrines. Instead, she hobbled about, making the camera follow her, enunciating each line as carefully as she would in front of a live audience. If she so much as gave a line a bad inflection, she would insist on a retake.

Sarah was the first personality of such mythic fame to leave so comprehensive a performance record. And yet the mechanically reproduced Sarahs multiply rather than reduce the ambiguity surrounding this most unpinnable of subjects. Just as Magritte added, to his hyperrealistic painting of a pipe, the painted caption *This is not a pipe*, one feels on watching Bernhardt's film *Queen Elizabeth* that this is not Sarah. It is only her tracks, an interpretation.

For three years after the war, she continued to write, lecture, and perform. She was in rehearsal when she passed into a coma. On awakening an hour later, she asked, "When do I go on?" She passed into a week-long period of semi-consciousness. Waking, she asked if there were any reporters outside. Told there were, she said, "All my life, reporters have tormented me enough. I can tease them now a little by making them cool their heels." These were her dying words. Here the legend, or the mechanically documented legend, ends.

But at the office Christmas party, where I was destined to come across so much that wasn't in the books, Mrs. Schreck, the immigrant cleaning lady, told me an extended version in a heavy accent that at several points thickened into incoherence. She told of how a relative of hers was one of those reporters cooling his heels outside the Divine Sarah's death chamber. This fellow bequeathed to his family an heirloom, repeated again and again over the years, the story of how at the eleventh hour, the Bernhardt repented of her cruelty to the gentlemen of the press waiting for word of her condition. She asked for one, chosen at random, to be brought in for an important message.

When Mrs. Schreck's cousin entered the room, he had to approach very close to the shrunken woman to hear her aspirated French. She looked up at him and asked:

—You've heard I lost a leg?

He smiled, and nodded. Then, with the air of imparting a great truth, she added:

—And yet, I still feel it there, though it was removed some years back.

With that, doctors led the reporter back to the foyer, where he was mobbed by his fellow journalists. He announced that the great actress had passed into unconsciousness, having said nothing.

This exchange is no more or less believable than the rest of Bernhardt's speculative biography. So much depends on an initial misunderstanding. Of Mrs. Schreck's cousin, I could find no documentary mention in any book on Bernhardt, nor any mention in any book on Ford, whose path he also claimed to have crossed in his role as reporter. No document remains of the fellow ever having existed except, if one allows, the photograph by Sander.

Chapter Fourteen

Conscription and Vocation

Chodounský was saying to Vaněk that in his opinion the world war was bloody nonsense.—JAROSLAV HAŠEK, *The Good Soldier Švejk*

THE FIRST TIME the two rotund gentlemen came calling at the tobacconist's widow's shop, Peter missed being arrested by the slightest of misunderstandings. It was late in September. Von Kluck's turn in front of a prostrate Paris had exposed the army flank that Adolphe would have been in had he not been skimmed for occupation duty. Gallieni and the taxicabs capitalized on the mistake, halting the German drive. The race to the Channel stalemated, and the armies of the Western Front settled in along a line that for the next four years would remain virtually unchanged except for the identities of those going over the top.

On hearing the bell to the shop door, Peter, who could dress faster than the widow, came out front. There, two old friends of apoplexy stood huffing and puffing and speaking in tongues. On seeing Peter, they produced a parody of High Dutch, which they flushed out with a variety of inventive hand gestures. Peter, too amused by the spectacle, failed to tell the fellows that he spoke German like the citizen he was.

Making sense of the fellows' performance was the most fun Peter had had since the war started. Under the influence of an initial misunderstanding, he soon solved the riddle of their primitive

Dutch. The pair circled back again and again on the same key-words: *zoon*, which, though pronounced with two syllables, could only mean "son," and *neet waar*, perhaps a quaint rendition of "false." He recognized the name Schreck only after some while, having slid back into the habit of being called Kinder since his return to Holland.

Having arrived at these clues, it was but a small leap for Peter to piece together the gist of the round fellows' concern: fake Schreck son. He let out a burst of air, part laugh, part aha.

—That would be Hubert Minuit, or Schreck, as you gents have him. I thought he might have the law after him. You can find him at his friend Willy Hoven's house on Schunk Straat. But be careful. They're both communist lunatics, as I'm sure you're already aware.

The interviewers, relieved at having made communication at last, forgot to be irritated at this sudden burst of fluent German. They thanked Peter, laughing at his warning. One, mopping at the water that sprang from the red splotches of his face, spoke an idiom the earthy equivalent of "naturally": "Thanks for telling us our pants are soiled."

As Peter turned back into the shop and began telling the to-bacconist's widow about the transaction, he wondered if what he had just done qualified as denouncement. He supposed it did, and felt a little sad at having betrayed Hub without intending to. Intent, it seemed, had little to do with cruelty. He stopped in front of a tin of loose pipe weed and spoke, to no one:

—So Hub has gone and gotten himself in serious trouble. I knew he would.

And he thought no more about denouncement until two days later, when the Bavarians returned. This time, he was out of the shop on an errand. The men took up their search with the widow, but she was less adept at the word-salad game than Peter. She refused to understand German and could make no sense of the High Dutch the men mangled. She refused to communicate in anything but the provincial Plaat dialect.

The twin Central European megaliths took to pantomime to make their point. First, one of them pointed a thick finger at the widow's breast and shook his head no, to indicate they were not looking for a woman. The widow thought her tits had offended them in some way. Too bad, she responded. Then the other fellow held his finger under his nose, symbolizing moustaches and, thereby, manhood. Now Peter could no more grow a moustache than could an infant. The widow had no opportunity to be confused by this, however, as she had already pieced together the conclusion that the two strangers were allergic to her breasts.

One German rolled his way behind the cash counter. The widow, in a fit, thought he meant to rob the till. Instead, the men began miming a dialogue between what was now clearly themselves and Peter. The one playing Peter made a comment that the other objected to strongly. The latter clapped the surrogate shopkeeper by the wrist and made a show of dragging him off. Then he made the universally familiar and recognizable gesture of shooting.

The tobacconist's widow yelped pitifully. The proceedings suddenly became clear. The veil was torn from her eyes. Peter, playing one of his endless pranks on the customers, had insulted these clients and they had come back to kill him. In this interpretation she was not far from the truth. She began chattering a steady stream of pseudo-German, ushering the beefsteaks to the door.

—Now you two sweethearts get along. Important folk like yourselves have weightier stuff to attend to. I'll give the young scoundrel what's coming to him, be sure of that. He'll be so bloody he won't be able to sit down for a week. Imagine getting saucy with caliber gentlemen. Good day, friends. Here's a smoke. Off now, and come back at week's end for the satisfaction of seeing the lad on crutches by my own hand.

She thought that by speaking loudly and inanely, nodding her head rapidly the while, that she could make the men understand her. Feeble and foreign had always meant about the same to her. By making them think she was on their side, she could trick them out of the shop and all would be well and all manner of things would be well.

But the Bavarians were not to be so easily dealt with. One struggled with the widow, resisting expulsion. The other restrained him with a shrewd look, considering the international ramifications of such scuffling. Instead, the men set up a checkpoint just outside the shop door. Here they scrutinized every client that entered. They flattened their faces against the glass and peered into the store, leaving a cratered battlefield of Bavarian greased nose prints on the pane.

As the day went on, the widow grew thankful for the boy's compulsive prodigality. Aware of the fat Germans lying in ambush, the widow prayed for the very behavior she had tried to beat out of Peter. At best, she hoped he had taken the errand money from that morning and drunk it down, passing out in a ditch somewhere. If Peter came back and the rotund gentlemen killed him, her shop would fold, she'd be pauperized, and worse, she'd have to train another man from scratch to play the sex game as well as the boy did.

When the sun went down, the Bavarians, evidently tired, hungry, and irritated, began arguing. The impatient one managed to convince the plodding one that they should break siege. Before they left for the night, however, one of them stuck his head in the shop and let off a last high-speed, mimed rifle burst. This much was at least unambiguous: they would be back.

It was well past eleven when the returning Peter at last made the shop bell jingle. He went straight back to the rear rooms where he and the widow lived, a broad, disarming grin across his equine face.

—Sorry about the delay, old woman. Those things you sent me after this morning were damn hard to find. But I'll tell you what, you old witch. They must have been damn easy to lose, because I sure as hell don't have them with me now!

His laugh might have been Hubert's horselaugh, childish and out of control but wisened up by the world. The widow, relieved of her daylong wait for catastrophe, was so punch-drunk that the laughing infected her as well. She laughed violently, thinking how this unscrupulous boy had a knack for nearly missing disaster, by always making the other fellow look foolish. She thought of the fat Bavarians waiting all day to kill this tramp, and laughed until she worried about bursting a blood vessel. Decency dictated that she tell him what was so hysterical. She managed to get the words out between explosions of spittle.

—Two men came by today to shoot you.

She and Peter set off again, laughing out of control.

—I know that, you old cow. Why do you think I was so late coming home? I watched them from across the way at The Spoon. Six hours.

This triggered another round of hilarity. The Spoon was a one-room dive that should have been called The Glass. The image of Peter downing beer after beer, aping the German garrison for the public benefit of The Spoon's patrons was more than the widow could stand. When she stopped to catch her breath, she managed to ask:

—What did you do to get those muttons so worked up? Shit in their sheets?

—Do, hell. They came by the other day. I thought they wanted my brother Hubie. Don't believe it, mother. I'm their boy. And I haven't done piss to them.

The widow cackled off again, now out of force of habit. The boy had a wonderful way of swearing, saying it as if he'd just invented it in his own mouth. She gasped and signaled him impatiently to go on.

—I thought I'd had done with those pork rolls. But when I round the corner this afternoon, who should be waiting for sweet Petje but your friends Mr. and Mrs. Matterhorn. So I duck into The Spoon to collect my thoughts. Heh. Two beers later, it hits me: fake Schreck son. That's me, too. These fellows have come to escort me to their war.

—War? Yee-God. What are you saying?

The woman performed a ritual that began as a sign of the cross and ended as a warding-off of the Evil Eye. She had planned, these last two months, on outliving the war, ignoring it until it went away. Now the boy had ruined that chance by speaking the word right here in her own home. Well, the place was due for a sweeping and disinfecting anyway. She would do it tomorrow.

—What's this about the . . . what you said. You're Dutch. You don't got to go to nobody else's war. You stay here. I need you behind the counter. You're Dutch. You're neutered.

—German, mother. Blood doesn't matter when you sign the papers.

—*Ach!* Papers will burn. Let them fight their own war.

—Not a bad idea. Stand them side by side, and they'll cover the whole front from Paris to Switzerland, with britches to spare.

—You don't go to no war, Petje. I tell you that much.

—I don't go to *any* war.

—What's this, Aristotle come back from the dead to wee on me? Six years of school and you're correcting your elders. I'll tell you why you don't have to go off to nobody's war.

—Why is that, woman?

—Because they *kill* people there, that's why. That illegalizes any papers you might have put your name to.

All trace of hilarity had drained out of the widow. Her eyes had become saucer-wide with her last pronouncement. What she had just said, apart from the anarchic grammar, seemed to Peter the unimpeachably logical credo under which the world should run. They both sat silent for a moment, transfigured by this bottom line of sanity. The only way they could hope to preach this gospel was to sneak him out of town.

After the war, the Kaiser would seek asylum in Holland. And in spite of having spent the last four years fearing daily for its survival, the little country refused to extradite the fellow to the victors. But in the autumn of 1914, before the national states of Europe entrenched themselves in political cynicism, the same policy of noninvolvement meant that Holland would not prevent German citizens from themselves being extradited. The widow turned to the task of packing a sack lunch for the boy's escape the next day: three chocolate sandwiches, a Dutch national food, and the only lunch Peter would eat.

As she worked, she puzzled over not feeling the requisite sorrow for such a sad occasion. The boy was invaluable to her, if not professionally, at least personally. She supposed she cared for him; he amused her tremendously. They were always laughing about something, laughing until they rotted. Mostly, she had gotten used to him. New habits would take so long to develop after he was gone.

But she did not feel sorrow. When she reminded herself of the seriousness of the situation, how in all likelihood she would never see the boy again, rather than recalling all the morose unhappiness of her past—the death of her husband, who had always treated her so well and to whose memory she had in a peculiar way remained faithful; the amputation in childhood of a favorite sister's leg at the knee; the loss of a loved goat to one of the first motorcars in Maastricht—she could remember instead only those habits of hers that she would now have to change. And in considering those outrageous, ludicrous, and often unspeakable habits, she could not help but snicker as she split the rolls and inserted the bars of chocolate.

She had learned this feeling many times before, learned it and lost it with each passing tragedy: war, global emergency never seemed so urgent as some stray, unrelated, insignificant memory. She'd learned it when, led from her husband's death chamber, she grew distressed over a spot of oil smudging her newly purchased widow's weeds. She forgot and relearned it at each local catastrophe: the private self never meets crisis appropriately.

And as she buttered and cut the sandwich bread, she snorted again and felt that such distraction was not so bad a thing. Where are joy and understanding, those first weak steps toward responsibility, except in public tragedy always being interrupted by the self's secret healing potions? She stuck the sandwiches into a paper sack along with a fifty-guilder note. Without knowing what she did, even as she forgot all that had just occurred to her, she lifted the sack to her lips and kissed it.

Peter left the widow's shop before dawn on a modicum of sleep. The normally resourceful farmer, now at a loss without hat or cane, set off for another dance entirely. Uncertain how to proceed, he made his way with little difficulty across the street and into The Spoon. That was as far as he got that day.

He sat at the bar and greeted the perennials by name, smiling at what a poor escape he was making. He attempted the difficult task of choosing between two headstones that delighted him equally: "He died bending an elbow," and "Say what you want, but he was a sociable fellow." In the end, he decided to leave to chance what words commemorated him, as he wouldn't be able to read them from his viewing angle anyway.

The Bavarians appeared at the shop forty minutes after Peter's departure. The Spoon's front window gave a good view of their activity. They banged in Teutonic rhythms on the door, but the widow was shrewd and refused to open. The cheer went up in The Spoon:

—Good for the old cigarmonger!

Then one Bavarian called the other's attention to a sign hanging on the shop door. The widow, disliking the finality of a "Closed" sign, always used one reading: "Patience. We'll be back before the hour's out." Peter hung this message on the door each evening at close. Patrons seemed to find it wholly palatable. But then, the Dutch did not have the long tradition of dialectical imperative that the Germans had.

The loyal covey of predawn Spoon customers watched the two agents with morbid fascination. In only a few short years, the public had become trained in how to watch such silent, jerky, comic *mise en scène*. The Spoon clientele recognized at once the fat-comedian duos who pratfell their way through so many one-reelers, already universally popular on the Continent: first A kicks B on the rump. Then B falls on oversized nose. B stands up to take a poke at A. A ducks and B slugs wall. Reaction take. It would go on like clockwork. Only the Spoon clientele missed, a little, the title cards.

—What do you suppose they're saying, Petje?

—The bright fellow is saying to his buddy, "Look. Says here they'll be back in an hour. We've got ourselves an infantryman."

—Hooray! They've got poor Kinder now.

The predawn gate at The Spoon, though small, was tremendous, given the hour. Much of Maastricht apparently was used to showing up for the whistle slightly oiled. In Limburg, beer was the first of medicines, administered even to infants and the dying. In spite of The Spoon's high spirits, Peter grew increasingly despondent as his friends finished their beers and filed out, wishing him well. He could not hope to outlast the two thugs. If he continued to spend the widow's legacy at the current rate, he'd be forced to turn himself in by noon.

It was in this condition of increasing self-pity and decreasing capital reserve that Peter was befriended by the gentleman Theo Langerson. Those with steady jobs had long ago left Peter and the bartender alone, one washing dishes, the other dirtying them. Periodically, a beat policeman, the girl Wies's father, stuck his head inside, ostensibly to keep the peace but actually for the half glass that had become his due at such times.

After noon, Theo entered The Spoon and established himself, as morosity commonly did, within earshot. Soon he and Peter, hardly introduced, had struck up a competitive game of "So you think you have troubles." Theo opened conservatively.

—What's it with you, *karel*? Whatever it is, it must be at least interesting. You are plainly too young to be worrying about getting it up, and you still have all the hair you were born with.

—Go suck.

—Really upset, eh, chump? The clap, is it?

—What is this, the Inquisition?

—As a fellow sufferer, I'm out to prove my moral superiority over all comers, or at very least to derive a sense of comfort from there being saps worse off than myself. So you see how a man like you, obviously in agony, is obliged to aid my condition, one way or the other.

—You? Problems? Your wife cold-fishing you, more than likely.

—I assure you, friend . . .

—Can you blame her?

—. . . that nothing so mundane . . .

—You've heard of prostitutes? They'll fix your moral superiority for a few guilder.

—Ha! If only that were it. No, *karel*, I'm afraid my superiority is somewhat more moral than that.

—What then? You were in an auto accident, yes? Now your friends won't go drinking with you because you talk funny, and you have to take your morality out on strangers.

—You're no stranger, child. We're fellow sufferers.

Theo meant to invoke the bond of pain only ironically. But his use of the word "child"—*kind* in Dutch—misheard by Peter as his old surname, shocked the boy into thinking that they had already met, probably introduced by common friends at The Spoon. The other fellow, assuming Peter had recognized him, must have been carrying out the entire conversation facetiously.

That changed the complexion of the situation entirely. Peter had now to play along, be better humored, pretend the whole prelude had been a put-on, and try to trick the man into revealing his name. For the all-important line had been crossed; Peter no longer dealt with a stranger he could abuse anonymously. The two now bore, in Peter's mind, the mutual responsibility of having been introduced to one another.

—Have your victory, friend. Since you'd drag it out of me, I'll give you a hint about my troubles. I'm being tortured by the G-E-R-M-A-I-N-S.

Theo winced at the spelling and took two slugs of beer. When he was this boy's age, he had nursed a dream about free public education through the twelfth grade. That had been some time ago.

—Ah! Point two that we have in common. Strange country, that; in the name of Bach and Kant, they torch the library at Louvain.

Peter wished he could place this stranger. He had once had a conversation with a gentleman who spoke much like this. The philosopher on the bicycle. That was long ago, before the world had turned heels-up. That conversation had been in Germany, in German. He moved his stool closer to the other fellow and listened.

—Am I to understand that you are suffering in the abstract? That you are being "tortured," as you so colorfully put it, by basic human indignity at the behavior of the Germans as a nation? That would be remarkable indeed. I can hardly believe that you've been tanking since early morning out of principle.

—Principle, hell. Bismarck and the Kaiser are waiting on my doorstep to take me on a vacation *en France*.

—Bravo. I knew there had to be personal involvement somewhere. We become more closely related all the time. But it seems I cannot claim the more serious suffering after all. To escape my creditors, all I need do is quit my job. But to escape yours it sounds as if you must quit your home, your friends, and, no doubt, your pretty little wife.

Peter had a healthy laugh at the last article. The fellow must not know him after all; they could not have met in some Spoon extravagance because these always contained a surfeit of rude jokes about Peter and the tobacconist's widow. Absolved of the duty of friendship, Peter could go back to his normal condition of cheerful cruelty.

To make up for lost time, he began by suggesting that half a million men would have leaped at the chance to quit their jobs before the Miracle of the Marne; if all the gentleman faced was debtors' prison, he'd best shut his jaws and be content with a relative heaven.

Theo protested; the "debt" he had mentioned was figurative.

Until two days ago, he had held down a safe and guilt-free position as journalist with a paper recognized by Peter as one of Maastricht's smaller dailies. For the last year, Theo explained, his job had been to sit behind a lovely teak desk and ghostwrite editorials for his alcoholic editor. In this capacity he had championed a thousand progressive causes: universal suffrage, land reform, mass production, minimum wage.

—Naturally, in recent months I've spilled more and more words on the outbreak of hostilities. Nothing like a good free-for-all to boost circulation. All speculation, you understand; by the time the news travels from the front to my beautiful teakwood, it's worse than hearsay—it's hopeless interpretation. That's where the editor comes in. Friday, the word is the British are in. Saturday, word comes they're out. Who to believe? Not important; I simply do a sidestep and crank out a masterpiece beginning: "While the world decides its future, can His Majesty and Lord Kitchener afford to abstain?" I don't have to bother with the facts at all.

Peter ordered another glass and counted his remaining change. He could not follow this journalist: had the bastard made his point already, or was he still winding up to it? Either way, it did not touch on his own problem, all he had ears for at present. Still, Peter had long ago learned the habit of keeping quiet and giving off the air of omniscience.

—But now the higher-ups have decided that the public will not go another two months on editorials alone. Our readers must have facts, they say. Ha! Can you imagine? A newspaper stooping to collecting facts. I tried to argue: we in the Netherlands have to sit tight and keep our hands clean. The minute we go about poking our observant noses into the matter, we are involved. And there is no involvement without complicity.

Peter produced a sucking noise on the roof of his mouth. He clung to the disk of his barstool and tried not to let any part of his body touch anything else. A recent conversation on fingerprints he'd had here in The Spoon left him panicked about the marks his body made wherever he went. As this fellow piled up words in front of him, Peter began to feel that if he deviated even slightly from the narrow arm movement that brought his glass to his chin, he would be drawn into involvement with the man's story.

—They can't be bothered with such petty objections. Instead, they search through the office for the ideal war correspondent, and naturally, their sights land on me. My editorials, be they ever so speculative, qualify me as the staffer with most experience in war reportage. So I give you Theo Langerson, off to the front, humbly reporting for duty. Drink to me, will you, mason?

At this conclusion, Peter began to laugh so violently that beer began to run up his nasal passages. The long and short was that he and Theo were in the same jam. Why hadn't the fellow said so at once? Peter immediately liked the man several times better for it. He forced the beer back down his throat, and in his old winning insolence, suggested:

—So bloody what? You tell those news bosses to eat a sausage. Then you take a walk and find some honest work.

—Absolutely, young man. *Sans doute*. And you, for yourself, can thumb your nose at the Huns, pack a passel of clean shirts, and set up house in some other town.

—But where would I go? Who'd take me on? I've no papers; I'm no good for anything but light farming and selling pipe smoke. I'd be in a gutter in three days. Anyway, the Hun would be onto me after a while, no matter where.

—My point exactly. I ask myself: I'm supposed to change my habits just because it's Armageddon?

—But it's not so bad for you. You'd be with the press. That's safety; a paid holiday. They can't shoot someone with press papers.

—Unfortunately, they don't always check your papers before shooting. Then there's fire, and falling masonry, and artillery shells. I've done a little calculating, in fact . . .

Theo pulled out of his mantle pocket a soiled sheet of scribblings. He began to explain his mathematics to Peter, who, after the first log, was left in the woods. Theo claimed to have figured out, with an exactitude remarkable in one without firsthand facts, his chances of being hurt as a reporter at the front if the war lasted another six months, as some extremists were now saying it would. He had proved, with floating statistics, a 17 percent chance of his being wounded and a 9 percent chance of his being killed. His countenance took on an editorial gravity.

—Clearly unacceptable risks, you see.

Peter did not see. Compared with his own odds, which he now gauged at somewhere well past certain death, 9 percent seemed a gambler's land of milk and honey. He refused to involve himself in other men's quarrels. But no other course freed him from being hounded into an active role at the front.

—I should be blessed with your problem.

It took the men half an hour more of the moral-superiority game to realize that in that statement lay both their salvations. The only place in the involved world where Peter could hope to escape being drafted was the front. Theo could only escape the burden of first-hand observation as he had always done: by sending a proxy in his place.

The two arrived at the idea at the same time, as if the climate and not their individual genius made for discovery. Then they went about systematically working out the details and addressing each other's objections.

—How will I pass for you?

—Easy: take my credentials, press gear, and la! Theo Two. No one in France would recognize me. You have only to fool a few officials, and being fooled is their vocation. I'm more worried about what I'm to do with myself. I can't very well go back home and abroad at the same time. The world is only beginning to accustom itself to absurdity, and my neighbors wouldn't be ready for that.

—Stay with the widow. She's on the prod patrol anyway. It won't be long. Three weeks of machine guns, everyone will be dead, and we can all go home. Stay in the shop, across the street. There's space, and even a fellow like yourself can learn how to stand behind a counter. But how am I to learn to write dispatches?

Peter fell back into morosity. The impossibility of the proposed switch came on him, and he saw the situation too lucidly to pretend it would work. Yet in arriving at this conclusion, he'd left out the variable of necessity. He had learned to be a Schreck, a Kinder, too, for that matter. He could do for a Langerson, under fire.

—Reporting? Nothing to it. Just put everything you have to say in the first sentence: who, what, when, where. . . . One more: what's that last one? Anyway, just write what you see, or what you can get people to tell you. Get as many proper names as you can: place-names, weapons, heads of staff. Count everything, and measure everything else. Write down any unusual words. When there's no news, get the nearest foot soldier's story. When you get a few pages, send them to me, care of your widow. I'll doctor them and get them to the paper.

Peter saluted, military style. This dress-up game had definite possibilities.

—Of course, your letters will have to pass the army censors. So to give them the air of credibility, at least for the time being, you can leave out the "i" in "Germain."

—What? Let me make a note of that. Who are you? What's today? Where are we?

—Good enough. How are your languages, by the way?

—Speak-ee the Dutch like a native, humbly report, sir.

—I mean foreign. How's your German?

—Why do you think they're drafting me?

—French?

Peter released a salvo of pursed-lipped *"lunes"* and *"soleils"* that reduced them both to hops-induced tears.

Having satisfied himself on all counts that the change of identities, if not plausible, represented his only way out of responsibility, Theo left to secure the necessary documents of transfer. Besides cards and credentials, he found the boy a notebook and pen: at least give him a nudge in the right direction. He also produced a winter coat and more cash than the boy had ever seen in one place. Theo had little hope for the success of the venture, but it beat the alternative.

The Spoon filled with the old regulars, stopping in after work. In twenty minutes, Peter trained all his friends to call him and think of him as Theo.

Chapter Fifteen

The Biographical Fallacy

There are people indeed—and this has been my case from
my childhood—for whom all the things that have a fixed value,
assessable by others, fortune, success, high positions, do not
count; what they must have, is phantoms.—MARCEL PROUST,
Remembrance of Things Past

OUTSIDE the Your Move Theatre, an enormous newsprint poster
bore a larger-than-life reproduction of Kimberly Greene dressed
as Sarah Bernhardt in her one-woman show, *I Dwell in Possibility*.
To the right of the enlarged photo, critics from all Boston's larger
papers joined unanimously in proclaiming the stage act to be the
most important thing since penicillin. Mays regarded the testimonials, trying to restore to the laudatory sentences all those words
that had been surgically replaced by ellipses.

He felt like an anthropologist, piecing together an entire pro-
tohuman skull from half an inch of jawbone. "Compelling. . . .
Arresting. . . . I was stunned . . .," Mays thought might have
first appeared in print as "By compelling me to go to this so-called
performance, my editor caused me to miss the simple pleasure of
staying home and getting stewed. Arresting Ms. Greene would be
a public service. I was stunned that such a racket could escape the
Better Business Bureau." " . . . One of the best shows of the season. . . . You must see it. . . . A piece . . . to keep you enthralled . . ." could originally have been "As a self-respecting
member of the press, I can call this one of the best shows of the

— 189 —

season, providing the appropriate persons send the usual amount to Box 35B, Boston Station. If you must see it, bring along a piece of string to keep you enthralled during the second and third acts." Anything could be made to mean anything given enough ellipses.

If his expectations for the show were slight, if he had become openly hostile to the idea of *I Dwell in Possibility*, it was because of how public the object of his obsession had become. He had walked past the giant marquee perhaps two dozen times since the Veterans' Day Parade, and he had never once associated the larger-than-life document with the three-inch antique redhead in his memory. His blindness was that of children playing the game of Find the Word on the Map: the first child might keep the second one looking an hour for the tiny C-O-M of Combrai, but she herself may never find the E-U-R of Europe, not thinking to look for something so large. The obvious, not the obscure, always gave Mays the most trouble.

Kimberly Greene, if the photograph reproduced her accurately, was even more offensively attractive than Mays had imagined. If he had gotten a good look at those high cheekbones and hazel eyes from his eighth-story window, he would never have taken on the search. An obsession, however difficult, must have some chance of success if it is to raise desire. Seeing her now, posted so publicly, made him lose almost all desire he had once felt to track her down. The dialogues he had practiced in private for the moment of denouement and mythical meeting now caused him acute embarrassment that he could only hope would fade in the weeks to come. Curiosity had gone from the affair. The only shred of dramatic interest left in his life lay in whether Miss Stark, whom he had actually had the temerity to invite to see the show with him, would turn up.

Yet every time he looked down the street for a sign of Miss Stark, he looked up again at the enlarged image of Ms. Greene. More properly, he looked at Sarah Bernhardt, at the curious compromise of the two, their divvying up and occupying the same body. Seeing for a moment the two-at-once, he felt all the force of the old mystery: not red hair, but paradox; not present beauty, but the hint of some past debt.

Panic descended like Pentecost when he saw Miss Stark approaching the theater from down the block. He had one hundred yards to recall her first name, which he'd had the foresight to get from her before leaving the lost era of The Trading Floor. He thought dimly that it began with A-L, and he suspected it played heavily on "I"s and "S"s. He ran through the permutations of A-L-I-S female names—Alice, Alicia, Annalise. Names, words, letters, and sounds were not his strong suit. He suspected his brain was dominated by its nonverbal hemisphere, except that analytical quantities terrified him equally. As A-L, and perhaps I-S, Stark bore down on him, he remembered a favorite maxim of Delaney's: those who can't do become reporters, those who can't do or say become editors, and those who can't do, say, or comprehend become technical editors.

But in the last few paces of Miss Stark's approach, his anxiety gave way to fascination as he noticed a quality in the woman's walk. Looking now at Mays, now at the pavement, now randomly about herself in exploration of the theater district, Miss Stark, decidedly un-Edwardian in jeans and a loose-neck wool sweater, approached with all the easy, practical grace of an untrained dancer. She moved with a delightful self-consciousness, as if she had direct knowledge of every colony of her body.

The transformation from lace to denim, her mock-sheepish look at having shown up for this off-the-cuff invitation, her obvious enjoyment of the situation's novelty, and not least of all, her beat-up oxfords' syncopated attack on the sidewalk combined to create in Mays a sensation he had not felt in months, a sensation beginning, he intuited, with A-P-P-R: apprehend, apprentice, approaching, appreciation. That was it. Appreciation.

Gratitude joined appreciation when Miss Stark, saving Mays from a potential fix, sallied up, saluted, and said:

—Alison Stark at your disposal. The enemy is some distance off, and it seems safe to take some brief entertainment.

—At ease, shoulder.

Before Mays could redden over his slip of the tongue, Alison laughed and drew in her collar in mock propriety.

—Have you bought tickets yet?

—No. I wasn't sure if you'd show.

—Good. They're on me. I've come into an inheritance.

She pulled out the twenty-five dollars from Bullock's tip, adding:
—Do your parents know you're dishing out this kind of money?
—Listen, that wasn't mine. That fellow I was with has this tipping system . . .
—Sure, what do you think I am, naïve? You're trying to buy my affections, aren't you?

She struck a pose faintly reminiscent of Horatio at the Bridge:
—Well, it can't be done for a cent less than fifty.

As she went to the ticket booth, it occurred to Mays that what had just transpired was good humor.

They took their seats. The sound of shuffling as the audience waited for the curtain gave Mays motion sickness. The opulent, dim house, the half arcs of seats reminded him of the endless concerts he had attended while the search was still on. Preconcert excitement always nauseated him. He had the distinct impression that all around him, people had smuggled in pocket scores to follow during the performance, letting out gasps of indignation if the orchestra so much as bent the definitive text. Those concerts had only been made bearable by the hope of red hair. But certainty had a way of doing in hope, and now he hadn't even that to buffer him from audience anxiety.

The atmosphere in the Your Move Theatre seemed even more gladiatorial than usual. This was a one-woman show—the height of virtuosity—and the fans could smell blood. Mays ticked off all the reasons he could think of why people would come to these things. Some burned off excess income. Some, giving up on the hopes of promotion up the corporate ladder, looked to the theater as another arena. Some, as Bullock would say, came out because yet another evening with the dinner dishes, television, and cards would prove positively fatal.

Looking over the gallery, Mays concluded that most people who came to the theater did so because it met all the requirements of what bygone eras had called "hobbies": it was expensive, it produced nothing useful, and it killed time. The problem with getting by was no longer that life was nasty, brutish, and short. Lately, the difficulty was that life had become comfy, ghoulish, and long.

Alison sat down next to him matter-of-factly. Mays thought he had never before seen anyone so totally at ease. He suspected at first that her calm was an illusion produced in comparison to his own discomfort. But no; her body fused into her chair, filling the contours familiarly. Mays's vertigo lessened when he looked at her. After reading over every square inch of her program, even the fine print and disclaimers, she began folding it into irregular polygons. Noticing Mays's eyes on her, she looked up and explained:

—I'm regressing.

In seconds, with a few deft twists, tucks, and topological upheavals, she transformed the printed program into one of those graceful Japanese folded figures—a swan or egret or heron, some near-extinct wildfowl neither of them would ever see. She held the bird by the throat and pulled its tail. The paper wings flapped in an imitation of flight.

Still flapping, Alison began making guttural noises—a motor revving up—and all at once tossed the bird several feet in the air. It came down three rows in front of them, on a veteran concert-going *grande dame*, who singled them out for an executioner's stare. Under her breath, Alison whispered:

—God*damn* it, Orville. I thought you said we had it this time.

Mays laughed. Without thinking of what he was doing, he leaned over, lifted the hair off the back of her neck, and touched his lips there. He sat up and did his best unknown-soldier disappearing act, thinking that might help him escape the consequences. Off to the side, he heard Alison saying:

—I'll give you a quarter if you do that again.

It didn't seem fair; people were supposed to have to pay for well-being like hers. Mays asked her about her job, dressing up and waiting on the movers and shakers at The Trading Floor. Alison answered as if it were the first time she'd ever been asked about the matter.

—Well, I used to be a Catholic, but I found I could get all the suffering I needed by going in to work. It's like this. When I first started, for three days I got a kick out of how lovely the place was, the old outfit, and all. Erotic, you know? Dreamy. After that wore off, for about three weeks I took pride in being a professional, knowing where the gravy boat went, which fork went on the outside, what not to say. When that went, for the next three years I was able to content myself with going home and counting my tips, stacking the coins in piles and figuring how far I was from the next hundred. A sexy element to that too, I suppose. But that ran out. Now I'm looking for the trick that will divert me for the next three decades.

Mays knew of no such trick, so he kept silent. Alison sat silent too, but not yet sullen. After a few seconds' thought, she volunteered:

—It's not the place, so much. The place is peculiar, but nothing that can't be worked around. It's the psycho customers. My job is to care for them when I can't really *care* for them. At least, not beyond basic human kindness. They're all basket cases. You can't serve them dinner without them going to pieces on you. They all want to involve you in elaborate drama. Like Mr. Krakow, the old guy you rescued me from. He comes in every other day, dressed like Old Vienna, with this endless story about bomb shelters and camps and a wife who I'm supposed to reproduce perfectly. Must be the costume: anything from that era. I can wait on him. I can even listen to him. I won't send him away, because I *do* care for him. But as a fellow human, not as a long-lost, dead wife. There are too many of them to serve as long-lost wife for each.

Alison drew up short, aware that she was now asking of Peter the same involvement she denied her customers. She bunched her nose.

—Don't mind me. Just bring me another sherry and the check. It's my own fault, I suppose. I insisted in majoring in Liberal Arts. History. I was told a thousand times that the degree would be worthless. You see, I had this crazy notion that being interested was reason enough to study a thing. If I were doing it over, though, I'd let interest go hang. I'd get some salable credentials. I'd get myself a technical background. Computers.

She pronounced the word as if to distinguish it from "commuters."

—Say, what do *you* do? For a living, I mean. You're obviously not a broker, or I'd never have agreed to meet you here.

The sudden strains of a Protestant hymn saved Mays from the embarrassment of answering. A good part of the audience turned around in their seats, trying to see the spinet and bellows that produced the hymn. Both Alison and Peter, however, raised on such

deceptions, kept face forward as the house lights dimmed, intu-
itively aware that the music was piped in.

Another instant explained the choice of tune. Solo in center
stage stood Kimberly Greene, in nineteenth-century dress, her hair
somehow darkened and pulled back in New England severity. The
program identified the first tableau as Emily Dickinson. Greene
began what would be a two-hour monologue in twenty voices with
the unassuming couplet:

> I dwell in possibility,
> A fairer house than prose.

And there in front of him was that magnificent, elusive item
that had lasted longer and done more to give a significance and
sense of purpose to Mays's days than any material interest, the object that had buzzed memory's reed, that had seemed the one
mysterious motive in an otherwise smothering routine of security.
He could see the very woman, not fifty feet in front of him. She
looked smaller in person.

Having Alison next to him for the last half hour had kept him
temporarily free from the recursive loop of speculation. Conversation had kept him honest, absorbed. But when the curtain went
up, there was no more hiding. As in a fundamentalist's view of
the Last Judgment, his vanity, compulsions, and peccadilloes had
all been permanently recorded, mechanically reproduced—not, as
the too-literal had it, on celluloid but in the fleshy record of an
actress's body—and he would be forced to watch every incriminating nuance.

In all his fantasies about finding the distant woman, Mays had
never given the redhead a voice. Speeches, yes; long, well-re-
hearsed conversations. But he had never created a quality of voice
to go with the words. Now here she was, speaking. In fact, as the
introvert from Amherst, almost all she did was speak. She went
stage right to a prop desk, sat, and spoke as she mimed writing
letters. She went stage left and gazed through a prop window,
speaking a description of an imaginary scene. She stepped forward
in front of the proscenium and spoke both parts of a mock dialogue. Mays felt at a loss to explain how a contemporary audience

could watch a contemporary actress play a historical figure mim- ing a dialogue for the benefit of an imagined future audience.

Kimberly Greene's round, professional periods rolled into every nook of the hall, and Hearing, the most abstract of senses, was the agent of Mays's shame. There was no more imagined antique figure, limping upstream against the parade. By speaking, Greene had unfolded herself as Greene.

Not that Mays heard much of what the woman actually *said*. He jerked out of his thoughts long enough to hear Miss Dickinson threaten to "pull society up by its roots and plant it in another place." He stayed attentive through the start of another quatrain:

> I never saw a moor,
> I never saw the sea,

but drifted in attention after these two lines.

As he watched this striking figure go through her stage act, he felt himself coming down with the stomach flu, symptoms of a bad conscience: he had forgotten to do something, or had done something he'd vowed not to. He was unwilling to let go, altogether, of the antique image despite the physical evidence of Ms. Greene. Hoping to clear his head and settle his stomach, he jabbed out impulsively and took Alison's hand. She started at his touch, but did not object.

Kimberly Greene's performance formula was simple and elegant. She appeared in the rough guise of an important, though sometimes little-known, female personality of the last hundred years. She'd speak a pastiche of the figure's written and reported words, starting and ending vigorously, encouraging the audience by her delivery to imagine that they were unobtrusive observers at the event.

Finishing each characterization, she would disappear from the darkened stage, replaced in the interlude by period music and photographs projected onto a back screen. Then she would reappear center stage in another role. The women replaced one another in gradual, chronological order. Aside from the technical considerations of projecting the photographs—images charged with the politics and privations of the century—the production was remarkably subdued. It made no attempt to outseduce film or TV. The show employed few props, hardly any set, modest changes of lighting, and no theatrical tricks.

In place of the thrill of being a spectator at an extravaganza, the audience at this chamber piece had only the lurid satisfaction of eavesdropping, of being a near-participant at an intimate affair. Most professional and amateur critics could not understand how such an understated show remained running while vastly more entertaining and lavish spectacles opened and closed a week later. The show was closer to dry essay than good drama. Its success could only be attributed to the phenomenon of Kimberly Greene.

Mays, for one, felt as if he were back in school. When Emily Dickinson disappeared and returned as Susan B. Anthony, he felt the old, cold, creeping anxiety of accountability. At the end of the last act, the ushers would collect all the programs and administer a multiple-choice exam on each character's contribution to history. He'd have to sit through repeated showings until he scored a 90 percent or better.

It had been some time since Peter had learned anything aside from the variations on a tneme he came across at work. At twenty-one, Mays decided that he no longer had time to learn anything new except what he absolutely needed to survive. But as any eighty-year-old can attest, that amounts to little more than how to cross the street without being hit by a car. Now he regretted his practical economy. He suspected that the only way he could rid himself of his fixation with the redhead wraith and appease his stomach (only temporarily abated by his latching onto Alison's hand) was to commit to memory the least action of these women moving across the stage.

By intermission, they had had, besides Dickinson and Anthony, Mrs. Pankhurst, Gertrude Stein, Emily Davison (the suffragette photographed throwing herself under the King's horse at Epsom, having said, "The cause needs a tragedy"), Marie Curie, Isadora Duncan, and Edith Cavell. This last dramatization took place entirely in a Belgian cell in 1915 as Nurse Cavell waited to be shot by the Germans (*fusillé par les Allemands*). By the time she mimed being led away, Greene-Cavell managed to say, "Patriotism is not enough." And Mays had arrived at an idea that would not leave him alone.

The precision of Greene's performance, its antique perfection, led Mays to three distinct notions. First, the entr'acte photographs—anarchists in coffins, colonials in Africa, dreadnoughts in drydock, revolutionaries in St. Petersburg, rioters in Chicago, doughboys in Flanders—allowed only one clear interpretation. The theme of the infant century was violence. But second, for whatever the last hundred years had done poorly, it had also begun—perhaps too slowly and fitfully—the restoration of half the race. His third idea, still in embryo, derived from Nurse Cavell's speech. He had far to go before he could articulate it so neatly, but it ran something like: no existence independent of others.

Greene's last vignette before intermission was her most virtuosic. Entering the stage as a youthful Sarah Bernhardt, she elicited a general gasp of appreciation for her now-unrestrained good looks and grace. The Bernhardt incarnation was drenched in sex and sensuality and self-possession, the animal beauty of a panther or constrictor. A voice that melted the house lights and a posture of arrogant, uncaring hedonism and high art added further to the figure's naked appeal. The Bernhardt did not ask for so much as demand adoration, and the house gave it to her without a murmur. And fifty feet away, Mays at last saw the image that had compelled him from eight stories up.

But these were only surface charms. Not until mid-monologue—nonstop trivial vanities and theatrical *mots*—did the Bernhardt legend begin to fill up the rented seats of the arena. For by some trick of posture, facial expression, or vocal inflection, Greene managed to devastate Madame Sarah with age, stiffen her joints, gravel her voice, crease her features until the audience grew nostalgic for the young creature with the golden lilt.

She spoke with glowing courage about the amputation of her leg, thereafter hopping about the stage with the most agonizing effort. Mays, taken in, looked for the severed and stashed limb. Then she was once again performing for the troops at the front, as she had seventy years before. And again, politics and violence gave way to the spell of a once-strawberry mop of hair.

She did not play a death scene, and made no allusion to dying words. She merely spoke again, on the darkening stage, her self-proclaimed and often repeated motto: "*Quand même*"—even though, or, in spite of everything.

When the house lights came up for intermission, Alison was in a state of extreme agitation.

—This is great. This is exactly what I was trying to say.

Mays could not remember her saying anything. But as he looked over at Miss Stark, he found he had not even remembered very well what she looked like, during that hour in the dark. Her face seemed somehow altered. Mays heard his mother telling him not to stare, or at least to be more subtle about it.

In her eagerness to get his attention, Alison was using their still-paired hands as a sort of mace to club Mays in the thigh. Suddenly aware of the familiarity—she did not even know this man—she extricated her hand and exploded in a beet-cheeked laugh.

—These women really got their hands dirty, didn't they? They had the goods and they went to work. But Liberal Arts just does not give you the goods. I mean . . . in my opinion . . . ever since Sputnik . . . technology . . .

She trailed off in ever-increasing nostalgic intonations, proving to herself the impossibility of her own ignorance. To Mays's mind, it was just as well that such a genuinely likable person should be stymied by an imagined obstacle than to realize, as he had, that even armed to the teeth with technical know-how, a person no longer had any possibility for consequential action of the sort Alison wanted, the sort they had just witnessed in biography. But he did nothing to argue this point with her. If she asked him again about his line of work, he'd claim a secret government post he was not at liberty to divulge.

—But this is really great. It's not just a show. You don't just look at it, you . . . Where did you hear about this? Or is it your standard place to bring pickups on the first date?

Mays laughed appreciatively over the pickup irony, thinking how just a few hours before this woman had accosted him and drafted him into the role of fiancé. He knew that Alison, too, at that minute was thinking about the old fellow, Krakow. Could *he* fill them in with the details on Nurse Cavell, or was that before his time? Mays, who knew exactly how many minutes it took to edit a paragraph of technical text, was totally incapable of gauging time in any clump larger than two-week pay periods.

—A friend recommended it to me. The one I ate with at your restaurant.

—"My restaurant"? I'm not guilty. You mean the Leopold-and-Loeb character who cut out and left you holding the bill?

—Well, it was his money.

—So you claim. A broker, right?

—How can you tell?

—They're always stalking something. Can't keep their eyes off the scope for ten minutes. They rely heavily on peripheral vision, and they all slouch, probably from carrying around Opportunity Loss.

—What's that?

—It's what keeps The Trading Floor in business. You buy a hundred shares of a stock. It goes up a point. To most anybody, that's a hundred bucks you can go blow on the Vineyard. But to a broker, it represents two hundred dollars Opportunity Loss, since you might have bought three hundred shares. The more you make, the more you're in the hole.

—How does that keep your . . . The Trading Floor in business?

—They like to watch the tape as they eat. What fun is dinner if you can't take a beating during it? Keep tabs on the Opportunity Loss. The more they don't make, the more satisfaction these guys get. But that's a male problem, isn't it? You like the virtue that comes with suffering. All you fellows try to come home and find your wife—how to say this delicately—diddling some stranger.

Mays blushed for both of them. One look at her eyelids confirmed that if "diddling" meant what he thought it did, it might just be pleasant with her. Alison talked in *opera buffa* style, which undercut any misanthropy she faked. She liked to talk. He very much liked to listen to her. Even her denouncements took on a quality of admiration and reverence. She belonged to the narrow class to whom no thing was separable from the complexity of the whole and all things were cause for surprise.

—You're a great one to knock ambition, after going on about work and contribution and all.

—Two different things. Brokers are after lucre, which is only about getting, consumption. The other—going back to school to study science and all—that's about making things. Use. Production.

Mays had trouble with this one. Production and consumption came to the same marketplace, and he could not see the virtue of one over the other. His mind was elsewhere—on Nurse Cavell, on Sarah Bernhardt, and not least of all on Kimberly Greene, who he wished had not turned out to be so substantial. His mind was on patriotism not being enough, politics not being enough, producing, consuming, all amounting to little in the climate of endless violence.

He sat and waited for the second act, thinking that if he kept still and patient long enough someone would take pity on his obstinacy and grant him the poorest of revelations: reveal what he nad chased in the window phantom, what he had thought to have seen in the distant Ms. Greene, why he was jeopardizing his sense of proportion on a vague feeling of ill ease. Reveal, too, the person next to him. They took hands again as the house lights dimmed.

The program announced that Greene would open the second act with Jane Addams. To settle the house, the piped music started up again—a George M. Cohan strain. Once again, projected photographs set the milieu: a view of Old Chicago, the street-poor, food lines, immigrants packed on New York's entry docks, two men boxing bare-fisted, signs offering jobs to anyone neither Irish nor Negro. Then, in a heavy attempt at contrast, the images changed abruptly to a montage of the turn of the century's very rich: Vanderbilts at dinner with a retinue of twenty, the banker Morgan, the summer-cottage mansions at Newport, a Park Avenue hostess walking on a lump of ermine.

The last entry in this Billionaire's Banquet was an unassuming newspaper photo, doubtless chosen for its caption: *One of World's Richest and an Heir?* The famous figure of Henry Ford appeared with his arm around the shoulder of a young man. The audience, to a person, let this image go by and settled into preparation for Jane Addams. Mays alone shot bolt upright. For the figure draped by Mr. Ford's arm, identified by the press as a potential beneficiary, was him.

Chapter Sixteen

I Dwell in Possibility

There is no [independent] mode of existence. Every entity is only to be understood in terms of the way in which it is interwoven with the rest of the universe.—ALFRED NORTH WHITEHEAD

ON THE EVENING of the office Christmas party, I'd left my boss's house much later than planned. Fat, slow snow was general over the South Shore. Despite having drunk nothing stronger than eggnog all afternoon, I was in good spirits over having, just this once, overcome the old-maidish qualities I'd been nursing since twenty that ordinarily turned my holidays into civil-defense drills.

If I had not been pressured into making a token appearance at the party, I would never have met Mrs. Schreck, so distinct are the first and second shifts in American business. Besides the clues that could at last move me forward toward the recovery of the photo and the oceanic sense of that lost day in Detroit, Mrs. Schreck had given me two hours of her life, talking at length on memory, the Great War, the experience of immigration. She was older than my grandmother and almost without English, but nevertheless I developed, in a matter of hours, an affection for her that I normally reserve for lifelong friends. On the train back to the city, riding north in the darkening snow, I thought again about how for months I'd gone after Zander, while Sander was there in my own office each evening, fifteen minutes after I'd gone.

On returning home that evening, I made a resolution to stay late at least two nights a week, pursuing my friendship with Mrs. Schreck to see what else I could learn from her. But as with those well-meaning and avowed resolutions I had made the day of the Rivera murals, I broke the resolution almost at once. My feeling of well-being, my urge to see more of Mrs. Schreck, did not last through the next morning. Rather, for the next several working days, I left a few minutes early, just so I would not meet her. After hearing the painfully pidgined stories—a childhood spent within earshot of the trenches, a family decimated by the system of national states, a second catastrophe and decimation, and the long trip to another country on a Ship of Fools—after hearing this history opened up to me, I did not want to see her in scrub uniform under the fluorescent lights of our common office. I could not connect one world to the other, and I did not want to see the two occupy the same place.

Perhaps I confused or hurt Mrs. Schreck by this retreat after so warm a first meeting. I quieted my conscience by insisting that we had made no plans to meet again in the future, and that I was sparing her, too, the shame of appearing in the dress of the present. The continued appearance of the sorry bonbons and, on the last working day of the year, according to Dutch custom, the chocolate letter P, my last initial, left me miserable. But still, I left early.

Her facts about the photograph—her privileged knowledge that could fill the gaps in my research, her personal experience that could at last cause my reading to coalesce—frightened me as much as the thought of seeing her under fluorescent light. Not that my curiosity had lessened. Every day as I rooted in the sock drawer, plowed the drifts on my way to work, or heated some instant item for dinner, I thought of the names she had given me and how they might flesh out and complete my image of 1914 and of the photograph. As familiar as I had become with the second-floor rear of the public library where they kept History, I could now, in twenty minutes, go straight to a print of those three farmers. The idea terrified me.

To begin with, I was afraid that Mrs. Schreck's information would lead me to a photo identical to but different from the one that had compelled me so long before. I had dwelled on the one in my memory so long that it was sure to have altered, to have taken on an authority of its own. I did not relish proving how undependable my memory was. Besides, Mrs. Schreck's personal involvement with the picture led me to believe that I had been vain in thinking of it as "my photo" and "my farmers." I was an egoist who dabbled amateurishly in the politics of another time—the life and death of ten million—strictly because it was more entertaining than the workaday. Finally, I was afraid to arrive at the final object of all my effort and, by succeeding, end what had been my only diversion.

So I circled back to Sander only gradually, with fake patience. Delaying the inevitable, I found myself reading a biography of Bernhardt. The story of the world's most famous actress matched most of Mrs. Schreck's details. Before I finished, I'd slipped back into the biographical fallacy—the addiction to eavesdropping on notable people's lives. I began and left unfinished a volume on the Kaiser, one on Max Planck, and a third called *Key Figures at the Battle of the Marne*. Soon I was back to the old books on Henry Ford, just to see what I had missed.

I had missed everything, seen nothing. I had missed the conspicuous link to the photo, to what had first caught my imagination in the museum that day in Detroit. The details that I had committed to memory then had already, in and of themselves, contained all the clues necessary to decode the urgent message of recognition in the picture, the plea for help from those three young men looking over their right shoulders at a photographer no longer present.

Ford's biography spelled out the connection between me and those three boys, only I was too careless or willful to see it on first reading. On going back for a second look, I was startled to find, in the story of this Yankee industrialist, evidence of an explicit subplot involving the three young men walking down a muddy road at late afternoon. (They walk leisurely. One sings: "Carrots and onions and potatoes. Such thin fare!") All the books agreed that Ford had been, however briefly, in Europe on his ill-fated mission to end the Great War by will alone. That, I now decided, was when he must have met my, or more properly, Mrs. Schreck's three farmers.

Biographies ask the question "How do the details of this particular life demonstrate the spirit of its times?" Making the life conform to the times sometimes involves editing the first, sometimes reinterpreting the second. In both cases, biography always involves much footwork to keep the biographer's footwork hidden. In showing the link between special case and collective times, the biography must be nonpartisan. But it is already partisan to assume that the link between personal and collective indeed exists.

All lives are messy aggregates: Ford the farmer, Ford the illiterate, Ford the mechanical genius, the progressive, the reactionary, the anti-Semite, the philanthropist. Modern times are, by definition, a few billion times messier. Linking one aggregate to the other requires a good dose of editing, and thereby temperament. When biographers say, "Here is what makes my subject great, a representative figure," as soon as they explain why they've wasted years in tracking down the subject, they begin to implicate themselves, their own temperaments, and, paradoxically, the outlook of *their* times.

No biographer has clean hands. Biographers differ from novelists only in the direction of their proof: a biographer starts from particular details of character and attempts to deduce the life's general, historical context. A novelist assumes the historical terrain and induces representative details of character. Both muddy their work with intention and temperament. Biographer and sitter tangle and interdefine. Biographers can demonstrate no objective link between a life and its times free of the biographical interpretation. Yet in a final vicious circle, that limiting interpretation must be, in part, a product of the biographers' own relation to their times. Even my own phrasing of this impasse is colored by the climate of the 1980s.

The paradox of the self-attacking observer is this century's hallmark, reached simultaneously in countless disciplines. Psychologists now know there is no test so subtle that it won't alter the tested behavior. Economic tracts suggest that Model A would be inviolably true if enough people realized its inviolability. Political polls create the outcome they predict. Even in the objective sciences, physicists, in describing the very small, have had to conclude that they can't talk about a closed box, but that opening the box invariably disturbs the contents.

These are the recognizable bywords and clichés of our times. Casual talk abounds with the knowledge that there is no understanding a system without interfering with it. This much I knew well. What did not occur to me until the second time through the Ford biographies is that this position is itself tangled. Generalized, it attacks itself: "All observations are a product of their own times. Even this one."

This recursion is critical, not because it places a limit on knowing, but because it shows the impossibility of knowing where knowledge leaves off and involvement begins. If there is no independent vantage point, if the sitter's life is not separable from the biographer's interfering observation, then each of the sitter's actions must similarly be tied to biographical impulse. The two are inextricably tangled. Describing and altering are two inseparable parts of the same process, fusing into a murky totality.

Now the zoologist on expedition to Africa to study the great apes is not freed by this paradox of the observer to make up figures or indulge in poetic whimsy. The scientist is obliged, however, to acknowledge that the presence of a field team and film cameras tells the apes as much about human motives as it tells humans about apes' behavior in the wild.

With every action, we write our own biographies. I make each decision not just for its own sake but also to suggest to myself and others just what choices a fellow like me is likely to make. And when I look back on all my past decisions and experiences, I constantly attempt to form them into some biographical whole, inventing for myself a theme and a continuity. The continuity I invent in turn influences my new decisions, and each new action rearranges the old continuity. Creating oneself and explaining oneself proceed side by side, inseparably. Temperament *is* the act of commenting on itself.

Hypothesis—"This action defines me"—fuses with experiment—"What would I be if I did this?" And just as this hybrid of action and comment defines the individual, so each life both theorizes on and works out the spirit of its epoch. Each discrete life examines and explains everything it touches in a constant exchange of mutual defining and reshaping. By living, we become our times' biographer.

Some misunderstand the hybrid by emphasizing commentary at the expense of action. Too aware of the signs of the times, too adept at pointing out the precedent of inherited situations, these people forget their own ability to alter their inheritance through action. To the enormous class of well-informed fatalists, the Great War began in 1871 with the German annexation of Alsace-Lorraine, and followed autonomously and unstoppably all the way through Versailles and the Second War.

Equally and oppositely wrong, others overemphasize action. They would change history by passing out pamphlets on street corners. Enthralled with their own consequence, they ignore the inherited context that binds and defines all possible outcomes. They are the camp who feel the Great War was not inevitable until it broke out. Yet, if on a muddy road in May they were allowed a glimpse of August, what could all their individual action come to?

No; the Great War broke out as a hybrid of legacy and acceptance, a combination of precedent and consensus. Everyone alive at that time acted as both claimant and executor of events. Subsequently, my uncle Robert died in World War II—permanently changing my father's and, as a result, my own life—because of the way a majority of Europe interpreted the armistice that Marshal Foch made Matthias Erzberger sign in 1918 in Louis Napoleon's boxcar. So much depends on the inability to separate empiric fact from personal necessity. They create each other, as making and understanding create each other.

Just as a legislator follows strict legal protocol to change legality, so my every act changes both who I am and how I see myself. Concluding that the act of living—building up a personal biography and sense of continuity—does not differ qualitatively from the historian's view of how one time passes into another, I began to search for the inevitable honesty clause. Because there can be no interpretation without participation, the biographer has to be accountable to some third party that is neither commentator nor subject, independent of the system under observation. If no such independent accountability existed, each judgment would stall in an infinite regress of self-judging. Although we cannot hope to pin down a view of our subject undisturbed by our observation, we can test if we have reached an optimal fit between the two.

One such test is unsponsored recognition. Each day as I sift through my many new experiences, I find a few that I recognize without having any memory or experience of them. I do not mean mystical *déja vu;* I mean the practical moment artists call epiphany and scientists call the instant of aha.

At this moment of recognition I temporarily stop taking part in the thing at hand and jump a level in the hierarchy of awareness, no longer looking at the object from my vantage point, but at myself from the vantage point of the object. This shift of awareness away from the looked-at to the act of looking creates the illusion of familiarity, since this moment of standing outside the observed system is common to all other such moments.

I am on a passenger train late at night, speeding through Pennsylvania. The conductor walks through briskly, swinging a ticket punch by its metal chain. "Next stop Linton," he says. "Linton will be our next stop." I suddenly fill with a warm pulse. I recognize the name of the town, though I am equally sure I have never heard it before: "Oh yes, Linton." I settle a little deeper in my seat, wrapped in goodwill for the miserly-looking fellow in the seat across from me, since he too must suffer through another revisit of a place neither of us has ever been. He notices my change in attitude. Catching my eye, he peels back his lips. I am not at all surprised to recognize a gap between his first bicuspid and canine.

What I am experiencing is neither precognition nor submersion in mystical vision. It is a by-product of the way consciousness is structured, the consequence of our unusual ability to make one level of our terraced awareness double back and appraise another. At the moment when the stuff holding our attention dissolves and gives way to an awareness of awareness itself we recognize a community with all the other similar moments we have gone through—a concord, or close fit, between hypothesis and measured result.

We are accountable to these moments. In them, we feel the logical fit of two interdependent activities—looking and knowing. By slightly changing our angle of observation, a copse of seemingly random trees reveals itself as an orchard. This specific angle of observation, then, has an independent validity, revealing an order not of the viewer's making. Such a surprise visit of the orchard effect is always pleasurable—filled with the delight of recognition, a sense of the community of all explorers who also touch base at this common spot.

I continually write my own biography by my actions, mixing involvement with knowledge, accountable to those moments when both drop away to reveal the act of mixing—something a priori recognizable. This process does not differ measurably from the way I come to understand others, my time, or past times. Memory, then, is not only a backward retrieval of a vanished event, but also a posting forward, at the remembered instant, to all other future moments of corresponding circumstance.

We remember forward; we telegraph ourselves to our future selves and to others: "Rescue this; recognize this, or not *this*, but the recognizing." If we constantly re-form the continuity of our past with each new experience, then each message posted out of an obscure or as yet unexperienced past represents a challenge to re-form the future. No action unchanged by observation. No observation without incriminating action. Every moment of unsponsored recognition calls me to return to the uninspired world, to continue the daily routine of invention and observation, to dirty my hands in whatever work my hands can do.

I had completely overlooked these possibilities in trying to recover the memory of my critical day in Detroit. On that day, I was busy writing my own biography, answering the questions "How did I get here? What am I after? How does this day fit smoothly into the sum of days that make up my past?" Then, without deliberation, I walked into Rivera's imagined factory, instantly more recognizable than any of the factories I myself had worked in.

To compound the instant of aha, I rounded the corner smack into the three farmers, more familiar to me than my own parents, though I knew beyond doubt that I had never seen them or their photo before. For the next several months I would be obsessed with finding the exact message the image meant to send *me*, mistakenly looking for it in names, dates, and places.

I had to learn that none of that had any real importance, did not in fact exist without active interference from me. The black-and-white print was less a document for archiving than it was a call to action. I was to understand that better on rendezvous with another memory I had posted forward the same day. This third memory would produce a moment of recognition equal to that brought about by Mrs. Schreck's farmers.

For on my way out of the museum, repeating to myself, "Zander, Austrian, Zander, Austrian," I passed a display case remarkable only in that it contained one of the least display-worthy, most common objects in the world: half a dozen copper pennies.

I did not stop to examine them, but the oddity—everyday objects put forward as museum pieces—made me take notice. I waited until the second time through the Ford biographies to read that note. A half hour from at last being able to unearth the photo, I stalled, going over the old material that had once seemed my only lead but had led nowhere. I read again—with all that Mrs. Schreck had told me about the farmers and the photographer never far from my mind—the passage, already familiar to me, describing how at the height of the First War the philanthropist Ford made plans to mint his own money. Once again, I read the story of how he had stamped several hundred coins, virtually indistinguishable from the Lincoln copper cent, except that Henry's profile replaced Abe's and the motto changed from "In God We Trust" to "Help the Other Fellow."

That was what the museum case must have held: the mundane transformed. But I did not know what I looked at until I came across the story a second time. Nor had the biographical detail seemed particularly relevant until I remembered my direct experience. The two combined to show Ford's stunt for what it was: a biographical act of incredible hubris and humor, a self-explanation as well as the posting forward of a memory to some future, as yet undisclosed other fellow. An act of commentary and involvement, an industrialist literally making his own pile, replacing the elected official with a self-appointed one, trusting not in God but in the active partner.

This time, I noticed that when America entered the war, Ford cancelled production after minting only a few of the intended run. Copper had a new importance by then, calling for a new minting of biography, a new relation of self to the century. Ford the mottoist became Ford the armorer. So it was that the armorer grew slowly and, in retrospect, continuously out of the fellow who, a mere eighteen months before, had been Ford the launcher of the Peace Ship.

The Peace Ship took on an entirely new character. The venture was another attempt to mint his own currency, to write his own biography and his times' history. Historians might agree that the adventure was tainted from the start by the ludicrous notion that a small band of celebrities could rewrite the largest mandate for violence in history. Yet these same historians still did not calculate for me the size of the celebrity band that started the war in the first place. Hidden in the furor over the ship was the old debate between the efficacious and the well-meaning.

And hidden in Ford's response, his creation of the first-ever "missile for peace," lay the love of a clean solution that would in a year turn him into a warrior, his factories into munitions lines. It was clear now that hidden in my historians' response to the Peace Ship was the same ambivalence, the same love of simplicity that dismissed the whole project with a perpetuating violence.

Also clear to me on a second reading was that Ford's action, however culpable or laudable, followed in a long tradition of Ships of Fools—the metaphor of humanity as a mixed, unseaworthy lot adrift on the ocean with no rudder or compass and only a dim idea as destination. He had done nothing less than rewrite the metaphor for his own time, and in rewriting the biography of Henry Ford—"Help the Other Fellow," "No such thing as No Chance"— he merely pointed out that there is no abdicating to another captain. We can only chart the situation, and sail. If he had been somewhat light in the charting, he managed, barring everything else, to show me that I'd been somewhat light in the sailing.

I had looked for my farmers in the wrong place. I had spent months hunting down the photographer: who was it that disturbed these boys on their way dancewards? What was this observer's intention? Why so unobtrusive when the boys are so obviously shocked and awed by what they see behind the lens? It was time I admitted that I had looked too long at the boys to discover what had happened that day. I had already interfered, and it only remained for me to follow that interference to its logical conclusion: mint my own coinage, sail my own Ship of Fools to the place where their amazement lay. I knew now that half their startled attention focused beyond the lens, beyond the photographer, even beyond the frame, on me.

Between jobs, between trains, in a strange city, busy with revising the way I presented myself to myself, the act of explaining and defining my times, I was moved by another's explanation.

Rivera had looked about, seen, and acted. Reaching back to the stuff of religious frescoes and forward to a vision of mass production, he forever changed my concept of both with his devotional piece to the machine, his act of biography. Rivera's work meant to fuse the world Rivera hoped for and the one he saw.

In the corner of that mural sat the biographical stamp of Ford: crabbed face in front of enormous dynamo, Ford, whose friend Burroughs writes: "Mr. Ford has expressed himself through his car and tractor engine—they typify him." They *are* him, the act of autobiography linking him to his times. But with the engines finished, Ford's act of biographical revision had to continue, moved by that elusive and never quite definable quantity, the other fellow.

Thirty million other fellows—three in particular—acting out and writing one another's biographies, violently forcing the old text into a new edition, moved Ford to captain the Peace Ship. He sailed his personal diplomatic mission to Europe for the express purpose of linking his destiny to theirs, theirs to his through some inconsequential, personal transaction. If there were no such transactions documented in the existing biographies, I would have to create them.

Plainly, I could learn nothing by tracing the photograph back to its material origin alone. I had also to descend into that shifting, ambiguous place of possible meaning, find why I recognized these farmers without ever having seen them. (They stand in empty countryside, proud, posing in Sunday clothes, just the barest hint of terror, of trapped animals.) To look anywhere beyond my own daily routine was to go too far afield.

Busy at our own biographies, anxious to uncover how the lives of all others touch ours, we one day find that by sheer number— billions now—they, the other fellows, have a much more persuasive argument for making us do the conforming. They wait for a peace envoy, wait in surprised, posed stillness, beyond them the vacant, blurred nothingness of country out of the depth of the lens. Along a muddy road, just beyond a white, right-hand border, out of the frame, they head toward either a dance, complete with young woman—call her Alicia—or that unmitigated act of violence called the twentieth century.

Chapter Seventeen

A Country Under Occupation

Every decision is like a murder, and our march forward is
over the stillborn bodies of all our possible selves that will
never be.—RENÉ DUBOS, *Louis Pasteur*

ADOLPHE was still recalling how he had argued with his half brother
Peter over the distant brass-band music, and how Peter had teased
him about Alicia being at the May dance, when the command went
up to arm and turn out on the street. Adolphe did not grasp at
first what was happening, and he continued to look at the photo
the Belgian girl had given him—*Jack's Mother Is Not Pleased with the
Beans*—demanding of it the reason he couldn't talk to his brother
just a little longer.

The shouting and shots cleared his head, and he knew, at least
as much as the other soldiers, what was afoot. He threw on his
uniform, trying to press out the wrinkles. He found the gun he
always carried while inspecting the Belgian houses and headed for
the barracks door. Waiting for Adolphe outside was a vision of total confusion: who was on which side? Why was everyone running? Adolphe had always preferred physical pain to disorder; here
things had blown well past disorder, and Adolphe, pushed along
on a sea of nervous boys in uniform, offered bribes to God—his
eyes, his money, his letters from Alicia—to return the town to its
state of logical peace.

In the darkness to the right, a clump of Germans trotted after their leader, a fat man in his fifties who panted and said "Shit" in rhythm each time his right foot hit pavement. As the gang passed, a young boy broke ranks and turned to Adolphe, his face drained of color, croaking above the gunfire:

—*Franc-tireurs!*

Coined in 1870, the expression, meaning civilian snipers, sounded, on the lips of this boy, the worst of juvenile terrors, a sort of surprise exam gone wild. The soldiers had talked of nothing else since occupying Petit Roi, and now it seemed they had created the situation out of their own fear. At once it occurred to Adolphe that if the Belgians had indeed used a secret cache of weapons to arm an uprising, then he, as Contraband Council, was responsible.

He tried to determine where the front was forming, but could find no clear-cut line. Rather, civilians and soldiers mixed freely, interpenetrating each other's forces. Nothing in his rushed boot camp or weekly lectures on The War So Far prepared him for the chaos around him. Behind and to his left, a dozen soldiers fumbled with buckets to put out a torch fire in the troop quarters. Five yards off, a girl of eight threw dish shards at an officer, who ducked and threatened with his weapon, repeating in unintelligible French:

—This is *le bayonet*. It *est* sharp.

Shots rained from second and third stories all up and down the street, although the darkness prevented anyone from actually aiming at anything. The air filled with projectiles—stones, brick, pieces of metal tool. Pain seared Adolphe's ankle, and he thought for a moment that he had been bitten by a dog: one of those big bulldogs, he thought, with pushed-in faces. But looking down at the road next to his foot, he saw a plain piece of broken picket fence, with nails protruding from it. He lifted his cuff and examined the holes where the nails had entered his flesh. He trickled saliva onto his fingertips and rubbed the wound. Then he pulled up his sock and pressed it into his ankle to stanch the bleeding.

He stood up, ashamed at his uselessness in the fight so far. If he could find the French Belgian who had wounded him, he could retaliate. But he had no training in restoring order. A melee formed in front of him. As he threw himself into the fray, the fighters were just discovering that they were all Germans. When Adolphe reached them, they were deciding that the best way to avoid future misunderstandings was to spread out and deal with the enemy separately, manfully. Again Adolphe was alone, unable to attach himself to calamity.

Soon he came across a pair of undeniable townspeople. An old couple, man and wife, they looked to be at least centenarians. They struggled with each other, the man trying to restrain his wife, who brandished a crucifix chained to her neck that she had sharpened in a point almost all the way up to the Savior's feet. She called out:

—A judgment! A visitation! Isaiah forty-two, Psalms thirty, Romans eleven. . . .

She reeled off several more random passages, and if her husband had not forcibly restrained her she would have stabbed the totally surprised Adolphe. For as he drew close enough to see them, he had frozen in place: they were the old couple from one of the bicyclist's photographs, spread out by the side of the road that May Day. Or were they? There *had* been a photo of an old couple, he felt sure. He very much wanted to compare memories with Peter or Hubert, to get to the bottom of this odd likeness.

He woke from his reverie when the old man, stooped in the back from scoliosis, yelled at him to take no notice of his wife: she was upset by the whole war, he explained, and by the death of a prize milk cow earlier that day. These two were as little accustomed to their roles of *franc-tireurs* as Adolphe was to his of suppressor. Still, as he lowered his rifle to the horizontal, Adolphe realized his edge of superiority over them.

—Go home, *opa.* This is no place for the two of you.

—A judgment! A visitation! Did God cast off his people? God forbid.

—Ignore her, sir. She's touched. She only sharped up the cross this evening when she heard there was plans. I'd of turned it in as a weapon otherwise. I swear it.

—Get along. Go home, close your door, and get in bed. You don't know what is happening out here. This is history.

When Adolphe pronounced this last word, the old couple looked about them in horror. That something so abstract could happen here on the streets of Petit Roi scared them more than Adolphe's rifle or the projectiles falling all about them. They thanked Adolphe humbly and withdrew, each preventing the other from looking back. He kept his eye on them until sure they were not doubling back. This, then, was civilian control.

Adolphe resumed searching for the commotion. He came across a fat gentleman in nightshirt who had hoisted his great bulk onto the reviewing stand the Germans had built in the square, commanding:

—Listen, everyone. This is your Mayor, Kruger. I'm ordering everyone home this instant. The situation is hopeless and can only lead to further unpleasantries.

The occupation force, finding in the tradesman Kruger the only town resident of undeniably German extract, had installed him as puppet head of government. Adolphe watched him strut on the stand; here was a man almost universally hated for being both a collaborator and a joke. If Kruger told the townspeople to go home, they would stay out and riot all night just to spite him. Adolphe would have to silence him.

—Go home yourself, you. Take your own advice.

—Please sir, I'm trying to control my constituency.

—Now, Herr Mayor. While you can.

—Thank you, sir.

Again Adolphe welled up with accomplishment. He would hear from his C.O. about this, his first action of the war. Already three Belgians had thanked him, proof that even the irrational nationalities could see the necessity of the German cause. Soon the French and Russians would feel the same necessity. And Adolphe no longer felt anxiety over the imminent end of the war; he had contributed.

But where had they gotten weapons? It had to be from the house he had checked that morning, the Després's. He had been thorough everywhere else, confiscating everything sharp—metal tins, chisels, even empty wine bottles that could be broken and used as daggers. Only at the Després's had he gone easy, because of the girl. He recalled the girl, how he had wanted her, how she had ruined it all with her belligerence. The print of Jack and his mother came back to him vividly: the familiar but unplaceable actress sinking her face into cupped hands.

A pointed stick grazed his shoulder, bringing back the present urgency. He struck his thigh with his rifle as punishment for forgetting himself. He was getting worse than Hubert, strangely unable to concentrate on what was at hand. He trotted briskly for the Després home.

Several soldiers, including the third-ranking officer of the town force, had beaten him there. They stood in a spacious front court, shooting out windows as if at a clay-pigeon competition. They took turns rotating shots until something flew out of a second-story window. The Germans hit the earth in unison, but there was no retort. The ranking officer sent Adolphe up to investigate. Proudly, without fear, the boy walked up to the object, a white linen table napkin, smeared with gravy. The house occupants were giving themselves up. One by one, men with high collars, dark coats, and soft hats came out the front door with their hands on their heads.

Adolphe grew uncomfortable. He did not want to be standing there when the girl, Comelia, came out. He, as Contraband Council, was responsible for the cache of weapons—from chicken wire to lead pipe—the house had produced. He edged away slowly from both soldiers and captives, trying not to call attention to himself. As he did so, a sublieutenant cantered up on horseback, addressing the ranking officer.

—The church burns pretty steadily, and we've struck up a spark at the library for good measure, sir. If I may say so, sir, it seems to have turned the trick.

This speech raised a collective hurrah from the soldiers. In the distraction, Adolphe slipped off. He would double back to the square along the town edge. If anyone stopped him, he would say he was headed for the common stables, to secure the horses and deny the townfolk mounts. The excuse would pass in the general excitement.

In the back streets, dark except for a gas lamp or two, he came across a Belgian boy of ten fighting with a German twice his age. The boy had gotten hold of an antique fowling piece and been sitting on his haunches in the gutter, propping the gun between his knees and trying to figure out how to use it, if such were still possible. The soldier came by and snatched the iron away. He now used it to whip the boy about the shoulders and ribs. He did not try to kill or knock out the child. He struck him repeatedly, as one hits a dog with a newspaper. On each blow, he called out, "No" or "Never." The child emitted animal sounds of pain.

Habit took Adolphe, and he did what he would have done on coming across the same scene in the Westerwald: he pulled the two apart, meaning to slug the bigger one. No sooner did he put hand to uniform than he recalled that hitting this fellow would be attacking the Kaiser's foreign arm. He stopped, confused.

—For God's sake, mind the commandments.

Adolphe said these words more wildly than he meant to, because the soldier's face took him by surprise. It was pretty, beardless, and without trace of malice, pity, or excitement. It was a blank summer's breeze, showing no emotion apart from slight shock at being yanked from its duty.

—What . . . commandment . . . do you mean?

Adolphe froze, staring at him. He tried to remember which commandment he *had* meant. He enumerated them, with the explications from Luther's Small Catechism, and was surprised to find that none expressly forbade pistol-whipping a small boy if it were done in good faith, for a reason. He released the soldier and ran from earshot before the next installment began.

The sky now shone a light, unnatural rose that made Adolphe think he was about to witness his second aurora. His first, four years ago, a spectacular curtain of light gliding over the heavens, made his stepfather declare it a sign that Frederick Barbarossa was about to wake from his long sleep in the Kyffhäuser. But as Adolphe closed on the town square, he found the light to be no proclamation of the old king at all, but flames from the library and church, as the sublieutenant had claimed. All fighting had stopped, the Belgians giving up their resistance to save their burning buildings. The Germans capitalized on the truce that they could not force by manpower and modern weapons. Ordering their ranks, they circled the fire-fighting townspeople, guns drawn.

Because the church and library occupied opposite ends of the square and because of the difficulty in transporting water to the blaze, the villagers had to choose between saving one structure or the other. All but a few elected the church, although their numbers gave them less than even odds of saving the foundation. A dozen others addressed themselves stoically and bitterly to the library, confined to such ineffectual measures as beating the flames with topcoats, succeeding only in fanning the pyre. Yet they stuck with the hopeless gesture, the act of voting the opposition out-weighing the small chance of success.

The churchists formed themselves into teams. One group commandeered several horses and milk drays, riding a shuttle be-tween church and reservoir, slowed somewhat by two armed Ger-mans riding in each cart. A second team formed a bucket brigade, unloading milk cans and passing them hand over hand into the sacristy. A third group routed them to the most needed parts of the church. The fourth group remained in the nave, keeping open a direct intercession with God until the heat drove them out.

Watching the blaze, Adolphe wondered if it were right of the sublieutenant to use such drastic measures to end the resistance. He knew there was some theological debate whether church buildings themselves were holy or only symbolic, but either way, razing one seemed close to insulting God. Of course, the Belgian sniping, which had started the terror, had not been moral either. The German attack had to cleanse these sins, fire for fire. One could not be both effective and pious at the same time. Efficacy now made way for piety later.

When the Belgians at last doused the fires, the library had been leveled, taking with it a rare, multivolume work on the area's flora and fauna. All that remained of the only church in Petit Roi, re-named Königen, were two and a third walls and a carbon outline of a steeple. A bell cable had burned through, crashing the coun-terweight and releasing a brace of chimes. Those picking through the rubble found some ecclesiastical paraphernalia of only nos-talgic value and a melted-down silver chalice.

Under the influence of the released chimes, the chalice finders claimed the lines of melted silver formed a small image of Christ on the cross. The chalice passed from native to native, polarizing the town: on the one hand, those who saw the image of Christ and found in it a promise of redemption in the aftermath of tragedy, and on the other, those who saw only melted silver, the handi-work of the Germans. Yet when the Germans rounded them up for the night's internment, miraclists and skeptics alike broke into spontaneous singing of "O Sacred Head Now Wounded," the Pas-sion Chorale.

Adolphe's fear over his personal guilt in overlooking the Després household during the weapons search was groundless. The fact never came out in investigation; there was no investigation. The troika of commanding officers concurred that unidentified Belgians must have opened fire treacherously on Germans, leaving no need to investigate the matter of guilt or culpability. Germans had been fired on; the whole town had turned out for the fray. Each individual was accountable for the behavior of the group. The objective truth—that loose masonry falling on the helmet of a jittery Prussian boy had caused him to fire on a knot of shopkeepers, who in turn had sent word to the stockpilers to bring out the pointed sticks—was of no importance now to either side, a detail lost to the past.

The final casualty count had eight Germans injured, one with tetanus and one with broken ribs and hemorrhaging. Four Belgians lay dead; many more had gun wounds. The nightmare's fifth death resulted a few days later when an eighty-four-year-old woman, refusing sustenance out of grief over the gutted church, died in bed, chattering to the Virgin.

Word came down the chain of command that the army's policy, not only in Petit Roi but in all Belgium, dealt totally and inflexibly with such costly civilian actions. It could not blanch from meting out retribution to any civilian involved in conflict. The power in Petit Roi, by order of higher-ups, elected the enactment of collective responsibility.

On the third day following what was now called "the incident," handbills began blooming. They covered over the old announcements describing the terror waiting for armed insurgents. Plastered on lorries, shellacked to posts, glued to the pavement, the new, clean face of textual history said nothing more than that everyone was to assemble in the square that evening at five. At the appointed hour, in the gray of late day, the entire village, on signal, poured out of a thousand doors in files, head down, without sound. Each parader, from the broadest burgher to the smallest infant at the breast, was decked in Sunday clothes. They dressed as if some archivist were to meet them to take a group portrait. This was an occasion, and everyone turned out in their finest.

The camera-ready files queued into an orderly matrix in front of the demolished and rebuilt reviewing stand. The soldiers,

Adolphe among them, formed an identical matrix across the square. Someone had thought to bring wooden chairs for the old, so they could sit up front and hear as judgment was leveled. Judgment was swift and to the point. The sublieutenant stepped forward and commanded the Belgians to count off by twenty and every twentieth to step to the center of the square. The first Belgian, a woman of thirty who made a living selling eggs, recognizing the intent of the new century without being able to rescue herself from the values of the old one, began by saying, "Twenty." The next man, an accountant, also said, "Twenty," without hesitation. The whole Belgian matrix followed suit, repeating, "Twenty, twenty," in a orchestra of accents.

'Dolphe stifled a grin and looked around quickly. He was safe; the other boys of the army of occupation still faced forward. He made a note of the event—the whole town breaking into heroic "twenties"—to tell Peter the next time he saw him. His brother would appreciate it.

The sublieutenant, making no display of temper, barked a few efficient orders to a cadre of men, who then combed the Belgian ranks, ejecting every twentieth by hand. Adolphe grinned, too, at this clever response to the Belgians' clever parry, and waited for the next move in this cat-and-mouse game. Another side glance showed his compatriots still face forward but obviously involved in this spectator sport. But just as he felt the well-being of belonging to a cause larger than himself, Adolphe suffered a sudden shock of involuntary memory. What of the girl, Comelia Després?

Although he had not taken her when he desired her, Adolphe felt that his desire had cemented him to Comelia. He had always acted honorably; if he had not been already married to Alicia, he would certainly have said *du* too to Comelia after the thoughts he'd had about her. And hadn't she given him something, the photo of Jack's mother? Or had he taken it by force? No matter; what counted was that they had something of the other's—she, his desire and he, her photo. So he had an obligation to watch over her as over himself.

He looked at where the cadre was just finishing thinning the ranks of the citizens. He could not pick out faces from the large group of the safe. Anxiously, he looked over the seventy condemned. She was not among them, and he felt the last check to his happiness drop from him.

The old commanding officer stepped off the reviewing stand to examine the seventy Belgians who were to be the example of collective responsibility. He nodded to the sublieutenant, saying the children would help make the point. He added something about how random subsets always made good cross-sections, and he returned to the stand.

—Let the Mayor, Herr Kruger, be added to these for knowing of a conspiracy and failing to tell the authorities.

The spindly-legged merchant was singled out and led from the community of the safe. The German boys near Adolphe snickered at the comical way Kruger walked. Kruger was needed so that the world press, so unfairly intent on distorting the German cause, could make no charge of German barbarity or favoritism. Kruger, though of German extract, had to suffer as any other.

—And let the family residing at Seven Narrow Street be added, as the suppliers of weapons for the incident.

The Després. Now Adolphe straightaway located Comelia as the cadre sought her out. She, in turn, seemed to return his gaze from across the open square, holding it as she was led among the victims. Reaching her preordained spot among the seventy, she took the hands of her family and faced the reviewing stand. The order came down from the stand, and with four commands from the sublieutenant, the boys of occupation were firing into the examples.

It took three volleys to bring all seventy to the ground. The safe group screamed some, but for the most part they, like the examples, kept still, thinking perhaps that keeping still and waiting was the best defense against a future that no amount of action or words could put straight. Day after day, their farm animals had shown that bringing to market was best and cleanest done when begun and ended in stillness.

For some days after, Adolphe found he could rest easier if he substituted for the face of Comelia, who often came unsponsored into his thoughts as he lay in bed, the face of the familiar actress behind the knotted hands playing Jack's mother. The memory of the photographed face was calming and soporific, and he fell asleep certain that the incident and post-incident made sense in some larger context he was not party to.

Once asleep, though, he advanced only fitfully. Often he would wake, trying to yell, "Run." But his enunciation of the word, as with the legs of the dream runners, blurred to a leaden stillness, and those startled boys waking next to him in the barracks could no more understand him than the seventy-odd he shouted to.

Late one night he awoke for a different reason altogether. He dressed methodically, refusing to answer his bunkmates' questions except to say he had business. Outside in the dark, he made his way to the commanding officer's quarters. The C.O. now resided in the home of Mayor Kruger, vacated after the post-incident. A twenty-four-hour guard rotated watch at the rebuilt picket-fence gate. Adolphe recognized the current guard as two friends from the Westerwald, one, the younger brother of the Jacob girl who had beaten out Alicia as May Queen.

—Daniel, Johann, let me in to talk to the colonel.

—Halloo, 'Dolphe. What's this about?

—I've news of the first order, confidential and for the colonel only.

—No going. It's after midnight. Can't wake the colonel for anything short of Germany's victory or another sniper attack.

Blanching at these last words, Adolphe sat down on the pavement, back to the fence and gun across his lap. He dug in and waited for his audience. Several times his friends tried to draw him out, but he would not talk. He refused offers of food, cigarettes, even contraband alcohol. When the boys' relief came, he did not even say good-bye.

In the morning, he still could not enter without identifying the nature of his mission. The guards pointed out that the name Schreck was synonymous with trouble, that in training, Adolphe had set a platoon record for number of times on disciplinary review. Adolphe protested; they could see he had reformed, given up practical jokes since the war. But the guards weren't taking chances in case of Adolphe's accidental relapse. Adolphe pleaded that the security of the Königen force, perhaps the whole army of occupation was at stake. The guards said they were plenty secure just minding their post, and would be less so if Adolphe started to pull tricks on the colonel. Adolphe had no choice but to play his bargaining chip.

—I have intercepted an enemy wireless message.

The guards stiffened and their eyes grew involuntarily wider. They knew of wireless, but the whole process lay veiled behind technological novelty. Only thirteen years earlier, Marconi succeeded in sending the letter S across the Atlantic, and only the year before, 1913, Armstrong patented the regenerative receiver circuit. The first commercial broadcast was still six years off, but the military had pounced on the new technology before the public, and every foot soldier knew that both sides somehow flew messages through the naked air, not perceivable to the ordinary individual.

Beyond that, the guards floundered. Their parents' generation had just grown accustomed to people mechanically reproducing their own images at will. Now came the even more alarming fact that people could reproduce their own voices, their own individual qualities, infinitely throughout the atmosphere, with no mark of the sending. They accepted the fact without comprehending it.

So Adolphe's claim had a terrible, profound impact on the two Westerwald farmers blocking the Kruger gate. They did not think to ask *how* Adolphe had gotten the wireless message. For all they knew, a crystal set could be built out of wire coat hangers and incantations. This wireless communication required immediate attention. They notified the colonel, and soon Adolphe was ushered into the house.

He went into a plush study on the first floor, filled with heavy dark wood furniture, the kind immovable once placed. Filling every free spot in the room were hundreds of toy mechanical banks— woodchoppers, circus performers, hunters, and bears—that all did tricks when coins were placed in their slots. The home was by all standards that of a well-off but not wealthy bachelor of questionable taste. Adolphe thought it a palace, the most opulent interior he'd seen. He tried to imagine what trick each of the mechanical toys did, and he had to be called to attention by the colonel, who sat in an overstuffed chair behind a breakfast tray, still in a pair of pastel Chinese pajamas.

—You say, soldier, that you have overheard . . . intercepted a wireless?

—That's exactly it, sir.

—Of the . . . ah . . . enemy's?

—The Russians, sir.

The colonel lifted one eyebrow and poked about in his poached egg.

—I was under the impression that our wireless operator was named Nederman.

—I believe so, sir.

—And you are his assistant, then?

—No sir. Adolphe Schreck, Contraband Council and enlisted man, sir.

—You've built your own wireless?

The colonel put down his silver and looked up with an encouraging grin. This was evidence for the superiority of the German cause, if an uneducated farm youth could get a hold on the new technology. He beamed at the boy, wondering what Frenchman could make the same claim.

—No sir.

—You have no crystal set?

—I have a metal filling in my back molar, sir.

This total non sequitur threw the colonel for a loss. He studied the peas on his plate a full minute before piecing together the boy's logic. Apparently the Contraband Council claimed that a mixture of calcium, silver amalgam, and something in saliva—salt, perhaps—could turn him into a human radio receiver. The officer thought back to his scientific training to decide if such a thing were possible, but could recall nothing but the number 6.02×10 to the 23rd power, something to do with chemical weight named for an Italian who sounded like a vegetable.

—And were you able to . . . crack the Russians' transmission code?

—They used no code, sir.

—You are able to speak Russian, then?

—Pleased to report, sir, they broadcast the message in Dutch.

—Dutch! That's . . . very curious.

Adolphe sensed the colonel was having trouble with the interview. Perhaps the C.O. didn't believe that he spoke Dutch. Adolphe was about to set his superior's mind at ease by telling him about Peter and Hubert but checked himself. It didn't necessarily follow that just because his half brothers were raised in Holland that he himself spoke Dutch. So he said:

—My father is half Dutch, sir.

Adolphe's first lie tortured him. But the situation required him to give his story some credence. Still, he began repeating silent contritions.

—And what was the nature of this Dutch wireless message you received from the Russians over your dental work?

—The Russians have secretly landed three divisions on the Channel coast. These have infiltrated our lines and one is not more than twenty miles from here.

The colonel, trying to unstick a piece of gristle from between his teeth, nearly succeeded in swallowing his tongue at this disclosure. The boy was obviously suffering from some mild dementia. Many such cases had cropped up along the front at the sights of the fiercer artillery duels. Perhaps the low-level bombardment audible at Königen was enough to bring on a light case. He did not for an instant think the story worth pursuing.

Yet, oddly, Adolphe's story had in each particular a factual counterpart. In the first year of the war, failure to transmit wireless in code contributed to the Russian defeat at Tannenberg and the Masurian Lakes. Throughout the century, people have claimed being able to receive radio over metal fillings; one famous movie actress reportedly broke up a World War II Japanese spy ring in Hollywood after hearing strange vibrations in her amalgam. And as for the phantom three divisions: all England in 1914 produced by hallucination not just three divisions but an entire Russian army being secretly transported to the Western front. Without any trigger from government or press, they saw full-coated, full-bearded Russian troops everywhere. Sober Englishmen reported them disembarking from ships, drilling, loading onto troop trains. For a few days, a whole country produced a whole army out of nothing. In a year given to hallucination, Adolphe's was modest.

Nevertheless, the colonel had reached a diagnosis. He took a piece of onion-skin stationery from the late Kruger's writing desk and addressed a few lines to the town physician:

I understand there is a new treatment out of Vienna for curing the varieties of light delirium brought on by the stress of day-to-day living. Will you please administer such to the foot soldier bearing this, as he seems to be wont to exaggeration of reality.

He signed the letter with a military flourish, affixing all the titles he had given himself on assuming command of Petit Roi. He sealed it and gave it to Adolphe, charging:

—Your information is of the utmost importance. I have written it down here as you told it to me. You must deliver it by hand to the physician Minguette on Acorn Street, so he can advise the civilian population. I shall notify our forces in the environs. Good day, soldier.

The colonel subscribed to the belief, held widely by officers and universally by statesmen, that the only way to cure delusion is to play along. He requested one of his personal guard to follow Adolphe at a distance and make sure he reached his destination.

Adolphe took the note with all due obedience and departed for the familiar streets of Petit Roi. He wondered, though, if the colonel grasped the urgency of the situation. Three divisions of Cossacks were not to be sneezed at. Sparing so much as one man on an errand such as he now served could only be a mistake.

Adolphe had never before considered countermanding a superior's orders. Whether on his stepfather's farm or at the Kaiser's front, he knew that the nation depended on each person accepting subservience to command. But here was a higher authority, a greater logic to which he owed allegiance. The survival of the town, the occupation, the front, and ultimately the homeland depended on his taking up a position in the field against this surreptitious Russian force. He swerved off the road and cut across a Belgian barnyard.

Walking across the empty field, he was visited by a strong feeling of resolve. His little mutiny would be understood in time, judged in a wider context and forgiven, even praised. The matter settled, he thought no more about the Russians or what defense he meant to put up against them. He was thinking about his half brothers.

He was angry with Hubert for filching, out of turn, the picture of the three of them, because it might be some time before they could see one another and he could get the photo back. Alicia so loved to have the picture on her press, next to her combs: that way, he could be home when he was not. He thought of the wireless message he'd received the night before over his tooth. What a remarkable, excellent society, in which people could reproduce their voices and images cheaply and mechanically for wide consumption. Photos, radio, the new forms of mechanical reproduction seemed to Adolphe further commandments to go forth and multiply, go and love the image of others as yourself.

He loved the image of his half brothers in his mind's eye. He loved the image of Alicia in his wallet. He loved the image of the child of his union with her, which had not yet appeared in the world. He loved Comelia Després, whom he imagined crying into cupped hands, as in the actress's image.

Someone called to him from the direction of Königen, but he could not turn back now. They would understand his little mutiny in time. Another call; perhaps it was the strange photographer on the bicycle, but he could not afford to stop and find out. How did that song of Peter's go? "Carrots and onions. If you'd fed me more meat, I might never have left home."

He would buy a gramophone after the war and play that song once a week for his child. Shots rang out nearby; the Russians, no doubt. Still Adolphe could not afford to stop. He found that through will and concentration he could force the bullets to bend away from him and explode at a distance.

A low-ranking officer of the occupation force was charged with the paperwork documenting the Schreck affair. This is the century for records, even records of the slightest individuals. Look it up, if the library has not burned: "And not answering several calls to halt, the deserter was fired upon." A medical examiner added excruciating detail concerning the perforation of the left ventricle. Neither saw fit to record that the deserter, for several minutes in the vacant field, before expiring, lay repeating: "Jack's mother is not pleased with the beans."

Chapter Eighteen

On the Windfall Trail

One custom Armenian-Americans observed was to paste in parts of photographs taken in Armenia to complete a family portrait made later in America. These composite photographs, with their artless additions, bear a child-like quality and testify to the living remembrance of sons and fathers executed in the massacres.—"A Poignant Portrait of an Oppressed People," in *The Boston Globe*, April 24, 1983

To THE BEST of his recollection, Mays had never posed with Henry Ford Senior, who had died a good decade before Peter was born. The extent of his contact with celebrities was his once having seen Dizzy Dean across a parking lot swarmed by little boys. But, as the truism had it, the camera doesn't lie, and there on the big screen at the Your Move Theatre stood a twenty-foot image of Peter with a twenty-foot Henry's arm around him.

They were coming out of a closed room together, unposed, startled by the camera. The slide remained projected only a few seconds, rapidly giving way to the second act. Mays snuck a surreptitious glance at Alison, whose hand he held again. She answered his involuntary squeeze of alarm with one of affection, but made no other sign of having seen anything out of the ordinary. Yet he could not bring himself to believe that he had fabricated the resemblance. The problematic caption, *Heir,* he could have dismissed as the sort of journalistic interpretation he did for a living if it hadn't been for a Mays family custom he'd never before paid much attention to.

So involved was Mays with explaining the photograph to himself that Kimberly Greene's entrance for the second act startled him. His sense of time had been so dislodged that he was shocked afresh to see in front of him the object of his long search. But that old enigma—Bernhardt swimming against the Veterans' Day crowd—at once gave way to another altogether, an enigma of identity related to the first in a way that Mays could sense but not force clear.

Greene's impersonations in the second half of *I Dwell in Possibility* ranged from Eleanor Roosevelt to Sylvia Plath to Mother Teresa, but her great finesse in all of them was lost on Mays. Bernhardt herself would have stood only even odds of breaking his absorption. He worked at rearranging; given this new piece of evidence, his recent past once again required reinterpreting. Mays sat in his seat and reinterpreted as if his life depended on it. Two opposing theories explained recent events. He named them loosely the Conspiracy and the Coincidence angles. In the first, all the confusing trail of motifs—Veterans' Day, the war, instrumental music, the exchange, Bernhardt, and now Ford—secretly conspired to mean something. In the second, they did not, but only happened to occur around the same time.

He found the second camp infinitely more attractive and consoling. Whatever connection the string of puzzles seemed to imply he must have read into them himself. Perhaps, as Bullock liked to say, he suffered from the number two killer of modern times: boredom. As the foremost living case of an uneventful life, he had had every right to spice things up with a little exotica. He'd fabricated an interest in the distant redhead because of her otherworldly manner. The whole chain linking Greene to the Great War to Nijinsky to Bernhardt was then an ironic by-product of the way history was structured. The Trading Floor's allusion to the same time merely reflected the present's fascination with nostalgia. The lies and dodges of Brink, Delaney, and Bullock had been random or unintentional. At the theater, pressed by reality, finding all the fascinating avenues of possibility dead-ending in an accomplished actress's stage performance, he must have made one last clutch at intrigue and concocted a vague resemblance between himself and someone long ago dead. Anything to keep busy, to stay with the search.

He would have been content to buy this explanation, to settle down for the rest of the act, to make the acquaintance of the delightful Alison if it hadn't been for one ugly detail: that bit of Mays family folklore. Continually as he was growing up, usually when bills came due or following some heavy, unusual expense such as a broken leg or hot water heater, in short, when the precarious Mays socioeconomic position tipped toward the pinch of poverty, the young Peter watched his mother push her scarf higher up on her head, take a breath and say:

—What Ford might have done for my family.

The saying was proverbial, simply something his mother *did*, like roast beef on Sundays and cards at Christmas. Peter found the phrase so familiar that for a time he even thought it was universal, akin to "If wishes were horses, beggars would ride." He used it himself in young adulthood when money got the upper hand of him. But his friends had always commented on the phrase's quaintness. Realizing that the expression belonged solely to his mother—a way of complaining that her ancestors might have done better by way of cash—Mays paid no more attention to it than he did to, say, his geometry teacher, who, when frustrated by his students' total inability to get from A to B using proof, invariably exclaimed, "I should have gone into embalming." But the Ford photo changed the old expression for good.

The Conspiracy camp, on the other hand, had God, Conan Doyle, or someone equally nefarious dealing him a hand as an exercise in deducing what cards were out. He rejected this possibility, though not on grounds of implausibility: he felt no virtue or logic in being a skeptic. Mays dismissed the God option because if it were true, he'd be led to water whether he believed or not, but if it were false, he'd never be able to prove it so. Best declare metaphysics irrelevant at the start and get on to checking other angles. After eliminating those, he could come back and tinker with scripture.

A notch below diety, there remained the chance that history—an unconscious, forward-moving sum vector—conspired to drop a revelation in Mays's lap. Again and again, a turning on the same concern: the Great War, the opening decades of this century. But his being singled out for a private connection with the long-forgotten past, or the past making itself known through him struck

Mays as unlikely. He flossed conscientiously, took public transportation, and never filed anything but a short form; destiny did not sit well on him.

The most likely conspiracy was among his friends and new acquaintances. From the start, he'd been put and kept on the scent by others' deliberate miscues. After he'd given up the Vets' Parade for lost, Delaney had called him back and pointed out Greene, who had appeared *ex nihilo*, red hair gleaming, as if by prearrangement. Later, Delaney had deliberately intruded on Mays's private search, kept it alive with the musical instrument angle. Doug tipped him to Caro, Caro to boyfriend Lenny, who just happened to have a photo of Bernhardt hidden behind his Standard and Poor's. Lenny tipped him to Greene via Alison Stark; even the old guy, Arkady Krakow, seemed implicated in an elaborate scheme to issue Mays a date and ensure his appearance at the Your Move. Finally Greene, as if part of her act, tipped him to the Ford photo. An impossibly elaborate, cumbersome solution, but one that fit each twist of the script.

Where was the denouement, the final tip? What lesson did this conspiracy of equals intend for him, and why choose such a gothic tactic when they might have manipulated him more simply? He looked again at each link in the chain of intrigue: never had anyone forced his hand. The others simply suggested; he had taken the ball and run on his own volition. They had perhaps stretched rules once or twice: Brink's pressure, Bullock's lie about the exchange holiday. But no one had interfered with Peter's free agency. The thought nauseated him.

Mays awakened from this reverie with the vague sensation of being attacked by Alison. The last twist of the knife: strangled noiselessly in a theater by an Edwardian masquerading as a modern-day working woman. She struggled with his hand, saying:

—You're hurting me, Turk.

Worked up over the Conspiracy theory, he had clenched his entwined fist tighter and tighter until Alison squirmed in pain. He extricated his hand.

—No, I didn't mean for you . . .

But he fought her attempt to take back his hand. He checked it to see if she had taken a skin sample or left a secret mark of Cain in ultraviolet ink. Then, in a rare moment of lucidity, Mays understood that if he were not yet over the edge, he would be shortly if he kept to the primrose path he now trod. The Conspiracy theory came down to pure paranoia. The machinations were too top-heavy, too susceptible to breakdown. Too much effort would have to go into the chancy prospect of convincing Mays he was an unwitting millionaire. And for what? What could anyone stand to gain?

Besides, the collaborators could not have known about his mother's pet expression, on which the whole scavenger hunt now hung. Peter took a peek at Alison's profile: the most beautiful brow ridges since Piltdown Man. He could not suspect Miss Stark, at least, of any duplicity. He dropped the whole Conspiracy angle, and with his freed hand, once again took Alison's.

Clearing his head, Mays focused on the stage, where Kimberly Greene, again in the New England severity of Dickinson, the prophetic hermit, delivered those lines about possibility being a better place to live than prose. Mays had his doubts, but the minute the footlights were doused, he rose to his feet with the rest of the house and applauded vigorously. This put him about four feet closer to Ms. Greene, the better to scrutinize her face. He had some questions for that face, up close.

The audience continued to applaud, stomp, and whistle until Mays grew disgusted with the whole narcissistic demonstration. After the eighth curtain call, he looked at Alison, who rolled her eyes to heaven, also fed up with the conquering hero racket. They slipped, by common, unspoken agreement, out of the rioting hall.

In the foyer, Mays looked for the entrance into the wings. Alison tried steering him streetward.

—I'll give you a quarter if you take me home.

—In a minute. I'm trying to find . . .

—Come on, don't be shy. I won't make any passes you can't catch.

—It's not that. Only . . . don't you want to do the receiving line?

—What on earth for? When the bullfighter kills the bull, everyone gets to go home. I didn't think you were the type to go in for idol-worshiping.

—Not to worship, just to . . .

—Get a good ogle? What does she have that I don't have, aside from looks, face, figure, talent, and mystique?

Mays wondered why Alison was so averse to his meeting Greene, but refused to sink back into paranoia. Sheer rivalry, perhaps. He overruled her objections, and soon they stood in the queue of admirers, the conga line that by theatrical convention always forms outside performers' dressing rooms. Nor were they, despite having slipped out in mid-ovation, the first in line. Half a dozen stragglers—a good cross-section of Middle America if ever there was one—beat them to it.

—They must have come out at intermission.

—Hell with the show. Give them greatness.

Alison and Peter broke off bantering when the star made her appearance. Gasps and polite applause rippled through the line when Greene opened her dressing room door in her Bernhardt getup. Mays drew up short: she had finished as Dickinson; why resuit as Sarah? She'd gone to great lengths to get back into the stays. Theatrically demented, she doubtless believed in transmigration of actresses' souls. Then Mays checked himself, remembering his own mission of transmigration.

Greene dismissed her admirers one by one, politely but perfunctorily. The ritual burdened more than it gratified her. But each fan was too starstruck, too self-conscious at being in proximity of greatness to notice being clicked off like groceries by a cashier. Systematically, Greene knocked off the first half dozen in line. Then she reached for, took Mays's hand.

And for the first time it fell to the star to be nonplussed. Greene's face lit with recognition, and for once, the easy words did not come. Mays, actually touching the flesh of his phantom, stayed remarkably calm. He no longer felt himself in the presence of the talented Greene, the fabulous Bernhardt, or even the enigmatic redhead; instead, he stood three feet from a woman who could give him a definite answer, a solid lead on the long-hinted-at legacy. He would not budge from the spot until she handed over the facts.

Flustered, Greene removed herself from his grip and walked to the back wall of her room. She favored one leg, limping, a nervous habit doubtless adopted on donning her Sarah duds. Mays craned his neck, making out her destination. The far wall, from floor to ceiling and flush to corners, was papered with clippings and photos, a vertical archive documenting not, as Mays first thought, Greene's career, but the general career of the last hundred years: the *Hindenburg* explosion, "Dewey Beats Truman," Dust Bowl migrants, the River Rouge plant, Lucky Lindy. Many were the sources of the slides in Greene's play.

As Bernhardt stood wavering in front of the collage, Mays could not believe that she meant to pick one from out of the overwhelming scrap heap. The altar of history, put up for her own amusement, had grown out of control, too big to sift through. Yet Greene stood in front of the document-wall, a weaving, hooded cobra, lifting one hand gingerly to strike the board. She limped back and pressed her quarry into Peter's hand.

—Here. This is yours, I believe. This is what you're after. Take it.

Mays looked down superfluously, already knowing what he held. The photograph of himself and Ford, from which the transparency had been mechanically reproduced, bore a short news sidebar.

—But where did you find it?

—God only knows. It's not dated, and the source has been clipped off. There's no telling where it's from. You know the man?

—Ford?

At Mays's ridiculous rejoinder, Kimberly Greene at last broke into a grin. Her features showed under the pancake.

—I mean the other fellow. If it's really you, you carry your age remarkably well. You can keep that, if it will do you any good. Thanks for coming backstage; when I first looked up at you, I had a lovely jolt of synchroneity.

—Pardon?

Mays felt acutely his total inability to say anything remotely intelligible. He wondered if a body could be sued for not holding up its end of the conversation. Things had strayed irretrievably from the scripts he had prepared for use in meeting this woman, and he could not ad-lib.

—Synchroneity. All times at once. My hobby.

She indicated the Bernhardt clothes, apologetically fanned her skirts, and curtsied lightly. Just as he took his eyes off her to look again at the yellowed newspaper scrap, the line of well-wishers moved him along inexorably. When he looked up, Greene was gracefully accepting the enthusiasms of two hockey players. Urged on by Alison, who stood impatiently on the sidelines, and by a baleful usher waiting to pounce on loiterers, Mays beat a retreat. The woman was too addled on the past to help him much anyway.

On the street, Mays crouched over the clipping. Alison nuzzled up for a look.

—Let's see what the pretty woman gave the nice little boy.

Both accused the other of blocking the light. Neither thought of bringing the scrap closer to a streetlamp. Mays read aloud:

—"Our on-the-spot cameraman took this snapshot of the industrial wizard Mr. Henry Ford and a friend after their emergence from a two-hour closed conference following the recent Peace Ship fiasco. Mr. Ford, cornered by the press, said, 'Europe does not want an end to war. I came to help ten million boys. One will have to do.' Well, Readers: would you care to change places with that 'one'?"

Mays flipped the scrap over, desperate for clues. Brittle flecks of aged newsprint came off in his hands. The flip side showed a partially obscured gramophone ad and an article quoting a Morgan broker as saying that certain investments had been rendered extremely attractive by the war, and as this was likely to be the last European War, the small investor would do well with spot buying. Again, Mays flipped the scrap over to see if the photo or caption had changed since he read it.

—Look here. It looks like it's been penned in.

Indeed, the early reproductive process showed traces of carbon litho.

—I don't get it. This is supposed to look like you, is that it? I can't see it.

—Come on. Really? Here, look. Seriously. Look closely and tell me you don't see a resemblance.

Mays crouched down to Alison's eye level and held the photo up to his ear. He tried to assume the precise facial expression of his double in the photo. He was strongly conscious of being on a rain-emptied sidewalk with a strange woman, long after the ball was over, taking the final dive into absurdity. Yet he did not much miss his sanity. As he awaited her verdict, he looked over her features with reciprocal intensity.

—Nope. Sorry. I just don't see it. For one thing, the guy on the left is only two inches tall.

Mays grinned, despite himself. Whether Alison was teasing, lying, or blind, he was glad she could not see a likeness. It restored the healthy aura of speculation to the venture, the element of doubt that, as a child of midcentury, was his familiar inheritance. The time had come, he deliberated, to do something impulsive. For thirteen seconds, during which period Mays formulated the working hypothesis that moist, warm things were more pleasurable than cold, dry ones, he postponed asking Alison if she'd ever heard the expression "What Ford might have done for my family." At the end of the evening, he was twenty-five cents richer, but no closer to an answer.

In the morning, he decided against going to work. He called Caroline, saying he had some family business to attend to. She was remarkably solicitous, saying she got more work out of Delaney, and thereby Moseley, when Mays didn't show. Mays suggested a parity program: every day he didn't come in, he'd get paid double. Brink said she'd look into it. In a husky voice, she asked him how he'd liked Madame Bernhardt.

—How do you know about that?

—Lenny told me the whole story. He also said he suspected you did *not* go to the show all by yourself. Any rumor to that truth?

—I want to know why my private life is turning into a round of "Telephone." Tell Lenny there's still a couple over in Charlestown who don't know how far I got with his waitress. And while you're at it, ask him if he can recommend any good books on Ford.

Immediately on doing so, Mays realized the impropriety of yelling at and hanging up on one's boss. He didn't care; *Micro* could go hang. He didn't see how they stayed in business anyway; the other two trade rags must subsidize it, to preserve the balance of power. Mays put the place out of his mind and commenced packing.

Through years of exhaustive research, Mays had reached the inviolable conclusion that sneaking up unannounced on his mother's home in Chicago represented a physical impossibility. He'd given up trying some time back when, as an earnest computer science undergraduate (like Alison, he too once believed the way to true contentment lay in technical know-how), he'd made the five-hundred-mile trip home on a Wednesday morning in mid-February, even coming up the back way, only to find his mother outside in a down parka, seated on a lawn chair, saying, "I knew you'd never make it through the semester."

She *always* knew, either through maternal resonance or eternal vigil. Perhaps she subscribed to a network of homeowners who, like the freedom fighters of the French Resistance, kept one another posted on the slightest disturbances of Chicago's South Side. In any case, he long ago ceased bothering to inform her about his visits. She'd only resent the early warning anyway, preferring to rely on her gift of precognition. Anticipating the infrequent, unannounced visits of her son provided her only entertainment. This time she met him midway between the front door and the point on the block where a body first becomes visible from the house.

—My Jesu, Petje, are you dead?

Mays never knew how to answer his mother's questions. Somehow a simple no didn't seem emphatic enough. But if he said more, his mother would look hurt and say, "I was only asking a question." Of several hundred rejoinders, he settled on:

—I'm fine, Mom.

—You lost your job?

—No, but I'm working on that. I didn't tell my boss I was flying out here.

—Do you think they're going to like that? You know, Petje, most places don't look kindly on employees leaving without saying anything. Come in the house. You can call them from here. I'll pay the charges.

—Mom, it doesn't matter. Listen. You know how you always say, "What Ford might have done for my family"?

—You need money and you say it doesn't matter if you lose your job?

—Forget it. What's for lunch?

And the two of them, arm in arm, sauntered up the flagstones, with Mrs. Mays explaining how she had just finished making several bologna sandwiches—his favorites—on the hunch that he might be flying the twelve hundred miles from Boston some time that day.

Although it meant paying uncountable dues, Mays enjoyed being home. He enjoyed it partly out of pure hedonism, for the perpetually clean linen and hot food so lacking in his life in Boston. He enjoyed the scent of memory that clung to the place, the after-stink of tar pitch that sticks to freshly washed hands. The paint-and-putty jobs his mother continually administered to the walls—she did not work, and had nothing else for her time but "keeping the place up"—never completely masked the atlas of nicks and bruises that stood for the various accidental joys of Peter's childhood: the place where he punched the door in a Christmas rage, the fat hutch's mass-marks in declivities on the floor. The smells of eucalyptus and vanilla extract, the constant clack of radiators, the yellow, irremediable tape marks, random rectangles from a siege of postcards and mementos.

Mostly he enjoyed returning home to sample the monastic sadness of the middle class that he loved. Mrs. Mays held down the fort in solitude. Her husband had died while Mays was still in his early teens. Of his father, Peter chose to remember only demonstrations of extreme emotion: anger, when loosening his belt in the threat of discipline; hope, when reminding his son privately how much depended on getting a solid, scientific training; or love, when administering maudlin, affectionate cuffs on the ear over three-handed pinochle.

Of sustained scenes involving his father, Mays remembered only one: the last three hours of life, when, the color and texture of a steamed clam, the man lay in a canopied bed in the back bedroom in an anaesthetic, camphoric haze, regaining consciousness only long enough to say, "This pain in my chest is driving me crazy." Since then, it had been just the two of them, and after Mays departed for the professional world, his mother took up permanently her solitary confinement.

Mrs. Mays and her son agreed that the pleasure of monasticism surpassed the sensible commodities of the world. She cared for nothing better than to hover perpetually at the picture window, never more than a few steps away from the lunch meat in the eventuality that her lingering hunch concerning her son's return should come true that day.

For sustained solitude, no house beat this one, and no neighborhood beat Chicago's near-southwest side. Although the houses were smaller, the lawns less spacious than on the affluent North Shore, a more profound gulf separated each living room. The residents here still lived in the shock of immigration. They came from Eastern Europe in the floodgates of the 1930s and '40s: Latvians, Czechs, Slavs—"Loogans," as the boy Mays generically lumped them, enjoying a one-generation edge of superiority.

Whether they lived in fear of having their green cards revoked, or whether, in interpreting the events of the last half century, they unanimously concluded that the only valid national state extended just as far as the cellar steps, few neighbors ever ventured out on the streets except to trowel their lawns in the anonymity of Saturday. The only proofs that the endless, cramped two-deckers—each with widows' walks and steep stone porch steps—had occupants were the clean doily curtains and plaster Holy Mothers haunting each window. Infrequently, sidewalk graffiti proclaimed that *Lithuanians Are Rising*, but if they rose they did so invisibly, perfidious as bread leaven.

Mays liked to come home to this universal respect for isolation. He liked to spend summer evenings sleeping in the rocker on the screened front porch, or, awake, molding his mind to concord with the crickets. Arriving home and answering his mother's questions, which ceased abruptly when she felt all was well, he could go out into the backyard, or up into the front loft overlooking the street and nurse the idea of total oblivion: the next best thing to being hopelessly lost. The more a person exercised nonfeeling, the more pleasant it felt. Mays, his mother, the Loogans, all loved this nothingness for the same reason: they had become used to it. It was what they knew.

But for this visit and perhaps a good deal longer, the old charm of loneliness lay outside his reach. He'd have to put isolation away awhile. Several months back he had started to form, for want of a better word, a concern; and as an oyster trades off size for smoothness in converting sand to pearl, Mays had made larger and larger gyrations to live with that concern until he had finally shelled out the two hundred dollars and sacrificed his job to fly out and ask his mother, over breakfast, what she knew of the father of modern mass production.

—"What Ford might have done"? I've been saying that for years. I got it from my mother, took it over as my birthright. You can use it if you want—no patent.

—Right, Mom. But tell me how your mother got started saying it. And don't say "thin air." She had to get it someplace.

—I forget. That's ancient history, Petje.

—Think. It's important. Believe me.

—What's the matter? You need money? I'll sell the furniture. What do I want for furniture?

—That's not the point, Mom.

—You need a place to stay? You come live here.

—It's not healthy for a grown man to live with his mother.

—What health? You're going to give me tuberculosis? What do I need for health?

Although devoutly Catholic and even an occasional Infant cultist, Mrs. Mays took a Yiddish syntax from the tutor who had taught her and her parents English. She was intelligent, but not highly educated. The other leading influence on her speech, the tabloid press, she scoured religiously each week, particularly for articles about the new advances of medical science. As such, her good, Anglo-Saxon word-hoard lapsed at times into purple, polysyllabic technobabble, a startling "piezoelectric" or "multivalence." She wrote more than she spoke. She lived for mail, sending twenty letters to her son's one.

—Look, Mom. I need to know where this phrase comes from. I'll explain it to you better when I understand it myself. Now as far as you know, your grandpa never worked for Ford. It wasn't something silly like that?

—Your great-grandpa never set foot in America.

Mays saw the irrelevance of the answer, but took it as a solid no. Right out of the gate he discovered what every researcher comes to admit in time: tracing folklore is largely speculation, even from the source's mouth. He began to suspect that the news photo was a coincidence. Perhaps his mother's grandfather lost his farm in the hard years following the war for want of a Ford tractor. But

Mays could not drop it there. Bernhardt had to be accounted for, Nijinsky, Armistice Day, Nurse Cavell, The Trading Floor.

The time had come to roll out the big guns. Peter had avoided asking directly to the point, equally terrified of both yes and no. But he had nothing left to find out except what he was after.

—Did any of my ancestors ever meet Ford?

—Are you joking me?

—Is that so impossible? The man wasn't a god. He probably met several little men in his life. Rumor has it he was a little man himself, once.

—Don't get fresh with your mother. My father was a poor policeman. He only met one celebrity in his life, the town funnyman named Bauble. He had to stop the fellow from killing his wife.

—So you're absolutely sure?

—"Sure" is for statesmen.

—I'm looking over the old stuff anyway.

—It's all yours. See if you can't throw some of it out this time. It gives me the willies, all those old papers yellowing. I can hear them.

Five hundred pounds of fire hazard in the house eaves made up the Mays family memorabilia. Mrs. Mays could not hear it yellowing because it had long ago yellowed. Nor did it give her the willies, and she did not really want any of it thrown out. Both she and her son shared a fondness for the old archival junk. The attic-treasure enforced their solitude. On those rare occasions when Mays mucked about in the memorabilia, he had liked not so much to look through it as to sit in and smell it—naphthalene and wood alcohol—and remind himself of how many people were already dead. Yet both mother and son felt obligated to denigrate the junk when speaking of it, ashamed to care for something so fully lost and useless.

The keepsakes filled the apron made by the A-roof where it ran past the verticals of the second story—not the attic proper, but more like two unfinished closets running the length of both eaves. In houses of this design, such superfluous space normally gets filled with insulation. So was the old stuff for the Mayses a sort of accessible insulation. The mementos divided chronologically: in the west eave, the material covering the last two generations—Peter and his folks. The east eave held everything earlier.

As a child, Peter was not allowed to enter either eave. When the constraint was lifted in adolescence, he satisfied the curiosity of the forbidden by spending an entire weekend there. After the initial orgy, his tastes settled and he grew to prefer the west. Peter liked his own records, photos of himself, not through any unusual narcissism but because he recognized what he was looking at. He liked to relive, this time consciously, those tiny triumphs of and over inconsequence: baby's first tooth; first unassisted toileting (Kodak, 1957). These records lay nearest the cubbyhole entrance to the crawl space, the easiest to dip into and the easiest to leave.

On more extended trips, he would crawl deeper into the west eave to visit his parents' documents. He liked the pictures of his mother as a child, posed in Wild West outfit on a four-foot pony, or smiling, back to rail, as her family sailed into New York harbor. Looming behind her in this milky, Brownie camera exposure was not the expected Statue of Liberty but the Ellis Island detention camp. The composition always made Peter more aware of the taker, presumably his grandfather, than of the subject, his mother. But he did not linger long over the photos and reproductions of his mother's life. He spent most of his time in the west eave getting to know his father.

From keepsakes Peter learned that his father—also a first-generation immigrant, judging by the quantity of letters with foreign postmarks—had come to this country as an orphan (passport) and had attended grade school at a charity organization (six report cards from Waterloo Ohio Home for the Homeless, gentleman's Cs, with some trouble in English, History, and Penmanship). He'd worked first for the railroads (medical record; insurance payment for tie dropped on and breaking his shin). Near the end of the Second War, as he came of age, he joined the service (volunteer, identification, regimental, and honorable-discharge papers). He served domestically with the Engineers (photo; insignia) after being rejected from the Air Corps as too short (personal letter).

A box of unsold samples attested to his first failed business venture, a cheap brass souvenir ashtray stamped *Welcome to Chicago*, bearing several intaglio views of city highlights: the Water Tower, the Science and Industry Museum, the El and Loop. Meticulous sales records in his father's hand attested that business had never been brisk. Chicago, as his father wrote sadly to a friend, never became the tourist mecca it should have been.

Finally Peter's father hit his stride as an actor on radio. A producer discovered him at a community Bingo game, calling out numbers in what could pass for a German accent. Once heard, his father was by all accounts easily remembered. Radio gave him a faceless notoriety. He became Herr Gustav, the Gentle German, who interrupted *Mystery Tonight* to beseech the home audience to "drinken op de bier dat is gut ver yoo." In the late forties, the Germans went from being the most feared to the most comical national group, and Mays's father capitalized on that change.

On an old machine the size of a large suitcase, Peter had several times listened to two-minute samples of his father's work. The distortion of radio and tape combined to make his father sound as far away as Sputnik, but close, too, as close and familiar as the crawl space, the west eave: the world's most German non-German, talking on in tongues as if he had never died. With the waning of commercial radio, he gave up the accent and became a reader of weather reports, with no one in the home audience any the wiser.

Beyond his father's keepsakes lay the end of the eave and a stepladder. Three crouched steps and Mays penetrated the broad attic under the A-pitch of the house. Here resided nothing of interest: old furniture, a globe still showing Manchukuo and Siam, and a Victrola that reproduced nothing earthly. Mays headed for the far side, where another stepladder descended into the east eave. He did not so much as turn his head to sniff the mementos of the more recent Mays family. This time he crawled for antiquity.

He went down the ladder and fumbled for the pull cord that lit the east eave. The light came on at a fraction of its original wattage, yet bright enough to show the material at hand as still too modern. No records of his father's family existed; he had arrived in America orphaned, without documents. The boxes around Mays held materials contemporaneous with his mother's earliest records in the west eave, only focused on her parents: identical boat-rail shot in front of Ellis Island, mother substituted for daughter. Mays had more hands and knees work before reaching relevant terrain.

Mays kept to the attic side of the low, pitched ceiling, edging his body forward in the manner of a coal miner. He could smell the artifacts getting older. A tilt of the head to either direction showed a bridal veil, a swatch of funeral gown, an oval frame around a hunk of hair, a piano roll titled "Heerlijke Opa." Warm and warmer. The molding holy host of printed material—the licenses, letters, certificates, lapsed insurance policies—multiplied into a babble of tongues.

He stopped to open a cardboard box: ten pounds of stereoscopic views, once popular with the spending public. Two photos of nearly the same scene—usually the Eiffel Tower, an auto show, or the boardwalk in Antwerp—sat shoulder to shoulder on stiffened cardboard. Whoever saw fit to save the views did not preserve the hand-held viewer, so Peter could only hold up and gaze at a few of the slightly skewed scenes and imagine how parallax transformed the two views into three dimensions.

A shade farther along, he opened a similar box filled with commercially reproduced *cartes de visite*, percursors of the modern postcard. He flipped through them randomly until hitting on one that made his blood go to zero: Madame Sarah lay supine on a sofa, not dead, but doing a convincing imitation. At once, he wondered how Brink, Bullock, Delaney, or even the silent partner Moseley could have broken into the east eave to plant this here. When the suspicion faded and he gazed on the rapturous, pliant face of the actress, he once again filled with desire, the urge to unmask, but not Bernhardt or the convincing Ms. Greene. He wanted to reveal the woman who had sat next to him, whose hand he half felt, half fabricated: Alison.

He could still abandon the east eave, reverse his quick flight of this morning, show up on The Trading Floor, and put himself at the mercy of the lacy Edwardian. Only a yard and a half of keepsakes still faced Mays, mostly unpromising trinkets and bric-a-brac. The printed matter had produced nothing promising so far: no famous names, no mention of America. For a moment, Mays thought the last four feet could promise nothing that Alison couldn't deliver in spades. She seemed to like him, even without knowing he was a tech writer. And she had cheekbones like you read about.

Peter debated the matter in his head while flipping through the primitive postcards. Each showed a celebrity; many he did not recognize. He thought it strange that his ancestors had a hundred photos of celebrities and none of themselves. But then, one could buy twenty Madame Curie prints for the price of an original gelatin. Mays thumbed through all the regulars—Edward VII, Victor Hugo, the Kaiser. Reaching Ford, he merely lifted his lip a fraction of an inch and started to pass on when he noticed that the identifying caption had been heavily scored in and underlined in fountain pen. Though circumstantial and insignificant, the detail forced Mays's hand.

Sometime later—he could not say how much later—he had turned over the entire east eave. He'd pored over print and private letters in four languages until he, who knew at best a smattering of Fortran, imagined he could almost understand them. Coming across an unassuming envelope marked *Sparen,* he knew that someone had posted the contents to an indesignate point in the future, had ordered subsequent generations to bring it intact through whatever public calamities the century served up.

The envelope held only three items. As Mays opened it, the smallest dropped to the floor. He held up the scrap to the light but could not read it. Whatever had been written—apparently a single word—was rendered forever unreadable by the softness of the pencil, paper grease, and years of folding that rubbed it out. Mays carefully replaced it in the *Sparen* envelope.

The second, much larger item lay folded in quarters. Mays opened it gingerly, revealing a photo badly beaten and defaced. He spread it flat. The rough handling did not obscure an image of three boys walking down a muddy road, nearing twilight. Mays withdrew the Greene clipping from his pocket and lined it up next to the large print. Even by attic light, Ford's heir and the middle figure on the road were undeniably one and the same.

Afraid of stroking out, Peter acted with deliberate slowness. He removed and unfolded the last article from the *Sparen* file, a doubled-over sheet of once-crisp heavyweight bond. Dated May 1, 1916, it began: "Dear Mr. Langerson." Mays looked up and thought: his mother's maiden name? But his mother's name had been Mays; his father had taken hers when they married because his was the same as that of a notorious Nazi war criminal. Mays checked his memory of the Reich for a Langerson, but all he could recall was that either Hitler, Göring, or Goebbels had only one testicle. For the fifth time in as many weeks, he kicked himself for his historical ignorance.

He continued reading:

> I said publicly on more than one occasion during my recent attempt to bring sanity to Europe that you were the only fellow I got any sense out of, and that I owed you one.

Mays quit reading, for medical reasons. He checked the signature before replacing the letter, although such a check was superfluous. In remarkably less time than it had taken him to crawl in, he freed himself from both eaves. And going downstairs to where his mother sat over a game of patience, Mays felt solitude rushing back into the house—the smell of an old friend.

Chapter Nineteen

The Cheap and Accessible Print

. . . Those who came into contact with the machine process found it increasingly difficult to swallow the presumptions of "natural law" and social differentiation which surrounded the leisure class. And so society divided; not poor against rich, but technician versus businessman, mechanic against war lord, scientist opposed to ritualist.—ROBERT L. HEILBRONER, *The Worldly Philosophers*

IN ONE of those apocryphal stories that make up the official history of Hollywood, a strapped producer tells a director who wants to take a film crew on location to Africa: "A rock is a rock, a tree is a tree. Shoot it in Griffith Park." The budget-conscious fellow knows that locale is created only partly by the on-screen jungle. The rest of the work is done by the million collaborators and African explorers inside the confines of the darkened theater. Reproduced on celluloid and given the lightest excuse for a narrative frame, Griffith Park can beat the deepest heart of darkness, even if the audience themselves have passed the same park on their way to see this same show.

A sophisticated adult might spend ten hours a week in Griffith Park, know every slab of granite and each graffito. But frame the place with a camera, crop it, mask the boom mike and bordering expressway, put two boys in the mud with gray fatigues and shallow bowl helmets, and add the persuasion of an artillery barrage produced by firing pistols into a trashcan, and this same sophisticated viewer will think: "So that's what Verdun looked like. It must have been horrible."

We explain such willingness to believe by pointing to the improving technology of reproduction, the growing accuracy of the mechanical facsimile. According to the theory, our machines have become so good at mimicking the sound, texture, and color of the original that it takes only the smallest suspension of disbelief to fall for the illusion. But this explanation is not enough. Boccaccio reports that Giotto's contemporaries often mistook his frescoes, which don't even employ rectilinear perspective, for the real thing; and viewers reportedly collapsed in dead faints at a scene in *The Great Train Robbery*—a film, in its best print, jerky, silent, black and white, and out of focus—where an actor takes a potshot at the lens.

Early audiences did not fall for clumsy illusions out of mere technical naïveté. For even the hyperproduced photographs and films of the 1980s come no closer to actual verisimilitude than did Giotto. A camera cannot begin to approximate the way an eye sees the same image. It changes the scale, focus, field depth, dimensionality, perspective, field of view, resolution, surface modulation, and luminosity of the image. Film color is restricted to discrete, subtractive values of the three primaries, and only approximates the continuous spectra of human sight. Each color print is unique, its tones not reproducible at will. Technological reproduction of images has certainly improved beyond all expectation. But our most advanced images are closer to Giotto than to the image a three-dimensional object makes in the eye.

Besides, if photographic technique were really powerful enough to make us confuse the image with its source, then we would at once say to ourselves, "Those are actors in Griffith Park," not "Those are soldiers at Verdun." For the park we pass daily would be so perfectly reproduced that it would force our recognition. The true power of photography and motion pictures, the trick that allows us to live imaginatively in the frame, is not the perfection of technique but the selective obscuring of it.

The strange persuasion of photographs rests on selective accuracy wedded to selective distortion. The reproduction must be enough like the original to start a string of associations in the viewer, but enough unlike the original to leave the viewer room to flesh out and furnish the frame with belief. Photography seems particularly suited for this precarious hybrid. It produces a finger painting in light-sensitive salts, but one regulated mechanically—simultaneously the most free and determined of procedures. One's shutter can only be open or closed, yet the resultant image can never be fully previsualized, corrected, or repeated.

Because the lens works so much more quickly and permanently than the eye, the result surprises even the photographer in its particulars: "That sign to the left on the building—I hadn't noticed that." Because the process mixes mechanical control with the surprise of light, and because the product mixes technical exactitude with veiling and distortion, the viewer's response is a cross between essayistic firmness—"this, then, the dossier, the facts"—and the invitation of fiction—"What can we make of it?"

Early photography had to educate its audience to this mixture. Editors of old pictorial journals, attempting to introduce rotogravure prints into their copy, met enormous resistance from readers, who found the old line engravings more realistic and dramatic. But by 1939, the public could see not Queen Elizabeth nor the anemic Bette Davis nor even a silver-gray, flat, underexposed and oversized phantom, but a hybrid of all these, tailored by the individual ticket holder.

Since inception, the medium implied that the only material difference between audience and artist was the possession of a camera. The technology first arose out of the desire of amateurs to record a scene independent of the unreliable hand. The *camera obscura*, an eighteenth-century tracing box, while reducing the need for special skill, still betrayed whether clever Hans or clumsy Franz did the tracing. One needed a device to place the Swiss Alps or the Grand Tour directly on the glass as it now stood. That need, and not the larger one of "seeing" better or improving on the Old Masters, precipitated the development of photography, although all the mechanisms had been known for some time.

And when, as often happens, several people at once evolved a process whereby light left its own register on the receiving frame, there arose an art not of talent or wizardry but of pure composition, vision, and decision, not of technical execution—the machine managed that—but of conception. Yet composition, vision, and decision are precisely the skills any intelligent viewer uses when standing in front of and appraising a finished picture. The process of making the thing becomes qualitatively indistinguishable from that of appreciating it. As Walter Benjamin puts it in his seminal essay, *The Work of Art in the Age of Mechanical Reproduction:*

> . . . the distinction between author and public is about to lose its basic character. The difference becomes merely functional.

With the advent of the cheap, hand-held, self-focusing, automatic camera, even this functional difference became negligible. The burgeoning, moderately privileged classes carried at their hip a machine that made it possible to select, edit, and preserve moments of reality at their own choosing. They did so by the trunkload, until no home was complete without crateloads of photo albums on display or stashed in the attic. Every family became at once the subjects, the photographers, and the editors of these albums, making the small jump from author to authority.

The enormous popularity of photography and movies comes from their having arrived at a gratifying hybrid of the expository and the participatory. The effect of a filmed image depends less on its content than on weighting, pacing, contrast, and other editing. Quick cuts between a man walking down the street and a woman, across town, anxiously looking at her watch affect us less in their content than their composition. We go to the matinee each Saturday less to see what perils the script inflicts this week on Pauline than to see how we and the director will get her out of them. As Benjamin states:

> The audience's identification with the actor is really an identification with the camera.

A thinly disguised Griffith Park cannot, by technology alone, pass for Verdun. Our enjoyment of the film comes partly from our *knowing* it is Griffith but making it serve as the battlefield. It resembles the battlefield enough to trigger us to build a symbol table in the mind, a table indistinguishable from the photographer's table of editorial and technical decisions. We are children, the photo, the germ of a story told us by a parent that we must elaborate, expand, repeat to ourselves to keep from falling asleep in the threatening dark. Listen to two people describe the same scene from a recent movie, complete with gesture, montage, directorial flair, but never one the same as another. Witnesses at a crime, they have forever sullied the facts with their own involvement.

We build our own symbols into the image, encouraged by the autonomy of the machine-made image. Although photography offers the possibility of manipulation—tinting, retouching, solarizing or mis-exposing, collage, assemblage, painting on the negative— such tamperings rarely fool the eye, let alone the mind. But under the auspices of the limiting machine, viewers give credence to their own free editing.

The nineteenth century adored the formal photographic sitting for three reasons. First, it could do, cheaply, the work of oils, which had been the reserve of the wealthy. Second, a print gave a good likeness without a painter's mannerisms. Third, the customer enjoyed the multiple pleasure of being subject, audience, and—by commissioning, posing, and selecting the final work—*auteur*. The photo-buying and soon the photo-making public saw in the studio portrait the perfect accomplice for its lifelong autobiographical projects.

With a shorter life-span and a heightened awareness of death, the nineteenth-century middle class also found in the daguerreotype and photograph more persuasive remembrances than the customary swatch of hair or inherited necklace. A newspaper ad for one portraitist's studio urges, "Secure the shadow ere the substance fade," and with this slogan hits upon the true selling point of the portrait: the shadow, infinitely more pliable, can mean more to the survivors than the substance ever did.

The shadow lends itself better to the continual act of biography the viewers weave in understanding the subject. Oval portraits, religious icons, stand on dresser-altars, remembrances rounding out the interpretive biography. The nature of the image takes second place to the associations of those who took, or feel that they took, the photo: "We had this taken on Stephen's tenth birthday, two months before he passed on. The photographer took a dozen, but I chose this one. His face clearly shows what he might have become. I made copies and sent them out to the aunts and uncles."

Running off copies—identical except to the trained eye—rather than decreasing the value, as with stamps and rare coins, multiplies it. There can be only one Ghent altarpiece, but there can be as many photos of Matthew on the back steps as one has the machine make. The monetary value of the Ghent altarpiece lies beyond calculating, while Matthew weighs in at twenty cents a print. But to the audience—the artistic consumer—the singularity of the altarpiece renders it unfit for anything but worship: five minutes at the museum rail until the folks behind begin "hemming"—a distancing proposition at best. On the other hand, one can possess, alter, love, own, and archive a print. When the *Hindenburg* explodes, it's not enough to look over someone's shoulder on the train and see that the thing has gone off. Buy a copy of the newspaper carrying the photo, and make the reality your own.

While the commercial value of a thing varies inversely with its ownability, this century nevertheless has declared that the book price counts for little against the identification of ownership. The autobiographical impulse—the true measure of worth—must stamp the object with the viewer's mark. One cannot interact with the "Mona Lisa" while standing behind the chain. But the machine has manufactured enough Betty Grables for everyone's personal consumption.

Certain reactionary photographers have tried to preserve the value of their prints at the expense of their consumability, creating limited editions and swearing on a stack of Stieglitzes that they destroyed the negative after fifty prints. But photos have always been the Model T of the arts. The man who wants to be buried with his five-hundred-dollar Ford because it has pulled him out of every hole so far also wants a five-dollar photo of his wife so that when she passes, he can pull her out of her hole and place her firmly on the dresser. A rock is a rock, a tree is a tree, and a profile does fine for the original.

This ability to reproduce limitless, virtually identical images without manual intervention seems either the greatest debasement or the fullest promise of the machine age. Machines strip processes of any value aside from the result. Packing plants, cameras, and motorcars care nothing about the way from A to B; they only want to get there sitting down, in the easiest manner possible. But the most expedient path is never the most delightful: the two are by definition distinct. We must choose between the getting and the going, the journey itself or the material outcome, aesthetic transport or mechanical transportation.

As a result, a large segment of population in each age attacks the machine as dehumanizing, moribund, ruthless, stultifying, uncontrollable, banal, ugly—in short, the worst sense of "mechanical" and "mass-produced." To these people, an object's value is the measure of humanity poured out and lavished on it. Reproducing destroys the unique quality and value of things. The cult of beauty judges by difficulty and effort: the clumsiest painting holds more value than the most striking photo, as the first came about through the more revealing, because more arduous, path.

For these believers, replacing the simple and beautiful with the mechanical and expedient—tractor with plough, horse and carriage with Ford, saber with musket and then carbine—starts a process of self-replicating escalation that ends only when our tools, regardless of our own say, seek an outlet of power and mechanical efficiency in an act of violence. No one can deny that this century's wars have been exercises of mechanical power, nor can one doubt—equivocal theories of deterrence notwithstanding—that the mere existence of fifty thousand nuclear warheads raises the possibility of annihilation above zero. But this camp takes an even stronger antitechnological stand: mass reproduction of photographic images represents and initiates those values that would destroy beauty, singularity, and all that is human and humane.

To others squared off against this line, mass production and reproduction provide a welcome liberation from the tyranny of privileged aesthetics—an "art of five kopeks." This camp, including Benjamin, believes that equating rareness with beauty, worshiping art in museums instead of using it in homes, keeping the market free of imitations to drive up the price of the original have for too long deprived too many people of the natural material necessary for contemplation and betterment.

In this light, photography—mass reproduction and distribution—at last provides a means for popularizing and democratizing artistic value. For the first time in history, copying an image is no more difficult or expensive than enjoying the original. The previously hallowed barrier between maker and appreciater breaks down. The anti-mechanicals lament the debasing of author to the level of mass audience. The pro-mechanicals celebrate the elevating of mass audience to the level of authority.

To the pro-mechanicals, rapid and unchecked proliferation of printed art, rather than negating or diluting value, promises untold practical and aesthetic worth for unchecked, proliferating mankind. As Benjamin suggests:

> . . . the newsreel offers everyone the opportunity to rise from passer-by to movie extra. In this way any man might even find himself part of a work of art . . .

What of the anti-mechanicals' accusation that the machine's concentration on results over process, on ends over means leads to a state of violence, where domination grows naturally out of efficiency? That mechanical technology creates weapons of unthinkably violent potential lies beyond doubt. But pro-mechanicals counter that our spirit of using or denying machines, rather than mechanics itself, causes or avoids conflict. Just as proxy battles and corporate shakeouts mean to solidify—by conflict—antagonists' holdings, so wars between national states, say the pro-mechanicals, mean to preserve and expand the material value—the uniqueness—of the state while asking the constituency to pay in doughboys.

An art of the few rather than the many, equating beauty with commercial rareness, only perpetuates those material motives that underwrite wars. Says Benjamin:

> If the natural utilization of productive forces is impeded by the property system, the increase in technical devices . . . will press for an unnatural utilization, and this is found in war. The destructiveness of war furnishes proof that society has not been mature enough to incorporate technology as its organ, that technology has not been sufficiently developed to cope with the elemental forces of society. . . . Imperialistic war is

a rebellion of technology which collects, in the form of "human material," the claims to which society has denied its natural material.

The choice is clear: shoot snapshots or shoot rifles. Produce and distribute widely available images that answer the material needs of the world, run off universally available, obtainable stock certificates, or enforce the old system of aesthetic ownership with violence. We have the choice of politicizing aesthetics with the aid of cameras or falsely prettifying political reality, which, according to Benjamin, leads only to war. Treating current events as art or reading history as romantic fiction must result in revering conflict, too, as a formal beauty.

Thus both extremes in the debate of mechanical reproduction accuse each other of stances that result in catastrophe. Between these two groups, the vast majority of us go about using cameras without realizing the consequences at stake. We make our albums, take our snapshots, at times out of a love of rare beauty, at times out of a documentary impulse, but mostly as a healing charm against death. We try, with the aid of the lens, understanding neither technical mechanism nor philosophical import, to beat the annihilation of time, shore up against loss, not just loss of the subject matter—our late aunt Sophie, or last summer's vacation in the Balkans—but the death of the instant of vision, the death of the eye, which, without the permanent record made by the machine, gradually loses the quality revealed to it in the moment of seeing.

Every photographic print invites identification with the photographer, forces re-creation of the values implied in preserving the vanished image. Viewing becomes a *memento mori*, a reminder of the death of the subject matter, landscape or portrait, long since passed away but remade in our owning and involving ourselves with the print. For the viewer, contemplating the lost scene of a photograph lies well outside the aesthetic *or* the political. Hannah Arendt explains this in her treatise on violence:

> Death, whether faced in actual dying or in the inner awareness of one's own mortality, is perhaps the most antipolitical experience there is. It signifies that we shall disappear from the world of appearances and shall leave the company of our fellow men, which are the conditions of all politics.

Every full appreciation of a photo, every alignment of ourselves with the lens creates in us the profound awareness of such a departure. For we have left, we have died away from the conditions of the photograph's moment. Every mechanical landscape, interior, or portrait comes to the viewer over time, a memory posted forward from the instant of the shutter waiting to come into conjunction with the instant of viewing. Noticing the image, observing it at once implicates the viewer as a partner in that memory. Looking at a photo, we act out and replay, to a copied phantom, parallels of the very decisions and criticisms of the photographer. We ask: "Who would I have to be, what would I have to believe in to have wanted to preserve this instant?"

And just as our daily autobiographical revisions resemble collective history and allow it to write itself, so the act of seeing and loving a photographic image calls us to action, but action circumscribed by the image's historical context. Interpretation asks us to involve ourselves in complicity, to open a path between feeling and meaning, between ephemeral subject matter and the obstinate decision to preserve it, between the author of the photograph and ourselves.

The idea that we look *at* the sitter or subject matter begins to lose its credibility. We look *over* it, attempting to locate something else. When a movie editor cuts from a woman turning her head to a midrange shot of the shops across the street, we follow her gaze, having of our own volition turned our attention to look with her. To make sense of a montage means to reassemble the cut, in reverse, using the editor's criteria. We remake the montage dynamically, as an act of looking.

The same applies to still photos: the lens slices a cross-section through time, presenting an unchanging porthole on a changed event. The frame invites us to feel a synchroneity with the photographer the way museum-case glass, slicing through a beehive, invites us to live in the colony. We cannot worry too much over what lies to the right or left of the restricting frame. If the path between sense and significance opens, it will open in those moments when, momentarily delighted by some overlooked detail or construed resemblance, we become aware of what lies in front of the plane of the photo.

We scour *over* a photo, asking not "What world is preserved here?" but "How do I differ from the fellow who preserved this, the fellows here preserved?" Understanding another is indistinguishable from revising our own self-image. The two processes swallow one another. Photos interest us mostly because they look back.

Time and again in Sander's unfinished portrait gallery, *Man of the Twentieth Century*, painfully aware of the serious business of the lens, his subjects abandon hope of portraying their individual peculiarities and instead take up the heavier obligation of representing their upbringing, social role, and class. They focus their gaze distantly, well past the photographer, on a farther, more important concern. When we come behind the photographer's shoulders into conjunction with that gaze, we have the macabre feeling of being its object, the sense that the sitters mean to communicate something to us, to all posterity.

Yet this sitters' arrangement is the very opposite of what is commonly called posing. Sander deprives his subjects of the studio pose, the refined posture meant to convey character. With the cataloging urge of a natural scientist, he treats them as specimens, and they can at best buck up and make themselves presentable. Normally, the subject, desiring immortality, makes an appointment and appears at the studio. Sander reversed all that, bicycling to and pinning down his unsuspecting species where they grew. Depriving them of their active desire to be photographed, Sander enforces his subjects' accountability to the camera. They are caught in the act of revising their own biographies under the examining eye of history, which is the lens.

A fish and child on either side of aquarium glass react to and modify the behavior of the other: a finger jab causes fluking causes a delighted squeal causes a surprised flushing of gills. We, on the far side of the glass, adjust ourselves similarly. The subject of *Man of the Twentieth Century* is this constant interplay between the small self and the larger portrait gallery. The subject of *Man of the Twentieth Century* is us.

Sander, in depriving his subjects of the ability to pose heroically, deprives the viewer of the same evasion and gives even the casual museumgoer the sense of being summoned. When just before the turn of the century, the police photographer Jacob A. Riis brought out his volume of images called *How the Other Half Lives*, he removed the subjects one degree more. His sitters were both unwilling and unwitting, not even aware they were being photographed. Riis and two assistants skulked about at night, clandestinely taking flashpan photos of criminals and the extreme poor. Following the blinding discharge, the photographers would have to disappear just as suddenly, often pursued by startled and angry crowds.

Riis meant to expose the squalid conditions of New York's Lower East Side, to show the poverty and degradation of the human flotsam there. He could do so only surreptitiously, without his subjects' consent. In one startling image, robbers, some bearing cudgels, peer threateningly down their narrow alley hideout at the dazzling phosphorus explosion. Decades slide past the ground glass, and they look out on the scholar, museumgoer, or nostalgist, who has taken the part of the original intruder.

Perhaps Riis intuited that a comfortable, propertied class would believe the debilitating conditions he documented only if they saw, as collaborative evidence, their own unwillingness to look reflected in the poor's unwillingness to be looked at. Riis, in showing the local decrepitude of one city, succeeds in showing the true face of humanity when unable to prepare itself for the record.

The removal of the sitter's pose from the finished portrait becomes complete in the work of Eugène Atget, who photographed Paris early in this century. Tens of thousands of plates show deserted streets, shop windows filled with bric-a-brac or headless mannequins, empty doorways and arcades, and barren cafés waiting for a clientele conspicuous in its absence. The scenes catch the hushed, paralyzed aftermath of tragedy. Atget's empty streets are portraits without sitters, calling attention to a foreground surprisingly vacant. They are the clichéd snapshots of relatives in front of public buildings, only this time the viewers must supply their own relations.

The aperture of a camera forms a two-way portal through which both subject and viewer peer into another time. The subject, conscious of the permanence of the document, posts forward a memory. The viewer, aligning with the memory at some later date, works to preserve the sight from disintegration. Both are present at both moments; both experience the revelation of being adrift in time, sampling it laterally.

The moment of recording and the moment of interpretation lose their basic distinction. Somewhere in time, observer and observed reverse roles. Conscious of being watched through the asynchronous screen, both modify their behaviors, presenting their best profiles: interpenetration of looker and participant, audience and authority, aesthetic escape and polemical display, welded together and mechanically propagated through time.

To look at a thing is already to change it. Conversely, acting must begin with the most reverent looking. The sitter's eyes look beyond the photographer's shoulders, beyond the frame, and change, forever, any future looker who catches that gaze. The viewer, the new subject of that gaze, begins the long obligation of rewriting biography to conform to the inverted lens. Every jump cut or soft focus becomes a call to edit. Every cropping, pan, downstopping receives ratification, becomes one's own.

Consider a print of you and a lover standing by the side of a house. You can shrink or enlarge it to any size. You can print it on matte, glossy, or color stock. You can mask the negative, tint it, print it up as Christmas cards. You can crop it and edit out your mate or yourself as appropriate. Finally, you can take a twelve-dollar camera and repeat the scene with a new lover, as many times as it takes to get it right.

And a new technology, already on us, extends this ability well beyond still photography. Every home is about to be transformed into an editing studio, with books, prints, films, and tapes serving the new-age viewer as little more than rough cuts to be reassembled and expanded into customized narratives. Reproduction will make the creation and appreciation of works truly interactive. These exotic technologies, like the camera before them, will enlarge the viewer's understanding of the maker's act.

We feel the process of looking most powerfully when not distracted by the object of attention. On a busy street, a normally perfunctory businessman stops on his way to the office and cranes his neck to relieve a crick acquired by sleeping with the window open. The woman behind him stops too, looking up with a voyeur's curiosity. Soon a whole crowd gathers, refusing to miss the excitement, looking up into absolutely vacant sky. Some demand, "What is it? What's happening?" Others imagine: "There; I saw it, just behind that building." Still others feel an oceanic gratitude come over them: "So this is me, on a July morning, stopped a moment, looking into the blue." Then they shrug shoulders, straighten shirtsleeves, and remark to themselves, "A curious thing, consciousness," before heading off to their appointments.

Here at last is an explanation of why we can be moved by a scene clearly filmed in Griffith Park. We respond not so much to the events on film as to the thousand reels we concurrently edit in our mind—movies of our own hopes and terrors. Griffith Park, Verdun, the empty streets of Paris, or three men on a muddy road matter less than the mechanical decision to involve ourselves, to retake the composition and extend the story.

On a Wednesday afternoon, just after one, the drizzle of a false January spring began slowly, imperceptibly to crystallize into a flurry of snow. I had skipped work, calling in a lie about my returning to the Midwest for a family emergency. The couple in the apartment directly above mine were also home and fighting, as was their natural idiom. The woman alternately screamed and laughed in pleasure. The man begged, pleaded, threatened, and destroyed furniture. I could not hear the issue.

Across the courtyard, a baritone sax rehearsed chromatic scales—the music cartoons use to portray seasickness—missing the same notes it had missed daily since I took the apartment. In the street, a man wearing two bulky, oily coats stood stock-still, repeating, "The hell you did; the hell you did" to no one in particular. I had, in my neck and forearms, the warm distress that marks the onset of the flu. I decided to take a walk, not to get outside before it began snowing in earnest, but to get a good, solid, raging flu if I had to get one.

I prefer walking to any other means of getting from A to B. It's a perversity on my part, pure and simple, but I enjoy the feeling of even the smallest, ten-cent errand taking up twenty dollars of my prorated time. The availability of the private car makes it absolutely unaffordable to use any cheaper transportation. But on this day I had not been able to walk fifty dollars worth before the snow became so heavy I could no longer keep my eyes open. In a fraction of an hour, the day had gone from delicious spring—the stink of earthworms and returning vees of geese—to a winter storm, knocking out power lines, blocking streets, and blanketing everything under whites and halftones.

For some minutes I was unable to move. I shielded my eyes as the neighborhood disappeared into gray outline. A car jackknifed nearby and thudded softly into the curb. Snow obliterated the scene, but the air, strangely, did not feel especially cold. It had that odd cusp quality that occurs at 68 degrees, again at 50, once more at 32, and finally, say the adventure stories, at −40, where the temperature osmotically matches the body, cradles it without being felt.

I stood motionless, seeing nothing, distracted by nothing, feeling nothing but the leading edge of my illness. Suddenly, I felt an overwhelming urge to quit my job: the most trivial, self-evident decision in my life. I had no idea why I wanted to be rid of it, or what I would do to survive. I felt like traveling. I bent down and scooped together the first accumulation of snow, pressed it into my cheeks and eyes, and let some drop into my collar and down my shirt.

A memory stirred just out of reach of my thoughts, some name, place, or event pressing in from the outside that demanded speaking. As the snow lifted slightly, I half expected to confront some tableau—a Model T, perhaps, sliding on the new layer of white, or a vision of antique petticoats, high-laced boots, and strawberry hair requesting a photograph while the snow obscured the outline and era of the city.

What I saw was nothing so remarkable. I had sprung a slight nosebleed from jamming the snow in my face. With a little imagination, I found I was in Mrs. Schreck's neighborhood. It was still early afternoon; she could not have left yet for her evening cleaning stint at the office. At the staff Christmas party she had urged me several times to drop in if I was ever nearby. Well, I was nearby. Perhaps she would not mind my dropping by for something to stanch the bleeding.

For months I had gone after the source of the photo—names, dates, places—hoping, by pinning down the biographical fact, to alleviate the hurt and mystery of the thing. Yet in the time I'd spent trying to dispose of the memory, I'd become something of a martyr, thinking of it as "my photo" and "my farmers." But it was not mine; I had done nothing with it except try to explain it away. Mrs. Schreck had far better claim on the image, not because she had met the photographer, shook his hand, or bought the image directly from him. That was incidental chance.

Mrs. Schreck's claim on the image rivaled even Sander's. She had made it her own; at the instant of seeing it, she had construed a relation between one figure and a friend of hers whom she had loved more than life. For half a century, she had honed that resemblance, elaborated on it, edited it, despite not one of the fellow's other acquaintances ever being able to see a likeness.

Perhaps she would not mind my stopping by for a lesson in how to see.

Chapter Twenty

Out-of-Town News

He thought that by distilling the sludge he could trap the *Weltgeist*, or Universal Spirit. By chance he observed that the residue left in the retort when heated glowed in the dark even when cool, and he named it *phosphorous* ("bringer of light").— BEAUMONT NEWHALL, *The History of Photography*

AFTER SWEATING OUT the first few checkpoints, Peter settled down and stopped worrying about how little he resembled the picture of Theo Langerson on his official papers. Aside from superficial similarity of hair color, skin tone, and bone structure, the two men could not have been less alike. Theo was a good fifteen years older than Peter, had high cheekbones and narrow forehead, and looked saturnine where the other looked impish. Although only two inches wide, the photos on passport and press papers could never pass for Peter without the most generous assistance of the inspector.

When his group of neutral physicians, diplomats, and reporters from Maastricht reached the border of occupied Belgium, Peter, seeing how meticulously the German officials and Belgian collaborators went over the travelers' printed documents, gave up hope of pulling off the switch of identities. But at the precise moment when he prepared to turn back and reboard the train for Holland and probable conscription, an examining line opened up and a boy his age, in the uniform he should have been wearing, asked him to step forward. Peter advanced and offered his papers. He hoped the amusement of the boy's confusion would help compensate for the penalties. If the fellow asked him any questions, he would answer with the echo game so beloved of the tobacconist's widow.

The Kaiser's foreign arm fussed a great deal with the written material. Peter suspected that he, like Hubert, was more polemical than literate. But coming on the photos, the fellow at once looked up and nodded in approval. He did the same with the second, identical print, then waved Peter/Theo into the occupied country. On the far side of the checkpoint, Peter, amazed, inspected the images to see if they had changed.

Now inside Belgium, trying to recross the Meuse was just as dangerous as pushing on to Paris. So he kept to the original plan, sticking with the band of neutral pilgrims for extra credibility, traveling to the front to escape the front. After repeat performances at various checkpoints, he began to think, incredulously, that he might make it. Number Four stopped his heart by holding the photo out at arm's length next to Peter's face and squinting. After an unbearable length of time, the ersatz Mr. Langerson suggested:

—Haircut.

The official gave a knowing "aha" and passed him on. Number Seven, a stubby, good-natured Hanoverian, who all during the inspection professed a love for the Dutch, stopped short at the photo.

—You must have been on a bender for this one.

Peter did his best to look sheepish and charming.

The real test, he knew, would come at the first French checkpoint. The group was to leave from a free Belgian port and arrive at Le Havre, making an end run around the trenches and sailing under a clean bill of health from the German submarines. Peter thought the photo would not pass the French as easily as it had done the Germans. The European war had come about because the Germans were too industrious to be observant while the French were too observant to do anything, and two such radically opposed temperaments could not exist side by side on the same map. But the first and only Frenchman to inspect his credentials before whisking him on to Paris merely lifted one eyebrow at the ridiculous likeness.

—Old photo?

The strain of the journey had worn away Peter's resistance.

—Actually, sir, it isn't me.

The *poilu* affected a dry laugh, as if to say, "We French may be getting the shit kicked out of us, but no one can say we don't like a good joke." In this way, Peter Kinder, become Schreck, made his way through the world conflict to a besieged Paris, completing the first step in his transformation to Theo Langerson, Dutch war correspondent.

The Parisian authorities issued him a cold-water flat and kept him in close check. They required him to report each morning at ten to a makeshift International News chamber, to have his name marked off a roster, and to stay for an optional official briefing on the hostilities to date. His first such session featured a sanitation worker who, in Gallieni's already legendary defense of Paris, had had a three-inch lead pipe blown through his brain, entering at the frontal and exiting at the parietal lobes.

The briefing covered how the fellow had undergone massive personality changes and claimed to have come from another time. The French authorities gave the press carte blanche to interview the man, providing, of course, their accounts passed the usual wartime censors. At this first briefing, Peter realized that, even if he were interested in covering the war, the official French news conferences would be of no help.

He tried to see the sights of Paris, but gave it up after only two hours when all the famous structures began to resemble Les Invalides. The city had been prettier from a distance, in the rotogravure. He did not feel at home in this city of the homeless, largely because, though transient, he was there not as a person who could not find his turf, but as one who took to each new climate too easily. In Paris, one really had not to belong to belong.

He left his flat each morning with just enough time to reach the press parole board at ten. He skipped the ensuing briefing, taking off immediately for no place in particular. For the deal with Theo never stipulated that Peter take seriously his war reportage. Their arrangement was equally convenient: both saved the other's skin. Theo could not bargain for much more. Yet Peter, grateful for his delivery from the two rotund German agents, tried to satisfy the requests made of him by the pact—from what he could remember, to keep eyes and ears open, send back numbers and geography, and stay out of trouble with authorities.

Theo had explained to him that most reporting consists of

elaborating on extremely small quantities of facts. A good journalist could get by with almost none at all. Theo called it "restoring the context," and pointed out that the public liked a vivid description of an artillery barrage more than statistics and kilometers. Who knew how long a kilometer was in wartime anyway? "Gallant stand" and "wavering defense" cut a better figure with the fellow spending his news guilder than "position x, position y, position z."

And so, from a few offhand observations Peter picked up and forwarded in his first weeks' walking around Paris—observations running from "Men in shirtsleeves try to use opera glasses to spot the front from upper windows" to "My concierge found a shell fragment on a picnic"—the real Theo, living a happy life among cigars and the widow's fat folds, put together an editorial called "The Boulevards Under Siege." The title took longer than the copy itself, which he created by bringing the bones Peter pitched him into line with a few facts from a single-volume encyclopedia.

The article caused a sensation, boosting the paper's reputation a head above the other Maastricht regulars, who relied on dry strengths and maneuverings plagiarized from one another. A negligible government agency cited the article as "outstanding in bringing the war home to the Dutch people," although the citation did not go on to explain why such an activity was commendable.

Peter's humble war correspondence, rising no higher than "Generalissimo Joffre announced publicly today that the French are winning," would have trickled out altogether after a few weeks if it weren't for a perversity: he adored the strange sensation of posting a letter to himself. To address an envelope with his name, care of the widow's shop, gave him the exquisite pleasure of receiving inside word from the front, although in his role of sender, he knew the word to be worthless. He felt he was the first to communicate from beyond the grave, or from one time to another. His propriety unhinged each time he posted correspondence to himself, and the novelty of standing detached from his old self refused to diminish.

The wartime authorities of Paris, however, soon intervened. One day, not six weeks after his arrival, Peter was summoned for a hearing before the military censors.

—Mr. Langerson, it has not escaped the attention of our copy readers that the stories—and I use the term literally—you send back to your home country are the briefest, most sporadic, and least accurate of any foreign editor in the city. Is it your paper's policy, Mr. Langerson, to turn the gravest calamity in all history into a bowl of steamed tripe to serve up over breakfast?

—Over breakfast, sir?

—Dinner, then, if you will. I assumed that your paper, of which I am blissfully unaware, has no afternoon edition.

—No afternoon edition, sir.

—Well then, my friend, we understand one another. Now ordinarily we would not interfere; we allow anything to pass not libelous or injurious to our cause. Let the public hang its sources, is our motto. But in your case, it smacks of suspicion to have a foreigner nosing about Paris, never once visiting the front he is supposed to be covering, sending abroad infrequent, speculative notes not fit for the sports pages.

—Not fit . . .? I'm new to this sort of reporting, sir. I used to do . . . the *other* sort of reporting, you understand? I mean, our first war fellow was killed, poor sap, at Liège. Bloody mess up there, sir, as I'm sure you're aware. Our second went down in Alsace. We had two gents die with the Germans from eating canned brats. Finally, I was the only one left. I used to do the "Society Chat" column. You know: who's poking whom, and who cares. I just can't seem to adjust to this whole . . . world conflict business, sir.

—Quite. You understand our position, however. In wartime, everyone's conduct, particularly our guests of the state, must be beyond suspicion. Or they are deported or tried as spies. The Germans shoot civilians, you know.

—Thank you, sir. I'm sorry, sir.

Peter used these two phrases instinctively when in trouble, as his mother had always drilled into him that good manners can save a man's life. He suppressed "much obliged," the third in the trilogy, only through a mighty effort of will.

—That's all, Mr. Langerson. And if you are looking for the war . . .

The chief examiner pointed a finger northeast. Peter left the room and building heading in that direction, so as not to draw further suspicion. It did not take a great leap of insight to see that the revelation that he worked under an assumed name and sent his copy to a tobacco shop would not bode well at a spy trial. He had, it seemed, to creep still closer to the front to escape it.

His copy increased and improved suddenly and considerably, for one with only a fifth-grade education. Pushing deeper into the war zone under armed escort, he discovered a thrill in being there as a noncombatant. He took a voyeur's, even a collector's, pleasure in knowing the soldiers' routines without having to follow them himself. He was allowed to reconnoiter only on those days when a visible lull hung over the lines, and his presence always noticeably moved the troops. They swelled and mugged for his benefit, competed for his attention, reporting a garden variety of acts of valor that, albeit small, had, each assured him, radically altered the war.

As he and his notebook traveled about the lines, Peter could not at first adjust to being the center of attention. He'd always played the *Lümmel,* and the respect of all these earnest men left him with the overwhelming urge to tell, with visual accompaniment, the joke about the fellow whose bowels wouldn't move. But the slightest donnybrook and he was hung for espionage—the only draftable German behind French lines. To compensate for the old nihilistic urge, he grew even more formal, reserved, rigid. This, in turn, led the common *poilu* to lend more authority to his act, and they badgered him all the harder with personal histories.

Although not school-bred, Peter possessed enough native intelligence to see that his new dispatches, although vastly improved in range and detail, were no more accurate than his old reports concerning his concierge's inside information about a pact with Italy. First, he only saw those areas not directly involved in conflict. He had never witnessed, even from the safety of a nearby hill, the actual mechanics of slaughter. So long as the French government controlled his movements, he could not hope to look directly at the war but only at its by-product—the reflection of an eclipse in a pinhole shadow box.

Second, the troops obviously altered their behavior for his benefit. On seeing him, they went from shelled silence to singing the *Sambre et Meuse.* From grumbling about meat-maggots, they rallied to brag about the battering of the Boches in the last encounter. Peter wondered about the nature of the camps in his absence, but dismissed the question as meaningless. He could not report on what he did not know. He could know only what he saw firsthand. Yet his firsthand presence forever altered the observed.

When he had used Paris simply to stay out of the service, Peter had felt no qualms about the quality of his military reports, doing no more or less than needed to preserve his adopted identity. But compelled by the authorities, for form's sake, to draw closer to his subject matter, he began trying to close in on it. Over several visits to the lines, he befriended a frequent escort, a Breton sergeant, in the hopes of finding some hard data less suspect than his subjective interviews with cooks, MPs, and carbine grist not yet knocked out of their *cran* and *élan vital*. One day, he asked the sergeant casually:

—Tell me about the war: what drives it? How will it fall out? I know so little.

With a curious look and an ironic salute, the sergeant packed him into an unreliable staff car and assaulted the top of a nearby hill. The two left the auto and stood overlooking the lowlands, teeming with the unknowable movements of the hive. The sergeant stood at attention, and with almost Germanic, paradelike precision, extended his arm and index finger, describing the grandiose arc of a porcelain music-box ballerina, calling out:

—The Germans came down on us in a large, circular scythe. To our far left, nearest the Channel, came Kluck and their First Army. He was to set the pace, being the circumference of the wheel. Next in, Bülow had the Second. Then came Hausen with the Third. They went through Belgium like *that*. Some titled gents headed up the Fourth and Fifth: the Duke of Württemberg and the Crown Prince, Frederick Wilhelm. Now facing them are our men: to the left, the Fifth, under Lanrezac, the Fourth under . . .

The text had already been printed, bound, reviewed, and only awaited events to catch up before being shipped to bookstores everywhere. Peter stopped the sergeant just before he reached the pitched battle marking the end of the war and the final cleansing of the world.

—*Pardonnez-moi, monsieur,* but do all these names belong to people? These fellows are the war?

—Of course not, sir. Patience, and give me a chance. I'm getting to the matter of the British, and the affair in the East. A great disappointment to us, the Russian steamroller. Then there's the small countries in the Balkans, but I'm not too up on that.

—So Kluck plus Bülow divided by Lanrezac equals all those men back at hospital who want me to know that they didn't scream when the mine blew off their big toe? That's what I'm to write home to my paper?

—Sir?

The sergeant gave Peter the fossil stare he reserved for cutting off a draftee's obtuseness. He attempted comprehension, rallied, attacked, wavered, and at last retreated from the discussion in a rout.

—Don't the Dutch enjoy reading about commanders? I'm not a politician, and it's a little late to be bothering about causes at this date, sir.

Insulted, the sergeant returned gruffly to the auto. On the way back to Paris, he declined to answer questions, saying only that there wouldn't be any Germans on French soil if officers could fight rather than give tours.

Peter wrote to the original Theo for pointers on improving his journalism. He wrote delicately, to keep from alarming the French censors:

> Dear Peter, I hope that as my managing editor you enjoyed my last reports from this side of the war. The French are more than helpful with material, yet I think I can improve my work. I want to write the story of the real war—I mean the father's, wife's, son's war, the small businessman's war. Can you give me any help? Any word an old paper-hound like yourself could give would be gold to me. Theo.

The old Theo, alarmed by the recent dramatic improvement in Peter's articles, grew terrified at this letter. Everything had been so perfect; by sending a proxy to the front, he'd escaped a shrewish family and publisher, and learned more about cigars than he thought possible. Editing was easier than ever; studying the rival papers, he could transform Peter's scraps into eyewitness accounts that involved all Maastricht. A good feature took only half an afternoon.

But when the dispatches began including facts, Theo worried that Peter, by enlisting another's aid, had jeopardized the whole system. Confused by the euphemistic tone of the note, the over-subtle Theo jumped to the conclusion that Peter was blackmailing him: the small businessman's war; every word being gold. Obviously, Peter had gotten a cushy protection, and no longer needed him. The veiled threat: pay up, or I'll tell all. Panicked, he did not know whether to write the new Theo or make out a will for the old one. The widow was no help:

—Let the scamp try thing one and I'll go to the front and teach him how to cover the war.

The old Theo had been content to let nations reach their moment of crisis while he sat on the neutral sidelines editing observations. But the belligerents came to claim their own, it seemed. His life as a small shopkeeper lay ruined. The little bell on the shop door, formerly filling him with the delight of potential sale, now made him flinch and turn his face involuntarily. The bell ringer—his publisher, the widow's husband's corpse, his own wife perhaps, Joffre, or the Goblin King—was after him.

All Holland knew that Germany, having drawn Britain into the war by violating Belgium and Luxembourg, stood to lose nothing but two days in swallowing up the Netherlands. But these worries did not alter the armchair editor's feelings of having been singled out for persecution. He would rather have the war come to him than have to go to it. He wrote to Peter: "Stuff your war and your stories. You can't threaten me." Peter, too confused by this to be hurt, thought he was ready, with some spelling help from a censor who had studied Dutch at the École Normale, to send his articles directly to the paper in Maastricht.

Hearing no response from his double at the front, Theo felt more than ever that the jig was up. For months he refused to leave the shop, even to take the air. When customers entered, he ducked behind the counter and called out, "Who is it?" in a high, squeaky voice. He dreamed of assignments in New York or Khartoum, but he had no identity papers. Theo Langerson was a minor celebrity for his Paris by-lines; Peter Schreck was wanted for extradition. And with fifty thousand names a day being erased, aliases were at a premium.

The strain of waiting for history at last caught up with the hack-cum-clerk. He left Maastricht and hitched to the North Sea. Unable to book passage without proper papers, he rented a single shell and attempted to scull to Sweden. On May 1, 1915, the first anniversary of Peter, Hubert, and Adolphe's photo, a German sub picked him up and impressed him into service. Six days later he helped bring down the *Lusitania*, more capable of adjusting to the times than he thought.

Reporting directly to the paper, Peter grew more aware than ever of the injustice his stories did his readers and the events. He wrote increasingly cavalierly about the facts of fighting, making them up or ignoring them entirely. Had the French and Germans accumulated the territorial gains he claimed, they would have been in Moscow and Tulsa, respectively. Had his casualty and ammunition counts been right, the war would long ago have trickled down to two fishmongers slapping each other with carp yanked from the Somme.

Yet he caught the effect of an artillery barrage: "Put your ear to the engine block while your neighbor cranks for twelve hours." In short, halting sentences, he described the first, flimsy flying machines a hundred feet above the lines, how half the men clapped their hands in rapture, while half, terrified, trained their guns on the unknown. Peter was the first to suggest in print that both sides use insignia, so troops would know which side strafed them.

He relied more and more heavily on direct quotes. One foot soldier confided: "The best thing about mass formation is that you stop worrying about your smell." Another said: "It's all waiting; first I wait for something to happen, then I wait for it to end, then I wait for an explanation, but that passes quickly. Now I wait to be hit, which seems the real comfort. Everything's been dealt; I'm just waiting to see the down cards."

Gradually, nothing he wrote seemed to the point except these direct quotations. He especially liked second-hand quotes: "I overheard Captain M. saying . . ." He trusted these more than lines composed for his benefit. In daydreams, he built a mechanical eavesdropper that allowed him to quote at a distance those words that would never have been said in his presence. Such a machine would turn each person into his own journalist, and everyone would be the subject of an article.

Without such a machine, Peter recognized his own fraudulence enough not to trust his own telling of the war. Convinced that his subjects could tell their story better than he, he turned his reports into little more than pastiches of overheard conversations.

Hungry for quotes and paraphrases, he wrote the Schreck farm in the Westerwald:

> *Volken*, please tell me where I can write 'Dolphe and Hub, too, if you are in touch with him and he has gone to war. I'm not cross at Adolphe; by accident, he did me a good turn. I'm not so silly as before, as I now have a vocation. I will come back after the shooting and tell you. There is something remarkable in this world war that people reading the papers cannot know.

Peter knew he risked arrest by posting this letter. If this signed confession did not bring the authorities down on him, the letter, even routed through Holland, stood little chance of making it from one belligerent to the other. But his desire to get his brothers' firsthand accounts side by side with the enemy's was so great that he took the risk. Receiving no reply, he blamed the censors or suspected that the Schrecks disowned him for running out on the Kaiser.

The newspaper's home office complained to Peter/Theo on two counts. After causing their initial stir, the Langerson articles began losing their readers to other, more impersonal and strategic reports of thrusts and reconnoiterings. For newspapers have always served the same purpose as memory: to repeat the dry, physical fact again and again until it no longer threatens the individual. Peter's quotes, by involving the readers too deeply, did exactly the reverse, and so slowly lost popularity both with the public and the paper. The paper also suspected that by excessive quoting, Peter meant to avoid the work involved in saying something for himself.

These criticisms hurt Peter deeply, and he soon found out how quickly dedication can turn to cynicism under resistance from the home office. But he did not capitulate just yet. He had another plan for sending home the war in a literal and undeniable package. With his thoughts increasingly on his brothers after his abortive letter to the Westerwald, he was ripe for an unsponsored memory.

It came one Wednesday as he descended the stairs of the press detention center. As he had on countless days previously, he put his hand on the wooden rail leading to the street. But this time, because he touched the rail while sidestepping a puddle at the bottom step, he received the electrifying impression that he held his old cane and stood in the muddy road on that May Day so long before the start of history. He thought of the photo and how easy it would be to carry a box camera all the way to the front if need be.

Even the larger papers at that time still relied on engravings for their principal illustration, a preference largely habitual and partly economic. The halftone process, decades old, permitted cheap, fair-quality mass printing. Even a poorly taken, poorly reproduced photo could surpass an engraving in information. But the papers rarely used them, aside from oval portraits of Archduke Ferdinand, John French, or the Czar, preferring the block-diagram map and bold arrows marking out wishful thinking.

Peter's idea—the one great insight often given to the inconspicuous—was that, by using the incontrovertible evidence of an amateur's photos, he could prove that the war had nothing to do with line-drawn maps. He did not know, in fact, what the war *had* to do with, but felt certain that what went through the lens onto the plate would be it. His pictures would be forthright beyond editing, too naïve to be faked, taking both subjects and viewers by surprise.

To purchase his machine, Peter resorted to the time-honored method of not eating for four days. He did not want to requisition money from Maastricht; that would take too long and blunt the surprise. Hunger seemed small hardship; four days left him hardly faint. He bought the camera and rudimentary instructions. He made a few experiments, including the obligatory box-at-arm's-length self-portrait. He felt ready.

He did not know what image he looked for or where to find it. It seemed best to keep strictly to his old routine. He had an appointment to visit a British field hospital staffed by nuns and teen-aged girl volunteers. He set out for the site as usual, only now carrying his machine at his waist.

With novice's luck, Peter came on his image almost at once. Trucks carrying wounded arrived just after his own escort. The doors opened and out came the casualties from the second Battle of Ypres, the first gas victims of the war. All hands at once began bearing stretchers. Of the first three soldiers removed from the camions, two gurgled in the backs of their throats and the third had already died. With no time to crate the corpse someplace more circumspect, the bearers simply tucked it out of the way by the rear wheels of the unloading truck. There it lay exposed to the air, without so much as the grace of a sheet. It posed itself in the simplicity of agony, showing more than anything how wrong the old masters were about the moment of death.

Neither horror nor an explorer's excitement came to the first-time photographer. Rather, Peter calmly recognized, as if by prearranged signal, his subject matter. Surely and quickly, memory dictated to his fingers; he did as he was told. Then, mechanically, he hid the camera where it would be safe, freed his hands, and pitched in with the unloading. He took no more photos, nor did he enter a single note into his books. He spent the day assisting the camp medics, thinking no more of reporting until back in the safety of his Paris flat.

There, under the guidance of the technical manual, the image came into existence out of a dark closet and the stink of chemical reagents. Peter watched the image develop, and at the precise moment dropped the print into the stop bath. A corpse huddled up near a truck's rear axle. It was, at the same time, precisely what Peter had seen through the viewfinder and yet radically different. So much more took place in the picture now than then—the play of detail, the crumpled form in halftones, the thing's utter silence. More than he'd seen in the original, yet exactly what he'd imagined on opening the shutter.

He had done the work of his assumed identity, the work he had been sent to the front to do. In this simplest possible snapshot the noncombatant observers would see finally, unequivocally, without interpretation, the dance of 1914. No word could gloss the effect. This photo would show the onlooker what the war was about. It was about this corpse, this latest in a long history of Pietàs, with truck axle standing in for mother. As with every new addition to a tradition, it did not call attention to itself so much as point to all the past Pietàs, ask what they now meant in this changed world.

All he could tell the news-hungry audience in Maastricht was that the war was this dead fellow, and leave it at that.

Peter put the print on his windowsill for two days, as if it were the studio portrait of a near-relation. Then, pressed to give the thing away, he carefully wrapped it in brown paper and twine and sent it to the home office. After, he felt vacant and acquitted. The final report had been submitted, and he only awaited a reply.

As with all replies of consequence, his was unexpected. In two days the censor board summoned him for a closed conference. Peter appeared in the old work clothes he'd last worn at The Spoon the day he met Theo. The same petty official who had earlier reprimanded him for slack reporting, threatening spy trials, now launched another magisterial dressing-down.

—Mr. Langerson, we on the board have all seen and admired your photo of the unfortunate British fellow. Gas victim.

—Thank you, Your Horseface.

Mumbled, the crack passed for "Your Honor." Peter's dead-pan and the old adolescent smirk confirmed the Hegelian dictum that opposites meet.

—Quite a bit of artistry, we all agree.

—The gas?

—The photo, young man. May I remind you that you stand before this body as a guest of France.

—Just as I stood in front of the other body.

—Quite. We've arrived at the point, then. It has been the policy of the Entente Powers to ask newspapers to oblige us by not printing photographs showing visible corpses of either side. Nor are the Entente releasing any such photos to the press of neutral

— 277 —

nations. This war, you understand, will be won or lost by the morale of the civilian populations.

—No dead bodies?

—No photographs of visible corpses of either side.

—You're to keep the citizens happy by denying the dead bodies?

—Not denying them. Just not serving them up for dinner.

Peter searched one end of the council to the other for a cracked smile, exposing the whole, extended joke. His mouth hung slack in incomprehension.

—Gentlemen, in my village, that's called shitting your pants and blaming the stink on the cows.

—That's as may be. But you are forewarned that failure to comply or further attempts to print the photo will lead to immediate deportation at the least. Perhaps after the war, God willing, you will find a taker for your fine piece of work. I understand your frustration and your hostility. Good day.

There was nothing for it but to bow out of the room. Surprisingly, the rage called for by the circumstance did not creep up on Peter either at once or in the days to come. Having consummated his work as a journalist, he gave up the pretense and lost whatever modicum of conscience or motive he had had. He had had his great insight and moment of articulation. He had taken his photo. Back in the incarnation of Peter Kinder, congenital *Lümmel*, he no longer cared what became of the image. Now he needed diversion.

Directly on being dismissed from his finger-slapping, he crossed over to the Left Bank and Montparnasse, where he traded his topcoat for a hip flask and some change. Outside an unassuming cabaret, the Left Bank found him. Two suspect young men— apparently avoiding the draft on grounds of acute hemophilia— both with spoons strapped to their shoulders to resemble epaulets, neatly accosted him and wrestled him to the pavement. One, wearing a pointed felt hat, seemingly superior in rank, spoke first:

—Art thou that which governs, the so-called Prime Minister, he who rules those lessers that comprise his constituency?

Peter, normally poor at answering questions, could not even recognize this as one.

—You pushed me down!

— 278 —

—He shows, in truth, the logico-physio-nuclear faculties of he who governs.

—It is! It is the Prime Minister.

—My Prime Ass, I am.

—He admits it. We've got him then.

The overeager junior partner sans cap, whose nose threatened to set up a populist rebellion from the rest of his face, began to grab Peter. The first speaker checked him with a cuff on the ear.

—Keep silence, you who are second in command. If it is, in truth, the Prime Minister, then he must know that which men call the logico-mechanical purpose of this interview.

Recovering from his rough handling, Peter began to get the spirit of the thing. Unable to match the floridity of his interrogators' diction, he went to the opposite extreme, cursing them out in Dutch. He started with a phrase meaning, loosely, "Chop up your genitals and use them for stewing meat," working up to bigger and better as he warmed.

—Eh? The Prime Minister is a partaker of the German nation-alogicality? That explains much, does it not, Petit?

The capless one rubbed his tremendous nose and laughed. His breath smelled of paint thinner.

—*Jawohlt*. The whole logico-mechanical war. The Prime Minister of France a German. *Très bizarre*, geopolitics. But who are we to demand that things make sense?

Peter stood and brushed himself off.

—Listen to me, rubes. I'm not your goddamn Prime Minister.

—What? But you as good as admitted it.

The capped one calmed the nosed one and, by gestures, asked to be allowed to handle the crisis.

—It's you who had better do the listening, bub. We were sent to fetch the Prime Minister and bring him back, and you're it, or we'll bash your bob in.

—I abdicate. Find another.

—What? Another? Among all these . . . these . . . Pri-mettes?

The grand anemic dismissed all humanity with a great gesture, so startling one or two passers-by that Peter laughed despite himself.

—Buy us a drink and we'll talk about it.

The capped fellow looked confused, and consulted his assistant.

—Drink? What means this "drink," Petit?

—That which men swill, Your Dregness.

The man's shout of recognition loosened his spoon-epaulets and sent them jangling to the streets. With general hilarity and back-slapping, the three headed off as if old comrades.

The two took Peter to the catacombs under Montparnasse. On the way, in their tortured, inextricable syntax, they explained that a dozen or so artists—"reality modulators," as the cancerous nose termed them—had banqueted underground for the last seventy-two hours, sleeping in shifts and taking turns going aboveground to buy that which men swill and that which men swallow. Only an hour before, someone had pointed out that they had no guest of honor, no one to throw the banquet for. Ruling out Genghis Khan and Simon Bolivar as ineligible on grounds of death, they settled on the Prime Minister. Since guests of honor customarily attended their own bash, Charles and Petit were dispatched to fetch back said official or suffer emotional agony and verbal abuse.

Taking this in, Peter reflected on how in a short time he'd been Dutch, German, Dutch again, and Parisian expatriate; gone by Kinder, Schreck, and Langerson; had been a derelict, farmer, tobacconist, newshound, and now chief governing official of France. It all seemed, as the reality modulators were fond of saying, logico-mechanical.

The student-artists had stumbled upon a section of the old Roman catacombs beneath Paris that was not on the state tour system. The caves made a perfect if fusty and moribund draft dodge. Charles lit a candle and led on into the tombs, with Petit prodding Peter from behind. The stone wall harbored periodic cavities that Peter chose not to look into too deeply. An occasional *objet trouvé*— a bicycle chain, shower nozzle, commode fragment—each bearing a placard reading *The Path of a Proton*, or *I and We: the Metaphysio Pronouns*, indicated that an anonymous reality modulator had taken on the task of sprucing up the crypts.

The sounds of clinking and speechifying grew more distinct, and a moment later the party of three pushed free into a cavern that, although hewn from rock, leaking water, and stinking of slime mold, passed for an elegant dining hall. A dozen men and women lay about in varying degrees of oblivion. Thick smoke hung in the air and debris from food and drink littered the room.

The guests broke off singing and fell silent at Peter's entrance. Finally one fellow, the tacit ringleader judging from his tux and tails, the single ugliest, most hirsute gentleman Peter had ever seen, rose in trembling gravity and bellowed in stentorian voice:

—The Primatique Minister!

This coinage signaled that "logico" and "mechanical" were now passé, and words ending in "matique" would hold court for the next forty-eight hours.

Peter was feted, toasted, and forced to drink a liter of wine without coming up for air. Everyone wanted to stroke the Prime Minister, and some of the women rubbed him so hard that he got an erection, which two of them promptly announced to the crowd in official tones. The hairy fellow rose, looked stern, and demanded:

—Speechify. Tell us about the war. The people demand of he who governs to inform them of the course of the war.

Much yelling and concurring followed. They dragged Peter to a rock slab that served as a podium.

—Friends, Frenchmen. The plans of the war are to . . . to keep . . . the plans of the war . . . very, very secret.

The crowd broke out in boos.

—Tell us!

—Trust us. We're as mum as the dead.

—One thing I can tell you, however. I have it on the highest authority that we'll keep fighting until either they are all dead or we are all dead or both they and we are all dead or they stop fighting and say it's all right for us to stop fighting or they stop because they thought that we stopped or until they say that they aren't going to stop unless we say that . . .

—Bravo!

—*Exactement.*

—*Liberté, égalité* . . .

The banqueters broke into hymns; some, "The Marseillaise," others, "You Should-a Seen-a Lina." In the confusion, the ringleader took the podium from Peter and demanded silence.

—After the informatiququitive speech of our beloved Primatique . . .

—Encore!

—There is little one can say. Yet I might add that word has reached us from aboveground via this delightful and generally accurate paper called . . .

Pulling a newspaper out of his tuxedo, he held the banner close to his eyes.

—. . . Le . . . Monde, that we reality modulators are not alone in trying to remake the world on proto-willpower. It says here that a certain Monsieur Henri Forte, famous American motorist and car driver, has invented a torpedo that is right at this minute sailing across that which is wet with the intention of blowing up that which is old, Europe, and starting a new Golden Age of Peace. Equals, may I propose a toast. To Peace.

—To Peace and Diplomacy.

—To Peace and Diplomacy and Motorcars.

—To Peace and Diplomacy and Motorcars and those pretty packages rolling papers come in.

The cumulative toast worked its way clockwise around the party, each adding another toast and obliging all to drink. But the self-replicating, self-improving chain broke at Peter, and the hilarity drew up short. For the Prime Minister had snatched away the copy of Le Monde and was reading it furiously.

Chapter Twenty-one

Catching a Connector

I don't blame any person but the system—HENRY FORD

MAYS LAY IN THE TUB shortly after 2 A.M. The bath water, scalding when he'd drawn it a few minutes before, now seemed tepid to his touch. Peter had noticed the phenomenon many times since childhood: had the water actually cooled, or had his skin just adjusted to the status quo? Neither answer made him any warmer. The situation called for less metaphysics and more hot water.

If opened to full, the house's plumbing went into bronchial seizures. Mays's mother slept fitfully upstairs after the emotional scene a short while before, and he did not want to wake her. At her son's insistence, she had exposed the worst scar tissue of the family's last four generations, and now needed the recuperative power of dreams to heal once more.

To avoid the poltergeist of pipes, Mays reached back into the flotsam of memory and recollected an old childhood trick. Lying back in the porcelain, he applied a light tangent pressure to the HOT with his left big toe. This loosened a washer gasket rotted these twenty years, trickling hot water out of the pipe housing and down the tile wall. Draped on the other foot, a terrycloth face rag intercepted the stream and directed it down Mays's leg into the tub. If he loosened the drain plug a shade, the whole system achieved dynamic equilibrium: out with the cold, in with the stew. The system was technically perfect, and if his mother had not stuck rubber daisies on the tub bottom following John Glenn's 1960s shower accident, daisies that left a corsage on Mays's back after prolonged soaking, he would have stayed in for good, slowly ossifying, fingers pruning in the hard water of the Midwest.

The tub had always been Mays's palace of simplification. Slack in the pellucid water, he would dwell on his recent traumas, replaying them from every possible camera angle, stretching misery over ceramic tile, steaming it clean in the tub vapor. Memory and hot water scrubbed his self-image clean. He never soaped himself but only soaked, avoiding the sullying intervention of his germ-laden hands.

But this bath, even helped by the oblivion of 2 A.M., could not settle the conversation he and his mother had just had, no matter how often he replayed it and waited. For however skilled he and a hot tub were at smoothing his own biography, they could do nothing to the inherited biographies of the Mays family tree.

A product of immigration—the American nonclass—Mays had never paid more than lip service to his ancestors. He felt only distantly related to his parents, more like a ward of the state. And he knew nothing of more distant progenitors. That evening, for the first time, his mother sowed the macabre suggestion that he actually shared genes with strangers. He was indebted to people he had never even heard of. The effect resembled those dreams in which he discovered unknown rooms in the old house.

The letter from Ford to Mr. Langerson and the photograph of the three turn-of-the-century dandies on a muddy road, one of them Mays, brought on a violent reaction from his mother. She heaved, hyperventilated, and repeated, "I didn't know." Didn't know of the stuff's existence? She had put it there. Didn't know that this was what her son was after? Even her fifth-grade education sufficed to draw that connection. Didn't know that Ford had provided for her grandfather's descendants? She had only to read the letter.

Recovering from her fit, she launched, over her ruined game of solitaire, involved excuses why she had never before told him of family history.

—For your sake, Petje, most of what happened back then was awful. You can't imagine how their lives went; you've had it easy. And why not? Why raise the old devils? The children have got to cast off the old burdens.

Mays, making the evolutionary step from tub to dry land, re-

— 284 —

called that she pronounced "burden" as "burthen." Had that been the form in her day? He had only a vague notion of the speed and degree of language change. Shakespeare was Greek; his mother came up with corkers: somewhere along the line, English had arrived at the telegraphic perfection of *Micro Monthly News*.

Toweling dry, he considered that mores, too, had evolved some before reaching their present finality of perfection. The details that his mother withheld for his sake—that his great-grandfather had deserted family and country and that his grandfather had been born out of wedlock—instead of shaming Peter, delighted him. But beyond the color, outside his mother's outdated moral concerns, lay the real trauma of family history.

He padded on shriveled feet into his old room and closed the door to put an extra barrier between his own sound and his mother. He had an unshakable desire to call Alison. He had long ago concluded that desires could only be lessened by giving in to them. First, however, he pulled on briefs and a pair of pants. Four generations of phone use had not bred from his family line the belief that one ought not to place a call in the buff.

To further deaden the rotary pulse dialer, one that got its thunder from the surrounding silence, he put the phone in the bottom drawer of his now hopelessly boy-sized dresser, wedging it in boy-sweaters his mother still kept in the shrine. He threaded the receiver out through the crack and closed the drawer until snug against his upper arm. He dialed blindly, feeling for the holes, amazed that the number Alison had given him the night before should already be in his fingers. He tried to check by counting the clicks of the released wheel, but he could not hear fast enough. After half a ring, a frightened voice at the other end demanded:

—Yellow?

—Alison?

—Who is it? Who's dead?

Peter suddenly realized that it was after two in the morning—three, East Coast—too late to call anyone, let alone a relative stranger. But it had been a night of relative strangers and strange relatives.

—I think I am.

During an audible silence, Mays recalled that carbon monoxide was supposed to be painless. When she spoke, Alison sounded as naturally affectionate as on their night out.

—Oh, it's my date. Come over to play?

—That might be tricky; I'm in Illinois.

—Illinois? Jimminy. For the benefit of our listening audience, I am now crossing myself.

Mays heard a fumbling as she held the phone to her chest. He found fallen-away Catholics infinitely appealing.

—Listen, Alison. I'm calling to see what you think about marriage.

—As a concept?

—As an institution.

—Not as amusing as other arrangements we might invent. Why?

—Well, it's just that . . . I mean . . . I'm about to come into some cash and I could use a tax dodge.

—Hank came through for you, huh?

—In a manner of speaking.

—Well, I'll take it under advisement and get back to you. In the meantime, have you considered municipal bonds?

Under her flippancies, Alison betrayed a genuine interest in the detective game. Mays, in a voice too steady to be natural, explained the treasures excavated from the east eave, and his mother's subsequent explanation. His great-grandfather—a shady figure in family folklore—had somehow ingratiated himself with Ford. To reciprocate, Ford did what he did best: set up a trust fund for the fellow and descendants.

—Let me guess: a twenty-five-dollar Series E savings bond.

—Close. Five hundred dollars cash. The price of a Model T, accumulating at more than nine percent since 1916.

—When do you dine with the Vanderbilts? What does that work out to?

—Perhaps the figure of a quarter million dollars means something to you.

—You're kidding. Jesus. You know, you could have called me at full rates then.

—Sorry.

—A quarter . . . ? You're kidding. Say, how did you do the math for that?

—Compounding? One of the few things I remember from calculus.

A suck of breath at the other end informed Mays that this woman, who had barely flinched at a sum that would have endeared him to anyone else, would forever hold him in reverence because he knew some math.

—So it *was* you in that photo.

Mays corrected her:

—My great-grandfather.

—Hows-a-come nobody in your family ever drew on this little nest egg?

—For one, they, like you, failed to grasp the miracle of compound interest. And two, my mother and grandfather disowned the old guy as a family scandal. They agreed to sweep him under the rug. Fortunately, my mother could not bring herself to throw out the only two documents of the man's existence.

—Still, a quarter million sitting in an attic smacks of the implausible.

—There were other terms. The principal could not be touched for thirty years. That knocks out the great-aunts and uncles from the legacy. Then, it could be milked only by a blood descendant who shared the same profession as great-grandfather's at the time of his meeting Ford.

—Which was?

—Journalist.

—And you are . . . ?

—A quarter million richer.

—A writer? You know calculus, and you became a writer? Jesus. Some folks just flush their lives down the toilets.

—Well, it is technical writing, if you'd like me any better for it. So how are things by you?

—In the forty-eight hours since we were together, you mean? Etsy-ketsy. Wages, tips, salaries. The usual.

—How's my buddy, the old guy? What's his name? Herr Krakow.

Silence at the other end told Mays he had stepped on something.

—Why do you ask?

Alison's voice had turned metallic.

—Look, it was only a lark, to make you laugh.

Only partially reassured, Alison described how Arkady had noticeably deteriorated over the last two days.

—Not to blame it on you, but he keeps asking after you.

—What's so awful about that?

—He wants to know how our son is. His and mine, he means— you. Wait; it gets worse. He speaks to me almost exclusively in funny languages. He slips back in time, every five minutes another year. He's stuck in the twenties at present, currently under the impression that the restaurant is a Viennese coffeehouse. He goes around asking the brokers what they think of his lovely young wife.

—Meaning you? He *has* lost it.

—Don't joke, assuming you're joking. Peter, do you suppose he's dying? That he's going systematically backward through his life until he unwinds it all?

Mays, unable to recall any formulas from calculus that explained this nonlinear regression, did as he did for all urgent questions: he kept silent. Alison had to pick up the slack.

—So, what are you going to do with your pile?

—Bequeath the Peter Mays Traveling Scholarship for Technical Education. Is "bequeath" a word?

—Sounds like a book title. Drop everything after "Education," though. How does one apply?

—Just sign the papers.

They had talked for almost an hour. Peter made a note to leave his mother a check for the toll call—not that she'd ever cash it. Their banter bred like mink; they could not bring the call to an end, could not give up the pleasure of reminding one another that someone outside themselves existed. It was Mays's only pleasure of late. He finally got around to saying good night by way of saying good morning.

—Sure you don't want to come over?

Alison gave the invitation such a lazy, curled-up tone, as if long distance were the same as adjacent theater seats, that Mays had an overpowering urge to drop everything for another close-up of this woman who treated Edwardian dress, the banalities of The Trading Floor, an obscenely late phone call, the mystery of calculus, the disclosure of an enormous windfall, and concern for a fellow come unstuck in time as equal elements in a huge, improbable, improvised experiment.

Mays felt briefly the old suspicion that Alison played a part in a labyrinthine conspiracy leading him to his windfall. But he at once concluded that if there were a conspiracy, he was the culprit, not she. As they said good-bye and he opened the drawer to replace the phone in its cradle, dullness came over him.

The anaesthesia he felt on hanging up seemed the dominant condition of his times, a condition that could not be escaped. A person might say, "I am drugged," but, being drugged, will not want to detoxify. For his generation, so Mays thought, like morphined patients, *knew* of their loss of feeling without by definition being able to feel it. For them, memory without catharsis, history without recognition.

In Bernhardt, in Veterans' Day, he had sought something long denied him: an experience, a sorrow, an antianaesthetic emetic. And he had come up with only a fortune—another soporific legacy that seemed to be the final reward of all searches. The silence of his boyhood room in his mother's house closed around him until he felt the lateness of the hour, sitting bowlegged in front of the phone as a cultist in front of a shrine, still moist from the bath.

He could hear Alison's voice distinctly, although modified by the present silence. She alone seemed untouched by the general anaesthesia of the present, the terror of occupation. Bullock had his puts and calls, his late-night lawn mowing; Delaney had his vaudeville and his mania; Brink, her expertise; Moseley, his compulsive privacy; Kimberly Greene and Arkady Krakow bowed out to nostalgia. Alison alone found time for a broader curiosity.

But she had one rub—her admiration and ambition for technical expertise. Mays wondered why this rankled him. Had the camera, car, and computer induced the general anaesthesia of the times, or were they the by-products? Perhaps in going from A to B sitting down, one lost the experience of travel. Yet she had to come of mechanical age—come to terms with the terms. There was no value in innocence or avoidance. But he wondered if even her congenital affection, her easy way with feeling could survive a good dose of technical know-how.

Too tired to feel fatigue, he swept the papers of the Ford file off the dresser and collapsed in bed. He gave the 1916 letter to Theo Langerson only a perfunctory rereading and a grunt before he sent it sailing down to the floor. Nothing there but the facts. If the folks in Motor City would accept the trade press as journalism, he could stop by anytime and pick up his fortune.

Already the prospect seemed unreal. He looked again at the old piece of newsprint foisted on him by Kimberly Greene—the *Heir* photo. He had examined it too often for it to be of much interest any longer. The shock of seeing himself embraced by one of the century's most influential men had worn off. The sight of his own face in the guise of his great-grandfather's put him off, with its smirking surprise, its lack of presence of mind in the face of the documenter's flashpan. The young man looked like a child caught with its hand in the epochal cookie jar—a ringer in the archive of history.

Peter found Ford's face more interesting—shrewd, deranged, the face of a visionary or lunatic intent on teaching a billion human beings the laws of celestial thermodynamics. What was this dangerous fellow doing in Europe? Shouldn't he be stateside, minding the first fully automated plant or keeping the home fires burning?

Both the caption and the letter alluded to some service rendered by the unknown boy, a service providing the only check to a substantial setback that Ford had received in Europe. What could the world's leading industrialist have suffered that a sprout of a journalist could in any way mitigate?

Although curious, Mays felt these questions touched the main issue only tangentially, an issue that grew fuzzier the longer he stayed with it. He threw aside the article and picked up the last item in the impromptu dossier. At the last analysis, he came face to camera plane with the image of three farmers on their way to a dance. He could derive no greater clue to the mystery of the regeneration of experience than his physiognomic resemblance to one of these boys, boys in the deliberate surprise of a day long ago, irretrievably lost, preserved by the treachery of the lens.

Because it had been stuffed in an envelope and hidden in the east eave, no one had seen the print for decades. Was this the original print, the one first pulled from the photographer's negative?

Were the heavy creases in the print the work of one of the subjects? The question made no sense. A print was by nature only a print, entirely interchangeable with any other print, antique or contemporary. As a commercial object, it had no verifiable bill of lading. The thing served as a portal to alternate places only through its content, the record of light passing through the lens.

This image content captured Mays, and he stared at it until it went through the hazy deformation of things stared at too long. He blinked, looked away, then tried again. With no clear idea of what he looked for in the picture, Peter nevertheless felt compelled by its detail. The tilt of hats and canes, the minute facial blemishes, the fold of the coat cloth, the hair combed and uncombed, the draped cigarette, the worn shoes, all invited Mays to speculate on the scenario, to invent a fiction behind this documented incident stretching out over the years in both directions, without beginning or end.

The first several times that Mays examined the scene, the left hand of the center figure—the one resembling Mays, the Theo Langerson fellow—puzzled him. Thumb and forefinger closed in a ring, forming an imperial affectation out of keeping with the figure's face and bearing. After prolonged staring, Peter saw, or thought he saw, a new detail that made sense of the shape. A faint line, perhaps only a flaw in the negative, outlined a black object—handkerchief or pair of gloves—that dissolved into the protective coloration of the lead boy's coat.

The new interpretation made sense of the area: the hand did not form a ring of negative space, but instead closed around something actual. Yet the photo lacked definition precise enough to reveal whether the new way of seeing the area corresponded with the reality of that day. Perhaps that question, as with the authenticity of the print, had no meaning.

Mays held the creased yellowed paper in his hands, trying to precipitate a memory. He didn't know if what he tried to remember came from his own past, from the three boys', or from only ten minutes before, when he had had a small insight. With an equally sketchy notion of *what* he tried to recover—whether animal, vegetable, or mineral; a place; an idea; or just the ability to experience without irony or acute self-consciousness—he stood little chance of success. He redoubled his efforts to locate the remarkable in the picture, but the intensity of his effort chased off recollection the way a swipe at a falling sheet of paper only succeeds in blowing the sheet farther away. What he was after would have to settle down unchased. At some point that he did not mark, the violent act of memory gave way to sleep.

He dreamed that since his early childhood he had participated in a research project run by a large public university, a mammothly funded, mammothly staffed venture stretching out over several decades and outlasting its founders. The experiment called for everyone in a certain medium-sized town, including Peter, to appear once every few months throughout their entire lives for a studio portrait. The resulting photos were then edited into an organically growing filmstrip documenting what the decades did to each subject's changing face.

Mays woke early, more fatigued than when going under. When she rose to find her son packing and calling for ticket reservations, Mrs. Mays jumped to the conclusion that the family secrets, so carefully hidden for half a century, were driving Peter from the house.

—Petje, what are you doing? You've hardly gotten the moths out of your suitcase. You've no cause for shame; you're the same person as before I told you anything.

—What? What are you talking about, *Moedi*?

—You know, Petje, your grandfather was neither the first or the last of his ilk.

"Ilk" was one of those rare birds Mrs. Mays culled from the tabloids. Mays tried to figure out what exactly his mother meant to say.

—You mean collaborationist or bastard?

Mrs. Mays's right hand flinched and attached to her collar button. She had long ago stopped crossing herself, to keep Peter from giving her the voodoo lecture. But unable to break an old habit, she contented herself with grabbing her collar button, a brief, atrophied holdover of evolution like the tailbone in humans or front legs in snakes.

—Everyone in Holland collaborated in some way. You don't know, Peter. You've never lived under occupation.

Peter felt bad at having upset his mother, and shame at the

truth of her words. But he could not answer her; the reservation clerk at the train office had booked him into a holding pattern complete with piped-in music—a soothing, classical piece Peter remembered from his concert days when his object was still the redhead, and the redhead was still a clarinetist. Prehistory, a wasted search, except that now it made waiting for train tickets infinitesimally more interesting.

The train system had a few years back become seminationalized, meaning it now enjoyed the extortionate rates of a private business *and* the bankrupt, bureaucratic ineptitude of a government agency. Waiting on the phone listening to phantom concerti could easily burn up more time than the ride back to Boston. Each time he traveled by train, Mays swore he would fly or hitch the distance before boarding another silver liner. Yet he had jumped town without notice and could not expect a job on his return. That made airfare a bit dear. That he would pick up a quarter million on the way had not yet registered with him. The smell of bus seats nauseated him, and he did not have a pair of shoes strong enough to make it across Ohio, so he kept quiet and listened to the tune.

The clerk reconnected at last, saying Mays could make it to Boston via a Detroit connection the next morning. Mays made a reservation for the Early Riser and went back to packing.

—Look, Petje, you stay home a little longer. We'll play some cards; you'll fix that gutter pipe you've been promising. Everything is the same. A few days, and you won't remember anything about this.

—It's not the stories, *Moedi*, really. I'm not ashamed of my ancestors. None of them did anything that a million others in the century haven't done.

—So stay a few days. The place needs you. What do you need for Detroit? Is it the money business in the letter?

—It's not the money, exactly. It's just that there's so much of it.

—What, five hundred dollars at nine percent? That hardly covers the train ticket.

The night before he had tried, violently, to explain to her how much cash was at stake, but it was no good. To his mother, 500 dollars at 9 percent was 545 dollars.

—I didn't raise my son to be a fortune hunter.

—What did you raise your son to be?

—Don't start with me, *kind*, or I'll finish with you.

The threat that terrified Mays as a child now never failed to delight him. He liked to hear the old undercurrent of maternal violence creep back into her voice, even though she induced it now mostly through method acting.

—What will you do to me, *Moedi*?

—I'll break your ribs, honey. I didn't raise you to grub for money. I raised you to be a good man. A blameless man. Any guff with that?

The Early Riser made one unscheduled stop on the way to Detroit, somewhere in the desolation of Indiana. The view from the window—endless acres of scrub and stubble—resembled Bikini Atoll. A uniformed party boarded the train, apparently looking for a stowaway criminal. For a sickening interval, Mays worried that he would have to show some identification. As the last remaining individual who refused to use credit, he had only the two shots of his great-grandfather for photo ID. But the unsuccessful officers disembarked as quickly as they had boarded, into the vacant nothingness of harvested fields.

In Detroit, the train belched Mays into a grandiose but dilapidated train station, now functioning at a fraction of its heyday size. Mays had called the Ford offices the day before and secured an appointment with a Mr. Nichols, a dime-a-dozen PR man, for that afternoon. Then he had booked a connection to Boston on the Technoliner. He had two hours to kill.

Falling out of the station into downtown traffic, he felt time sitting on him and despaired of killing it on his own. He considered sightseeing: the fabled Renaissance Center, or a view of Canada. These he vetoed: one drab municipality looked like any other. The art museum? He'd sworn off cult objects until he came into his pile. After all, this was Detroit, and Peter could think of nothing more apropos than sitting and watching the cars.

Mays arrived at Mr. Nichols's office a good half hour early. The secretarial pool stripped him of his Ford file and forced him to wait in a criminally modularized foyer. There, a band of photos and artifacts rounded the room at eye level, exhibiting the sequential history of Henry Ford: Ford as young farmer, as apprentice mechanic, as an engineer for Edison, his 1892 car, the charter for Ford Motors, the first Tin Lizzie, the automated factory, the five-dollar-a-day bombshell of 1914.

Mays paused in front of a photo of Henry on the boarding ramp of a ship stenciled *Oscar II*. The caption read:

> In 1915, Ford formed the ill-fated Peace Ship, attempting to staff it with luminaries and, without official sanction from the United States or any other power, sail it to Europe, fully intending to break the diplomatic deadlock of the First World War.

With a sudden blow, Mays's own deadlock broke and scattered. Concentrating on the tacitly implied failure of the mission—the ill-advised, ironic, ridiculous, obtuse, commendably absurd attempt to take history into his own hands and act, even if only clownishly—Mays found he could make his chest and throat tighten. The muscular waves thus brought on fed back into the photo, and the escalating surf of emotion would certainly have had to find outlet in some demonstration if a voice calling his name from the inner offices had not thrown oil over it. Mays turned to witness the face of a fellow who could have passed as centerfold for *Orthodontia Today*. He took hold of Mr. Nichols's hand and tried to make sense of what he was saying.

—. . . the expense of your coming to see us here in Detroit. The letter—quite a prize, you know, a signature of value—checks out, in a manner of speaking. Mr. Ford did indeed provide for your great-grandfather's family, but not in the way you no doubt hope.

Chapter Twenty-two

The Immigrant's Essay

The past tense, which inhabits our lives as it fills the pages of history, can claim significance and urgency only if it insinuates a concurrent present. Given the courage, we live by moments of interference between past and present, moments in which time comes back into phase with itself. It is the only meaning of history. We search the past not for other creatures but for our own lost selves.—ROGER SHATTUCK, *The Banquet Years*

I FOUND Mrs. Schreck's apartment without difficulty, and as I had hoped, she had not yet left for work. She greeted me at the door, warmly but surprised. With maternal efficiency, she whisked me inside, dabbed my nosebleed with a lace handkerchief, and produced two towels from a hidden place.

—Dry yourself before you end up in the snowman's morgue.

She stood, a drill sergeant in attendance, as I removed my layer of snow, indicating that young men don't understand the urgency of such matters. She had lived at a time when pneumonia, consumption, and tuberculosis were real, when people died from sitting too long by a drafty window.

If I took my time toweling dry, it was not out of disrespect for Mrs. Schreck's medicinal theories. When I first put the robin's-egg-blue antique towel up to my face, a pungent smell greeted me: a painfully enjoyable scent—a mix of pies and spices, mildew, wallpaper paste, human odor, starch—yet one lying outside the reach of its individual smells. It smelled of use—long, continued, loving use.

I thought that I knew this smell from somewhere in my past,

and I tried for a moment to place it. But I soon realized the truth: the smell itself was the memory, and I was anthologizing and sending it to the future. If I were to smell anything faintly resembling this amalgam in the years to come, I would be at once transported to Mrs. Schreck's foyer, toweling dry, just in from a snowstorm.

So I lingered with the towels, stretched the process out more than necessary. But each pass under my nose only succeeded in replacing the urgent with the familiar, and at last I surrendered the goods to my hostess. She ushered me through her suite of rooms back to her kitchen, where she began preparing lethal doses of herbal tea. The towel scent proved to be no isolated case: the whole apartment was a temple to aroma: eucalyptus, rosewater, mothballs—more than I can name. I sat at an ancient deal breakfast table. My eyes must have glazed over with the stupor of pilgrims visiting Chartres because the old woman said:

—I have been living in this place thirty and more years.

Accents seem arbitrary, independent of how long or willingly the speaker has embraced the new language. A sixty-year-old can erase in six months what a child leaves intact after twenty. Mrs. Schreck's was surprisingly heavy for so veteran a speaker, although it showed signs of a struggle. Her "have" came out "hep," while "this place" might have been "dizzy plots."

—But the block was so different then. Everything frail, jolly. Ah, but heaven shuts off at sighing. How goes it with you?

Her "how" was a "who," her "with" a "mit," but the combination was expressive.

—Not too bad. Only I didn't go in to work today.

—Good for you. A body's got to play hooky now and then.

I had to laugh at "hooky" for enunciation and diction. Delighting in my delight, Mrs. Schreck said the word again: hooky, hooee-e-key. We laughed, and she added, as if narrating:

—We laughed until we rotted.

—Yes. Only I didn't mean to drop by like this, all unexpected. I don't want to make you late.

—Maybe I play hooky too. I tell them I can't make it in the snow. And you did mean to drop by, or why are you here? Drop polite; I'm too old a lady for polite.

— 297 —

It was true; she, who had survived the worst part of the century, did not need my pleasantries to protect her. The old need honesty, not deference. I looked at her stoic grin, mirrored it, and forgot about apologizing for dropping out of touch after the Christmas party.

I let my gaze wander around what I could see of the apartment. Here, accumulation of things had taken over. Yet there were none of the common shrines of the propertied—food processors and stereos, or those watchdog carpet runners and antimacassars, where the thing proclaims its value by being above use. Every square foot in the place was stuffed with things so worn down and handled that many had died the death of functionality. Three overstuffed chairs in the adjacent room carried the composite shapes of bodies long since vanished. Her bric-a-brac garnered and identified its old users as clearly as a burnished mirror.

Normally, technology creates new goods that create the need for themselves, until in a short time consumers cannot do without a good that did not exist a few years before. But Mrs. Schreck's thing-hoard implied that she had bypassed this assimilation altogether, simply by making no distinction in value between a pinecone picked up on yesterday's walk and a rare, ancient floor-cabinet radio she now caught me eyeing.

—The best thing about old radios? They are all of wood. Then, when they break down and refuse to run, you took them to the carpenters, who worked cheaper than the electricians.

She put her fist to her lips and convulsed lightly over her joke. Her hand wrapped around a lace doily, impossibly old and embroidered in a foreign tongue.

—Mrs. Schreck, you have some valuable antiques here.

—Value? They say that if the rich could pay others to do their dying for them, the poor could finally make a decent living.

She went on to explain that when the old radio worked, its value was in the working. Afterward, when it was dead and long overdue for the heap, she found she had nicked it up too badly to part with it. The cash she could get for it would not compensate for the loss of so perfect a road map of all her accidents and angers along the axis of time. She explained, with a shoulder shrug, that the value of memorabilia—value in general—lay beyond anyone's ability to say anything meaningful about the matter.

Mrs. Schreck served tea, but did not drink directly from her teacup. Instead, with a quick jerk, she poured a small amount into her saucer. Using two hands, she managed the flat plate up to her lips for a quick sip without spilling. She caught me staring at the process.

—I do this the Old World way. Also, good for the shakes.

An overhand wave of the palm assured me not to take her seriously about anything.

Age varies as widely as accents. Growing into a new body resembles learning a foreign language. Some inhabit their final years with the grace and ease of native speakers. Others retain the obstinate accent and diction of an earlier tongue, adolescents imprisoned on cytology's Ellis Island. One waits for sixty to go instantly doubled over; another centenarian thinks ten nimble sentences for each one she speaks.

Mrs. Schreck, over eighty, instantly appeared to me at the office Christmas party as one who, having lived through the century's spectrum, simply adds each decade to an expanding repertoire. If she were sillier today than on that evening fingering the hole in the ambulance driver's cap, it testified that the old have behavior as rich and diverse as their years.

The view from Mrs. Schreck's kitchen window revealed her building's courtyard, a spur of the street, and a vacant lot beyond. Snow continued to fall, fat, thick, and general, even heavier than at my recent blinding, falling so rapidly that it created the illusion of falling upward. Believing that the snow's continued fury made the threat to my health even greater, Mrs. Schreck made me drink my tea to the dregs and towel yet again until my skin went raw under the persuasion of linen. Only then did she spring into action for herself.

—Hemel. Now I really got to play hooky.

With a quick step equal parts anxiety and joy at the world's coming to an elemental stop, she left the room to place a call to work. I heard her negotiate with a superior in a language midway between English and German. I took the opportunity while she was in the next room to poke around. Aside from the old cabinet radio, the only other substantial piece of technology was a massive player piano, pedals down and roll threaded. The bench housed many rolls ranging from a nineteenth-century song, "Mijn Kleintje," that could not have been played without crumbling into pieces, to a relatively recent one called "Henry's Made a Lady Out of Lizzie," complete with lyrics sheet describing Ford's overdue abandoning of the Model T in favor of the Model A.

I closed the lid and continued my surprise inspection. A narrow bookshelf held a few cheaply bound books in Dutch, German, and French. The only English books were a cookbook, a pamphlet of religious devotions, and, inexplicably, a newsstand book on Ted Williams written in the 1950s when the Red Sox were in the heat of a pennant race. The path of even the straightest of lives winds strangely.

About the room, a thousand trinkets and bangles lay in various states of antiquity: a stereopticon with views of the great cities; a singing, alabaster angel. A moldering boxed game from 1920 promised "All the excitement of a great railway journey." A cast-iron plane perched destructively on the cover, bearing the torn-away decal, "irit of St. Lo." Nearby, a gum-arabic print showed a young version of Mrs. Schreck in the steerage of a passenger liner. I had only explored the smallest fraction of the hoard when Mrs. Schreck returned briskly.

—They beg me to stay indoors. I say, "Who will clean?," but they beg me. They think I will slip on the ice and break my hip. Old people are always breaking hips. Then the insurance finds out they hire someone above retirement age.

Then, with a troublemaking squint of her eyes, she added:

—I said *nothing* about your whereabout.

And she pressed something into my hand that turned out to be a chocolate bonbon.

—Now we really play hooky. Sit and talk. You tell me, first, why you came.

—Well, I . . . thought we could start that friendship we talked about.

—Ha. Friendship never in all history brought anyone out on a snowstorm without help.

She jerked her palsied thumb toward the window, indicating the storm. I pictured being snowbound here a few days; it would be almost fun, picking through the mounds of memorable chaff. The never-predictable Mrs. Schreck could entertain me for the duration.

—Perhaps you'll like I should tell you my story of the Peace Ship some more.

I nearly swallowed my lungs at this piece of telepathy. At the Christmas party, I had trotted out for Mrs. Schreck the whole elaborate story of my obsession with the Detroit photo. She, in turn, had given me everything—photographer's name and correct nationality, date, location of the image—all the facts I needed to put my obsession to rest. If I had come now, as she suggested, to hear more of her other tale of that evening—the Peace Ship—it was because the facts behind the photo were not enough. I was the laboratory researcher, repeating the experiment long after the data are in.

—When I remember the Peace Ship, I smell onions. I peeled onions to help my mother for dinner. I was fifteen, just like the century. The boy I loved went already into the service and I knew I wasn't to be seeing him again. And I didn't.

Hearing her talk, I realized how unlearnable are a language's idioms. I concentrated on her sense, not her words.

—My father came in with an evening news. He was Socialist then, only secretly, to keep his job on the police. He used dinner to criticize government in privacy. Politics is Europe's sport. Here, we have baseball, there, talk.

She mimed the swing of a bat and then the flap of a mouth, laughing at the ludicrous equation of the two. When memory again invaded her, she quieted and continued.

—But that day's news had him nervous. Father sat us to dinner and said the prayer. Then he told us—my mother, two brothers, sister, I was the young one—how the great Henry Ford was sailing by Europe to stop the war. The War: *total* war, they called it; *total* meant against the people too, and the full work of the nation, with guns bigger than houses and guns in the air and water and under the water, and who knew if it went on another year or forever? At the start, they said three weeks, then three weeks and another three weeks, then three weeks of three weeks, and no one believed anymore that it would end ever.

—But people believed Ford could end it?

—Who is people? Probably no. But for my father, Ford was like a god. For the Socialist, because he built a factory around the time and size of the worker, where the machine came to the man and men worked together on one production. He raised up the worker. So he promised this thing about the ship, and people would laugh him to the ocean bottom, but not my father. Because it was Ford who spoke, and because every person with sense wanted to end the war the same way, even stupidly. My father believed; at dinner—still onions to me—he said the Peace Ship needed only enough listeners and they would be heard. Each day for a week, my father reads another piece of news on the passage.

Involved in her story, I sat on a stuffed chair and nervously fingered a coin bank fashioned after Jack and the Beanstalk. Jack held out beans to his mother, who cried into her hands. When one dropped coins into the hidden slot, Jack dropped the beans, a stalk began growing out of the soil, and Jack's mother looked up, smiling. Still another machine I had overlooked in my count.

Fidgeting with the machine, I hung on each word of her story. I didn't care a cent for Ford or diplomacy. I wanted to know what would happen to this policeman and his daughter.

—We follow the news each day on that ship. More people talk and hope, so others begin to talk and hope. Then something happened, I don't know what. The news talked about fighting on the boat. Some said this; others said the other. What was it? They had different plans for peace. Then even my father, who always held the belief, knew it was all up. If the doctors and ministers and famous folk on a country just the size of a boat could not keep from fighting, what hope for the sons of bakers and butchers on the bigger map?

She sat silent, hands in her lap, with only an apologetic grin betraying any sign of life.

—The news made a mockery big enough to put their own disappointment in. They laughed the Peacemakers through Holland all the way to their committee. The word "committee" killed the last hope. My father grew bitter. He blamed all—the news, the governments, the peacemakers, too. Everyone but himself and the man who made cars. He stayed a Socialist for twenty years until dying by a broken heart.

A subtle shift in posture and she no longer talked about history but about experience, direct personal experience, that commodity that grows more endangered daily.

—To have my hopes disappear into committee was not the last disappointment. Three weeks after the Peace Ship came in, the boy I wanted to make a life by, who went to the front without even enlisting, gets killed by his own side and buried into a ditch. When or where, nobody knows. For a long time, I blame the Peace Ship for not being sooner or stronger. Ford was the enemy. Not for the laughable, but because he was not even more laughable. I hated everyone I saw, because they were not laughable enough to act. And myself, too, for many years, became the enemy.

—But what could a handful of private citizens do against a war forming for . . . ?

My own voice surprised me, and I broke off, sick of the old debate between fatalism and activism. I had no fresh line, nothing to add, no peace plan for the hundred-year war between the private citizen and the mechanized state, no argument that Mrs. Schreck, who had seen sights well beyond argument and counter-argument, could use.

—Forming for how long? Two years? Since 1870? Since gunpowder or sticks? You are right, friend. Which is why you didn't come to talk about the Peace Ship at all. You came to get out of the snow, stop a blood-nose, and see if I will show you what you are too lazy to walk to the library to see.

Instantly she regained her playful composure, her mercilessly sly look. Just as quickly, she was on her feet pulling at my arm and dislocating my shoulder socket. She would allow no resistance; I'd have to see the photo now. And if my memory had so altered the image since I first saw it, if I could find nothing of the old urgency in the print, then memory would simply have to change to match the facts.

Bringing me to vertical, she shoved me along until we entered a perfect example of those ancillary bedrooms found only in the homes of the very old. Always impeccably clean, always aromatic, with floors that slope in places. The bedspread of white chenille with embroidered knobs gets changed once a week, metronomically, on the canopied bed that waits for one who will never sleep there. The room always adjoins the dining area, through a door invariably three-quarters closed. Inside is always a twilight of heavy curtains and dark mahogany.

But shoved into this room, I noticed none of these details. For on a heavy bureau sat a glass frame making a square-foot shrine. Enough adrenaline rushed into my limbs to prime me for a fist-fight. Two perpendicular creases, where the photo had been folded into quarters a half century ago did not mar its identity: my Detroit photo, to the smallest shade of remembrance and halftones.

If anything, the three farmers on their way to the dance that was the year 1914 shocked more than on first viewing. Just as Rivera's murals prepared me then, so the year of guesswork, research, and delay leading to the snowstorm and Mrs. Schreck's private narrative filled the Sander photograph with an even greater urgency. The moment had come to name these farmers.

Mrs. Schreck did that for me for all time by placing a palsied finger on the left-hand trailing figure in the parade of three, the rumpled, old-mannish boy with cigarette hanging from mouth at a dangerous angle.

—There. That's him. My Hubert Schreck. The person who in a ditch bittered me to all the Peace Ships and the world.

The skin on my skull tightened into gooseflesh. My voice was not all under control.

—Schreck? But I thought you said . . .

—That he died before we married? He did. What am I doing with his name? I stole it. I got it by Ellis Island, when I came over. I land. This big fellow in police jacket asks for the name. I give him my father's name, my birth name, but he frowns and says, "Too long." So I give him the first name coming into my head, which is always Hubert's, even years afterward. He wrote the "Mrs." down; all good women in this country are married.

—Then you've been single your whole life?

Her face filled with dry, mock opprobrium.

—I wouldn't say that.

I looked back at the photo, seeing facial detail I had not before noticed.

—He looks like a roughneck. Was the photo taken near your hometown? How long before the war? Where was Hubert headed that day?

—Oh, but it's not truly him.

Again the gooseflesh. This time I looked so alarmed that Mrs. Schreck had to sit down for laughing. Trying to look contrite, she attempted explanation.

—I confuse you, I know. But I never meant it was really my Hubert. I got this picture after the war, after Hub died. I went by the Westerwald for a last trip before America. An odd German fellow on bicycle stops me and my sister by a dirt road and asks us for taking our picture. We are so suspicious until he put out other photos on the roadside to prove he was a photographer. Here I saw this photo the first time. Boys the right age, taken at the right time, and this figuring looking maybe a little like the man I lost to Henry Ford's failing. But you have to make your eyes like this:

She squinted exaggeratedly and held the picture within an inch of her face. She had a natural talent for burlesque.

—I had to have it. I didn't want anybody for the whole world to see it, only me. I pay so much for this and a second copy he showed that I didn't have enough for my own picture. I burned the second and folded up this one to put in my day book, one, two. No one to see it but me. Later I learn about photographs. He could make a hundred, thousand . . .

—Hang it in museums . . .

—Ja.

That "ja," silent and resigned, communicated a life. She invited me to fill the monosyllable with meaning, to make it an affirmation equal to her photo-affirmation of the lost Hubert. History, Hubert, had disappeared before she'd ever once handled his would-be portrait. As I worked, in my mind, toward the same conclusion, she said, without a trace of accent:

—No one owns a print. The machine just makes another.

She curled her finger against the plate glass, scratching as if to develop out some further picture. But her finger-rubbing neither produced nor removed anything. The simple portrait, worshiped for half a century, most of a lifetime, had no real connection to her except as an act of imagination. She did not know the actual boys pictured there, but had, rather, invented, out of her own need, a whole story linking them to herself by means of the pliable image. After years of trying to monopolize the print, she had at last to surrender the question of authenticity not to the photographer nor even to the indiscriminately reproducing machine, but to the tampering darkroom of each viewer's imagination.

I understood at last that if we have sacrificed the old aura, the religious awe of a singular work of art, we have, in mechanical reproduction, gotten something in compensation. If the photographer is as powerless as we viewers in giving authenticity to a print, then we viewers are at least as capable as the photographer of investing a print with history and significance. Mrs. Schreck had done so; I would have to also. What matters is not the slice of history on the emulsion, but our developing it.

When Mrs. Schreck broke the silence, her accent had returned to its full thickness.

—The photo has not once, not even once told me who my young man would have become. *I* had to do it all. In here.

She held a finger to one aged eye. In her complaint was the suggestion that nostalgia can be cured only by taking more pictures, that living is the process of preparing to join the permanent archives.

Outside, the snow continued to lay a quilt on the courtyard. Children poured outdoors, eager to put down tracks and mark the place with their presence. One lay in a drift and, waving arms and legs, made the time-tested shadow of a snow-angel. Several overstuffed coats of uncertain sex planned a bombard by stocking up snowballs. Everyone was in a hurry to enjoy the storm, conscious that it could not last long so close to spring.

Mrs. Schreck's manner brightened. Sensing I was about to go, she offered to give me the photo. But the idea of owning the thing now, depriving her of husband, even an imagined one, horrified me.

—But you must take something with you, and one thing more each time you come back to visit, or all this junk will squeeze me out until I live on the back porch.

I timidly suggested the piano roll about Ford and the overdue Model A. She gave it up gladly. Seeing my interest in the player, she suggested we give it a whirl. First, she warned:

—A mouse ate a hole in the blower, so we must pump hard.

We kicked in unison, each taking a pedal. I had never heard the tune before, and felt disconcerted to see the keys go down automatically in perfect, unpremeditated chords. We kicked it hard, trying to move the tempo-gauge needle to Presto, but could not. Letting the needle slip to Allegro, Andante, and finally Adagio, we watched the punched dots roll past, each mapping a key. The tune changed considerably at each new tempo. For all its being a preordained thing, we varied it greatly with our kicking.

—Here, boyo. Try this. Put your fingers light to the keys. Then, when one goes down beneath you: baf! It's almost like playing.

I did. And it was.

Chapter Twenty-three

No Such Thing as No Chance

Write anything. Truth or untruth, it is unimportant. Speak but speak with tenderness, for that is all that you can do that may help a little.—JOHN BERGER, *G.*

SO PETER'S ASSOCIATION with those who called themselves that which is the *avant-garde* ended before it could result in any found masterpieces. Yet he would always thank the reality modulators for accidentally putting him onto the Ford peace delegation. Aside from his run-in over the corpse photograph, nothing newsworthy had happened on or behind the static front for ten months. Here at last, in the Ship of Fools, was something worth talking about.

Peter wrote to the home office in Maastricht. At this point in his journalistic career he could almost spell, and with a little help put together a fee proposal. He received an enthusiastic reply with enough of an advance to get to Oslo and become the self-appointed welcoming committee to the self-appointed diplomats.

He arrived in Norway before the *Oscar II*. While he waited for the Peace Ship to come in, Peter was amazed to find both journalistic and civilian interest in the matter eroding daily. Of course, there had been the wireless reports of the on-board squabbling, picked up and ridiculed in all the world's newspapers, but Peter failed to see how that altered or detracted from the worth of the mission.

Then it occurred to him that most people measured this crossing of the Atlantic in a small boat strictly on its prospects for bringing about a true and lasting peace. Peter, who had visited the front and photographed its by-product, found this hope laughable. He had now reached the advanced stage of thinking that considered peace as nothing more than the continuation of wars by subtler tactics. From the beginning, Peter had never laid great odds for two hundred clergy, industrialists, and students against mustard gas, massed infantry, and repeating rifles. The Peace Ship had from the start signified one and only one thing to him: a chance to meet the man who had automated the automobile.

On that May Day when, impatient with how long it took to reach the dance by foot, Peter had teased Adolphe about his shiny car back in the Netherlands, he'd lied. There had been no auto then or ever. But he had loved the concept of speed so greatly, had spent so much time gratis under the hoods of friends' machines that he had, in truth, become a first-rate amateur mechanic. In his more poetic moments he imagined a bright, metallic future where goods and services whipped instantly from origin A to need B.

Even in his first days as Theo Langerson, when reporting names, dates, and places had bored him to distraction, he still generated enough interest and expertise in the new military hardware to become fluent in the vocabulary of makes, mechanisms, calibers, torques, velocities, firepowers, chambers, and gauges when many of his colleagues still kept an eye out for the apocalyptic cavalry charge. The home office duly criticized his copy for its lurid fascination with the species and capabilities of weaponry.

In Norway, he was to come face to face with the greatest machinist of the day. Peter had read about the world-famous automated factory—the machine that made other machines, while workers served as midwives in the act of reproduction. He imagined it—across the sea in the American Canaan—as a mechanical hay-baler. On one end, conveyors fed in a steady stream of sand, coal, iron ore, and black paint. At the other, people queued up as if for an amusement park ride, paid their five hundred dollars, and drove off as each car plunked down the exit ramp.

And he, ignorant Dutchman, was to interview the genius who had brought about this miracle. Peter briefly wondered whether the genius Ford—capable in his mind of just about any trick—might not, in fact, be sailing to unveil some secret, self-replicating peace-machine. That altruistic hope gave way to the daydream that the world war—Louvain, Tannenberg, the Sopwith, the *Lusitania*—might be the means to his first very own auto.

By the time the *Oscar II* docked, most of the reporters sharing Peter's vigil had settled into the cynicism of crushed hope. Peter alone saw in this mission of sanity a cause that every day seemed more ridiculously sublime. A pack of newshounds turned up on the docks to hunt for additional burlesque. Ford came aground shaken, ashen, and even more gaunt and tubercular than usual. A cadre of bodyguards whisked him off, promising the jackals of the press a news conference the following day.

Those of the already incredulous press corps who understood English were in no way prepared for what came out at the conference. Ford threw them all a Yankee spitball by starting out:

—Those of us who came out to see what we could do about this murdering want to thank those of you who backed us by turning out.

What was this fellow saying? Did it have anything to do with the catastrophe facing all Europe? One year before, these same reporters had had a field day with the unofficial French plan of war called "*le système D*", for *se débrouiller*, or muddling through; now this American tinkerer was proposing a peace "Plan A," for "All for peace, stand up and holler." Only those few of the conference attendees with a more global sense of history knew that this was not the first time that the fate of nations depended on the emperor's clothes syndrome.

—My colleagues from the Peace Ship intend to stay in Europe and establish a forum for continuous mediation by neutrals.

Ford read from a prepared speech, obviously written by someone else. The word "mediation" itself tripped him three times. Reading out loud, the schoolboy oral-reporter made a big, public grimace at his inability to get through the Ivy League words, a look that said, "Just between you and me, folks, this can't go on." He looked up and proceeded in a more natural, if still nervous, tone of voice.

—Now I myself'll be heading back home to the States the way I came, because somebody's got to mind the store. If everybody'd stayed home and minded their own store we wouldn't of been in this state. But one thing I'd like to tell you fellas before I go, and that's to spread the word to the powers that be on this side of the Atlantic that they stand to garner a whole lot more profits in manufacturing the weapons of peace than the weapons of war. And just to start the ball rolling, tell them that I'm leaving the design of my tractor unpatented, so that they can make it themselves freely without paying me so much as a penny. Now I'd like to talk over those same plans with you, briefly like.

The reporters could not have been more stunned if the enemy had suddenly come up over the top at them. This disbelief would be repeated continually in press conferences down the century, well past the Great Depression when the same Henry Ford went on record as saying, "These are really good times, only not very many people know it." The world press would learn, through a series of incredulous sessions with Ford and a whole breed of new luminaries, that public personalities, too, were somewhat changed in the emerging age of the masses.

Whatever Forditis or hopes for a quick peace the international reporters had brought to Oslo Ford now proceeded to quash with talk of pistons, rings, and internal combustion. Increasingly agitated, the reporters began to realize that the prospect of European peace and the cheap, widely available tractor were not distinct in this lunatic American's mind. One fellow, a polemical, troublesome Frenchman, took the floor and asked:

—Mr. Ford, are you aware that two towns the size of your Dearborn are lost here every day?

—Well, I don't know as to the exact figures, but if that's the case, well then, it's a tragedy pure and simple. And it's exactly to the point that I've been making. If the warmakers would beat their machine guns into tractors, then none of us would be in this damn hole, would we?

The situation deteriorated. The grumbling in tongues increased. Another journalist rose up and in commanding voice addressed Henry:

—Mr. Ford, would you care to draw any parallels between the passengers on board the *Lusitania* and those good folk traveling on board your own Peace Ship?

—Those people on the *Lusitania* were fools. They were warned, weren't they?

This brought the house down, but not in laughter. The conference threatened to lapse into a free-for-all. The journalists split into two opposing camps. The majority malcontents protested vocally, attempting to shock the would-be peacemaker back to reality by citing the most gruesome statistics of the war. On the other side, a lone, crazed Dutchman asked Ford about gear ratios.

Finally a Danish correspondent, legendary among neutral and protagonist presses alike, stood up and announced:

—I have the headline for my next edition's story: "War Continues Despite Tugboat."

He saluted Ford, turned on his heel, and left the hall. A general murmur of agreement rippled through the ranks. They paid their respects and departed. Ford was crushed. His staff busied itself with the unprecedented task of putting his ego back together. This was the first serious check to self-esteem the mass-producer had yet encountered. Before this, people would have followed him anywhere, out of gratitude for the new car on their curb.

In a barely audible whisper, Ford asked why the papers always employed so many Jews. At last his eyes focused on the back of the hall, where the Dutchman with the technical questions still sat. The sight of this boy—the existence of at least one other person who loved cars more than war and politics—did more to cheer Ford than his whole legion of paid subordinates and volunteer diplomats.

Against the urgings of staff and physicians, who thought that under the circumstances the best strategy was to beat a hasty retreat to the hotel, Ford decided he had to talk to this fellow, if only for ten minutes, to gain a renewed sense of his mission on this ungrateful earth. He had already scuttled his plans to play world peacemaker. He would leave the continuous mediators in dry dock and go back to America and stay close to the factory. He had made his foray into political history. Now, half a world away from his factory, the mechanic wanted just to spend a couple of minutes talking autos.

Of the actual conversation, there is little to report. The departure of the interpreter with the rest of the press created a language barrier that neither of the unschooled men could hurdle. Only an occasional adverbial phrase, pushed over by hand gestures, made it across no-man's-land into the other's understanding. Yet the two communicated quite handsomely, if not facts, then at least a common passion. They recognized in one another the fundamental love of nothing better than things that work right and run fast.

Ford drew some sketches of converters and assembly lines, explaining nonchalantly all the while, convinced the boy could understand him if he spoke loudly and slowly. When at a loss for commentary, Peter simply buzzed his lips, imitating an engine revving. Ford would nod, grin, and copy the sound, the two of them making motor noises and slapping their thighs, while outside of the little rented hall a stunned world underwent a bloody cesarean.

Outside the hall door, a cadre of photographers lay in wait, banned from the conference proper. They hoped to get one picture of the great industrialist, and stood patiently amid tripods and magnesium flashpans. A few put their ears to the door, only to come away puzzled.

—Sounds like they're running a road race in there.

Finally the door worked loose, and an ambush of flares and shutters went off all at once. But the plates were ruined. Ford had not come out of the room alone, as everyone had hoped, but with his arm around a boy of completely uncelebrated face. They asked him to stand for his portrait again, this time alone, but Ford, stunned from the first round of flashpans, ruined these plates, too, by appearing almost epileptic. He recaptured Peter/Theo and bade him good-bye, with one of the photographers doing the interpreting.

—You've given me something more than the rest of Europe put together seems likely to. I hold that a gentleman always returns a favor. Now what is it that I could give to you?

When the translated, edited version reached Peter, he answered without hesitation.

—A Model T.

—Write down where I can reach you. I'll do better than that.

Peter could not write the address of the Schreck farm or the widow's shop, two worlds now closed to him. He gave, instead, the journalists' bureau in Paris. Ford waved the scrap and announced with backwoods bravura:

—Gentlemen, a beneficiary.

And so their first plates were redeemed, at least for a Names and Faces column inch or two. Peter himself never read the papers, and he did not discover his fame until he received the letter from Detroit. He took the letter to a polyglot friend in the Paris newspaper ghetto, who rendered a liberal, stylized translation in hybrid Dutch-German. Peter got the point, or thought he got the point: if he could survive the universal destruction that the new century still faced, he would be a rich man.

Although Peter had always cultivated a careful indolence, living for speed, consumption, and those rare luxuries that sometimes fall to the lower classes, the prospect of gentility derived from compound interest did not much move him. For one, he could multiply only approximately, using schoolboy tricks. The exact size of his fortune lay a few digits to the left of his comprehension.

Additionally, the Ford legacy failed to excite him because he knew he would never grow into his inheritance. Ford had failed to stop the war; it would go on forever. Both sides, pressed for manpower, would dispense with the luxuries of reporters and photographers and swallow their observers into service. Naturally, he would be killed in action; there could be no other ending.

If the war ended that afternoon, however, it would be just as disastrous. He could not maintain the identity of Theo Langerson in peacetime. There was little future for an illiterate reporter. He could not stay in France without the excuse of a career, and he could not, as an evader, return to his adopted Germany without prosecution. And his place in the Netherlands had, by all appearances, been more than adequately filled.

So the prospect of the Ford bequest seemed altogether dim. But Peter knew of a better use for the letter. He folded the crisp American document carefully and inserted it in his next mailer to Maastricht, to be forwarded to the policeman's daughter, Wies. He enclosed the self-portrait that he had made by holding his new box camera at arm's length in front of his face. She could identify him by that, if she remembered his face from the day in the widow's shop. If Wies ever received this letter, it might go a long way toward expiating the one guilt he carried around inside him, if the love not extinguished by a single act of desire could best be called guilt.

Wies found in the terrifyingly legal document an expiation of her own. She had had a son; whose was no matter. She had failed to secure him a father. She had borne him into relative poverty. She had passed on to the child an undiagnosed neurological disorder that left him subject to fainting spells and loss of balance. And worst of all, she had conceived him in the world's final days, in 1914. Before the arrival of the Ford letter, she had no compensation to offer the infant for these multiple sins except, when the time came, stories of a heroic father who, on principle alone, went to fight and be killed in a war that had not summoned him.

But this legacy would be better than stories of heroism. Wies went to the back of her press and extracted a folder secreted there. She withdrew a folded photograph, prematurely aged. She compared the new portrait of this fellow Theo to the middle figure in the larger print, although she needed no such comparison. She gazed at the triple portrait a little longer, trying to place it in time. Then she broke off the exercise as meaningless. She folded the American letter and replaced it and the photo in the folder. On the front of the folder, she meticulously crossed out the name "Schreck" and wrote the name "Langerson."

The child, who had been duly christened Hubertus Johannes in full, watery ceremony, went from that moment on by the name Peter Hubertus. He was none the wiser. And his mother, Wies, never tired of remarking how the child seemed destined to become a reporter like his father. His first full-time job was writing the obituaries for a small-circulation Maastricht daily. For extra income, he faked letters for help that his colleague the advice columnist printed and answered.

In 1934, at the age of nineteen, the boy repeated the sin that ran in the family line, but rectified it without drawing notice by making a clean and expedient marriage. The union produced a healthy, plump baby girl. Each day brought new responsibilities to Peter Hubertus until by the age of twenty-five, he was, aside from ever-increasing neurological problems and fainting spells, a model citizen.

As his father, the older Peter, had feared, the war was still raging when the boy reached his majority. It had started up again after a brief armistice. And a hitherto friendly neighbor, in the horror of the 1940 occupation, exposed to the authorities—whether out of greed or fear is irrelevant—Peter Hubertus's German ancestry.

Thus revealed as German by descent, Peter Hubertus was conscripted into the service and deported to the Westerwald. There he was put in charge of a work farm for young men of many nationalities, primarily Dutch. The camp aimed to engage the young men—too unreliable for active service—in demanding but generally useless work. They built roads that inched outward from nowhere to nowhere. They leveled hills and filled in gullies, then dug the holes out somewhere else.

Despite its motto—"The Laborer Governs the Earth"—the camp was little more than an armed prison, Germany's peculiar solution to the age of masses. Conditions were relatively soft by 1940 standards: campers were fed regularly, and although they received no medical treatment, they were not excessively tortured.

Most of the young men held up well, goaded on by group morale games, as when they all grew parodies of Hitler moustaches. Peter, invariably the one who had to make the men shave off the parodies, fared the worst of all. His fainting spells grew more frequent and serious, and while ostensibly a camp administrator, he merited no more medical attention than his men. He took to wearing dog tags with the familiar medical insignia of those with chronic problems, only his read: "Do not trouble about me. I will be better shortly."

What traumatized him even more than his collaboration, which he could get around fairly well, given the circumstances, was his knowledge that the world was facing its critical cusp in history, and that he could observe or alter no more of it than these few acres in the Rhineland where he and his men tore down hills and built their ambling roads to nowhere.

One day a man about his age appeared at the camp office in a spanking lieutenant's uniform. Peter Hubertus felt relieved that the cursory execution he had always expected had come at last. But the young man identified himself as Peter's cousin Adolphe, the son of Adolphe and the widow Alicia Schreck of a nearby farm.

Wies had traced the surname that Hubert had scribbled on the ancient scrap of paper, informing the boy's only relations of his internment. Peter Hubertus Langerson knew nothing of any such relation and denied it vehemently.

A heated and confused debate followed, with neither young man willing to give in to the other's objections. Adolphe, the more completely informed of the two, could not make his explanations stick until he produced a photo of his father, whom he himself had never seen. Peter, seeing in it the perfect double of the rightmost figure in his mother's old trio print, finally gave in and embraced his cousin.

Under the strain of new relations, Peter Hubertus suffered a violent blacking out while the young Adolphe stood by, helpless. On recovering, he recounted to his alarmed cousin a full medical history. He explained that employees and even employers at the work camp merited no treatment by physicians.

The young lieutenant, who had commanded troops in the *Blitzkrieg* on France, had long before, while living on his grandparents' farm to which Alicia had returned following her husband's death, completed two years of veterinary school. He hoped to employ the new veterinary technology to improve husbandry on the farm. He gave up the course to defend the fatherland. But he retained enough medical knowledge to convince his newfound cousin that his suffering might be relieved by a rudimentary mastoidectomy. He volunteered to do the operation, and Peter, desperate for aid, agreed.

For the next three hours in a locked room, the vet removed a chunk of the Dutchman's skull behind his ear without benefit of anaesthetic. He operated with penknives run under hot water nowhere near sterilizing temperatures. He closed the wound with handiwork closer to latch hooking than sutures, and dressed the wound as ably as possible.

A ranking camp officer, alerted by the long closed-door session, broke in on the proceeding's close. Not believing Lieutenant Schreck's claim that the dressing covered a minor infection, the agent lifted the bandages, revealing the incision beneath. The vet and his unconscious patient were sent to their separate punishments.

The military tribunal presiding over Adolphe's case felt grounds for particular harshness. If a lieutenant took it on himself to defy so small and easy a rule as that prohibiting medical attention for laborers, would he not soon be tempted to acts of open insubordination of greater consequence?

The young Adolphe was assigned to a disciplinary officer notoriously without those means—such as wit and marriage—that most people use to channel their sadism. The officer told Adolphe that he had been condemned to death by live burial. He brought Adolphe to an open field not far from where his cousin's work force built their monumental and worthless earthworks. Three enlisted men dug a trench and made Adolphe lie in it. They buried him in loosely packed dirt. When the dirt had not been on him more than a minute, the disciplinary officer instructed the men to dig him out and revive him.

The officer told Adolphe his sentence had been rescinded in favor of the more humane execution by pistol. Adolphe was made to kneel in the dirt, forehead to ground. The officer put an unloaded pistol to his nape, and fired another into the air. At the explosion, Adolphe crumpled to the ground under the impression that he was dead.

When the disciplinary officer began to prod him with a boot toe, Adolphe came to the ambivalent conclusion that he could still feel. He was told to wait in this field without moving; if he so much as altered his posture, his punishment would far exceed what he had suffered so far. The other men piled into a waiting staff car and departed.

Outside time except for the gradually fading daylight, Adolphe could not tell how long he had waited or how much waiting lay ahead of him. His mind could not be bothered with such complex concerns. For without the normal distraction of activity, all he could do was reproduce, again and again, the details of his mock executions. On his knees, face down in an empty field, he could not remember if the executions had occurred that morning or deep in history. He was totally alone; the other fellows would not come back. Gradually, the atmosphere of the planet he alone inhabited filled with the terror of memory.

This son of two semiliterate, earthbound peasants would never have survived the ordeal without a remarkable intervention. At that moment—which was not for the lieutenant a real moment, since he lay outside time—when his brain threatened to collapse into aloneness, a shape emerged from a nearby copse of trees. He focused on the form, his link to the material world. A thin woman in white pinafore, sporting a parasol and the most glorious strawberry-red mop of hair Adolphe had ever seen walked slowly to within a few yards of where he knelt. Adolphe at once returned to his senses, though alarmed that the woman should be dressed in clothes a half century old.

—A pleasant evening, sir.

The woman spoke in impeccable French, nodded once, and keeping to her pace, disappeared into another grove. Stimulated by this shock, Adolphe managed to fight off the remainder of the prolonged sentence. When the punishment ended, he resumed his duties in the service.

Remarkably, the son of Adolphe and Alicia suffered few long-term scars from his eternity in the empty field. When the war ended, he took part in the Economic Miracle, becoming a prosperous businessman. His only two residual agonies were a fetish for collecting Limoges porcelain figures in petticoats and an unrestrainable need to chase after redheads in crowds.

For his part in the forbidden operation, Peter Hubertus, on regaining consciousness, was stripped of his administrative duties with the camp and shipped by boxcar to a civilian jail for sentencing. The sutures behind his ear were left to fester and rot out as they would. Peter helped them out with a fingernail.

He sat in solitary for an incalculable amount of time, fed irregularly, overlooked by the authorities. He no longer despaired of being absent at, unable to observe the cataclysm of the times. He developed a pastime to sustain him in his confinement, a game increasingly seductive with repeated playing. By enforced concentration, he devised an entire town, peopling and arranging it from his raw imagination.

Twelve hours in the cell collapsed into one as he invented, laid out, and named roads, farms, businesses, family trees, intrigues, trysts, scandals, births, deaths, political maneuverings, dances, careers, estates, accidents, traditions, auctions, awards, wars—in short, all the records and events that made up a small society. In prison, he created lives and stories based on the figures and countryside in his mother's triple photograph. He set this miniature world in the first decade of the century, peopling it with all he knew of the First War and its generation. He came to revere and be thankful for the isolation thrust on him. He would never have come to know his father and imagined uncles so intimately otherwise.

When tired of building up his town's history, he took to predicting its future. He laughed to see how different were the real events of his town from how they came to be recorded in the documents and annals of subsequent generations of villagers. In this way, he passed a year and a half awaiting trial.

Following the Allied victories in the Ardennes, a flurry of desperate German bureaucratic activity turned up the forgotten prisoner, whose crime had gone unrecorded. The authorities summarily routed him to a death camp, where he was duly stenciled and prepared for execution. Thirty hours after his arrival, Hitler shot himself in his Berlin bunker and the press declared victory in Europe.

What Peter Hubertus saw in those thirty hours confirmed that everything that mankind can do, it will. Whatever horrors the body makes possible will, given sufficient time, come about. Peter concluded that to survive, a body had to concentrate on the bearable permutations and forget the others. He did not consider this an evasion, but a sort of journalistic, practical categorical imperative. Soon, the same belief began cropping up among his uncles and other prominent figures that inhabited his imagined town.

Returning to Holland, he received a half-day sentence for collaboration with the Nazis. The morning following this act of clemency, he read in the papers about the first explosion of a nuclear device on a civilian city. In trying to conceive of the detonation, he imagined it going off above the town he knew and cared for more than any other—the one he had invented in prison. He could not grasp it, it did not seem historically continuous, this device. It could not be fit into context. Soon, he forgot its existence. He took to wearing long-sleeved shirts to hide his serial number. He wrote again for the paper: the gardening column.

His mother, Wies, had died during his incarceration, *fusillé par les Allemands*. She left him absolutely nothing in all the world but a greasy piece of paper with penciled surname, a letter from a celebrity, and the photograph that showed three fellows who had become more familiar to him than life, with explicit instructions to spare all three.

His plump daughter married postwar Dutch money, and in the 1960s, managed to secure a green card for entry to the United States. The couple brought along the prematurely old fellow. They carted him up to the Catskills for ski vacations. There the waiters asked if he wanted the Beef au Jus or the Duck à l'Orange, but getting no answer, and perhaps noticing the serial number on his arm, removed themselves deferentially.

His daughter and her husband had no children, and so the line ran out in the New World. Peter Hubertus did not like this end to the story, so in the Catskill evenings he devised another. He had brought his mother, wife, and young daughter to America just after the war—or better, just before. They escaped in time. They stood before the immigration officer at an Ellis Island of an earlier day, one he had read about in texts. The officer demanded his name. Hesitant, he spilled out:

—Peter Hubertus Kinder Schreck Langerson van Maastricht.

The immigration officer pressed his temples and responded curtly:

—Peter Mays.

As for the first Peter, the father in the photograph, he decided to stay in Paris illegally. There were other Great Personalities to interview. He would find the reality modulators, have them hide him from the authorities in their catacombs. They seemed the types to enjoy sheltering an illegal alien.

He would approach them about an idea he'd had: an artwork, a documentary time capsule to be buried and opened somewhere toward the century's end. Besides the usual records—photos, legal papers, schedules—would be a miraculously preserved, unaged human being.

He would have to work out the details for the live burial. For the time being, he was once more excited about his own immediate future. He was beginning to feel, though less articulately, how the dead poet Rupert Brooke had felt in 1914, just two months after the May Day photo: "Well, if Armageddon's on, I suppose one should be there."

Chapter Twenty-four

And We Have Come into Our Heritage

The world image contains no observable magnitudes at all; all that it contains is symbols. . . .—MAX PLANCK, *The Philosophy of Physics*

BEFORE MR. NICHOLS called him into the inner office, Mays got an idea for what to do with with the legacy money. He hadn't given the matter much thought until arriving in Detroit on the Early Riser. When Alison asked him outright over the phone about his plans for the cash, he'd had no good answer. The quarter million was still an abstraction to him, the unlikely payoff for pursuing red hair seen from a window. It remained an emblem only. That he could spend it had not yet occurred to him. He lacked the connective thread that led him to the sum and could not realize that he was, by second-generation immigrants' standards, rich.

But standing in the offices of the Ford Motor Company, he at last comprehended the sum. Although not excessive by 1984 scales—it would not, for instance, buy him a house on Big Sur—the sum drew more interest per annum than Mays could comfortably spend. He could buy his mother those new rain gutters, send Alison through tech school, buy some Trans-Air to placate Bullock, and still not touch the principal. He had a real problem on his hands.

Banking it, spending it, or giving it away seemed equally arbitrary and deplorable. Mays felt—trained by his father's rise from penniless orphan to minor celebrity and his subsequent fall to an indesignate rung between the two—that what mattered was neither credits nor debits, production nor consumption, but a healthy fit between the two. Efficiency counted for more than expansion, and the idea of running at a surplus annoyed and obligated him.

The question that concerned him as he browsed through the Ford archives while waiting for Nichols was what this fellow Henry did with his excess capital. Ford's case was on a somewhat different scale than his, but Peter nevertheless found a certain similarity of concerns as he buzzed the photo museum in the foyer outside Nichols's office. For the first time, Mays considered philanthropy on a larger plane than being kind to his cellmates at *Micro*.

Cleverly programmed into the human body, he reasoned, was the capacity to feel pain. After a debate with a hot plate as a small child, Mays gained a deep respect for the survival value inherent in the trick of physical trauma. Mays could think of no cleverer teaching device or mechanism for instrumentation and process control except that equally ingenious flip side, pleasure. He envied nature in coming up, by mere trial and error, with systems that he himself could never have come up with in a billion years.

Grudgingly, he conceded that having developed cognition, an organism could find similar survival value in anxiety. The capability to suffer, too, had to be selected for evolutionarily. The trouble, in Mays's unschooled view, was that evolution was entirely and eternally incapable of selecting between valuable and excessive ability to suffer, and could not select for mechanisms that felt the one and ignored the other. Between survival pain and the level where pain shut off at last lay a good deal of room for surplus anguish.

Now if people suffered an epidemic or an earthquake, that upset Mays, but such pain seemed an unfortunate by-product of a necessary, selected-for capacity. Grief, too, served its purpose. But avoidable or inflicted suffering was another matter; sheer surplus anguish offended Mays's sense of efficiency. Surplus production of pain—unusable and indistinguishable by natural selection—had to find a match in some surplus consumption, a surplus buying power somewhere.

That, thought Mays, as he killed time over the photographic

history of Ford in the foyer, was where philanthropy comes in. Meeting up with his pile that afternoon left him with two options: he could invest the surplus loot, nurture the sum, watch it grow—increasingly indebting society out of all proportion to his needs or worth—or he could blow the sum on buying up some surplus pain.

This was what Ford had tried to do. Standing in front of an image of Ford and his buddy Edison on the dock among the *Oscar II* festivities, Mays read of how Henry had funded, out of his own pocket, the first-ever missile for peace. War, extracting payment for services denied, produced unusable suffering well beyond those debts. Ford, in a private parity program, tried to buy up that surplus and stabilize the market.

The photo caption implied, however, that far from reducing the surplus, Ford's privately funded floating nation actually increased the anguish, sadistically raising and then crushing the hopes of both combatants and observers. If the mighty Ford, one of the wealthiest men of his day, could not buy off any surplus pain, what hopes could Mays pin on a pile that couldn't even buy him a beach house? He knew the answer to that one.

Only one stockpile in all industry was capable of consuming enough pain to make a dent in the supply. That capital was, for whatever the word meant, humanity. Mays could define the word only circularly: humanity was a sop for surplus pain. And the answer to what the sop could or could not achieve, the best way to exercise it lay hidden, he now realized, in the remembered and documented past.

A redhead in antique clothes limps upstream in a dispersing parade, one commemorating the survivors of an old bloodbath, ancient sacrifice. That was his search: to find, in the concurrent past, the lost context of surplus anguish and attempted action that informed the shapeless quantity called humanity. And his search had proved that the past could be recovered only by a deliberate reading-in on his part.

For every bit of history he had tracked down, he had also been empowered, condemned to add to. To observe was already to change. The power to consume excess pain that Mays called, for want of a better term, humanity could do what evolution could not: go to the past, interpret, and select for qualities that would make people less susceptible to the unnecessary.

Memory, thought Mays, was a reminder to change something in the future. And photos—the one of his great-great uncles on a muddy road; the ones he browsed through now; even the window-framed long shot of Kimberly Greene—were more or less recognized memories. Seeing the photo of the Peace Ship, he remembered, and that memory initiated his plans for philanthropy. It would be modest and of almost no consequence. But small was best, when all was figured. Nothing smaller than affection.

He had an idea: the No Overheads Restaurant. He could subsidize subscribers from all over the state to mark their houses with a distinctive sign. Other subscribers, passing by while traveling, could then stop in and share a meal at cost. Mays seriously doubted such a scheme's feasibility. Even if the tempo of contemporary life permitted the reintroduction of the open inn, it would never fly with the IRS. Still, he felt attracted to the idea, saw it as a move in the right direction.

Here his thoughts on the matter, straying dangerously close to philosophy, began to break the emotional deadlock of his recent months, welling up as immanent feeling in his chest. The more he looked at the photo of the industrialist on the dock in front of his ludicrous Peace Ship, and the more he thought of those lost farmers walking along the muddy road toward disaster producing a descendant as ludicrous as he, the more his chest and throat informed him of how much more ludicrous, desirable, and necessary hope was than the press made out.

The voice of Mr. Nichols called him back to the things of this world. Turning, Mays heard the man next to him, sounding several blocks off, welcoming him to his appointment. He added something Mays did not catch about things never turning out as planned. So much depends on an initial misunderstanding.

Mr. Nichols led him into an office mocked up as a captain's quarters. A framed degree from Annapolis diagnosed the dementia. Round windows, bulkheads, stuffed seagulls, navigational maps, cork nets, and obligatory sloops in bottles conveyed the general ambience. Nichols ushered Mays to a desk chair. Only through a mighty effort of will did Peter resist the temptation to shiver his timbers.

Nichols spoke so appealingly and cordially that Mays at once put up his guard. The PR man held up the letter from Ford to

Theo Langerson gingerly, reverently, treating it as a cult object, grinning in disbelief.

—We've checked the letter over thoroughly, and it's on all accounts the genuine article. This is an authentic early correspondence signed by the first Mr. Ford. Stick close to it; it's valuable.

What was a hundred bucks against a quarter million? Mays felt seasick; he wanted to tell this guy to stop flashing his bridgework and batten down the hatches before the cabin pitched over entirely. Mays realized that the two of them were now reenacting the age-old ritual of hack versus flack, PR man versus trade-press journalist, two out of three falls. The flack began round two with a weak side gambit.

—Of course, your family's changes of names, the difficulty of getting solid documentary records from Immigration, and your virtually untraceable great-grandfather does make your claim of descent tough to verify.

Mays, ambushed, felt his blood rising to the fight. He had not expected this; Nichols had been sent out to skirmish with the claimant, bar him on a technicality. Nichols, and the Ford brass behind him, belonged to that perennial class Bullock liked to call "the big boys." Lenny's other aphorism, "The big boys play hardball for keeps," so impenetrable to Mays in the past, took on a material freshness and clarity as Mays stared at the wool, three-piece perfection of Mr. Nichols.

—Compared to some of the digs our research department has to make, this one is recent history. But a curious thing about research: the further back in the past an issue recedes, the clearer it becomes. Everybody agrees about the Greeks. But get five experts together to analyze yesterday's speech by the President, you'll have a fistfight.

The more pleasant the guy became, the more Mays ached to do a little plastic surgery. Peter had arrived in Detroit indifferent to the cash, thinking the legacy an unsatisfactory resolution to the mystery still buried in the past, in the perimeter of the Great War. Now the mere thought of this Brooks Brothers baboon rendered Mays, whose second-grade teacher once sent a note to his mother suggesting that there might be a somatic reason for his sluggishness, seething for litigation. He'd calculate the interest on the five hundred dollars to four places and sue to the fraction.

—Mr. Nichols, I don't know why I rate this long lead-in. The only reason I can figure for the executive velvet glove is that you are preparing to hop down the nearest loophole.

The flack's face twisted to keep its grin.

—I beg your pardon. I thought you might be interested in some of the details of this case.

—I've done without details for some time. Now I'm more interested in your paying up.

—It's a little more interesting than that.

As it always is. Simplification was the age's mortal sin. The situation with Nichols reminded him nostalgically of a ghoulish scenario back in the days of his beat. He was interviewing a vice-president of a leading New England computer firm while another vice-president in the adjoining office was being fired. The firm, conscious of every amenity, had hired a professional extricator to "facilitate the transition." The executive came to work to find a man sitting in his office speaking soothingly about his demise, using every psychological trick in the grab bag to calm him. The pro would say, "It's my job to help you do this as smoothly as possible." "Don't baby me; I know how to behave." "You don't think so at the moment, but you can jeopardize your future job search by inappropriate behavior now." Mays's interviewee tried to carry on the talk as if nothing was happening. Mays left the office with a new appreciation of just how rational, inarguable, and inexorable social cooperation had become.

Now he sat face to face across the walnut from a spokesman of that corporate principle, and all he could do was think of names to call him. He hadn't expected Ford to weasel out, yet he was not surprised. Bullock had done backflips to get Mays to put eight thousand dollars in Trans-Air paper. Ford, with thirty times the outlay at stake, would do thirty times the acrobatics. And Nichols was the preliminary screen.

—But the letter is definitely from the first Mr. Ford. His signature checks, and the proposal—the principal set at the cost of a Model T—bears his personal stamp. The first Mr. Ford had his characteristic way of doing things.

Characteristic or not, Mays intended to make the fellow sponsor his No Overheads Restaurant.

—The existence of a plausible genealogy and the fact that the letter has remained in the possession of your family through the century should settle hesitations on that score. There was some objection to your current position meeting the journalism stipulation . . .

Mays jerked. So that was it; they'd called *Micro* for employment verification and Brink must have told them that as far as she was concerned, he was picking up checks in a line down on Columbus Avenue. They'd gotten him on a technicality. Like any good animal in a trap, he kept still and waited.

—. . . but it was generally agreed that the trade press met the spirit of the first Mr. Ford's bequest. After all, the trades were the only magazines he could stomach. No, that wasn't the real prickler.

—What is, then?

With admirable resilience, Mays had bounded back from guilty silence to righteous indignation at the first hint of insinuation.

—Well, we naturally had to find the corresponding paperwork in our own Trusts department, a labor more difficult than you might think. The biggest crisis facing today's larger businesses is paperwork space. In the eighty years we've been a company we've never had so much trouble building a car as we've had managing information. Thank God for electronic filing. As you can imagine, a small trust opened in 1917 was not in the first closet we opened.

Mr. Nichols laughed winsomely. Mays tried to imagine the same grin without any teeth.

—Small trust? I wouldn't call a quarter of a million small, would you, Mr. Nichols? Buy a few cars, even at this year's sticker.

—Precisely. Compound interest. Rothschild called it the Eighth Wonder of the World. Well, we did locate the account papers, with the help of one of our retired clerical staff, an ancient Dutch woman who had been with the firm forever.

—So you've found your documents. I don't see why you're hedging over the check.

—Will you excuse me a moment, Mr. Mays? I think a visual aid might make this a little easier.

And without waiting for a nod of assent, the flack left Mays alone in the room. Too exasperated for bafflement, Mays sat and stared at a photo of the River Rouge plant, the one Ford converted to a munitions factory following the failure of his cruise for collective responsibility. When Nichols returned, he carried a safe deposit box. Mays glimpsed an armed guard lurking about the hallway.

—First, I'd like to assure you, Mr. Mays, the Ford Motor Company would never renege on a liability accrued by the first Mr. Ford.

Peter figured out what he hated about business. They knew what you were thinking better than you knew what they were saying.

—But the trust papers in the account state clearly that the principal deposited in the account shall comprise five hundred dollars worth of these.

He reached into the safe deposit box and withdrew a penny roll. Cracking it against his desk, he removed one copper and handed it to Mays. At first, Mays failed to see anything remarkable in the coin, and was about to throw it back. Then he saw the portrait, and stiffened: not Lincoln, but another emancipator, the man whose mechanical reproduction had infested Mays's life and irrevocably changed it. Feeling the No Overheads Restaurant slipping away, he asked in an unconvincing parody of indignation:

—So?

—So don't you see? Since the principal deposited was not legal U.S. tender, there can be no accumulation. Rest assured we've checked that with our lawyers.

The hoax spread itself out with merciful clarity in front of Mays's eyes. He had been victimized by an act of monstrous egotism. The way back to the past lay blocked. He looked at the penny's date: 1917. The decade ruled his life, but he could not reach back to unhook himself without snagging on one Great Personality or another. And there was no way forward except complicity, collaboration.

He fingered the copper piece—the exact size and weight of all those coins he never thought twice about carrying around in his pocket. He had one last maneuver.

—What is the market value of one of these?

He tried to remember the name for coin collecting: Nubian, Namibia, pneumonia—numismatics.

—About five dollars.

Five hundred dollars times a hundred cents per dollar made fifty thousand Henry Ford cents. Fifty thousand cents at five dollars each was still a quarter million. He did the product again, taking care with the zeros. It checked; his fortune was still intact, and he said so out loud. Mr. Nichols shook his head sympathetically.

—I'm sorry. The trust papers expressly say five hundred dollars *worth of* Ford cents. We've run this past the legal department, too. At today's market price for the coins, that comes to exactly . . .

And he handed over two rolls of coins; one hundred. One dollar, and not even legal tender. Mays felt cheated by some equivocation he could not name. But the real equivocation, the one that would never be uncovered without subjective interpretation, had taken place long before he had been born. He sat weighing his inheritance: small, metal, heavy. He looked over the cent again, unable to grasp his rise to poverty. For a motto, in place of "In God We Trust," the coin had "Help the Other Fellow."

Chapter Twenty-five

Looking

The form that delights the eye is significant.—BEAUMONT NEWHALL, *The History of Photography*

MRS. SCHRECK and I continued to kick at the player piano, experimenting with different tempi and deforming the antique tunes. I came to the conclusion that making music with even so slavish a reproducing machine was, if nothing else, at least an improvement over silence. I began to suspect that even this bellows pumping was an act of limited partnership. Those familiar tunes coming out of the roller, unrecognizable because of our playing, were stamped with evidence of manual (I should say pedal) intervention.

Technology does not remove the human role from music making; it just weaves the old give-and-take among actor, editor, and audience into a new whole, blurring their distinction. Since the discovery that pounding on a hollow log nicely supplemented the human voice, tune and tool no longer had independent existences but were bound to one another.

The present fears that mechanically reproduced music threatens to supplant rather than supplement our own competence at the keyboard. That may come to pass, but it was far from Mrs. Schreck's and my mind as our feet kept the pedals going, our hands curved over the keys in the illusion of virtuosity. To us, there seemed still an enormous amount of editorial leeway in selecting a roll, setting the stops, and choosing a style and speed of pumping.

When we finished playing, the rhythmic flap of the roll faded out into our snowbound stillness. I excused myself awkwardly and got my coat. At the door, Mrs. Schreck's parting words predicted her own disappearance:

—Some things no one will ever be able to prove. Your sharing tea here today is one.

I did not understand what she meant. Playfully defiant, I held up the piano roll she had given me—"Henry's Made a Lady out of Lizzie"—as evidence to the contrary. She laughed a horselaugh and said only:

—Perhaps.

On the path outside her apartment, I saw she was right. It was well after sunset; if anyone came or went in the drifted neighborhood, I could not see them nor could they me. Drifts would obscure my footprints by morning and melt in two weeks. Nor did the roll prove my visit: I might have picked that up at any rag shop specializing in antiques and collectibles. Any document of a second presence I had left behind —a ring-stained teacup; a cushion out of place—would be lost in the general anarchy of her rooms.

There was Mrs. Schreck herself, of course. Under oath, she could be made to testify to my visit. But she herself was already fading, well beyond the point where essay or documentation could rescue her. Disappearances ran in her family: there were her parents, swallowed up by the work of national states. And her never-husband, dispersed without benefit of studio portrait.

She had spoken once of an older cousin—slightly resembling another of those three farmers—a journalist present at Marconi's first transatlantic letter S, at Ford's only European press conference, and present, too, cooling his heels outside Bernhardt's death chamber. This man, a firsthand witness at some of the century's most newsworthy events, disappeared on the eve of Europe's second great catastrophe, leaving behind a cryptic note reading: "Penicillin was discovered by accident; one must keep the petri dishes ready."

Yes, Mrs. Schreck herself was genetically slated for disappearance. Soon, she would be missing with no traces. What, after all, did I know about her? She was an immigrant with an assumed name, in this respect indistinguishable from anyone else. As Margaret Mead has said, everyone who has arrived at this end of the century by way of Hiroshima and Nagasaki finds themselves immigrants in a new land.

And all whose living rooms fill each evening with television

— 332 —

signals reporting violence in no longer remote corners of the globe find themselves citizens of an occupied zone. History is the army of occupation, and we are all collaborators. Having begun her disappearing act, Mrs. Schreck could not be picked out of any dossier, so universal was her condition of assumed citizenship. I could not with certainty say whether a given photo documented her or some other immigrant in a country under occupation.

Mrs. Schreck would disappear. My visit to her would disappear as surely as the notes we'd pumped out of the old player disappeared into the surrounding silence. Only on one count did I have proof of ever having met the woman: only through my having shared Mrs. Schreck's story could the photo of the three farmers *auf dem Weg zum Tanz* be so thoroughly and permanently changed. I would never again see the old image in the same way. That was my proof that the woman had existed.

Not that her personal interpretation of the three subjects had diminished the fascination the picture held over me. I felt more eager than ever to get hold of a print, to pore over *it* and not so much the accompanying and identifying tag. I wanted to comb over the forgotten details, the too-fleshy noses and too-ample ears, the arched sanguinity of the eyebrows; in short, to indulge the fallacy that the looker can extract personality, social class, and that elusive quantity, "type," from a few mechanically reproduced halftones.

I badly wanted to return to the photo (the same in the Detroit museum as on Mrs. Schreck's bureau; no print is the authentic one), armed with all I now knew of Sander, Bernhardt, Ford, the period of the Great War, to see if a certain notion could hold up in the light of visual evidence. For since Mrs. Schreck's disclosures, the trailing figure on the left of the image began in my mind to acquire the creeping stain of her Hubert. I'd already devised half a story for him, he half for me. For no good reason except proximity, the middle figure flirted associatively with her cousin the interviewer, the one who had disappeared with the advice about readiness. And the third figure, the nervous, conservative leader of this lost parade: as I had suspected that initial day in the Detroit museum, his was *my* face out of another time.

This new notion I had about the photo did not displace my

sense of the three actual pictured boys. More than ever, I was aware that the photo's real subjects had led lives as verifiable, if not as well documented, as any of those Great Personalities I had pored over. Perhaps someone still knew these boys; they had not yet disappeared into the past. But Mrs. Schreck's involvement with the photograph forever changed it for me by laying alongside the factual image an interpreted one. One context did not replace the other but existed concurrently, like the two views needed to create the illusion of depth in a stereoscope.

As the dog breeder-turned-good soldier Švejk aptly observes: "There are really very few dogs who can say of themselves, 'I'm a thoroughbred.' " The farmers on the muddy road had become, in the process of my tracking them down, hopeless amalgams of history, association, bias, and measurement. For photographs, like the genetic material in each living cell, represent coded material from the past, an encrypted solution to the problem of survival.

And just as genes are retested in the crucible of individual experience, so must the photographic code be reinterpreted with each viewing. The end of this retesting and reinterpreting is to add to the code, improve its survival value. Mrs. Schreck had improved the Detroit image for me.

With two slightly different views of the photo—the essayistic and the imagined—side by side, I needed only the stereoscope itself to bring the image into fleshy three-dimensionality. Walking home through the drifts in the dark, I began to imagine what shape that machine might take. I saw the thin film of the image spreading out in two directions, back through the past, through catastrophe, to that idyllic day that had brought the taker and subjects together, and forward, far forward in time until the product of that day crossed the path of one who, like me, took on the obligation of seeing.

Perhaps this third element, the viewer, would arrive at the notion that the photo carried some personal legacy for him, a message woven into the complex personal history of his work, family, and love. Or perhaps he would simply seek in it the way to finally put to rest, after seventy years, the destructive residue of the Great War.

But there is no escaping the destruction of this war. Photographs, like DNA, if they mean to advance the code of survival,

must record in that code the memory of each trauma. Memory itself is the antibody, curing snakebite with poison. There is no way
around the memory of the First War, that dance lying just to the
right of the photo's frame. There is only going through it. Švejk,
the perennial, hit on the key to survival: experience the world's
catastrophes at arm's span.

> "When the war's over come and see me. You'll find me every
> evening from six o'clock onwards in the Chalice at Na Bo-
> jišti . . ."
> "Very well then, at six o'clock in the evening when the war's
> over!" shouted Vodička from below.
> "Better if you come at half-past six, in case I should be held
> up somewhere," answered Švejk.

No dog is a thoroughbred. The final mystery of photography
is that taker, subject, and viewer, each needed for the end product, circle one another warily, define one another in their own
terms. Mrs. Schreck's farmers, my imagined and implicated viewer,
the flesh-and-blood Sander and the actual boys of his photo are
each at work reconstructing each other, even going so far as to
postulate a biographer such as myself. And I am certainly no thoroughbred.

I had considered dropping the mouthpiece altogether, resorting again to the voice of authority, rounding out the outcome of
my visit with Mrs. Schreck, telling how from that day on my relations with my contemporaries improved. But I am every day more
convinced that it is the work of the audience, not the author (whose
old role each year the machine wears down), to read into the narrative and supply the missing companion piece, the stereo view.
Ford, often willing to be wrong in good faith, was once quoted by
reporters as having said:

> History is more or less the bunk. We want to live in the
> present, and the only history that is worth a tinker's damn is
> the history we make today.

Three farmers walk down a muddy road: the time being, that
will have to do.

By the time I plowed through the drifts and arrived at the obscured entrance to my apartment, I saw clearly that Mrs. Schreck would disappear; she was already gone. As I entered the warm confines of my rented room, I understood that I could no more see her again than I could return to 1914 to interview the farmers for their authentic story.

I had only the print or, rather, the print was its own authority. The important thing was that Mrs. Schreck, before leaving, had forever changed the way I looked at the print. I hope that anyone who has come this far in *my* account will have to say the same. Only through the direct complicity of another, an interpreter and collaborator, can we extend the code of survival hidden in the past. The form that delights the eye prescribes action; the eye's delight is its own best telling.

Chapter Twenty-six

The Mechanical Moment

Safe though all safety's lost; safe where men fall;
And if these poor limbs die, safest of all.
—RUPERT BROOKE, "Safety," *1914*

THE FIRST PLATE is ruined because Hubert, wanting to be photographed with the cigarette dangling from his fat cherubic lips at best angle, accidentally lets his butt fall and bends to pick it up just as the photographer opens the lens. Peter curses Hubert and Hubert curses Adolphe, from whom he got the cigarettes. The eccentric photographer curses all three boys equally and prolifically.

He threatens to pack up, and for a moment it looks as though the moment for the photograph is lost. The boys, appealing to the man's vanity, placate him and convince him of the merits of taking the photo here, late afternoon on the muddy road, with three such interesting facial types. Peter flourishes the exaggerated jawline that had so interested the man. The strange fellow in wide brim and gaiters relents, but warns that any further foolishness will spoil his last glass plate.

Adolphe, ever practical, mentions that the sun is going down quickly and if they are to take the picture they had best do it at once. Actually, the sun descends no faster than usual for that time of year, May first, pagan holiday and proletarians' annual. The photographer agrees, impatiently.

—If you boys will hold still in the center of the road and try to look easy, the way you were when I came upon you, then we can take this and have done.

Peter will have none of it. He marshals his companions into a semblance of heroism, or the outward trappings of it, pushing down Adolphe's shoulders, pulling out Hubert's chin.

—Look here, jawbone. What are you doing?

—Humbly beg pardon, sir. Just helping the camera out.

—Helping . . . ? The camera needs no help from you, thanks. It works perfectly well by itself.

—You mean you're just going to turn it loose?

—In a manner of speaking.

Peter is stunned. He cannot see the artifice in a photo where the subject just stands there. He takes his place in the middle of the processional, pensive and shattered. He studies his shoes, wondering how he ever came to find the style attractive. The photographer waits for him to emerge from his funk and look up, but he does not. He remains the reticent fellow in the police lineup, guilty by virtue of looking away.

—Jawbone, would you mind much not sulking and giving the audience some small odds of seeing your features?

—Who's sulking? And I thought you didn't want me to pose. Adolphe, suddenly ashen, adds:

—And what do you mean, audience?

Hubert alone remains unperturbed. He plays with his cigarette as if he has just invented smoking. His eyebrows go up and down in infant calisthenics. He parries with his cane, knocking at the others' ankles the way he torments captured squirrels.

The photographer rushes to assure Adolphe, who has taken a dose of stage fright, that the photograph will not go into any large shows; it will serve primarily as a scientific document, part of a growing archive of information, a collection of different categories of social classes, facial types, and economic roles spanning the whole hierarchy of man in the newborn century. The faces of Hubert, Peter, and Adolphe—even this trivial scene of young men on their way to the May Fair—will fill a small but significant gap in the project.

The boys listen in silence, awed by the sweeping undertaking. Hubert blurts out a question, and is reassured that revolutionaries are given a special section in the catalog all to themselves, and that the poor worker is positively highlighted. The scope and cleanliness of the plan appeal to Adolphe, and he unconsciously draws himself taller in a posture of Teutonic severity. He has a new respect for the eccentric bicyclist, whose hands push back, bits at a time, the general loss of this forgetting world.

The man's plan makes Peter think of maps. Photographing society reminds him of making maps of unknown terrain. It provides a key, a way of looking over a place without having to go there. This man's plan—to build up a document of categories and subcategories, even more precise and encompassing with each new photo—is like increasing the scale of the map. One mile to the inch is clearly better than two to the inch: more detail, and truer to the real estate. Perhaps this fellow on the bicycle, as incurable as he is about posing, might, by taking enough photos, improve the map of Man of the Twentieth Century to the scale of a few hundred yards to the inch, a few hundred faces to the photo.

But Peter does not take this hope of increasing exactness to its logical conclusion. A map of one inch to the inch, which cannot be spread without covering the countryside, shows nothing that the place itself does not show just as well. In order for this encyclopedia to become completely authentic, it would have to include a print of every living face, an impossibly cumbersome file and one replaced nicely by the faces themselves.

Nor does it occur to any of these four, who between them can boast only twenty years of schooling, that the subject matter of the project—Man of the Twentieth Century—will accelerate numerically, far outstripping any attempt to document it. The undertaking is doomed to the abstraction of the frame, as is this moment on the road.

—You see, the plate is more for science than for celebrity. You need have no fear; your parents will not punish you for becoming famous. Oh, perhaps you'll hang in a museum in a hundred years! But for now, strictly the archives. But if you fellows would like to meet me here next Sunday, we can arrange about a print for you.

Hubert demands to know how that is possible. Would they have to share the photo with the archive, say on an every-other-week basis? If so, they should be given a substantial discount toward purchase.

The photographer explains that an infinite number of prints, all unique in some small way, can be pulled from the original plate without harming the image. The boys' imaginations hang on that tremendous potential—an effortless, machine-run burgeoning, free from the uncertainties of the human hand, a godly process that, with the switch of a few dispassionate levers, creates cheap and available doubles, not just of people but of moments, this moment. One could paper the world with a moment that had not yet even been a moment until the camera ripped it out of time and printed it.

Aware of passing a threshold, the technology of outdoor photography, the boys automatically bring themselves into an agreement of postures—the decorum and propriety of churchgoing, with the camera serving for altar. Choosing this instant as his proper subject, while the boys radiate a knowledge of his project, the photographer secretly opens the shutter.

Through long practice, he has developed the ability to see almost as well as the lens, to previsualize what will appear on the developing-out plate. He knows instantly that this one is good, that the three farmers, in their suits saved for Sundays and holidays, here in the vast expanse of Westerwald nothingness, have dropped their obstinate masks of individuality and taken up the more serious work of the tribe, the pre-posed, awake look of being outside time. This, the taker of the image sees; the young farmers, interrupted on their way to a dance, see something else altogether.

For that haunted, blessed look of innocence could not have come into their eyes without benefit of vision. They become aware of the open lens, of light streaming from them into the box, drawing with it all memory of the moment and of their own outwardness. All three see it for the briefest interval hovering above and just beyond the photographer's shoulders: the third party, a vision of billions. They see a movie, played out instantly on an infinitesimal screen, of machine-inflicted suffering on a scale incomprehensible to these three rustics. Then, without any time passing, the lens opens as a clear portal, and they look past the photographer on countless people who, museumgoing, file by clinically, uncomprehending, curious.

This is the vision the lens arrests; it explains the quality in the subjects' eyes that so haunts and transcends. Their look fixes on the numbers and suffering of future viewers. They look forward—and back.

When the photographer caps the lens and emits a satisfied shout, the boys' vision of masses dissipates. Tacitly, they agree not to speak of what they have just seen; they make no mention or look or questioning sign. In keeping it to themselves, they hope to lose it altogether by the time they get to the fair.

Hubert is first to shake off the sight of collective horror. He picks up a piece of chick-pea gravel and attempts to brain a sparrow. Peter feels a new camaraderie with the photographer now that the image is done. He vows to pick another fight with the man, and this time let him win.

The photographer begins to pack away his gear, urging the boys on to the May dance but reminding them of next Sunday's appointment. Still, the boys dawdle, reluctant to remove themselves from this scene of great tragedy. They kick about. Talk springs up: politics, current events, the idle rumors of war people use to kill time. Adolphe takes offense; the photographer puts a question to him—the Kaiser's 800,000—the sandy irritant that will stay with Adolphe until the end, producing a bright and terrible pearl.

The photographer gathers up his sample portrait gallery from where it lies spread out by the roadside. He packs the prints snugly on his bicycle. Peter watches with disdain.

—Tell me again, Mr. Plato, why is it that an obviously well-off fellow like yourself doesn't own an auto?

The same ironic smile comes to the photographer as when he told the polemical boy to avoid organizations.

—A car is for getting from start to finish as quickly as possible. But I earn a living by pointing out what happens between.

The fellow mounts his portable workshop and pedals back along the muddy road, dipping and snaking through the hidden, dead spots of the Westerwald, but managing always to stay threaded, tethered to the spire of Cologne Cathedral. The three farmers watch him disappear. No waving; only the increasing ocean of solitude, the fallow, reticent fields.

It falls to Peter to rouse the boys from despondence back to the material world. He accomplishes this by the time-honored technique of insults and practical jokes.

—Hu-ub, Hubie. Your face looks like something we trained the dog not to do indoors. A-dol-phe. You think Alicia will want to tinker around?

And so on, every few hundred meters.

—A-dol-phe. No Alicia will want to dance with someone with a big spat of mud on his jacket tails.

Adolphe turns two complete rotations to see the spot, Peter goading him that it is just out of sight. Hubert, curious, adds his own erratic orbit: a solar system out of kilter. In a leap of insight, Adolphe takes off his coat and checks it in front of his face. He is furious at finding no spot. He restores the coat in silent shame. A moment later, he fears that the game might have been a setup; panicked, he checks his billfold. It is there. All is right in the empire.

The boys stray close enough to the fair to hear, carrying across the still tempera of May, the subdued sounds of a village celebration. Peter teases Adolphe a final time about the locals' quaintness, how most of them are just now hearing that a new century began fourteen years ago. Hubert scowls, showing the pachyderm skin of progeria, premature aging. The curls of hair, the forehead stretched to reach from temple to temple, prove how close innocence lies to violence.

—Luden, Luden. Burn it down and redistribute the wealth.

—An equal handful of cinders to everyone, eh, Hub?

The infant old man grins: a patted puppy. He is thinking about something the photographer said: until politics becomes a science, it will remain bloody. But the boy misunderstands; he takes this as a sanction. For the first time, a strawberry birthmark across the bridge of his nose becomes evident.

He asks Peter once more about the pronunciation of the Russian word "Soviet." He cannot accept that Peter—almost his brother—and Will, the brickmaker—almost his father—disagree on the pronunciation of this central word. He is divided between these two authorities.

The boys walk in silence, remembering the moment of the photograph. They keep to one side of the wheel ruts or the other; the road there is easier on their shoes. They resolve to pool their money and keep the appointment with the photographer next

Sunday, buy a keepsake of a world that will not survive the next three months.

They walk in single file; Peter again leads. Adolphe adjusts his hat with an eye to the other's angle: now too sober, now too cocked. Hubert lags behind, digging, with his well-worn heels, drainage canals and earthworks in the standing pools.

An observer coming over the western rise and spotting them unnoticed would have the distinct impression—there, the three of them in black suits, dragging their feet, keeping a morose silence—that they formed a tributary feeding into a swollen funeral river, instead of the truth: three boys walk down a muddy road to the first celebration of spring.

This near, the music issuing from the copse that hides the May dance is plainly a brass band. Adolphe glances pointedly at Peter, winning the argument. The taller, fuller figure—half mirror of the eye arch and equine nose—returns an impish look, whining:

—It's not Vienna after all, Adolphe. You promised you would take us to Vienna.

A bass drum followed by a tuba blast shakes the walking sleep from Adolphe. The violence of the downbeat stirs up fresh in his mind the already forgotten vision of catastrophe over the photographer's shoulders. Adolphe stops, one foot off the road, brought to a standstill by the shock of memory: countless people on the far side of the frame. He sees it again, as at the moment of exposure—a night scene whose contours stand out briefly in the flash of a phosphor pan.

There will be a terrible birth, and then another: violent obstetrics. He will marry Alicia, exercise his military privilege, but he will have no harvest. He will come back after a long while to find the house burned, the photo albums destroyed. But before Adolphe has the power to call out, the print of his vision fades as quickly as the original. He will not see it again.

Adolphe can take no step toward the dance, so paralyzing a fear has come over him on the empty fields. He cannot even check inside his coat to see if the thief has left him his billfold. The fear comes on him from nowhere, from a memory. He fears neither the passing of the old order nor his own foreseen death, but something much more trivial.

—Peter . . .

The jaunty, arrogant figure leading the parade freezes too. He recognizes in the tone an allusion to the shared vision of a moment before. He hopes the prim one will talk no more explicitly about it. He squeezes shut his eyes.

—Eh?

—Peter, will we be hurt?

There it is; the crisis Peter hoped to avoid. He laughs and gives a goosestep.

—Sliced down the middle.

He tries to laugh again, but his voice is strained. He would like to tell his soon-to-be brothers that he loves them, but it would only alarm them by being too out of character. The fear will pass momentarily; if he waits it out and plays dumb, he will save them the embarrassing effusion.

—Hurt?

Hubert speaks. He stands in a puddle, one lace untied. He looks, in his sadistic innocence, for all the world like the stone carving of a saint on a northern cathedral. A blessed saint of muddy puddles and complicity.

—Hurt, you say? What of it?

Three figures walk down a muddy road toward evening, two young, one an indeterminate age. The sun sits late in the sky, laying down long, weak lines of uncertain light. The black material of their suits scuds up at the elbows as the figures swing their arms. All three carry canes, though none needs them. Canes are the height of fashion this year, though they will soon be scorned as the props of the limping old.

The music of the dance is almost upon them. The dance is almost upon them. The lead figure keeps the parade moving. He swings his cane, cups his hand around a dark kerchief, and pushes his hat to a rakish angle. He keeps his companions moving with threatening good humor.

Just outside the fair, the music stops. The brass band is between numbers, or the notes have been swallowed up, fallen into a hidden ravine in the changeable Westerwald landscape. A look of ill-concealed horror crosses the three faces, then passes into nervous laughter. To fill the oppressive silence, to commit the moment to memory, the lead figure begins to sing:

—Carrots and onions. If my mother had served up meat, I might never have left home.

Then, by association, another tune:

—How long you've been away from me. Come home, come home, come home

Chapter Twenty-seven

Arrival at the Dance

To perceive the aura of an object we look at means to invest
it with the ability to look at us in return—WALTER BENJAMIN

IN A DARK BOOTH at the back of The Trading Floor, Mays spread
out his penny rolls on the table and hoped the place did not insist
on U.S. legal tender. Even if he still had a job, he would never
have been able to swing a meal there, much less afford the Bul-
lock-style gratiuties. He had wrapped three Ford cents in a tissue
and given it to the dapper host who welcomed and sat him.

But when the costumed fellow returned to his post, the sound
of metal rolling about The Trading Floor indicated the tip had not
met with approval. The fellow had not looked closely enough at
the coins to see the imperfection that made them valuable. The
divergences from the original were after all slight: just the profile
and the motto.

Mays would have been better off, if he intended to spend the
Ford Cents, cashing them in at a coin dealer in the nearby financial district. But he had gone directly from South Station to the
restaurant on hitting town, not even stopping at his place to drop
off his things. In an extreme hurry to arrive at his one, last, open
channel to the past, he jogged from the train to The Trading Floor,
baggage and all.

He played with the penny rolls until awakened by a discreet,
dry cough. The headwaiter stood at the side of his table, intro-
ducing his waitress: his favorite Edwardian after Bernhardt. Seeing
Alison again in the flesh, he even felt inclined to rerank these top
two. Throwing decorum to the pit, he gave in to the urge that had
possessed him when first dining here with Bullock. The stuffy fel-

low introduced Miss Stark, and Mays blurted out:

—Pleased to meet you, my dear, I'm sure.

Neither costumed figure so much as twitched a muscle. Alison looked blankly down at the linen she was spreading. Mays had the sickening feeling that she did not recognize him. Her face showed so perfect a void that he began to wonder if her features did, indeed, match the woman he'd met only days before.

The closer he looked, the more discrepancies between print and original he found. As in the child's game of "Find the Differences," two images side by side, so identical at first glance, reveal, with study, that they have nothing in common.

With the dry cough that prefaced his every action, the headwaiter withdrew. The alabaster Miss Stark continued to lay out the table setting. Just as Mays was about to convince himself that he'd never seen this woman before, she said, in affected cockney:

—Let's see: fork on the right, knife and spoon on the left? Or is it knife on the right, fork and spoon . . . oh screw it. You can do this your mizmo.

A sudden release shot through Mays's chest. He spared the woman a public display of affection, confining himself to reaching out and feeling her up. She laughed, fended him off, and continued setting.

—So you're rich now?

—In one word, not exactly.

Alison found the disclosure satisfying, even amusing. But she did not look at him or break stride in preparing the table. Her features were once again her own. As at every other moment of his life when a feeling of well-being overcame him, Mays went rigidly and helplessly inarticulate.

—So . . . how are you?

—Not bad in the clinch, as I hope you take the opportunity to discover.

—Listen. I'd like to talk to your friend Arkady. Something to ask him.

As she had over the phone when the old fellow's name came up, Alison missed a beat. Mays covered, nervously.

—He's a . . . civilized man, wouldn't you say? A . . . civilized one?

Mays had meant to say "cultured," "worldly," or "experienced," but not finding the right match in these fell back both times on "civilized," though the choice surprised him. He reached inside his travel bag and withdrew a heavily scored, ancient sheet of heavy stock. He unfolded it and spread it on the clean linen: three young men caught in the action of walking, looking out over their right shoulders at something—at an observer remarkably unobtrusive.

—I wanted to show him this.

Perhaps on the sheer weight of having been alive when the photo was taken, Arkady could tell him what it signified. Yet what could a doddering Austrian, floating in and out of sense, tell him of the hard-and-fast photo? Little. He might give the year according to the fashions, or—a long shot—the part of Europe shown in the indistinct background.

The odds of his finding out anything more about the photo from Mr. Krakow, or anyone else, were astronomical. An oil portrait might be traced to a national style, a school or movement, even to an individual technique. But a photo, especially one so without artifice, could have been done by anyone affording a camera.

Yet it was not the photographer's name Mays wanted to extract from Arkady. That held only clinical interest. Nor did he need to know more about the three subjects than the sketchy biographies his mother had supplied. He wanted to know what the boys looked at. From the instant he had come across the photo in the east eave, he recognized that faraway look: the viscous, rheumy eyes of Krakow, the past looking full-faced into the present and recognizing it.

Attempting to find the urgent memory that the past posted forward to him, Mays had gone the way of the Great Personality, the way of Bernhardt and Ford. He had been paid off in coppers, but was not satisfied. Krakow was his last, direct link back: an ordinary fellow who looked on the present without being able to shake the memory of the Old World, the old order. Krakow could tell him what it was these boys saw just over the photographer's shoulder.

Alison bent down over the creased photo. The same woman who could see no resemblance between Peter and Theo Langerson in the *Heir* photo now, without prompting, put her finger on the middle figure of the parade, saying:

—You look good in a black suit.

She straightened from the waist and regained her Edwardian propriety. In another accent altogether, she pronounced:

—He died the night you called me from Illinois.

For a strange instant, Mays thought she still referred to the middle figure of the photo. Then realizing that she meant not his great-grandfather but his one, contemporary link to that urgent look, he kept silent, not wanting to sully the old man's passing with something so silly as words. Guilt, remorse, relief, nostalgia, and appreciation, silent, all sound the same and cannot be told one from the other. Alison broke the emptiness.

—I am his sole beneficiary.

—His . . . ? Did you know?

—Out of left field. The wife thing, the delusion I first grabbed you to rescue me from. Jesus, Peter, he even wrote it in his will: "I am of sound mind. I know Miss A. S. is not my wife, yet the resemblance is so strong. . . ."

—That I'll leave her my estate?

Alison closed her eyes and nodded. Mays, fighting the urge to ask how much was at stake, heard her whisper:

—It wasn't much. He must have dug pretty heavily into the annuities to keep coming here for meals, to keep up the Old World grace. Still, there's enough to send me back to school.

Mays again reached for Alison's forearm, as if to restrain her. He grasped the worst: she would abandon him. While he sat morbidly tied up in the past, she had set her sights on the future and now had the means to reach it. She would collect that holy of holies—a technical education—on which Mays had never had more than a dilettante's grasp.

His leads to the past had died. He was too old to retool for the future. The only thing he cared for—and that, fiercely—was the present, and a chance to know this woman in front of him. And she was leaving. He forced himself to be adult.

—Computers?

Alison gave him a sardonic, lip-lifted smile.

—What do you take me for? That was last week. I thought I might study a few languages, then travel. See what's left of the places he used to ramble on about. It's his money after all. Know any good chaperones?

She gave Mays a look signifying that there's no such thing as

No Chance, or that the only history worth a tinker's damn is the history we make today.

Mays made out the shape of the headwaiter across the room, craning toward their booth, anxious over Alison's delay. Alison waved off his worry, suggesting the fellow could go stew in the house marinade. Mays looked up at this woman's face, once again trying to interpret her features. The Viennese, Krakow, had found in these features a hint of the long-ago lost. Yet neither wife nor waitress replaced the other; the old man had set them side by side, variations on an irretrievable original.

Here was the only possible explanation of the viscous look in Arkady's eyes when Mays had first met him. In Alison, Arkady had stumbled on one of those moments of intersection, the plane of the past cutting into the plane of the present and, in the side-by-side juxtaposition of the two, showing the closest hint of the three dimensions of the original template, which preexists the negative and lies outside time. He had read into Alison's face the forward-posted memory of his long-dead wife: they were concurrent. No observation without involvement; no fact without interpretation.

That same intersection of planes, Mays realized, lay behind the compelling look of the farmers on their muddy road. They looked over the photographer at *him*, at their own continued existence, the face of our time. The same compulsion lay behind his vision of red hair in the Vets' Parade: a past-in-present, the side-by-side interference of two worlds. History tips the second view slightly, and parallax combines the two into the full three dimensions of the original image. That original image, the only one possible, was the only and motionless dance.

He folded the print into its old four quarters and with a smooth motion swept up the penny rolls and headed toward the exit from The Trading Floor. Reaching it, he stopped long enough to remember that, under the strength of his insight, he'd forgotten something important. He focused on the stunned Edwardian across the room. Loud enough to carry, he called out:

—So does he get the girl?

Judging by the pall that settled on the business lunches and Boston money peering out of the dark wood and damask, the propriety of the place was forever compromised. Yet the phosphor ticker above the bar showed no dip at this calamity. The staff went apoplectic, eyes on Miss Stark. She said nothing.

—So when do we sail?

Mays's second bellow was louder than his first. The look that spread across Miss Stark's face suggested there would be time enough for travel, time spreading out infinitely in two directions.

Mays was to experience one more sense of concurrency that day, when he arrived at *Micro Monthly News* to find that nothing had changed since his departure. He threw his still-unpacked luggage under his desk and set to work, not on his "Accumulator" column or any editing assignment so hopelessly past due as his were. Instead, he marshaled his meager knowledge of grammar and began to draft a letter.

He hoped to employ the miracle of electronics to mass-produce a hundred copies of this letter and mail them off to celebrities, clergy, business contacts, even names from the phone book, enclosing, in each one, the first-ever Penny for Peace. But by two o'clock, he'd gotten no further in the letter than "A few of us would like to get together and try to keep the boys out of the trenches this Christmas."

At a quarter after, Brink, walking past his desk for the third time since he returned, did a double take. Collecting herself, she said:

—Peter, might I ask you to report your vacation days *before* taking them next time?

He gave her a three-fingered salute. If the Japanese were really serious about this Technowar, they could land an army of occupation unopposed. In the ensuing small talk, Brink let out that Bullock had left her and his job for place or places unknown. It seemed that the accounting books of a certain Trans-Air Transport, in which he had had all his clients heavily invested, had turned out to be masterpieces of creative writing.

Mays apologized, although he was almost certain it was not his fault. Brink, stolid, never far from the continual edge of happiness granted those born into their proper era, went about her job.

Duly notified of the return of another warm body to harass, the great, flightless, egg shape of Delaney swooped from nowhere in a flurry of cardigan, scattering papers over half of Mays's desk. Peter braced himself for the worst. Instead of the obligatory vaudeville, Dougo contented himself with picking over Peter's belongings. Coming across a commemorative cent, he eyed it suspiciously, then slapped his hand down hard on the desk in imitation of a quiz-show contestant hitting the ready-to-answer button.

—Henry Ford.

He made his own bell clang, and awarded himself the coin as prize.

—And these three rubes . . .

He picked up the print from Mays's desk, the spot normally reserved for enshrining the dead or members of the immediate family.

—. . . are Stalin, Churchill, and Roosevelt at Yalta.

The plant barricade around Moseley's desk rustled, and out of the crack in the foliage peeked the rare species in question: on all sides of Mays—here at hand, across town at The Trading Floor, even so far away as on a muddy road in a decade that would never again open except to the cheap and readily available silver halide print—lay that most elusive, universal, persistent quantity, always in need of foreign aid, the Other Fellow.